War Between Brother Kings

Lara MacGregor

A Wings ePress, Inc.
Contemporary Romance Novel

Wings ePress, Inc.

Edited by: Jeanne Smith
Copy Edited by: Joan C. Powell
Executive Editor: Jeanne Smith
Cover Artist: Trisha FitzGerald-Jung

All rights reserved

Wings ePress Books
www.wingsepress.com

Published In the United States Of America

Wings ePress Inc.
3000 N. Rock Road
Newton, KS 67114

What They Are Saying About War Between Brother Kings

5 Stars!

An exciting romance built around a handful of souls who bond as if a family intent on encouraging good fellowship...a tender relief from today's world of human hardship.

Lara MacGregor has that knack of painting her characters with such flourish, yet somehow illustrating love and mateship in a trail of doubt and question, an envious ability.

Its sense of mateship and care for friends is persistently warming.

—Kev Richardson

Award-winning author of numerous books, most recently the Soul of Australia series

Dedication

To all my friends. You have enriched my life.

* * *

List of characters:

Corentin Brodnik (Cory): an author and rightful king of his country; banished to America as a boy

Katarina Reynolds (Kat): Cory's great love, a bass player and chemist

Gunther: Katarina and Cory's long-term best friend, a motorcycle mechanic

Asher: Katarina and Cory's long-term best friend, a rock-climbing instructor

Brendan: Katarina and Cory's long-term best friend, a paramedic

***

Jaromír (Jon): Cory's younger brother, a prince and archaeologist

Goran (George): Cory's older half-brother, current king of his country

Queen Mérane: Cory's mother, deceased

King Jakab: Cory's father, deceased

Lothar: Cory's uncle (brother of Cory's mother), a king of a neighboring European country

***

Zahra Reynolds: Katarina's mother, a chemist

Liam Reynolds: Katarina's father, a chemist

Molly Reynolds: Katarina's little sister, deceased

***

Mérane Zahra Brodnik (Merry): Cory and Katarina's first-born child

Liam Corentin Brodnik: Cory and Katarina's second-born child, Merry's twin

Adorée (Addy) Katarina, Dominic Jensey, and *Aleksei Jaromír Brodnik*: Katarina and Cory's triplets, born after the twins.

Grace Reynolds Brodnik: Katarina and Cory's youngest daughter

***

Madison (Maddy): Lead singer in Katarina's band

Bernadette: Lead guitarist in Katarina's band

Treena: Drummer in Katarina's band

One

Honeymooners on the run

Katarina, his new wife, took Cory's hand in bed in the motel room. Finally, after much agony, she told him, she had decided to trust that someone could protect them despite her ominous premonitions of Cory's death. For years her nightmares had kept her from admitting she was in love with him.

Breathtakingly beautiful, she gave him the smile that made him stupid. Her eyes grew thoughtful. "Wow, you're a prince. Had I known, I might never have proposed marriage to my best friend, the unknown orphan with whom I fell in love."

Cory, Prince Corentin of Carasivia, true heir to the throne of his country, frowned. "My love, if the king hadn't forbidden me to speak of it…I feared for your safety. You don't mean that, do you?"

She gazed at him adoringly. "No. You're everything to me."

His heart swelled with joy. *Woman of my dreams…*

"Are we insane for doing this?"

He held her hand possessively. "Insanity would have been living a life apart." Sudden laughter arose from his gut. "I'm your husband!"

She laughed briefly, then her happy eyes turned serious. "Will he prevent us from growing old together? I hope you won't have to become something scary to face off with him."

"Sweetheart..."

"Realization keeps hitting me in the face. A king is hunting us." She grasped the red blanket.

"I'm so sorry." He rolled onto his back and stared at the dingy ceiling. "What did I get you into? We should be living in that palace, helping millions of people. Instead, we're in this shithole situation, being chased down like animals."

She put her hand over his, on his belly. "I'm glad you came to live here in America as a boy and became my best friend in eighth grade and are my husband now. Don't think I ever want you to change. I love you the way you are. I only ask that you fight a darkness that will someday destroy you if you let it."

He turned onto his side facing her again and dragged his fingers along her curves, causing her to shiver. "I'll get a grip on my—"

"Buried rage?"

He nodded curtly. "—if you'll try not to..."

"To what?"

"To whine and doubt yourself. I love you, but it tests me."

"What else?"

"Really?"

"Yeah. I want us to work." She kissed his shoulder. "Lay it out."

He interlaced his fingers with hers. "Your habit of keeping things from me has got to end. It has driven me bat-shit crazy for years. You're my wife now, so I expect you to be upfront with me."

She smirked. "You've pushed my buttons too, sometimes acting in haste, on pure emotion, making you act uncharacteristically, but because you want what's good for the people, you're meant to be on that throne, not that despotic brother of yours, King Goran, *George*," she added, saying his nickname. "Promise me, if something happens and even with your gift I don't get out of this alive, you'll still fight for your throne and save your people."

He shot up. "Don't talk like that!" He swept her into an embrace.

"Better me than you."

"Stop! They'll have to go through me to get to you!"

"No, Cory, if you die too soon, it won't be only me that will suffer. The thought of you not saving your country terrifies me."

He didn't respond.

"Cor?"

"Me too." He released her and swiped his face. "Jon gave us a thousand dollars to start. He regrets he has to keep this low key to increase our chances of staying off the radar. King Asshole has friends in high places looking for us in the finer places. And if Jon spent a lot of money with nothing to show for it—" Cory smiled briefly thinking of his younger brother. Jaromír had gotten used to the American nickname Jon. Cory silently thanked him for helping them run.

"Tell your baby brother we can get by on less."

"Baby?" He chuckled. Jon, at twenty-two, was only a year younger than they were. "Play me something."

"Now?"

"Yep."

She slipped on panties and a bra and retrieved her bass guitar from the corner. She sat on the edge of the bed and played. Her silky black hair dusted the hand holding the fretboard.

He watched, sucking in sharply. "Damn, you're one sexy heavy metal bassist chick."

She rolled her brown eyes, grinning.

"That's new."

"A wedding song for you. I just came up with it."

"You're talented. Your bass lines are melodic and evocative." He got up, slipping on boxers, and opened his laptop.

"What are you doing?"

"You'll see." He tinkered with the computer. "Bring your bass here. Let's record your song. I challenge you to do what J.S. Bach did and—"

"Write a musical composition in every key?"

"Yes."

"That will keep me busy."

"I'll write stories. I can't submit them yet, but when we're safe, I'll give them to my agent."

"Great! But will we ever be safe?"

He frowned. "If Jon finds that evidence to clear my name and get me on the throne. We have to believe."

Doubt and fear cast their shadow over her. "It's more likely the king will kill us."

He touched her shoulder. "Sweetheart. When Jon calls, I'll ask him to get me a guitar and some *how-to* books. I'm going to learn. We'll make music together."

She put her hand behind his head and pulled him into a kiss.

~ * ~

Kat cracked open the door looking down the dim hall. *All clear.* "I need a soda."

"Mm-hmm," Cory said sleepily, a satisfied smile on his face.

She grabbed his wallet and padded toward the vending machines by the doors. She looked through the glass, up at the full moon.

"Excuse me." A man in a hoody bumped her sideways then pushed through the doors.

She stumbled then reached for Cory's wallet in her pocket. It wasn't there. *No!* Cory's words came back to her: *Don't doubt yourself.*

"Hey!" She darted through the doors and across snowy grass, jumped, and tackled the thief.

Cory's wallet flew three feet away. She scampered for it and had it in her hand. The man punched her on the side of the head, sending pain shooting down her face. He snatched the wallet and scrambled up, opening it. She recovered and jumped to her feet. His hood came off, and she lurched for it, having it in her grasp.

"Give me back my wallet or I'll call the cops." She wouldn't really, but how could he know that?

He dropped it. She let go of his hoody and he ran. She took up the wallet and waved hello to a couple staring. Her head throbbed as she made her way inside to the vending machines. She opened the wallet and stared, sick to her stomach, at the gaping emptiness where several hundred-dollar bills, hers and Cory's food and shelter money, had once been.

"Fuuuuuuuck!"

Cory ambled over, rubbing his eyes. "I missed you." He paused as he made eye contact with her. "Oh, no." He ran to her and took her by the arms.

A chunk of snow fell from her hair. She shivered, her clothes wet. Her lip quivered. "I'm sorry."

His frantic look brought tears to her eyes.

"What happened?"

"He took our money! I just wanted a soda. I should have taken only soda money, but I'm a dumbass and brought it all!"

"Are you *hurt*?"

Pain radiated down her jaw.

"Tell me!"

"Our money is gone!"

"I don't give a damn! Are you fucking hurt?"

"A little."

His posture stiffened. "Where?"

"He punched me in the head when I chased him." She touched her face.

He whipped his gaze over the empty snow-covered grassy area and swore a string of curses in his native language then looked back at her. He gently touched her head. "Are you okay?"

She winced. "I'm fine."

"I'm sorry. Did he...do anything else to you?"

"No."

He wrapped an arm around her shoulders. "Come inside, sweetheart. Describe him. I'll search the neighborhood for the man who hit my wife."

"No way. You'll beat the shit out of him for punching me, and we have to be low key."

He sighed. "You weren't low key when you chased him, but what pisses me off is that you were hurt."

"You told me not to doubt myself."

"I didn't mean for you to go after criminals!"

"I'm sorry."

In the room, dried off, she got under the covers. He gave her a kiss, feathering his fingers over her cheek.

She smiled. "It's all better now." She raked her fingers through his hair. "I love your brown hair. It kind of matches my eyes."

He took her hand in his. "It's my fault you were hurt. I let you go alone."

"You didn't *let* me do anything."

"Please don't do that again. We're being hunted."

"He looked young, and I didn't see a weapon."

"Still. When I saw you standing there with snow in your hair, and a look of injury on your face—"

"All right. Jon's not meeting us for two days. He's stuck in Carasivia. This room is paid for through tonight. At least we have bags of chips."

He kissed her, climbed under the blanket and held her. "I'm just glad it wasn't one of George's men you ran into. You would probably be...gone. I was nearly asleep when you left. I dozed and woke with a start and went to find you."

The next night, they slept in a park, under a tree, shivering and holding each other. He called his brother, but Jon didn't pick up.

She pointed to a cooing pigeon. "Pretend that's a turkey. Happy Thanksgiving, Cory."

He kissed her head. "What I'm most grateful for is right here."

Come morning, they gulped water from a drinking fountain. Their stomachs growled. Cory rationed out their last bag of chips.

When the exceptionally handsome Jon found them at the meeting spot, he paled. "You two look horrible. Here." He shoved a bag their way.

Kat pulled out two sandwiches. She handed one to Cory and tore into hers, taking a big bite. "Thank you," came out muffled.

Cory ate a sandwich and told Jon what had happened.

Jon shook his head. "King Goran, the asshole, *George*, was watching me for days, or I would have returned your call."

George thought the nickname was an insult, but Cory had told Katarina it wasn't. *George* was just the closest translation for *Goran* he could think of.

"I flew back here from Carasivia this morning," Jon continued. "It was difficult to escape his prying eyes. I have bad news. I have only a hundred dollars for you today. I can get more every few days but not as much as I have been giving you. I'll do what I can manage without arousing George's suspicions."

Cory frowned. "It's hard for me to find work under these circumstances. You said George is monitoring my publishers, paid an insider, so I can't write under an assumed name. I could try a new publisher with a fake name, but that takes time."

"I'm sorry." Jon shook his head again. "He's monitoring my friends and colleagues as well, determined to find you. I had to do some fancy maneuvering to meet you here."

Cory turned to Kat. "What have I gotten you into?"

She touched his wrist. "Knock that off."

"But—"

"I want to be here, problem solving with you."

A sad smile tipped his lips. "You're a sweetheart."

Jon gave them a grave look. "Previously, I put everything you two owned into a hidden storage facility and paid the rent on Corentin's apartment for a year." He shrugged. "You never know if you'll need that place again. George found out and froze my accounts. I gave you the American money I had on me and even exchanged my Carasivian currency. George is only giving me a tiny allowance, which I'll give to you. I can't tell you how sorry I am that he did this to you."

"Please, give my parents a message for Christmas. Say I'm fine... celebrating my honeymoon in bliss, and I love them," Katarina said.

"I'll do what I can. I can't stay long. I don't want George to hear about this meeting. I can usually outmaneuver him, but you never know."

Cory touched Jon's shoulder. "Thank you. Please, tell me he didn't...punish you for storing our things."

Jon glanced down. "No, of course not."

"Look me in the face and tell me."

Jon lifted his face. "One beating is nothing—"

"No!" Katarina cried.

"I'm so sorry." Cory closed his eyes briefly.

"I'm fine. I'm more concerned for what you two are going through. Besides, I can look *that* brother in the face and lie. I swore a public fealty saying I had no idea where you were. The servant at the ducal mansion who gave you away, well, my men caught him. He's imprisoned in the mansion's basement until it's safe to release him."

Cory took Katarina's hand. "Thanks to you, Jon, we're okay." He glanced at Katarina. "We'll get by."

Jon looked at Katarina. "I had a colleague tell your band you'd be gone a while. Your parents, of course, are still touring Europe. My friend said they needed you, and that you gave your apologies. Your band wants you back as soon as possible but will use a temporary bassist."

~ * ~

Days later, Kat took out her wallet to get bus money and stared at a temporary paper copy of her new I.D. *Katarina Lenore Brodnik*. "Remember when I was Katarina Reynolds, what...days ago?" She smiled. "I like my new name."

Cory glanced at the paper copy. "I can't wait until Jon picks up your mail at the P.O. box and hands you your new official I.D."

~ * ~

For three weeks, Cory and Katarina had to spend some of their nights shivering in parks or other places they could find because the little bit of money Jon had managed to slip to them hadn't been enough to provide a motel room for them every night. On one of their "outdoor" days in an out-of-the-way café, Cory held Katarina's hand over a small table in the far corner of the room. People chatted around them, paying them no heed.

Katarina gave Cory a weak smile. "Tell me about your country. Something I don't know."

He let go of her hand and rested his bent arm on the table, propping his cheek against his palm. "Well, you know the royal palace is on a beautiful mountaintop. We have some gorgeous lakes and forests as well."

She took a sip of the small coffee they were sharing. "Tell me something cultural or historical."

"Tea is more popular than coffee there. Cats and dogs are common pets, as are rabbits."

"Rabbits, huh?"

"Yes. The royal family had them a hundred years ago, and it just...stuck."

She lowered her voice. "How long have your direct ancestors been in charge, the Brodnik Dynasty, on the throne?"

"About three centuries," Cory said softly and sat up straighter, glancing around. He lowered his shoulders, looking relieved that no one was listening in on their conversation.

"Impressive."

"What would be remarkable is putting our future daughter in charge someday. She'd be the first woman in the country to rule because I will change the law."

She reached for his hand and squeezed it. "The Brodnik Dynasty would end, assuming she would marry."

He gazed at her. "Same family."

"With her husband's name."

"If she chooses."

They chatted until closing time, then made their way outside, cuddling on a park bench.

~ * ~

Days later, they strolled the aisles of a small library—out of winter's reach. Cory cracked open a political science book and compared American politics to that of his country. Unknowledgeable in the field, Katarina asked him many questions. He answered and asked her for her theories on various topics. After two hours of a lively conversation, she dragged him to the area containing music books, showing him pictures in a fascinating tome of the progression of the bass throughout history. She explained music theory as well. They stayed until closing time, eating the sandwiches they felt grateful to have, and then headed out.

The next morning, sitting at a bus stop, Katarina pulled a half loaf of bread, a jar of peanut butter, and a plastic knife out of her bag. "Breakfast time. Pretend it's not what we had for lunch and dinner yesterday."

"I'm starving and have a great imagination."

She slapped some peanut butter on bread and handed him a sandwich.

"Thanks," he said. "Mmm, mmm. This is the finest..." He glanced up in thought then brought his gaze to her. "...stack of mouth-watering waffles I've ever had. Melted butter, maple syrup..."

She laughed and made herself a sandwich.

He handed her a water bottle. "Let's get an orange at a convenience store today. Don't want to get scurvy."

She scoffed and took a sip of water.

He shrugged. "Am I wrong?"

"An orange sounds good."

He finished his sandwich and patted his stomach. "Thanks, sweetheart. You're a good cook!"

She chuckled and dipped into a bow.

Always on alert over the next few weeks, they only dared to enter places after scoping them out from a safe distance. But they had to keep moving, daily, on foot or on the bus. Cory regretted that neither of them had owned a car before this started, and Jon couldn't safely find the opportunity to provide them with one. He hoped that could change in the near future.

One night Katarina and Cory lay stretched out on the bed of their run-down room.

Katarina glanced at the stained wallpaper then back at Cory and smiled. "Aw, a nice, warm room. Sure beats the outdoors in winter. I like having a roof over our heads."

"And a bed." He gave her a heated look.

"Yes." She ran a finger over her new I.D., smiling.

"Nice. One dream come true—making you my wife—more to come." He kissed her.

Later, Kat looked at the pine branches in the windows Cory had carefully arranged to add Christmas cheer. He used toilet paper to make bows for the greenery.

"Thanks for that." She cuddled with him.

"I'm glad you like it."

"Hey, did you see that dollar store? Can we go?"

"I don't know—"

"I'm bored. I finished two books."

"Katarina—"

She flipped onto her back.

He chuckled. "Okay, whiny one."

She sat up and hit him with a pillow, smiling.

"We'll have to be very alert."

She took his hand and pulled him up. "Come on."

They crunched over snow and darted across the street. Once there, they looked around and saw nothing out of place. They browsed. She snatched up a little sewing kit. "I'll take this."

He picked up a craft book and opened it. "Hm, interesting." He took Katarina down to the cooking section and grabbed salt and cornstarch.

"What are those for?"

"Can't a man have any secrets?"

She gave a playful scoff.

The next night in bed, Cory pulled the covers up. "This blanket is shorter than yesterday. I wonder why the cleaning crew gave us a smaller one."

Katarina snuggled. "I'll keep you warm."

On Christmas day, Katarina pulled something from the set of drawers in their small room. Cory slid something out from under the bed. Both gifts were wrapped in toilet paper.

Cory handed his to Katarina. "Merry Christmas, beloved."

"Merry Christmas, love of my life."

"You first."

"What didya get me?"

"Open it!"

She tore open the paper and gasped, looking at a homemade, faux pearl necklace. "It's beautiful...how?" She dragged her fingers over the pearls.

"That's what the salt and cornstarch were for. They let me boil water in the motel's kitchen. I made the clay, shaped the pearls, poked holes in them, let them dry, and then strung them with thread. You really like them?"

Her eyes stung as she touched individual pearls. "Yes. That must have taken a long time. I can feel your love in each of these."

"Look on the inside. I traced a message."

She read, "I will love you always. I'm grateful beyond words that you have agreed to spend your life with me."

She wiped away tears. "Open yours."

He tore open the paper. His face lit up. "Slippers! Thanks! They look awesome." He put them on and took a few steps. "You *made* these?"

"Yep. Stitch by stitch, when you were on that errand, apparently in the motel's kitchen, and bit by bit afterwards."

He looked at their shortened blanket then at the slippers and chuckled. He kissed her.

"They're comfy. Multilayered."

"And infused with my love."

"Sweetheart—" he trailed off.

She went to her bass. "Time for Christmas songs."

They performed their favorite holiday songs while recording them onto Cory's computer.

"You can kinda sing," she said.

"Thanks! Dance with me." He played the music back. They slow danced next to their bed and sang along with the music, harmonizing.

After the music stopped, he looked at her.

"What?" she said.

"Our show should be starting now."

They stretched out on the bed on their bellies, and laughed at a 1950s comedy rerun on the little television. Static crossed the screen.

Cory reached and banged the side of the TV. Police sirens screamed outside. A flashing red light hit their blanket.

"That's the third siren this hour," Kat complained.

"Yeah, but the red light is Christmasy."

"Nice silver lining, husband."

He wiggled closer. "I love it when you call me *husband*." He grabbed their early dinner off the small table. He took a bite out of the two-dollar noodle bowl they were sharing and pointed to the screen. "This part is great!"

"He's so astonishingly predictable!" Kat smiled before taking a bite. She nudged Cory. "Hey, you took the longer noodle!"

He dropped it from his chopstick. "My pardon!"

"No, you can have it—"

He cut her off by picking it up and shoving it into her mouth.

She chewed, stifling a laugh. Later, they faced each other cross-legged on the bed, with their instruments.

"More music. Hope you don't mind."

"I'm having a great time!" he said cheerfully. He concentrated as he played.

She smiled. "I said the key of F, not W for 'What the Fuck.'"

He chuckled. "Give me time, sweetheart. I'm not a natural talent like you."

"I think I perceived a nice melodic line coming from your guitar yesterday. Perhaps we have a ghost in here?"

"Ha ha, my wife. You're hilarious! To the moon, Alice!"

They laughed, dropped their instruments, and rushed into each other's arms, making frantic love. Sweat-drenched, they lay entangled, her hair spread over his chest. From around her neck, she fingered the necklace he had made.

"We need more condoms," he said.

"Mmmm. If I'd'a known sex was this good, I would have jumped you a few years ago. You're...motivated."

He kissed her. "It's so good with you, it blows my mind."

She traced a finger over his chest, drawing a bass clef. "It wasn't that good with other women?"

"No."

"Why?"

He tickled his fingers down her arm. She quivered.

"Because I'd die for you."

She sucked in sharply.

"I don't know," he added. "I just...come alive everywhere when we're doing it."

"It's mutual. We uplift each other."

They were silent a while.

"Cory, you're amazing."

"Are you happy? Even though we live in a series of shitty rooms and are malnourished? Wash our clothes in the sink?"

"There's nowhere else I'd rather be. I don't care about our poverty."

"But what if this carries on for years?"

She kissed him. "Yeah, these places suck, but they're better than the cold, a lot better. Also, you went outside without me, slipped in snow, came back in here wet with chattering teeth, a handful of pine branches, and a huge smile, so I could have greenery for Christmas." She paused. "You're what I'm most grateful for. The definition of a good husband. You gave me a priceless pearl necklace that has so much love in it, touching it makes my heart flutter. If it takes years, so what? If it takes forever, oh well. I'm with you, Cory. I *love* you. You'll just have to put up with my whiny little ass."

"You'll just have to put up with my chivalry—old-fashioned by U.S. standards."

She traced his jaw with her fingertips. "You know I was raised to respect other cultures, and of all the men I know, you're the most respectful towards women—that's saying a lot because Gunther and Asher are real gentlemen."

"Women are awesome. They should preside over the world."

"You respect them but are protective. I love how wacky complicated you are."

"It's because of my mother. *She* should have been in charge, and she was murdered in front of me." There was a sad pause.

She squeezed his hand. "I'm sorry."

He sighed. "First on my agenda as king—"

She tipped her head. "What will it be?"

"Women's rights. King Goran is a sexist douchebag."

"Thanks for the finest Christmas I've ever had."

He looked at her with such love she shivered. "I'm going to give you epic Christmases in the palace, once I'm proven innocent and can figure out how to best the tyrant. Wish he'd meet me man-to-man."

"I look forward to those Christmases, but none will beat this one."

"You're astounding, wife."

"You're sexy, husband. Finish your new story tomorrow."

"Yes, ma'am."

"Let's add ten minutes to my language lesson too."

"Fifteen. You speak it like I play guitar."

"Hey!"

He kissed her temple. "You say *yes* and *no* okay, so let's focus on your understanding. I want you to understand enough to answer conversational questions."

"Okay." She yawned and closed her eyes.

"I wouldn't push you so hard except that I intend to win my throne. Damn, you belong there beside me, doing awesome things for our citizens, our sacred duty. We're going to change the world for them."

"They won't mind an American queen?"

"No. You're good-hearted like my mother was. She was a foreigner too, and they loved her." He looked down at the bad scars on Kat's belly and thighs and feathered his fingers over them. "Hero," he muttered.

She smiled, wiggling closer, and fell asleep in his arms.

~ * ~

When they were about to check in at the next motel, a man harassed them in the lobby about buying drugs. Cory politely turned him down. The man insisted they buy something.

"No," Cory said, firmer. "Not interested."

"I don't care." He touched Katarina's shoulder. "Damn, you're gorgeous."

She stepped away.

He leered at her. "A trade."

Kat saw red in Cory's aura. His hands were fisted, and he was trembling.

"Oh shit," she muttered.

Cory had gotten into many fights growing up and was about to go ballistic.

"Let's go, sweetheart." She dragged him away and to the bus stop.

The next morning at a dilapidated motel, as Cory walked into their room, Katarina sighed. "Coffeeeeeeee! Ugh. Why doesn't this shithole have any?"

"Good news, my love." Cory handed her a foam cup. "I helped a guy load bags into his truck when you were sleeping, and as payment he gave me this coffee he said he bought from the gas station two miles down the road. You won't have to tweak now, getting your fix," he teased.

She grinned. "Thank you."

He smirked. "Anything to avoid your whining."

"Screw you," she said, on a chuckle.

He kissed her. "I tasted it, and it didn't kill me or give me some weird reaction."

"What a thoughtful husband you are. Oh, wait." She stepped back, feigning shock. "You're sprouting another head!"

He smiled. "More good news."

"What is it?"

"Our neighbors in three-twelve are homeschoolers, traveling."

"And they brought their child to this place?"

"The father is a big man. Didn't look like he worried about protecting his family. They broke down. Car's in the shop. The boy was at the picnic table looking at papers. Math, my subject."

"Languages too, word genius."

"Thank you. I only know three, though."

She rolled her eyes.

"When he seemed confused, I introduced myself and offered to help. He was shy at first, but I looked at his assignment then helped him solve a problem. His parents are going to pay me ten dollars to tutor him for an hour."

"That's a lot of money. Can they afford it?"

"Yeah. Soon, you're getting a great cup of coffee."

"You're the best."

His lips turned up at one corner. "It's my pleasure, My Queen."

"Any word on Jon's progress looking for that evidence that will clear you?"

"Not yet. Sorry."

"For what?" Her brow crinkled.

"We might be doing this for the rest of our lives."

She sat on his lap sideways, resting her head against his chest. "You were more optimistic before."

"I waver."

Later that afternoon, they spread out multi-colored candy pieces on their room's little table. Katarina arranged them in rows and columns. Lining up the right-hand column, she used green pieces. "These are the noble gases." She pointed to the top one. "This is *H-e*. Name it."

He scratched his head. "Helium."

"Good. Now this one. It's—"

"Wait…neon."

"Good! For someone who suuuuuuuucks at science, it seems you *can* learn chemistry."

"Says a lot about your teaching. Without you, it falls apart."

"Learn the whole periodic table, and I'll reward you with a nude, full body massage and a happy ending."

He pointed to the column. "Argon. Krypton, Xenon, Radon, Ununoctium."

"You're driven."

He shrugged. "I want you naked on my oiled body."

She grasped his shirt, lifted him from his chair as she stood, and scooted the chair aside with her foot. Pushing Cory, she watched him stumble backwards. She shoved him onto the bed and straddled him, bending down to kiss him. So passionate in her lovemaking, she had him gasping as he gripped her arms.

The next day, they sat on the bed strumming their instruments. She wore his black and purple jacket with only the pearl necklace under it and panties.

"You're so hot it's hard to concentrate."

"Impress me and play an A." She smirked.

He played an A chord, and she played a bass line under it.

"E."

They did the same thing, playing several progressions. She nodded, and he hit the final chord as she hit her final bass note.

"Beautiful. You've made progress."

"Thanks. You liked my suggestion about changing F to F minor in the middle, then doing that diddly do thing?"

She chuckled. "Diddly do?"

"That melodic thing." He hummed.

She smiled, shaking her head. "You're great. Yes, I liked that. We just wrote our first song together."

"A momentous occasion for me."

She looked into his eyes. He was serious.

"What shall we call it?" She tipped her head sideways.

"How about...*My wife is so damn precious.*"

"Okay. Do you want to practice *My Wife Is So Damn Precious* again?"

"I'd rather show her." He put his guitar down, went to her, took the bass, set it down, and then pressed her to the bed, kissing her.

She leaned her head back, sighing. "We're perfect together."

~ * ~

As they approached the next motel, bags in hand, Cory froze.

"Sweetheart?"

He closed his eyes a moment then looked at her and shook his head rapidly.

"You did your psychic thing, didn't you?"

"Yes. We have to get the *fuck* out of here. You'd die here."

She gasped.

Later, tired, they arrived at another motel. Cory set his bags down on the discolored carpet, sighing. "I need a shower. That was a filthy feeling, sensing your death." Without a word, he went into the bathroom and turned on the shower.

Cory was drying off in the bathroom when someone tapped on their door.

"Cleaning service."

Katarina glanced at Cory. He was slipping on sweatpants and a T-shirt. Katarina peeked through the peephole and saw a muscular man with a cart of supplies. She and Cory had just arrived but could use more towels. She opened the door then was wrenched outside. The man glared.

"Oh shit." Tremors raced through her.

"Time to punish the traitor."

Two

Katarina swallowed a scream. The angry man wrapped his hand around her neck, pushing her against the motel room door. Cory marched toward them, pointing his cousin's gun at him, deadly intent in his eyes.

The man lowered his hand and sneered. "Just having a little foreplay. Go ahead and run. We'll find you." He got into a car and drove away.

Cory swept Katarina up, kicking the door closed, and sat on the bed. He held her against his chest.

"Let's just...get out of here." She trembled. "I can't be here now. I think we can maybe get our money back or at least part of it if we tell them we were harassed."

She looked into his tear-filled eyes, which were burning with rage. She leaned on him as they made their way out. He didn't say a word, not even when they arrived at the next place. They sat on the bed, and Kat saw trauma in his face. She assured him she was all right, even as he tried to blame himself.

"I opened the door of my own volition. You can't okay my every move."

"But—"

She cut him off with a kiss. "Stop," she said against his lips.

He reclined back and used his psychic gift, like he did each morning and night. He put his hands on his belly, closed his eyes, and drew a deep breath. His eyes came open moments later.

"Sweetheart, I don't sense your impending death." He released a held breath, relieved. "We can stay put for tonight."

"I wish the alien mask had given you a gift that worked on yourself as well."

"I'm just glad I can use it for you. But I wish I could use it to predict injury or other disasters."

She snuggled against him. "They must have someone watching us now that they've found us. Jon won't be able to get us out of the state. Maybe we can lose the bad guys."

"We can always hope. King Asshole will likely toy with us. He played mental games with me as a kid as well as hurting me, being six years older and not restrained by my father's hand."

"Whatever happens, at least we're together now and married."

He kissed her tenderly. She drew him into ardent kissing.

"I can't stand how much I love you," she said.

In the morning while she was combing her hair, he popped into the door with his hands behind his back. He whipped his hands around with a smile. "I've procured protein for my wife." He handed her a peeled boiled egg.

"You're a genius!" She put it whole into her mouth, while he watched wide-eyed.

"Thank you, sweetheart!" he said. "After all your compliments on my male prowess in bed last night, it's nice to know you value my intelligence as well!" He gave a cheerful but somehow sad bow.

Her chewing slowed. She chewed a little more and then swallowed hard. "Please don't tell me we were supposed to share that egg! You got one, right? I'm sorry…I was just so damn hungry."

He put his arm over her shoulders and pulled her against him, kissing her temple. "I ate mine already. Fear not, my lady."

"Thank you for that delicious treat. How'd you get it?"

"I stole it." He winked at her.

"You're too thin," she said softly.

"You too," he said, with a frown.

"Let's write a story."

"Cool."

They sat on the bed.

"Was that your stomach rumbling?" she asked.

"Naw. Main character of our new story."

"A guy, twenty-three, like us," she said.

They exchanged ideas, and he brought his laptop over, taking notes.

Later, he nodded. "I like it. A woman's perspective adds a nice touch. Let's make a habit of this."

"I'd love to. Talk to me about Carasivian politics."

"Excellent."

~ * ~

Carrying their bags, they shivered and headed to the bus stop, crossing an empty parking lot. A car screeched to a halt in front of them over slushy snow. Two large men got out and were before them in a flash, holstered weapons at their sides. Cory and Katarina dropped their bags. Cory shoved her behind him and reached for his gun. Katarina stumbled back. The men were close and lunged before Cory could reach his weapon. Everything was a blur, but Katarina, paralyzed by fear, saw flashes of Cory fighting savagely.

"Katarina." Cory shook her gently by the shoulders.

She blinked then looked into his face. A cut from his forehead and his lip were bleeding. His cheek was starting to bruise. He shook out his fists.

"Sweetheart, are you okay?" he asked.

"Am...*I* okay?"

"Baby, tell me you're okay!"

"Cory!" She hugged him.

"I'm fine. Dodged most of their punches."

She picked up a bag and her bass guitar then saw the two men lying on the ground. Their chests were moving; they were unconscious.

Cory picked up his bags. They strode away.

"You heard 'em say they were going to beat me like my father had done. I was holding bags, and they were so close. I think they bet I wouldn't have time to draw my weapon and so didn't draw theirs, and they were wearing vests—just wanted to hurt me at this point, not kill me, apparently...yet, or maybe beat me to death. They were right about me but didn't count on my ability to evade their grasp and whoop ass when my wife's well-being was on the line."

"You're a freakishly fast and brutal fighter...all those times you protected innocent people, victims you came across." She cast a glance over her shoulder.

He did the same.

The men were still out, and a bus was in sight.

"I have almost no practice drawing a gun. I should fix that."

"I'm glad you didn't have to shoot them."

He was silent.

"Cory?"

"Yeah, me too."

He'd gained years of fighting practice growing up in that American foster home in a rough neighborhood with a vicious foster brother. He hadn't been allowed to dodge his father's fists back home but learned to avoid those of the American bullies.

"They didn't know American street-fighting style. One of my bullies was a competitor. The douchebag taught me more than he knew. *These* motherfuckers were relentless, but I found I was unrestrained when my wife was being threatened."

He pulled bus fare out of his wallet. "I'm glad Jon was able to get us more money—not enough to eat like decent people, but enough to put a roof over our heads more often than not and let us keep moving."

"Yes. I'm thankful he can do that much. We've been able to get shelter on the coldest days. Good thing this state has some nice days in the winter." She offered Cory a small smile.

They got onto the bus.

~ * ~

Alert, they packed for yet their next cheap motel.

Cory counted their cash. "Our next room will be worse, and apparently, Jon is unreachable for the moment. He hasn't been able to help as much as he wanted to. He's trying to figure out a new game plan."

"Are you sure you're feeling better? I don't like that bruise."

"I'm fine."

"Thank God, but I wish we had some of that herbal healing liquid one of your childhood caretakers used to give you. I saw it work wonders on you later, throughout school. If I knew the chemical composition..."

"Really, I'm okay, sweetheart."

"I came up with a great idea for a song in E last night."

He dropped his wallet, taking her by the shoulders. "You're a queen. You should be living in a palace, playing in your own studio, the one I'm going to build for you."

"I'm a queen because you treat me like one."

"Sometimes I..." He gritted his teeth. "...can't stand what an inadequate husband I am." He glanced around at the torn curtains and the chair with the hobbled legs.

"Stop. You're the best!"

"No, I—"

"Don't argue!" She raked him with a sexy gaze. "And, you're my *really* hot bodyguard."

"You've been hurt twice now! This is intolerable!"

"They were minor injuries." *I'd suffer far more for you.* "The first two attacks were my fault, and you saved me from something very scary, twice."

"Katar—"

"Enough. You're a good man who's half starved, and you gave me your only source of protein. I think now there was only one egg. I ate it without sharing. You know I'm not usually that selfish."

"You didn't know, sweetheart. Allow your husband to provide, please."

She studied him. "You're from a traditional culture, and I respect that, so thank you. That egg was the best I'd ever had." She fingered the cornstarch pearls around her neck.

He smiled sadly. "Thank you for tolerating my backward ways."

"What kind of asshole would I be to disparage my husband's culture? I have a surprise for you, Cor."

"You do?"

"Yeah, you look like you could use some cheering up." She picked up her bass.

"You wrote me a song?"

"A special one, in C minor, then it moves into B minor with a beautiful lead-in. CB for your initials, Corentin Brodnik."

"When did you do this?"

"A phrase here or there, and while you were in the shower, the times I wasn't in there steaming up windows with you."

"Damn, you're good."

"Remember that the alien Mask of Truth enhanced my talents."

"It had a lot to work with. Let's hear." He rubbed his hands together.

"I wrote down instrumentation. The girls taught me how to write for their instruments, and I taught them the same for bass. Imagine a beautiful keyboard like this..." She played a riff. "Then add strings to fill it out." She played again. "Here comes the bass, like this."

She played and sang an epic metal ballad, dripping with love.

His mouth fell open. He dropped onto the bed and rubbed his hand over his jaw, mesmerized.

She continued her soulful, romantic piece, filling the room with her feelings for him. The last notes rang out.

"You liked it?"

"That was..." He cleared his throat. His eyes spoke of unconditional love. "...awesome."

He was grasping the blanket.

"Thank you."

"We need to record this. You rocked my world, beautiful."

She set her bass down, placed her hand behind his head, and put a gentle kiss on his lips. "Let's record it onto your computer now."

"So I can listen to it often. What's the name of it?"

"*I love Cory.*"

He grinned. "No, really."

"Really. Every note is like a pearl on this necklace you made me, infused with love."

His brow lifted. They recorded the song.

"So much comes through in your music, wife."

"Your story entitled *Five Oh Two* makes me cry whenever I read it. You're a brilliant writer."

"You're a brilliant flatterer."

She scoffed.

"Let's do something amazing in celebration of New Year's, really celebrate the greatness and generosity of life."

"You always surprise me. I *love* the things you've come up with."

"You'll thank me later. It will probably inspire you to write a song."

"Your ideas are *extraordinary*. I can't wait!"

The next day, at another place, packed up and ready to go again, Cory kissed her and told her to wait while he returned the key.

"Hurry up. Our bus will be here soon. Keep the door open, so I can watch for it."

"No. Peek out a window."

"It's a nice, sunny Colorado winter's day."

"Katarina—"

"You're not my boss."

He sighed and looked at the bed. "Then hold my cousin's gun."

"I don't like that thing."

"Do it anyway. A murderous king has his ruffians after us." He pulled the hood of his jacket over his head and proceeded toward the manager's office.

She glanced outside at icicles dripping from a tree and then looked at the gun lying four feet away on the bed. The drawn curtains made the room dim. She leaned low and stretched her hand toward the gun, and a shot exploded into the open door. She yelled out, grasping her upper arm. Blood dripped from under her fingers. She dropped to the floor, hearing footsteps pounding on the pavement.

"Katarina!"

"Arms up!"

"Katarina!" Cory shouted again.

"I'm fine!" Kat dared to scoot closer to the door and peer around the corner to see what was going on. Her arm throbbed.

The manager, a tired-looking man in a dull green jacket and jeans was holding up a shotgun. A man in a suit and Cory had their arms up.

The manager scowled at the assailant. "Get the fuck *outta* here! Bastard shooting at my clientele! Come around again, and you're dead. I'd call the cops, but I'd rather shoot a trespassing son-of-bitch like you myself."

The stranger slowly holstered his gun. "I'm leaving." He looked at Cory. "You should never have disobeyed your king and married that bimbo. I'll be seeing you. Hope you heard that, *bimbo*. I've been practicing my English. The bullet was meant for *him,* though. The shadow I saw inside just happened to be you." He got into an expensive car she couldn't name and drove away.

Cory tore into their room and scooped her up, shaking. Kat's heart sank. He was going to die because of her.

No. He wasn't.

"You idiot!" she screamed. "You could have gotten on that bus and escaped! Instead you ran *toward* the bullet!"

He squeezed her. "If you die, I die! My future does *not* include a life without you!"

"But you checked. I wasn't going to die today, but you could have!"

"Maybe you didn't die due to my actions somehow. Are you okay?" He leaned back, pale with worry, to check her arm where she was applying pressure.

"It just nicked me."

"Oh, God."

The manager peeked in. "You okay?"

"Can you take us to the hospital, please?" Cory asked.

He nodded. "We get a lot of criminals like that around here. I've been trying to clean up the place for years."

Later, when Kat's flesh wound was bandaged, Cory spoke to a nurse, worried, agitated, and petrified Kat's injury was worse than it was. Kat watched him as if from a distance, and closed her eyes, visualizing him lying dead at her feet. She opened her eyes with resolve.

"Cor, can I have some money for the vending machine?" Kat asked.

He turned to her, pulled out his wallet and handed her a few ones and some quarters.

"Thanks," she said.

He gave her a quick kiss then turned back to the nurse, with his concerns still pouring out.

Kat swept up her bass guitar and duffle bag.

Cory was so deep in heated conversation he didn't even see her leave the room. Kat approached the nurse's desk and asked for a pen and paper. She glanced at the young woman in purple scrubs who gave them to her.

"Can you bill us..." She was going to give them her parents' address.

"It's been taken care of. Your brother-in-law will be handling the bill. The police will be here soon for a statement."

Kat nodded and wrote a note for Cory:

That was terrifying. I can't live this way. Move on without me.
Katarina

Dizzy with regret and loss, she folded the note and gave it to the nurse. "Could you please give this to my husband?"

The nurse nodded and took the note. Kat dashed away and onto the first bus she saw.

Once off the bus, she found a pay phone and called Jon. He answered on the first ring.

"Hello?"

"It's me."

"Katarina! Corentin is going out of his mind!"

"I...just couldn't take it anymore. I'm sorry," she lied.

"I don't believe you. And neither does he. He knows the note was a sham."

"Believe me." She sucked in a deep breath. "Can you spare some cash? I'm homeless."

"I'll get some. Do me a favor, please."

"Sure."

"Tell me where you are. I'll have a friend pick you up in a yellow car. He has black hair, twenty-six years old, name is Sherban. He'll take you to the duke's mansion where you celebrated on your wedding night."

"Cory's going to be there, isn't he?"

"I sneaked him back there. Disguises, wild story. You owe him a word."

"No. He's a bad husband who put me in danger."

"You're a terrible liar. You fear for his life as long as you're in it."

She sniffled. "Goodbye."

"Wait."

She clutched the phone. "What?"

"Please, we're family now. Do this for me, and if you still want to leave, you can, under my protection."

"Promise?"

"I promise."

"All right." She told him where she was.

"You can say goodbye to your friends this time. I invited them back."

~ * ~

Trembling, she walked up the gravel path of the mansion. She walked past Jon's guards and knocked on the front door.

Jon greeted her. "Give him a moment."

She nodded, gearing up for battle.

Three

Jon led Katarina to a small salon then left. Cory stood there. He took several steps toward her, his face in an expression of agony. She held up her hand. He stopped.

"Sweetheart," his voice cracked. "Are you okay?"

"It's only a flesh wound, but now I'm traumatized!"

"You were hurt far worse when your sister died." He gazed down.

"That makes it acceptable?" she yelled.

"No! I'm *so* sorry."

"I can't do this." *Damn these tears.*

"Let me see you through this! We *love* each other so much it hurts!"

"Not anymore."

"Stop it!"

"I could have been killed today!"

He shook his head. "My gift said no. But it still terrified me to hear that shot and see that gun pointed into our room!"

"So, it's okay if I get shot, as long as I don't die?" she retorted.

"No! I fucked up," he said sadly.

It's not your fault! I love you! I'm glad it was me and not you! Thank God you had your hood up, your back was to him, you were down a ways out of his line of attention, and he thought you were in our room.

Cory stumbled back in despair. "I'm a horrible husband."

No, you're not! She coughed to help her breathe. "Cory—"

He stepped closer. "I'm not worth it, but I'll try. I'll try!" His hands came out in a plea.

She shook her head. *Oh God...* Her stomach cramped.

"Please, I'll do anything!" He leapt and grasped her hands. She gasped as he fell to his knees, pressing his lips to her hands.

"I want a divorce."

"No! Don't leave me!"

"We're through. Now you'll be free to marry whatever poor woman the king orders you to. I'm just glad it will no longer be me." The words barely escaped her throat. Thinking of him with another woman made her nauseous, but at least the king would let him live, dangling in misery, as he intended on giving Cory a wretched match, hating him so much. Something wet hit her hand. Tears rolled down his face.

She sucked in sharply. Aching to drop to her knees, embrace him, stroke his soft brown hair, and kiss him as his tears dried in joyous relief, she held her ground, picturing his headstone. She snatched her hands away. Black desolation poured over her. This was suicide.

He stood and swiped tears away, saying words she could feel from his heart. His lips parted, and his anguish came out. "You're ending me."

Her hand came to her mouth. She lowered it, clearing her throat in order to make way past her tears for words. "No."

He gazed at her, a memory in his agonized eyes. "Ten years ago, I discovered what emptiness was...when I met you."

Her brows narrowed.

"I hadn't known how alone I was until that first time you walked into that classroom, scanned the room, and your beautiful eyes lingered on me."

His pain showed in his eyes, his lips, his shaking hands, and made her ache with love.

"When I saw your scars and the tears rolling down your face, I knew I was looking at whom I prayed to God was my future wife." His sad voice forced tears from her eyes.

She rubbed them away. "We were only...thirteen."

"But I knew. And I know now...that it was mutual. All these years, all we've been through together, I dreamed that I'd be truly blessed and win over someone so..." He was grasping for control. "...lovely and good who would want her best friend, a fool like me. My heart *begged*. It was hell thinking I might have to watch you marry another man someday. And when you didn't...and you married me... part of me was so amazed I was terrified you'd later change your mind. But, after making love to you, I knew without a doubt, that you love me too. Now I only beg all that is holy and good that I'm not a stupid, complete, and utter fool for believing I was so blessed."

Cory! She fisted one hand in the other behind her back. *You're going to die if I don't do this. Think, Kat, of...that womanizing asshole you dated a year ago.*

The vision of her ex-boyfriend put steel in her back. "You disgust me. You say you love me but put me in harm's way."

"I'm so damn sorry. I love you so much! Please don't make my life a horror story and *leave* me! Don't do that to me, baby." His heartbreaking expression nearly unraveled her resolve.

She swayed.

"I'll protect you with my *life*. You know with the gift the extraterrestrial mask imbued me with, I can keep you alive, sensing impending death threats to you. I'll use it more often and—"

"But you can't predict your *own* death or keep me from crippling injury."

"Sweetheart." He coughed back tears. "Please! I—"

She'd have to attack his old-fashioned sensibilities of manhood. Her stomach turned. How could she do this? She didn't want to do this. "Man up already, and spare some of your self-respect."

His jaw dropped.

"I'm sorry. I thought your social position put you above me, but it turns out you're not good enough for *me*." She painted her desperate love with a cold stare.

He cast his blue-eyed gaze down. "I'm not."

His devastation cracked through her determination, sending the truth to her eyes just as he looked up and met her gaze.

Realization enlightened his features. He grasped her arm. "You're coming with me."

"No!"

"Your eyes just gave you away. You're...trying to save me, like you did before." A smile spread across his lips.

"Remove your damn hand!"

He released her.

She knew if she told him the truth but said she was leaving anyway, he wouldn't give up. And he'd be in grave peril. She took a deep breath. "You'd have to take me by force, kicking and screaming."

A long pause ensued. "So be it. Then you'll thank me for saving you from this bullshit lie."

"I'll scream for someone to call the cops!"

He studied her. "No, you won't. You gave me that extraordinary wedding ring. In all of Carasivia, to give such a ring happens once a decade. It makes front-page news. You knew that."

Do this or he dies.

"I changed my mind when a bullet struck me. That's when my love died."

He paled and shook his head. "Don't say that!"

His urgent plea forced her attention to the polished floor. Without those years of practice hiding her feelings for him, she would have failed, and squeezed him close to her heart. "I can't stand to look at you right now."

"I don't believe you—"

She shoved him. "You can't force me to come with you!"

"Enough! You love me!"

Yes. I'd rather die with you than live without you. Here it goes, my life for yours.

She screamed for help.

Jon ran into the room. She darted to him, slamming against his chest. His brow crinkled.

"Get me away from him!" Kat urged Jon.

He pulled away, took her arms, and gave her a beseeching look. "Stop, Kat."

Cory approached. "*Kindly* give me back my wife."

Jon stepped back.

"No! Either keep him away from me, or I'll flee into the night, and you'll never see me again!"

Jon gave Cory a piteous look. "I can't let her go out alone, homeless, penniless..." He held out his arms to Kat. She ran into them. He led her into the hallway.

Cory turned and strode toward the door. He stopped and punched the wall several times, yelling out. He ran past her in the hall. In a daze, she spun around and saw him collapsed in a puddle on the floor with his face in his hands.

I'll dream about you every day. No one will ever replace you in my heart. Tears splashed onto her cheeks.

"You'll beg me to take you back!" Cory's voice echoed against the walls.

She cried. Jon put a gentle hand on her shoulder. "Stay a couple of nights here, safe. I have men guarding outside. Soon I'll send you wherever you want to go."

She nodded numbly, and went to find her and Cory's best friends, Asher, Gunther and Brendan. Once she saw them, she apologized for disappearing.

Four

The following morning, Kat entered the kitchen and Cory walked in with the shadow of fatigue and misery covering his features. He dropped to his knees before her, taking her hands. "I beg you."

"Stop it!"

"No, you stop it!"

She curled her lip in feigned disgust.

He gazed up with tragic eyes. "Do you...hate me?"

Her lips parted. "No. I...just no longer..." *Oh God.* She put her hand over her belly. "Respect you."

Never taking his eyes off her, he rose to his feet, his pleading gaze turning into a glare. They took their seats, far from each other. She whipped around, wiped her eyes, and then drew a steadying breath.

Over a large breakfast table, the others gaped.

Brendan said, "Somebody talk. I hate this heavy silence." He ran a hand through his reddish-blond hair.

Cory looked daggers at him.

Brendan rubbed his face. "Oh, I drank too much last night. Fuck if I remember how I even got here."

"I saw a conversation between my parents in that weird mask and got another clue about the file." All eyes turned to Gunther. He took off his leather jacket and set it by his motorcycle helmet on the floor.

"What file?" Brendan asked.

"The puzzle my parents dropped into my lap when I was a kid. They had called from overseas saying they were pursuing interesting information. They had found an important file, the doozy of a mystery I've always wanted to solve."

Cory leaned forward. "Why open up to us now about your great secret?"

Gunther shrugged. "The mask said I should tell you all the truth, that I had important information to impart, so here it goes." He let out an audible breath. "My parents were corresponding with European royalty. There was a king and a queen and three young princes."

Kat turned to look at Cory. Steam from her tea rose, bringing with it the scent of peppermint.

Cory narrowed his eyes at Gunther. "Could this have been in Carasivia?"

Gunther frowned. "Is everything all right?"

"No, but please, continue. I'm enthralled," Cory said.

"Do you want to discuss what's on your mind?" Gunther said.

Cory sat up straighter. "Ever been in love?"

"Don't you remember that girl back in twelfth grade—"

"Ever needed a woman so badly you'd do anything for her, only to have her swear eternal love and then throw you away?"

Kat looked at Cory, her heart aching. She put her hands on her thighs and bunched her pants in her white-knuckled hands. She bit back bitter tears.

Gunther frowned. "What is it with you two? She loves you too, very much."

Cory tapped his fingers on the table. "Yeah, right. Ask her what the problem is."

Gunther turned to her. "Kat?"

She let out a small sob.

"Please, we're all confused here, I'm sure," Gunther said.

"I don't understand. You two are crazy about each other," Asher said. He combed out his long blond hair with his fingers.

Brendan scoffed at him, in the habit of playfully mocking Asher for what he called his *effeminate* ways. "Nice hair, bitch."

"Fuck you, savage," Asher said, chuckling.

"Maybe later, pretty boy."

"Asshat." Asher turned to Kat. "What's going on?"

"I don't think Cory wants me saying any more than I already have. We're all close but—" Kat dropped off.

"Be my guest, Katarina. These are our oldest and dearest friends," Cory said sarcastically.

"I'd say ten years of friendship going back to middle school makes us family," Gunther added.

"I—" She encircled her warm cup with her fingers.

"She thinks I'm a bad person," Cory blurted, patting the table. "A terrible husband, a weak excuse for a man, a threat that makes her scream bloody murder and run into the arms of another man."

Gunther and Brendan raised their brows, and Asher watched, frowning.

"Cory?" Gunther asked.

Brendan looked at Cory with disapproval and rubbed his jaw.

"Is it over between you two?" Gunther asked. "Already?"

Kat answered yes at the same time that Cory answered no.

"I thought you loved me, Katarina."

"Beyond words."

He leaned forward. "Sweetheart?"

She inhaled sharply. "I mean—"

"You're violent, Cory. Maybe she's afraid of you," Brendan dared.

Her gaze turned to Brendan. "I'm not afraid *of* him. I'm afraid *for* him." She bit her lip, mad at herself for slipping again.

Cory stood and took a step toward her, hope in his softened eyes.

"I mean..." she said to him. "You don't deserve the lingering love that keeps popping up against my will. I'm afraid for you to see the last of it die."

He drew in a deep breath and dropped with an angry sigh into his chair.

Brendan got up and sat next to Kat.

Cory grasped his armrests. "What are you doing?" Ice dripped from his tone.

Brendan gave him a glance and touched Kat's shoulder.

"I wouldn't do that if I were you." Cory's threat was unmistakable.

Kat gazed at him with sorrow. "Behavior like your unreasonable, jealous rage just makes things worse."

Cory visibly struggled to contain his anger, tensing.

Brendan nodded to him. "Relax. We've been friends for years. I would be here for anyone in our group, including you, if you hadn't ended our friendship."

Cory pointed at him. "You're insane! And fearless. You've come on to my wife before and then—" He turned away and pounded his fist on the table. "Fuck!"

Jon walked into the room, and Cory glowered at him.

Kat sipped her tea, holding the cup with a trembling hand.

Gunther looked at Cory, eyes narrowed. "Jon's not such a bad guy."

Jon walked over to Cory and placed his hand on his arm. "Corentin, please, your temper."

Cory shot up. "Mom would not have approved of you standing against me!"

The others gaped.

"You're brothers?" Asher said.

"Swear your silence about that, all of you," Jon said.

Jon turned to Cory. "I'm not against you. I love you and am your most loyal brother."

Kat was touched by the love she saw in Jon's face.

"I want to help you. I know you didn't kill our father, and I will help you prove it," Jon said.

There were gasps.

Cory spoke rapidly in his native tongue. Kat strained to understand and only made out a couple of words: "steal" and "wife."

Jon responded in the same language then turned and glanced at the others. "Let's speak in English."

Cory fisted his hands. "I don't know," he said in English. "You want her and plan on charming her away?"

"Corentin, search your heart. Remember how Mom raised you."

Kat imagined a younger Cory sitting next to a lovely woman in a little schoolroom in the palace. Her heart warmed. She sipped her tea, rolling the cool sweetness across her tongue.

"Having escaped Father's wrathful hand, his abuse, unlike me," Cory began, "you didn't—"

"You wouldn't tell us much about your past, Cory," Brendan said, and rubbed his temples.

"You're his closest friends. Will you all swear again to keep these secrets?" Jon asked.

Everyone nodded.

"He's the rightful ki—"

"Enough!" Cory snapped, pointing to Jon.

"Let's trust them." Jon looked at each person.

"Who are you two?" Gunther asked, looking at Cory and Jon.

"That's what I'd like to know," Brendan added.

"You know who I am." Cory tossed up his hands.

"I mean, who is your family?" Gunther asked, leaning back in his chair, making it creak.

"Well, Gunther, finish telling your story, and you may get some answers," Cory said. "I want to know more about this file your parents found. In a palace guest room?"

"Yes."

Asher took a sip of orange juice. "Tell us."

"Well," Gunther said. "I suppose it was lost with my parents in that plane crash, but perhaps there are ways to discover what was in it. One of my uncles was an ambassador, but he and his wife died years ago. They had no kids. My parents had spent some time with the Carasivian royal family."

Cory studied Gunther. "That was your family. I should have known. But you never revealed much about your parents and that mystery. I've never even seen a picture of them in your home."

"The aunt who raised me after that cried every time she looked at the pictures, so she put every one of them in storage. What do you mean by 'That was your family'?"

"I'm just...distracted." He slapped his hands onto his lap. "Oh, what the hell. Brendan knows."

Brendan shook his head. "What do I know?"

"Do you..." Cory began, "...forget our previous words?"

Cory's glare startled Kat. Would he hurt Brendan?

"Did something happen?" Brendan asked.

"Coward!" Cory shot to his feet. "Pretend and play stupid! The things you said you were going to do with my wife!"

"Cory, please!" Kat begged.

He lowered himself back down to a sitting position, huffing.

Gunther gave him a piercing look. "*You're* the kid my parents told me about on the phone, the haunted boy hiding behind palace corners. My parents died on the plane coming home from one of their political trips. The king had been killed, and my parents were visiting with the newly crowned young king, King Goran. I remember when I met you here in the States, Cory, when you first enrolled in our school. We two orphans became instant friends. You had a secretive past, and so did I, and we both accepted it."

"It drew us together like brothers."

Kat smiled, drawing a bass clef on her cup with a finger.

"What do you know? Please tell me," Gunther asked, leaning forward.

Gunther turned to Jon. "What's going on?"

"I defer before my brother. He is my elder and my k—"

"Jon, it's not like I'm going to leave Katarina—even if it's only a... one-way-love—and go home and rule even if I am proven innocent of killing my father, and the current monster ruling can be dethroned!"

One-way love. Kat's stomach turned. *If you only knew how far off the mark you were with that one...*

"You owe it to our country to return," Jon said.

"You go. Usurp that evil bastard. You're more fit to rule than either of us. Katarina thinks I'm a bad person!"

"I'm not a leader!" Jon said with wide eyes. "And you're not a bad person!"

"Yes, I am. My queen thinks I am," Cory said with a soft voice and lowered shoulders.

No, I don't. Katarina blinked away forming tears.

"So, you *are* a prince, Cory," Brendan said.

"He's more than that. Our father's dead," Jon said. "And our older brother is *literally* a bastard."

Cory gave Jon a clenched-jaw look. "My place is with Katarina!" He gave her a desperate look. "Give me another chance, beloved."

Waves of sadness washed over her.

"She doesn't want you," Gunther said gently.

"I *do* want him!"

Cory looked at her tenderly. He got up, went to her, knelt before her, and grabbed her hand. "You do want me, really?"

"I'm wavering, but I'm hardening against that."

He gritted his jaw. "Explain to me why you're ruining both of our lives!"

She tore her hand away and forced a mixture of fear and disgust over her features.

"Damn it!" He shot up and went back to his seat.

Jon studied her. "Kat? I failed you two. I couldn't keep you or Corentin safe. I beg you, forgive me. Let me try again. That's what it's about, isn't it?"

Cory turned, staring at her hard. "Say yes, sweetheart. I'll never give up on you."

Her breath caught. On the verge of saying, *Yes!* she had to bite her tongue as waves of terror—her premonitions—warned her. *He will die!* The same premonitions had screamed at her as a child warning her about her younger sister. She had ignored them, and Molly had died.

She thought of a look Cory had given a bully in ninth grade, Cory's impudent courage.

~ * ~

Do your worst, fuck face.

And the bully did. Cory missed school for days. Kat's parents, who knew Cory from his many visits, would drive Kat to the foster home to see him and chat with the house parents while their daughter visited with her new best friend.

Cory stretched a shaky hand toward Kat from his sickbed and smirked. *Stupid asshole taught me five new moves I'm going to use to whoop his ass next time.*

She cried.

He touched her arm. *Don't cry. Would you honor me with your smile? I could use it about now.*

I will see you through this, Cory... she had said. She handed him an icepack and then wrote down the answers to his homework as he dictated them. He occasionally winced in pain.

I have some ointment from my country. Please hand it to me. It will help me heal faster. He pointed to his dresser.

She retrieved it and rubbed some of the brown liquid gently on his face, neck and arms. She returned to do the same every day until he could return to school.

~ * ~

Katarina leaned back, giving Jon that same brazen smirk Cory was famous for. "No, Jon. I just need a reliable man." Her stomach turned.

Jaws dropped. Cory slapped a hand over his eyes, trembled while collecting himself, and faced Gunther. "The file wasn't lost in that plane crash."

"What?" Gunther said.

"When I was a boy..." Cory paused, "...I overheard your parents say they had mailed it somewhere because they didn't want it discovered on them. The thing is, I had no idea until today they were your parents. Where might they have mailed it? To your relatives? Washington doesn't have it. Jon checked."

"My mother was afraid. I saw in a mask vision that they were trying to decide what to do with it," Gunther said.

Jon approached Cory, dusting off his velvet sleeves with casual nonchalance. He took a seat next to him. "The men in Washington never did release to me the names of the agents when I asked if they had a file about Carasivia's royal family. But they questioned the family of their deceased agents. That led nowhere."

"My uncle and aunt, my only ones left..." Gunther shook his head. "They never said a word to me about being questioned, and I was just a kid. I don't have family besides them left."

"So, if they don't have the file, then who does?"

Gunther shrugged. "I don't know. What's in it?"

"Evidence to clear my name and put me on the throne, with my queen at my side."

Brendan looked at Katarina, then Cory and hesitated. "She doesn't want to go with you, so I won't let her."

Cory looked at him a long while. Everyone grew uncomfortable, shifting in their seats.

Cory's words came out soft and with resignation. "My hand is about to be forced, and I ask you all ahead of time to forgive me."

There were several gasps.

Five

Katarina stood and dragged Cory into a dim hallway of the ducal mansion where the others couldn't hear them. "Please tell me you won't do anything stupid."

"Why the fuck do you care?"

"Please!"

"Sure you're not going to scream rape or something? Some things I have no power over, but this I do. Brendan will make his move as soon as I'm out of sight, and even if I don't have you, he can't."

Her fingers curled around his arm. "Don't hurt him."

"You…" The blueness of his eyes reflected his agony. He stepped away from her grasp.

"Cory?" His sudden rejection alarmed her and sank her heart.

"Come back to me, or get out of my sight."

Tears spilled onto her cheeks. God, she wanted to touch him. Her hands shook.

"What do I have to do?" he said on a harsh whisper.

"Obey your king."

"It's too late for that. Wait, you're *admitting* this is what it's all about—"

"No, and no. We can get an annulment to erase our mistake." Hammer blows of loss hit her heart, the words the bitterest she'd ever said, but terror at the thought of his death pushed her forward.

"I will block you on this," he said.

"You will make an enemy."

He leaned close and looked into her eyes. "So be it."

A chill of fear sliced through her. "Goodbye."

"Katarina!" Panicked, he grabbed her arm.

She could see the raging, battling emotions turning him inside out. She leaned and gave him a last kiss, closing her eyes against burning tears. *Oh, my love!* "Farewell."

Brusquely, he turned and marched down the hallway. Kat rejoined the others. She lowered onto a chair, sick to her stomach.

Asher gave Brendan a concerned look.

"What is it?"

"Watch your back."

"Cory?"

Asher tipped his head.

"I'll be on guard," Brendan said, and rolled his eyes.

"Gunther, I'd appreciate it if you would bunk with Brendan tonight. I'm worried for his safety," Katarina said.

~ * ~

When Brendan had pressed that anger-infused mask against Cory weeks ago in the large kitchen, white-hot light had rushed him with fury. Funny how Asher had said he dreamt Cory had been poisoned. It didn't seem like poison to him. It ran through his veins, itching to be satisfied, making Cory feverish with dangerous intention. Cory's anger renewed upon waking. He shuddered with need.

As streaks of dawn cracked through a high window and landed on the stone-flagged floor, Cory opened his door and made his way to Brendan's room. He lifted his fist to the heavy door, and it opened. Brendan stared out with a derisive curl of his lip. Cory tipped his head, gesturing over his shoulder to indicate that Brendan should follow him. Brendan trailed behind him through a narrow servants' door. They entered a courtyard.

"Come," Cory said, walking across a small field near some pine trees. He glanced at security cameras then faced Brendan. "You and I have things to settle." His eye caught something white. He glanced to the side, seeing a white flower growing at the base of a stone bench.

His mind flashed to his wedding day.

Clasping his smiling bride's hand, he walked out of the courthouse, light on his feet, his heart expanding in a warm world filled with joy. Katarina paused.

"Sweetheart?"

"Hon, look." She bent to the ground, picking up a small white flower. "It's not the season. Someone must have dropped this. It's a sign." She straightened, tucking the flower into his jacket pocket.

He smiled. "A sign of what?"

"That our marriage, our love, is a miracle, like this flower in November."

The glow in her eyes, the faith in what they had, tripped up his tongue.

His heart softened. Anger had poisoned him, nearly driven him to do something he would never otherwise do. Cold shudders coursed through him.

"Hey, jerk-of-the-century." Brendan's voice tore him from his thoughts. "Katarina will never know how much I really hate you. I'll pretend I was a victim of the mask's influence. I'll say its poison had made me seem disrespectful to you and that I loved you like brother."

"She'll know you're lying. You'd never use the word 'love' and a man's name in the same sentence."

"I'll say you were my best friend, and I miss you. I'm going to hurt you now."

Cory's heart sank. *Think of the flower, of Katarina's love.* "We're..." he muttered in a harsh voice, "...on the border of this property."

"So?" Brendan chuckled.

"Step off it onto United States territory and stand where you'll be protected, so I don't have to lift my hand to you."

Brendan snarled and took a stride closer to the mansion.

Cory sighed. "Why? Is it the mask?"

"That's the story I'll give for my behavior."

Cory gulped past the lump in his throat. "For how long have you hated me?"

A flash of confusion flitted across Brendan's eyes.

Cory stepped closer to him. "Brendan? We're like brothers." Wild hope came to him, despite the fury he had held in his heart the day before.

"I've always hated you. Our friendship was a lie."

The air left Cory's lungs. "I don't understand. I would have sensed it. Sure, you've often messed with me, but that's what brothers do. And your chiding did not seem so bad until only recently."

Brendan scoffed. "I'm good at what I do. You were the weirdest new kid that school ever produced, and you disgusted me with your odd clothes and your fucked-up accent. When Kat, the prettiest girl in school, looked over at you for the first time, and her face lit with amazement, I thought I was going to puke.

"However, my closest friends liked you already, so when they dragged me over to talk to you, I had no choice but to tolerate you. Gunther and Asher lectured me about giving you a chance. They said either I do as they asked in that regard, or I could take a hike."

"I see. Why did you wait until recently to make your move?"

"Goran contacted me."

"What?" Cory stepped back.

"You never knew, did you? He offered me money. I told him I'd do it for free because I despise you."

"You're working for *him*?" Cory's throat narrowed with shock. In the light of day, he wasn't furious. He was heartbroken.

Brendan nodded.

"The mask," Cory said, then paused before speaking again, "told everyone good things."

"Oh, that simple-minded stuff about Asher and Gunther helping out a king is about to become canceled destiny."

"You could have just shot me."

"I want it to be more memorable than that. It's not time yet, anyway. Your grandmother is still alive. *He* went after you thinking she was about to die, but she didn't, and she just took a turn for the better."

A dash of relief soared through Cory.

"I wanted Kat for sex, of course," Brendan added. "I saw how you two looked at each other. I thought I'd wait until you consummated things. That way, she'd be *really* devastated, and I'd be more effective as her comforter, and oh damn, would it be exciting to look into her face while fucking her, knowing how badly I hurt you with my bare hands. Even now, I'm getting turned on thinking about it."

Cory's fisted hands pressed against his sides. "You've been a major asshole lately. She won't go near you. You fucked up, even if you do manage to kill me, which you won't."

An eagle called out, its cry cutting the air.

"I'll repent and be so sorry for the way I treated my *brother*. She'll take me into her forgiving arms."

"No, she'd never betray me that way."

"She would, because you're a lousy husband."

Cory's stomach turned.

"You know it's true. Now I want to beat you nearly to death."

"I can take a beating."

Brendan snarled. "I let you knock me out previously. Not this time." He pulled the mask from his jacket and slammed it against Cory's chest before tossing it onto the ground.

Cory looked at him through a sudden haze of red. "I can also *give* one hell of a beating. Say goodbye to this world, Brendan."

~ * ~

Gunther knocked on everyone's door, concerned. Brendan was missing. His overnight bag remained in his room. Everyone searched.

"Where's Cory?" Gunther asked.

"He's gone too." Kat touched her lips, worried.

Around dusk, Cory dragged himself up to the front door, with new cuts and bruises blending with the fading old ones across his face, and he slumped over in exhaustion. Everyone ran to him.

"Where were you? Where's Brendan?" Kat said, terrified.

He brought tired eyes to hers. "I was wandering around all day, trying to ease my torment. I have no clue where Brendan is."

"Cory!" Kat pulled him into a blue salon to the left of the main entrance. "Please tell me you didn't do anything!"

He glared. "So glad you're worried about him and not me!"

"C...Cory?" She blinked. "What were you doing?"

"I was considering making you non-royalty once again."

"Do you have political clout that allows for instant divorces or annulments?"

"No."

"I don't understand."

He remained silent a moment then said, "It's been a devastating couple of days."

Worry cut its demoralizing path through her. "Please don't. There's hope for us." *Fuck.* She kept on slipping.

"There is?" He held his breath.

I'd better anger you again. "I believe you can change."

His posture grew rigid. "Maybe it's *you* who needs to change," he said, in the crisp tones of his native tongue. He turned his tortured gaze from her.

The blue walls behind him emphasized the coldness surrounding him.

"Did you hurt Brendan?"

"You *dare* to ask me that?"

She could hear her heartbeat in her ears. "You threatened him."

"What if I did?"

She stepped back. "You...didn't execute him?"

His lips turned up at the corner, wickedly. "That execrable, abominable, abhorrent, son-of-a-bitch will *never* lay a hand on you. He pushed me hard. And you didn't give a damn about how it injured me!" He tapped his chest. "All you cared about was protecting your precious *Brendan!*"

She bent over, heaving. "You've snapped." She held out her hand against him. "Get the hell away from me!" This time, she meant it. "You're not the gentleman I thought you were." She stood straight and stepped back. "But then again, you were abused by your father."

"You throw that in my face!" He turned his head away, as if pained, then back. He chuckled in a mocking way.

"And you laugh. I shouldn't be shocked that the truth about you comes out after all this time. The ugly truth that you're a monster, like your brother and father, knocking off your own friend."

"You're shallower than I ever imagined in my wildest fantasies."

Her hands rested at her sides in tight knots. "I made a huge mistake marrying you! I should have fucked your friends before you ever touched me!" She regretted those words immediately but didn't dare retract them. She held her breath.

He stepped forward, shaking. She braced herself.

He leaned toward her with frozen rage but didn't lift his hand. "I feigned love for you to get you into bed. All my friends wanted you," he said, with venom. "Huh, my interest in you lasted slightly longer than average for all those women I enjoyed taking to bed in the past."

"Y...You said Brendan couldn't have me."

"A matter of manly pride."

"But...we...got married." Her lip trembled. Confusion whirled in her head. "To my disgust. Why'd you accept my proposal?"

His studying gaze chilled her. "To your disgust." He paused. "To defy that fucker King Goran, George the asshole. It was awesome. Oh, and I enjoyed killing Brendan. One of the servants disposed of the body."

Her world collapsed. She burst into a sob, ran to the nearest phone, and called the police. After getting her information, they informed her they'd look into it, but she should consider that a man in his twenties had been known to take off without telling anyone, and maybe he'd turn up. She slammed down the phone.

Images of Cory holding a gun on their wedding night, vowing to hurt Brendan, tormented her. She went to her room and tried calling Brendan's cell phone, just in case. His phone was disconnected. She cried herself to sleep. Days later, she phoned the police again and asked if they had any news. The officer told her Brendan's credit card had been used, and the signature on the slip matched the one on his driver's license. Also, a friend of his said Brendan had dropped by to say hello and mentioned that he was going to do some traveling. Kat sighed in relief.

~ * ~

Cory heard that when King Goran discovered Katarina had left him, the tyrant king was so delighted he lifted his lock on Jon's account, as well as those of Jon's friends, and redirected the spies he had watching them onto Cory. The king wanted to sit back, and for the sake of entertainment, watch Cory's ruined marriage play out.

Cory went to the apartment Jon had rented for him—back in his old building—and stewed in anger for days. He swiped up his gym bag and headed out. *All she cares about is Brendan! My wife has betrayed me.* He drew a deep breath, thinking of her directly. *I hate you for that, Katarina, you spit on me, just like my father had done.*

An hour later, he entered his apartment and threw the gym bag against the wall. A knock sounded at his door. He pulled it open. Katarina stood there, *the betrayer.*

"C...Cory..." She wrung her hands. "The police said Brendan used his credit card and contacted a friend."

"What's your point?"

"I just wanted to let you know that I know you didn't hurt him." She turned away to leave.

"You didn't come here to tell me you can't live without me." He gritted his teeth. "Your mind is ever on Brendan. Why the hell didn't you marry him instead?"

She spun to face him. "Maybe I should have." She glanced at his hand. "You took your ring off."

"Yep."

She looked at his hand for several moments. "Keep it off."

"Go away. My family paid the police and Brendan's friend to lie. Live with that one."

She gasped, turned, and walked out. He slammed the door behind her. He called Jon.

"Listen to what I have to say, Jon, and consider it a command from your rightful king."

"I see. Go ahead."

"If Katarina should ask you if you paid off the police and one of Brendan's friends to lie, you are to tell her yes or give her silence upon the matter."

"But—"

"Do not defy me on this. Understood?"

"Yes."

Cory hung up.

Six

Katarina went to Brendan's apartment. His stuff was on the street, and strangers were carrying it away. It seemed all the valuable items were already gone. She collapsed onto the curb.

Moments later, she got onto a bus and went to Brendan's mother's house.

A charming woman in her mid-forties answered, frowning. "Katarina."

"Can I come in?"

She guided Kat inside. They took a seat on the couch. *What can I possibly say?*

"I..."

Brendan's mother gave her hand a squeeze. "The police said he was out there somewhere, but why wouldn't my son call home? His sisters miss him. He was supposed to take them to the museum. It just isn't like him to disappoint those girls. And he got into his first choice of medical schools. Now he's missed the deadline. He told his sister he was going to become a great doctor and discover the cure for her diabetes."

Kat fought back tears. "If I hear anything, I'll let you know."

"Thank you. How are you? You look tired."

"I'm fine," Kat lied.

They chatted more, and then Kat left, heartbroken.

~ * ~

Cory hung up, happy. Jon had told him their beloved grandmother was still doing okay. At the palace, King Goran, *George*, and Grandmother played chess and discussed many things. Jon reiterated to Cory that George had assumed their grandmother was on the verge of death when he sent the men after Cory at the crappy motels. But since Grandmother was stronger, Cory had a reprieve. Since George had gotten wind of the way Katarina left Cory, he loved rubbing that in Cory's face, so much so that he allowed Cory to live. Cory had a stack of royalty checks from his books and stories that he could use, and his rent was paid. He had enough money from his small living to feed himself and pay his bills.

Cory went to Gunther's and sat on the couch.

"I wonder where Brendan went. What a weirdo," Gunther said, sitting in his grease-smeared chair next to his mechanic's tool box.

Cory visualized Katarina sitting in that chair recently and him beside her on the floor. He had looked at her hand, imagining sliding his mother's wedding ring onto her finger. His heart throbbed with the injustice of his loss. "Yeah."

"I'm sure he'll be back soon."

"Me too," Cory answered, shuddering with shame.

"So, you didn't see him?"

"I saw him. We threw down. I didn't trip in the street to get all the bruises I'm still recovering from."

"Yeah, I guessed you had fought, but I didn't feel it was the right time to say anything about it."

"He did damage. But I had taken more growing up. I can take a hit, as you've seen hundreds of times."

"Man, I'm sorry about that. I don't mean to imply anything, but what did you mean when you said your hand was going to be forced and you asked for our forgiveness ahead of time?"

He looked at his feet. "As I told Asher, I was considering suicide."

"You're fucking with me."

Cory gave him a direct look. "I am not. Losing *the one*—"

"Thank God you didn't do it. What stopped you?"

"The thought of helping seven million people in my honorable country some day and erasing that fucking institutionalized sexism George forced upon them. Rescuing them from a tyrant and giving them freedoms so glorious they'll dance in the streets."

Gunther grinned. "I'm fucking proud to be your friend."

"Thanks. When we were kids, did you and Asher lecture Brendan about giving me a chance?"

Gunther scratched his close-shaven head. "Not that I recall, why?"

"He said you did."

"Huh. Naw, he thought you were cool."

Cory narrowed his brow, confused. He shook it off. "You didn't freak out when you found out my family background."

"No, I've *known* you for years. You're not a murderer."

"Katarina said that because I was abused, and Brendan and I fought, I could do it."

Gunther shook his head. "My mother's old letter says otherwise about you. She said that you, well, the young, middle-born prince, made a wonderful impression on her and my father when they were there on a diplomatic mission. She said you were charming, kind, and gracious. You had a good energy. My parents believed in your honor, and so do I. Asher does too."

"You haven't spoken to the police about Brendan's disappearance?"

"No. Why should I? Asher and I believe the asshole just took off for attention. He did it once when we were kids. To add to that, he was probably so pissed off that you married Kat that he pulled this idiotic stunt."

"Thanks."

Silence hung in the air.

Gunther got up and crossed the room, looking outside his window. "Oh shit." He looked at Cory, alarmed.

"What is it?"

"Kat's heading up here. Your brother got her old place back for her, same building, different apartment. He even managed to help her get her old job back at the music store."

Cory inhaled sharply and stood against the wall, crossing his stiff arms over his chest. Gunther let Katarina in. She had dark circles under her eyes.

She threw herself into his arms. "I can't stand this!"

"Are you okay?"

"No. I hate him, Gunther!"

"No, don't say that," Gunther said.

"After what he did...Cory has darkness in him that I never could have perceived. What a horrible, wicked thing he did."

Cory glared, the sting of betrayal burning him up. Katarina leaned away from Gunther, turned her head, and saw him.

She paled. "Bastard."

"Give me back my mother's ring."

She snarled. "I have it hidden."

"Unhide it!"

She strode to him and lifted her hand.

He caught her wrist. "You never loved me, you bitch." He gave her an "I got away with it because I'm a king" look, smirking, then leaned and whispered into her ear. "Brendan's dead."

She wrenched out of his grasp and ran out of the apartment sobbing. Gunther tossed Cory a concerned look.

Cory gestured. "Do you want to comfort the goddess? Go after her, *if* you think I'm a guilty bastard."

Gunther sat on his couch. "I know you're not guilty."

"Gotta go see Asher." Cory clapped Gunther on the shoulder and made his way out.

He walked two miles to Asher's apartment. Asher let him in with a smile.

"Hey, Cor. How are you?" He walked to the stove and clicked it off. The warm, delicious scent of chicken soup permeated the room.

Cory heard *her* voice. *Coming from the bedroom.* He strode to the back of the apartment and turned the corner. "What the hell are you—"

The computer. He sat on the edge of the bed and stared at the screen. Asher entered the room, glancing at his computer.

"Just watching some old scenes of the gang."

"Turn this shit off."

"Wait. Look, you might find this interesting."

"For fuck's sake—"

"Do you remember last summer when we saw you off at the airport for your visit back home?"

"What about it?" Cory snapped.

"Look at Kat's face as you get on that plane." He rewound the movie then pointed at the screen.

Cory leaned closer.

Katarina was frowning. "I'll miss you, Cory." She reached a hand in his direction. "*Please* come back early."

Cory scoffed. "She'd have felt that way about any of us."

Asher raised a brow. "Keep watching."

Cory turned back to the screen. Brendan put an arm around her shoulders. She shrugged him off. "Don't. Why can't it be you that's going?"

"Ouch."

"I'd even take Asher or Gunther leaving. Why does it have to be Cory? A couple of months every year are ruined for me because he leaves."

"If he means so much to you, then why don't you learn his wacky language?" Brendan asked her.

"I went to the library and got tapes. I tried. I'm too dense to learn it well. So I watch Cory's face and his body, listen to his tone, and figure out things."

"You're not stupid, and that proves it. His language is one of the most difficult to learn," Brendan said gallantly.

"Hey," Asher said in the video. He pointed to a man twenty feet away. "There's one for you. He looks like he'd appeal to the ladies."

"Knock it off. I don't give a shit," she said.

Brendan's brows rose.

"Sorry, just trying to help," Asher said.

"Cory!" Tears ran down her cheeks.

Cory stared. *Did she only say those cruel words in a moment of angry passion? Did she feel sorry about them until I responded so harshly? I provoked her. She didn't mean it, did she? After all, I said things I didn't mean.*

"We suspected her feelings for you, but she denied them when we asked, so we thought maybe we were misreading her."

Cory nodded. "She was afraid." He watched the scene again. "Brendan was always trying to seduce her."

"She always turned him down."

"He was never my friend. He knew I *loved* her. How could he not?"

"I approached him about his actively trying to seduce her. He said that if Kat returned your feelings, even with certain looks and words she gave you, you'd have married when you turned eighteen. So, why not go for her if her heart wasn't truly invested in you? Sure, she showed signs, but she never made a move, and she denied it when asked."

Cory slapped his hands onto his face, annoyed.

"He had a point," Asher continued. "Though I don't think he was trying to hurt you. I think he just had strong feelings for her as well. Hell, if she'd gone to bed with the big idiot, I wouldn't have been shocked if he'd offered marriage. But—"

"He was not in love with her!"

"No, but he, like Gunther and me, has always cared for her deeply. A form of love is present. I have to ask you, and I want a fair answer, if you had to choose between your friendship with one of us, and a woman you desperately wanted, who would you choose?"

"You, my brothers, unless that woman were Katarina. I would not have jeopardized our friendship for anyone but her."

"Brendan risked pissing you off for the very same woman."

"But, damn it! I am the only one in love with her!"

Asher put his hands up. "I give in. Brendan is a dick, but he's still our friend. I now know that Kat has been in love with you for a long time, but I think she feared the depth of her feelings for you, and that's why she denied them. Is that the fear to which you referred?"

"Shut up."

"You must have known this!"

Cory bounded to his feet. "Maybe she would have slept with you had you pushed her enough. I'll never know for sure."

"No, she wouldn't have! You're being stupid. You're the only one she wanted."

"Her...love...is conditional."

"Bullshit!"

Cory's eyes widened. "Holy crap. I've never seen this side of you, hippie."

Asher seemed to blink away his frustrated anger. "Don't be a dumbass. You can't truly believe that about her love."

"She screamed bloody murder and told me to get the fuck away from her the day before we all met for breakfast in the ducal mansion."

"Tell me you figured out why."

"I..." He slapped his hands down. "I tried. I really tried to get her to admit it was an act, but she showed such vehement disgust and fear—"

"Hmm," Asher said.

"I couldn't *force* her to come with me. Then she made it clear she thought me capable of murdering Brendan. Do you think I killed him?"

"No! I told you that! He's a strange one."

"You think more highly of me than my own wife does."

"I doubt that. If I had to guess, I'd say you gave her reason to think you capable with angry, false words. Otherwise she wouldn't."

"Brendan probably took off to be the center of our conversation. He's capable. Remember when we were kids and went camping, and he disappeared for two days, the search—" Asher shook his head.

"Yep."

"And his damn excuse that he wanted to see all our faces."

"I wanted to wring his neck."

"He's a jackass for causing all this trouble now. He must be *really* mad about your marriage. He disconnected his phone. It may even take *me* some time to forgive him for this stunt when he returns."

"Do you remember you and Gunther lecturing him when we were kids, telling him to give me a chance?" Cory asked.

"Never happened. Why? He was resentful that girls looked at you first, but he thought you were the coolest kid in school."

A knock on the front door sounded.

"Asher, let me in!" Katarina cried.

Asher tossed Cory a concerned glance.

"Don't tell her I'm back here. Got that?" Cory demanded.

Asher nodded and left to answer his door. Cory stood by the bedroom door against the wall, listening intently.

Seven

"Asher!" Katarina sobbed.

"Let's sit on the couch. Talk to me."

*Do you wish for his...*comfort, *Katarina?* Cory wondered from his hiding place.

"This is destroying me. I can't sleep. I don't eat much."

"Allow me to help you. I'll lighten your load," Asher said in a husky, inviting voice.

Cory drew a deep breath. *Asher? What the fuck?*

"Wh...what are you saying?" Her voice came out in unsteady tones.

"Exactly what you think I am."

"What? I love you but, no."

"You prefer Gunther then?" Asher asked.

Cory scowled, pressing his hand against the wall, to repress the urge to storm out there.

"N...no."

"Why? It's just sex, Kat, and from someone who loves you."

Cory gritted his teeth.

She gasped. "I don't desire you or any of my friends that way."

"Are you sure?"

"Damn sure," she said, in crisp tones.

"Not even for revenge against Cory?"

"No!"

"How about Cory's ridiculously handsome brother, then? He could comfort you."

"Stop, I don't want another man!"

Cory heard the rustling of her clothes as if she were springing to her feet.

"Jon is boring and uninspiring compared to Cory," she said. "They all are, no offense."

"None taken. My future wife better see me that way, or I won't marry her."

Cory smiled. *You're a genius, Asher.* His shoulders fell in relief.

"It's too bad he gave in to his dark side. I'll never find another man as great as Cory again."

Cory's heart rejoiced in the compliment.

"I apologize. There's a credible explanation I can't give you now for the way I just disrespected you. Do you trust me?" Asher asked.

"Yes."

"Then please accept my apology, and I'll explain later."

"O...kay."

"Kat, listen to me. Cory did not do the terrible things you think he did."

"You weren't there. He's guiltier than the devil."

"You're wrong. Cory is a good man."

"Cory is evil."

Cory cringed. *Say something, Asher.*

"Kat!"

"He admitted his crime to me!"

"Was it during a fight?"

"Yeah, so?"

"He said it to you in anger then."

Thank you, buddy.

"Don't be stupid. Or blind."

"You're the blind one." Asher's tone edged harshness. "That asshole Brendan probably set him up!"

Cory raised his brow in surprise again over Asher's tone.

"You've never spoken to me this way before." Her voice came out so small and injured that Cory's chest tightened with protective love.

"I'm sorry about my tone."

"Brendan did not set him up. He lost his chance to go to his first choice of medical schools. His mother and sisters are crying over him. Everything he owned was out on the street, being carted away by strangers."

"Wow." Asher let out a sigh. "There's a credible explanation. There *has* to be."

"Stupid fool," she said to him.

"I'll pretend you didn't say that."

"I asked Jon if what Cory said were true about his family paying off the police and Brendan's friend to lie about Brendan, and Jon didn't answer. He didn't defend him! Jon and I are close friends. He knows he can confide in me."

Asher cleared his throat. "Don't you remember in the dining room of the ducal mansion that Jon said he deferred before Cory? Cory probably made him promise to do that, out of anger. Cory would only say those things to you because you not only broke his heart, but his famous fury took over."

"Those years of his father's abuse were shoved deep inside, and he finally exploded. And that awful foster home he grew up in after that. Remember how he'd come to school with a black eye or a bloody lip—bullies always egging him on," Katarina said.

Cory looked at the floor, regret-filled.

"I remember and recently heard about what his father had done to him."

Cory leaned against the cold wall.

"It still hurt him, but it wasn't an angry, vengeful pain I saw. I must have been wrong," Katarina said.

"You're wrong now and frustrating the hell out of me."

Cory's eyes widened, listening behind that corner. He remembered Asher once said how Kat brought out an interesting side of the mellow, goofball, hippie guy he was.

"I'm shocked at your behavior today," she said.

"Don't worry. I'm not going to blow and go kill somebody."

Cory's mouth dropped open.

She sobbed once. "You're mocking me!"

"No. I'm sorry. God, now I'm being the asshole. Forgive me. I owe you big for this."

"You're family to me."

"Yes. I'll always be there for you."

"Maybe the mask made Cory or Brendan snap."

"If Cory had a bad chemical reaction to the mask due to its elements and did what you're convinced he did, it wouldn't really be Cory's fault, now would it?"

She was silent for a moment. "In the end he chose darkness."

Cory pressed a hand to the white wall again, frazzled.

"Besides, the mask seems to bring out good things in most people, those who aren't inherently...troubled," Katarina said.

Asher scoffed. "What are your intentions?"

"I'm working extra hours, eating less, and saving every extra penny."

"Why?"

"To sue for divorce."

"If he wants a divorce, he'll see it through on his terms."

"He'd be abusing his power. He's a king, and I'm a peasant."

Katarina, you're not a peasant!

"He's not an acting king now."

"He thinks what he says goes. Well forget that! I have rights as an American."

"What are the laws here regarding divorce? I never had reason to look into that," Asher asked.

Cory strained to get a peek.

She shrugged. "Don't know. Been too exhausted to check. I figured I'd just save a bunch of money and then approach a lawyer to rid myself of that jerk."

Cory flinched.

"You're wrong about him. Did you ever love him, truly?"

A long pause ensued. Cory's fingers curled into fists.

"Yes. Powerfully."

Cory gasped and bent over briefly. "Katarina." *You did say those words in anger.*

"Do you *still* love him?"

Cory didn't breathe, hanging off their words.

"Desperately, but if you tell him, I'll kick your ass."

Cory let out a breath. Relief and joy flooded over him.

"You sound just like him," Asher said.

"You, an angel, should not approve of me being married to a demon."

"Good God, he's no demon!"

"I'm going to die."

Cory gasped. He did a quick inner search of his instincts but didn't feel the black cloud of her doom. *Thank God.*

"What are you talking about?" Asher asked in a stressed tone. "Are you...ill?"

"No, but my clothes hang on me. I play bass mechanically now. Sometimes I'm dizzy from hunger, but lawyers are expensive. If Cory thought of me for the barest moment, he'd know of my impending end. Maybe he's celebrating this."

Anguish sent shivers of regret through Cory.

"You're just as dark and dramatic as he is. You make the perfect couple."

"Fuck you."

Cory closed his eyes a moment.

"I will help you, as a friend," Asher said. "Promise me, for the sake of our friendship, that you'll not do anything foolish."

"I won't do anything foolish. I'm just starving."

"No," Cory said quietly.

"Allow me to help you while you're in this rut."

"No."

"If you care about me as a friend, you'll accept my help. No strings attached."

"How much do rock-climber instructors make? Not *much* more than I do at the music store."

"I make more than you think. Wealthy clients pay me for private lessons, and I'm great with my budget. Allow me to help you."

"Fine, but only with food."

"Come over tomorrow for dinner. Nothing fancy, just chicken or something."

"Okay. I gotta go. Weirdo."

Cory smiled. His girl was cute. Their kids would be adorable.

"Are you okay now?" Asher asked her.

"For the moment."

"I love you, Kat."

"I love you too."

"Oh, by the way, I need you to tell me the truth about something."

"What's this about?" she asked in a dubious voice.

"Jon told me some things. That day you left Cory, you left him because you feared for his life, didn't you? You thought if you were out of his life, he could annul you, marry some stranger that George picked out for him, and be allowed to live."

"I—"

"It's okay. I swear I'll never tell Cory."

There was a pause as Cory's heart raced.

"Yes," she said at last.

"I knew it!" Asher said.

I knew it too! Cory pumped his fists, smiling a wide, open-mouthed smile.

"And at great sacrifice to yourself," Asher added.

"Yes. It felt like I was stepping in front of a firing line for my husband. Right before I screamed for Jon, I said to myself, 'Here it goes, my life for yours.'"

Cory pressed his hand to the wall, dizzy with love and awed by her sacrifice. Tears stung his eyes.

"Wow. And?"

"Between us?" she squeaked out.

"Yes."

"Cory was the best husband. I wanted so much to go out there with him again. But I was terrified for him. He could have kept me safe, but I could not have kept him safe. I had to act like a crazy woman to get him to fall for it. I had to picture his headstone to be convincing, knowing I was sealing my own dim fate, losing him. But at least he'd still be alive. I thanked God for him. God must see me the fool now."

Cory brushed tears off his cheeks.

"Kat..." Asher said.

"I wouldn't recommend unconditional love. It's torturous. To already love a man, *so* much, and then find out he's...bad...but the love won't go away—"

"But—"

She sniffled. "I get flashes of him smiling or doing something heroic, like when he barely missed getting killed in the street, saving that little girl...the hero-worship look five strangers gave him... flashes of us all laughing together, of the time he and I were trapped alone downtown in the dark, but he took away my terror and actually made me laugh, of when he went out in zero-degree weather and came back dripping wet, half blue, just so he could add Christmas cheer to our shitty motel room with bits of pine—"

"Now that sounds like the Cory I know."

"Brendan wasn't the first I've seen him threaten to kill. He threatened that asshole Bart, from high school, beat him up."

"Kat—"

"Goodbye."

"See you tomorrow."

The door clicked shut.

Cory fell onto the bed and looked up when Asher entered the room. "Thank you."

"Here, I'll send you the movie." Asher typed into his phone. "There are other scenes you should see."

"Thanks." Cory reached into his jacket and pulled out his wallet. He removed a twenty and handed it to Asher.

"What's this for?"

"Buy her a meal and give her food to take home. If I had more, I'd give it to you." He put his wallet back in his pocket. "By the way, when I take my throne, you're getting rewarded, big time."

"No, that's not what this is about. I'm just protecting an innocent man, helping a wonderful woman, and doing what I can to save a blessed marriage. The fact that I changed your mind—I can see—is my reward."

"Thank you." Cory touched his shoulder, turned, and headed out for his apartment. Jon had gotten his stuff out of storage for him as well as getting him back the apartment, and Cory would go through things to take his mind off his stress.

On the way, a car with tinted windows lurked nearby. Tingling alarm told Cory they were the tyrant's men.

When Cory saw Katarina storming down the sidewalk on the way to her own apartment nearby, he approached her. They stood face-to-face.

"Katarina," he uttered.

"Get out of my face, scumbag!" She swiped tears away and dashed around him as fast as her little black boots could take her.

From the car behind them several yards away, Cory heard laughter. The car pulled away.

Eight

Cory went to his room, grief-filled. He lay on his bed. Katarina's raspberry mist spray scent wafted from the pillow. Her image flashed in his mind.

Eleventh grade...

"That was a nice thing you did."
She shrugged.
"Katarina, you really wanted to be in that science competition."
He leaned against her dresser, crossing his arms over his chest.
By dropping out of the contest held outside of school, a spot had opened up, and the shyest girl in the neighborhood—with Katarina's urging—entered her own project. Katarina had been working on her own marvelous endeavor for three months, first doing research and then spending time on its development. When he searched her eyes, Cory saw how the sacrifice pained her, but she brushed it off.
"I'll enter next year."
"You're always doing little things like that."
"Lighten up. It was no big deal."
He grinned. "You want me to lighten up, eh?"

Black brows arched over beautiful brown eyes.

He swung down, swiped up her pillow, and swatted her arm. She grabbed another pillow and wacked his side, laughing. He tackled her, tickling her sides and belly as they landed on her bed.

"Stop! I beg you!" She laughed.

"Make me!" He grabbed her foot and tickled it.

She shook her head wildly, laughing harder. "Stop tickling me, or I'll piss myself!" She reached above her head for a spray bottle.

Before he knew it, raspberry mist rained down on him. He released her foot, dropping it onto the mattress, and looked at the bottle near his face.

"I surrender."

"You can surrender, but now, sir, you are my prisoner. I'm never letting you go. But don't be afraid. I treat my captives well."

The euphoric smile of enduring friendship on her face burned into his memory.

He rolled over and punched his pillow. A corner of paper stuck out from inside the pillowcase. He pulled it from its hiding place and sat up, his heart pounding.

My dearest Corentin Oleksandr, Cory Alex, our wedding day is upon us. My love,

My gallant knight, from shadows you reside,

And me, in night, waiting to claim such love, unknown ere now, from my tomb to my life, in the arms of my love, my soul shall forever frolic under the glowing protection of my dashing, my beloved, my great, my wonderful groom. I love you, sweetheart. A thousand times, I love you. Now that our souls have connected, I shall never be free from happiness. God I can't wait to marry you.

His eyes stung with tears.

P.S. Sorry about the non-rhyming, amateurish poem, Cor. You're the writer, not me—unless you include rock songs! Oh, and whenever I touch my bass, I'm playing for you. Remember that. Always know you're my inspiration and have been all these years.

Cory imagined her smiling as she penned that part. He read the final piece of the letter, gripping its edges.

P.S.S. You never knew this, but do you somehow suspect why you're the only one to call me Katarina? A long time ago I told the others only to call me Kat. You're special, and you always were, and every time I heard my name—Katarina—come from your lips, I felt warm inside. I wanted to tell you years ago. Call me Scaredy Katarina and forgive me.

He pressed the love letter over his heart then grabbed his phone and watched the video Asher had sent. His four, make that three, best friends and an asshole, were doing silly things at a park, messing around. Asher waved and said, "Hey, Cor, hope you're having fun back home."

Brendan smiled and mouthed, *I'm sorry.*

Cory frowned. Brendan had glanced into the camera with a look of brotherly love.

"What the hell?" Cory muttered. What if the mask *had* made Brendan go insane? *What if...* Certain thoughts occurred to him for the first time. He froze in horror.

What have I done?

He didn't know how much time passed as he sat in the dark. He put the green alien mask on his face. Images flowed like a river.

He was speaking with Asher and Jon in his own apartment.

"She'll be miserable?" Cory asked.

"Yes," Asher said.

"I cannot do that to her. I will fight to heal her broken heart."

Jon gave a sigh of relief.

The scene forwarded to later. Shadows dusted the room in grayness.

Cory looked at Asher and Jon. "Do either of you know who approached me with that weird invitation to that costume party? The guy looked like me."

"Yes," Asher said. "The mask has powers and created the illusion. You had touched it without knowing, brushed your fingers over it on a bookshelf. The man you saw worked for your cousin, the duke. The messenger placed the mask near you and knew it would have this effect on you because he tried it on, and the mask revealed this to him. He appeared much like you, reflecting a sort of a projection of yourself, trying to warn you to be aware of your darker tendencies. You mentioned Kat seemed to think he resembled you too. She had touched the mask as well. You have important *work to do and must fight for your good side," Asher added.*

Jon nodded. "You're going to be great."

Cory said, "Jon, I don't regret what happened, getting blamed for killing our father and being exiled to America as punishment because once here I met my friends, I met Katarina. But why as an eighteen-year-old, newly-crowned king, did King Goran—George— send me to Colorado where Gunther lived?"

"George didn't know Gunther existed, but he wanted you far away and chose America. Not being familiar with too many places there, he told his men to send you to that state those damn agents who got killed in that plane crash—Gunther's parents—lived in, Colorado."

"Then George did me a favor, not knowing it."

Cory dropped the mask. Approaching Katarina wouldn't be enough. Even if he could get past her anger, she'd still want to protect him.

His phone rang. It was Gunther.

"Yeah?" Cory said, lying back on his bed.

"I was having dinner with my uncle and aunt. I mentioned my parents and their work overseas. My aunt started to say something, and my uncle stopped her from discussing it. She said my parents would have wanted the truth to be known, that they had courage, so why shouldn't she and my uncle as well? My uncle reminded her about the plane crash that killed my parents.

"I looked at them and said, 'You lied to our government about not knowing anything. What do you know?' My uncle's eyes grew hard, and he told me that my parents had been foolish, but he wasn't. Then he gave me a guilt trip saying that if I repeated that, I'd be responsible for their deaths when they got knocked off too, maybe even by one of the agents that would be assigned to protect them. Money went a long way, after all."

"Interesting," Cory said. He stared ahead, unfocused.

"I'm bringing Jon to visit them soon. He might be more persuasive in getting them to talk."

"Gunther?" He pinched the bridge of his nose. "Have they known, all these years, who I am? Did they put the pieces together?"

"If they did, they kept it to themselves. I've waited long enough to tell you."

"Tell me what?" Cory rolled over.

"Fight for her! You two love each other, and this is stupid."

"I miss her." He glanced at the chair in the corner of his room. She had sat there, lifted her skirt, and dragged her fingertips up her thighs. Her devilish smile had made his mouth go dry.

Cory clutched the phone. He shifted his gaze to a snow globe on his dresser. "Remember the time, our sophomore year, when we went ice skating on that frozen pond—"

"Yeah."

"Brendan called me stupid for failing a biology test."

Gunther chuckled. "Kat shoved him face-first into the snow."

"I'll never forget the look on her face when she turned to me, her cheeks red from the cold."

"I saw the look. The woman loves you. You still have that snow globe she gave you the next day at school?"

"Yeah." *With the words, 'Brendan is the idiot. Here.' And she shoved her little gift into my hands, the way she shoved that epic wedding ring into my palm, bursting with emotion.*

"Go see her, or you'll regret it your whole life."

Cory hung up and closed his eyes, feeling gut-wrenching love for his wife. He fell asleep and woke up in a cold sweat. *Oh my God, I was so pissed off, then messed up in the head. What if George had Brendan? Fucking anger causing me not to think right.*

He swiped up his phone and anxiously dialed Jon's number.

"Corentin? What's wrong?"

"Can you...find out, without George knowing, if he knows what happened to Brendan?"

"I already thought of that."

"What?" Cory sat up straight.

"My rigorous investigation revealed zero signs of George's and Brendan's connection. I think Brendan lied to you about knowing him. He probably overheard us talking about him, put other pieces of information together, and used it all to hurt you."

Cory sighed, disappointed at the dead-end lead but then closed his eyes briefly, relieved the tyrant king didn't have Brendan. He swiped his face in confusion. "Couldn't George have arranged this to punish me?"

"I could find no evidence of that, and I was motivated."

"Thanks. I'm sorry for everything. You're gifted and full of heart. You're my little brother, and I love you."

"Thank you. You too," Jon said gratefully.

He hung up and leaned with his head against the cold wall.

~ * ~

Over the course of weeks, the psycho bully George had called Cory a few times to laugh at him. He was enjoying getting reports of how much Katarina hated Cory.

One day, Cory gripped the phone, having no choice but to take his older brother's unkind words.

"Why does your wife despise you so much?" George asked.

"I—"

George laughed. "The drugs you gave her to marry you must have worn off," he joked.

Cory shuddered at the insult. What an awful thing to say!— for he knew George couldn't figure out how a woman as lovely as

Katarina could have married Cory. George knew nothing about true friendship and love.

Cory braced himself for George's reaction to his next word, a word he prepared to say in order to hear that reaction. "Brendan—"

"Who the hell is that? Some guy she fucked after you disappointed her in bed?" He roared with laughter.

George's voice sounded sincere. *He didn't know him.*

Cory's shoulders dropped. This confirmed Jon's findings and meant they really were at a dead end. They had no leads to Brendan's whereabouts. He'd have to think of something else. However, Cory could see the silver lining—Brendan wasn't at the king's mercy.

Cory listened to George's further abuse in silence.

~ * ~

Cory paced a hole in his floor, rereading Katarina's love letter again and again and watching the video even more. He wore the slippers she had made him, infused with love he could still sense. He pulled a box from his closet, shifting through old pictures. A class picture, ten-years-old, rested at the bottom. He picked it up, touching its edges, remembering something.

Eighth grade...

"Hey, commie!" the big kid with the freckled face said, shoving Cory back.

Cory slammed into the brick wall behind the school. He winced and rolled his shoulders back. "My country is not communist."

The jerk cupped his ear. "What's that? I can't understand you."

"My English is fine." He had studied it for years back in Carasivia and practiced with his brother Jon. He often wrote letters to Jon in English.

The bully smirked. "Not through that thick Russian accent."

Cory didn't fear him, but as a prince, he had never raised his hand against his father, the king, in defense. Angry, he curled his hands into fists. "Hey, ignoramus, I'm not Russian either."

The dickhead took a swing. Cory didn't sidestep fast enough and cringed when his lip split against the kid's knuckles. Coppery-tasting blood coated his tongue. A feminine gasp drew his attention to his right. He turned back, and the bully crumpled to the ground, rubbing his jaw and glaring.

Brendan stood there, shaking out his fist, grinning. "It's okay to fight back when provoked."

Before Brendan hit the bully, Cory had been about to deck the guy, rivers of suppressed rage coming to the surface, and get into his first two-way fight.

Brendan put an arm around Cory's shoulders. "Let me help you to understand that, and we'll work on that accent." He lowered his arm.

Katarina drew near, her ebony hair flowing in loose curls. She wore a white blouse. Her skirt shimmered in silvery pink with each step she took toward him. Little pink shoes peeked from under the hem. The flashy color of her skirt contradicted the conservative length of the garment. Cory was intrigued.

"Are you okay?" She put a gentle hand on Cory's shoulder. "I know we don't know each other well yet, but I'd really like to be better friends. You're the most interesting guy in school." She scowled at the bully getting to his feet. "And you—"

"Hello, beautiful."

Her chin came up. "Any enemy of Cory's is an enemy of mine."

The kid's features melted into a frown.

Brendan looked at her with interest. "Cory and I are buddies."

Cory grinned and glanced at Brendan, but he saw truth in his eyes. Cory looked back at Katarina. She held out her hand, and he took it. Something was in it. He pulled his hand away and looked at the tiny white flower in his palm.

"Cute, isn't it?" Katarina said. "I found it on the ground. Must be a sign. We're meant to be best friends."

Cory dropped onto his couch. *I was crazy to ever think I could live without you.* He coughed back tears.

~ * ~

Jon called days later and told him George had executed two men for allowing their wives—in Carasivia's capital city's main square—to push them around. George had said the men set a bad example for other men, and that women should know their place. The wives were imprisoned with the promise they'd be released if they publicly apologized and said they regretted their wrong actions. Cringing, Cory demanded that Jon take him there. Enough was enough. It was time to do something.

When George called a little later, Cory braced himself. "Goran."

"Congratulations once again on your wife hating you. As you Americans say, 'That's awesome!' Damn, this is fun to watch. That beautiful bitch saved your life by leaving you. I wonder what she'd say if I told her I'd let your pathetic ass live permanently if she came to me."

Cory gasped.

"Would she reject me to see me kill you?" George laughed.

Cory dug deep. He had to protect her from being kidnapped. He shuddered, preparing for the lie. "She betrayed me. You can have her. You can try getting her to submit to you to save me, but she'll probably just tell you to do your worst."

"Huh, well, at any rate, it's fun hearing that you walk around all pissed off about being rejected. It's entertaining seeing my view of you as a loser playing out." He hung up, laughing.

~ * ~

On Jon's private jet headed to Carasivia, Cory sat facing him. He clasped his hands together over his lap. "I want to beat the crap out of him. Killing those men was an awful thing to do, a disgrace!" he hissed.

Jon studied him then spoke. "I'm right there with you, but you can't. I can't."

Cory scoffed and leaned back.

"Corentin, even if you got the chance during a private audience to tackle him and do your worst, you'd soon be arrested, then be unable to do any good for our country!"

Cory grumbled.

"Besides," Jon added, "it's not what our people want in a king. *He* is violent. Carasivia deserves a peaceful king."

Cory rubbed his face and sighed. "You're right. I need to get a grip on my fighting urges, so I can rule Carasivia and Katarina's heart *with honor*. They deserve a man of peace. I will put my *all* into this."

Nine

Once in Carasivia, Cory embraced his grandmother, who was sitting up in her sickbed in the palace hospital.

"I love you, Corentin."

"I love you too."

George glared.

Grandmother turned to George, motioned him over, and kissed his cheek. "Thank you for these visits with him, Goran."

George nodded stiffly and bent to kiss her forehead.

Later, Jon and Cory searched Cory's childhood bedroom in the palace, unbeknown to George. The door opened, and a maid walked in with a duster in her hand.

She bowed before Jon. "Sorry, Your Highness, I didn't mean to disturb you."

"It's quite all right."

Cory smiled at her. "How are you today, Mary?"

She took a hesitant step forward, twisting the duster in her hands.

Cory frowned and approached her. "Are you okay?"

Tears glistened in her eyes. "As a guest of our prince, you've been nothing but kind to me."

"Why wouldn't I be? It's the way my mother raised me."

She dropped her gaze. "I know who you really are. I remember and recognize you, though out of fear like the others, have pretended not to."

Cory's eyes widened.

She looked behind her at the closed door then back at him. "You were always a sweet boy, hard-working, laughing with the servants. I saw you help the younger children of servants with their math homework at times, something a prince was not obligated to do. Also, you suffered your father's abuse and never took it out on anyone. You say it was your mother's influence, but I tell you, you were born good."

"You honor me. Thank you."

She curtsied. "The honor is mine."

"You're trembling." He touched her arm. "What is it? Don't worry, the prince and I will help, and he will protect you if necessary."

"Yes. What is it?" Jon asked.

Tears rolled down her cheeks. "I can't stand it another day. I was there, the day your father died."

"What?" Cory asked.

"I...was in the largest kitchen. I saw your father's cook preparing his soup. I was peering around the corner, unseen by him. I didn't want him to see me because he was my supervisor back then, and I was late for my shift that day."

"Go on," Jon said.

"I was late because my boyfriend, a footman, kept me. Little did I know that he followed behind me. I stood and saw my supervisor take a packet out of his pocket, not the cabinet like normal. He sprinkled powder into your father's soup then threw the empty packet into the hearth fire. I thought it was a new spice he had just gotten from a travelling merchant. Two maids shrank back in the corner, kneading dough. They disappeared shortly after the king died. Quit, I guess."

"Was the powder...yellow?" Jon asked.

"Yes."

"The poison that killed my father comes in the form of a yellow powder."

"My boyfriend was standing behind me in the shadows, filming me secretly as a prank. My supervisor was in the line of sight. He's on the film. After he left the kitchen carrying the soup, I ran into the main room. When the king died, I was terrified to say a word to anyone. I thought I'd get executed for seeing what I did and not putting a stop to it—but I didn't know! My boyfriend, who didn't know it was poison either, followed me in, laughing, focused on me. I posed for him, blowing him a kiss for his little movie. Behind me, on the wall, you could make out the bulletin board with the date. I hid the film, scared. My boyfriend said if we said a word, we'd be dead. But I look at you, and I feel so sad. I know you'll protect us now."

Jon stepped closer to Mary. "You can clear Prince Corentin's name. Please, give us the film."

Cory glanced at him. "No! It's too risky. We'll find another way."

"Corentin—"

"Forget it." He turned back to Mary. "Don't risk yourself for me."

"It's for our country, Corentin!"

Cory looked at Mary, offering a smile. "Don't tell anyone. Stay safe. I'm already in search of other evidence." He squeezed her hand and strode out of the room.

~ * ~

Brendan's mother called Kat in tears to tell her that Brendan's body had been found and she and her girls had held a private funeral for him. The police had told her they believed his death was accidental, while he was doing his so-called traveling, but she didn't believe that. She believed someone powerful had the authorities covering up the truth. Kat lowered the phone.

~ * ~

Cory called Katarina on her landline and left a long message of love and regret on her answering machine. For days, he waited for her to return his call, but she didn't.

A week later, after searching for any clue of the hidden file containing evidence, in disguise wearing a red-haired wig, Cory strolled down the capital city's main street, past a line of shops, kicking at the dusty road, melancholy. He walked into a bar, ordered a beer, and glanced up at the TV in the corner, watching the soccer game. It was very American of him to think of it as soccer.

A heavy-set man sitting next to him knocked over Cory's beer.

"Jackass!" Cory stood up to shove the man back.

The bartender looked at him sadly. "So much trouble lately. The king makes everyone edgy."

Cory's anger deflated. He sat back down mumbling, "Accidents happen." He ordered another beer and looked up.

Suddenly, the television screen went blank. Several patrons tossed insults at it about missing the game. A stream of light crossed the screen horizontally, and his brother Jon appeared on the screen.

Cory straightened and set his mug down.

"Greetings," Jon began. "I'm sorry to interrupt, but this is urgent."

The bartender changed the channel. Jon was on every one.

"Let's listen!" Cory said.

Everyone watched the screen.

Jon's voice was grave. "My brother, your prince, Corentin, is alive and well, and innocent of all charges against him. He was forced to leave the country as a boy. The king faked his death. Let's get our prince back here."

Cory heard gasps in the bar. He wiped his hand over his mouth. *No, Jon. George will kill you. You'll have to remain in hiding.*

"I repeat, Prince Corentin is alive and innocent."

When Mary came onto the screen, people watched intently. She explained in tears that she was a witness but that her boyfriend had destroyed the evidence years before without telling her. She told her story. A man about her age popped onto the screen and confirmed her account. Cory said a prayer for their safety, knowing Jon would have them in hiding. Perhaps this was being broadcast from outside the country.

The people around Cory burst into conversation. He heard snippets like, "As I've always believed," and "I read the books claiming it was so. Rang true to me. The boy prince was a real fine little gentleman."

"To Prince Corentin, wherever he is."

"Wish he'd come back."

~ * ~

He met Jon in a basement where Jon had his people working on a project entitled *Corentin for King.* Cory approached the tech guy in front of his computer.

"I'm ready."

"We've been waiting to hear you say that." The tech guy typed something.

Another man pushed a camera in front of Cory.

"Now," the tech guy said.

"Wait," Jon said. He gestured to the palace doctor.

First the doctor spoke toward the camera, introducing himself as King Goran's physician and telling the people he had DNA evidence that the man about to speak was Prince Corentin. He nodded toward Cory.

Cory looked into the camera. His heart raced, and he wiped his sweaty palms over his thighs. "Hello, beloved citizens." He paused. "I've missed you since my banishment, but I have visited often over the past decade, keeping apprised of life here. My heart is with you. I just wanted you to know that."

Jon came to his side. "Continue."

Cory nodded. He drew in a breath. "I wanted to come forward earlier, but because of the false accusations against me, I had to wait until I could be vindicated. We came upon our witnesses only recently. This country is suffering, and I can't stand to see that. Let me help you. Let me be your prince. You remember my mother, your loving queen. She gave me my values, as many of you know. Let me honor her by continuing her ways, and in so doing, I will honor you."

Jon smiled. He signaled to the camera guy, and they were off.

Cory and Jon collapsed onto a sofa, and the technical crew took random seats around the basement of the nobleman's home.

The duke, dressed in his tailored suit, took a seat across from Cory and Jon. He gazed at his cousins, and a knowing grin spread across his face. "My congratulations, cousins. That was excellent. It's about time we removed a tyrant."

The duke's phone rang. "Hello?" He nodded and muttered an "I understand," then hung up, looking at Cory and Jon. "That was a man in my employ at the palace. He keeps me apprised of the situation there."

"Important news?" Cory asked.

The duke offered a half-smile. "It seems the king is quite furious, as he ought to be. He ordered men out to search for you and kill you on sight. He has other men trying to discover the origin of the broadcast."

Both Cory and Jon frowned.

"Not to worry," the duke said. "I have the finest equipment and experts money can buy. No one on my end will betray you—not with what I pay them. But even so, I recruited men sick to death of the king's policies, as I am. And my tech people know what they are doing. None of this can be traced back here."

"He certainly won't suspect you," Jon offered. "Because of that scene at dinner you created for him last week. Brilliant," he said. "King Goran couldn't praise you enough for your intelligence in maligning Corentin, from everything from his poverty to his democratic ways."

"Yes," the duke said. "King Goran is under the false impression that I'm an insufferable snob allied with him. Also, I have employees watching to see if I need to take any extra precautions in order to keep suspicion off myself. I believe in my heart I'm on the winning side with you two."

Jon touched his shoulder briefly. "I know. I've known for a while that your views secretly align with ours."

"But," the duke continued, "it's advantageous that King Goran thinks I'm with him for now, not only for my safety, but so I can be of service to you. He has no idea I'm a fan of your policies." He sighed. "I'm also exasperated that he has threatened my land and titles three times in the past, merely for disagreeing with him in conversation."

"I would never do that to you," Cory said. "Not for simply voicing what you think and even if we should find our opinions diverging."

"I know," the duke said. "You're a true leader who listens to what people need. Even as a child. Many times I witnessed your honorable behavior." He paused. "Let my people give you better disguises. You'll be unrecognizable. Go out there and see the results of our handiwork."

"Good idea," Cory said. "Thank you for everything."

"Hail King Corentin," the duke said, with deep respect in his gaze. "I will give you whatever money and resources you need. Now that you've been proven innocent of regicide, I can finally follow my heart and give you my support."

~ * ~

The next day, Cory and Jon ventured out in disguise. All over the city, signs saying such things as: *We love Prince Corentin*, or *Bring back Prince Corentin* abounded.

Cory got the crew busy making signs of their own. He put out his policies, signs that said things like: *Equality for Women, Freedom of the Press, Prince Corentin is for citizens' rights.*

Soon, people took to the streets, chanting "Down with King Goran," and "Prince Corentin for king!"

Cory faced Jon in the hideout at the duke's home. The cameras were ready to roll again.

Jon greeted him. "George is a proud man. Challenge him."

"Pistols at dawn?" Cory asked with one sarcastic brow raised.

Jon scoffed. "Funny that you'd joke about that. Challenge him publicly. He won't turn you down."

"Okay. An intellectual challenge. I need to prove that reaching beyond my combative tendencies is now my way."

"Good. You're serious about what you said."

"Katarina needs to see this too. Contact the gang and get them watching."

"Yes."

"If George can beat me with questions relevant to our country, I'll turn myself over to his mercy."

"No!"

"If I win, he steps down."

"You...seem awfully confident."

Cory grinned.

"Let me make his bastardhood known. He'll be thrown out of the country for fraud."

"No, Jon, I've told you before. I don't want our mother's name involved in this," Cory said.

"She was a rape victim."

"I insist."

"Do you know what you're doing?"

Cory nodded. "I've done extensive research and have kept more up to date these past years than most citizens here."

"Okay."

"Let's begin."

Jon waved over the camera guy. "Get him on."

Cory made the challenge to George, asking him to meet him in the capital city's largest film studio.

When Cory and Jon arrived, they weaved through a crowd lined for blocks outside. Cameras broadcast on large screens outside. Cory and Jon ascended the elevated stage in a huge room. Lights shone, and microphones were propped up. George sat on the stage, wearing his gold, gem-studded crown. He rose from a portable throne, arms crossed over his chest, and glared murder at Cory.

"My grandmother is in a coma, so this thing between us ends today." His voice rang out in the silence of an enthralled audience. He looked at a chopping block to the left.

Cory trembled but thought of his people. "I'll ask you a question concerning the welfare of our people. You answer it correctly to get a point. Then you do the same for me. Experts are here to verify our answers. Five questions each, Goran. Then either I'll turn myself over to you, or you'll step down as king. If it's a tie, we keep going until one of us wins."

"Bring it on, dead man."

Cory steadied his erratic breathing.

~ * ~

Katarina and Asher were on his sofa laughing over a joke.

Gunther banged on his door. "Open up!"

Asher let him in.

"I just got a call. Your computer, now! Carasivia, big news. Live."

"What is it?" Asher asked.

"Cory challenged the king!"

"What?" Katarina said.

They went to Asher's computer, and Gunther found the site. They clicked on a link for English subtitles—perhaps Jon had arranged that.

~ * ~

"How many elementary schools do we need, nationwide, to keep the children at the level of education they deserve?" Cory asked George.

George sneered. "I get harassed regularly about this."

"As you should."

"There are one and a half million elementary-aged children in my country. An average of five hundred kids per school. To keep classes at twenty pupils per class, we need three thousand schools."

"Good. I'm glad you know that."

"I'm going to enjoy killing you."

Cory looked at him sadly. "Your turn."

"How many fish are in our great lake now?"

Cory's heart skipped a beat. "That's a question for the good of our nation?"

"The good of *my* nation. Answer it."

"Considering that there are laws limiting the amount of fish our hard-working fishermen catch to provide our people with a healthy form of protein...and ten years ago the count was ten million with an average loss of..." he paused.

George sneered. "You don't know, do you?"

"Well, they're allowed to take ten percent from our rivers and smaller lakes. They're allowed..." He thought of the percentages. "The lake holds twenty percent..."

Jon interrupted with a scoff. "Hah! Corentin is *great* at math."

"Shut up, pipsqueak," George said.

Cory looked at George. "From last estimates, and, listening to the talk down at the docks, I'd say, there are about...five million?"

George looked over at a guy on a computer typing away. The man nodded. "That's the latest estimate."

George gaped. "How did you..." He shook his head. "Never mind. Ask your next question, colossal loser."

"Who's the last woman to win the national prize for honorable achievement?"

George laughed. "Irrelevant. They answer to men now."

"It's not irrelevant! She started an orphanage."

"Next question. I've made it illegal for them to win. More men benefit from the prize money now."

"Even my father wasn't as ridiculously sexist as you are, and he was bad. Before that hideous law was passed, who won, Goran?"

"Ask a different question," he gritted out.

"Carasivians are generally too low in which essential nutrient?"

"Vitamin C. We need to import more fruits and vegetables, but I thought to spare my people the expense."

"That's a lie," Cory said. "I know how to get it without gouging the public, and so do you, but it would mean less money in the royal purse, and you insist, even though you're a billionaire, on taking a tax-supported salary. That's just plain wrong."

"You're an ignorant lowlife. I'm correct. Vitamin C."

Cory sighed. "Yes. Now your question."

"Who's my best army general, the one most likely to keep Carasivia's interests protected?"

"General Sarzakoff is the most competent, the best statistician, and the sharpest of mind."

"A month ago, I publicly stated that it was General Rivortz."

"But you secretly awarded General Sarzakoff the medal. I got a picture of it and put it into the public record. You only said it was the other guy to keep General Sarzakoff humble."

"Damn you and damn the pipsqueak prince for telling you. Next question, dead man."

"When does the bridge over our major river have to have maintenance work done to keep our citizens safe?"

"Beginning of next month. *My* citizens. Who's the biggest threat to Carasivia now?"

"Our northern neighbor. You invite war, Goran."

"Wrong! I sent them a note this morning, offering to marry the pretty royal daughter they just presented to the public."

"You're...getting married? Congratulations."

"They have yet to respond but have expressed interest in diplomatic talks. Their daughter is that pretty. Worth my change in policy," he paused. "Until after I get her to the altar," he said under his breath, smirking. He then lifted his voice. "You lose the point."

Cory rolled his shoulders back. "What is the most common female name among our citizens under the age of twenty-five?"

"Again with this bullshit?"

"I let one question slide. Answer it. It matters to our citizens because women and girls matter."

He rolled his eyes and slapped his hands against his thighs. "I don't know. Ivanna? It's all I ever hear around the palace."

"Wrong. Mérane, after our mother."

"I should have guessed. They loved her."

"That's my point. They approve of Mother's values. That's another reason why the question matters."

"Okay, dead man, name my favorite meal."

"Why does it matter?"

"A ruler does his research. Prove your worthiness, or do you suck at your preparation as much as you look like you do? If you can't handle the little things, how do you think you could handle the big ones? A ruler can handle the pressure."

"A writer knows how to research, Majesty." Cory studied him and thought of the conversations he used to have with his mother.

"What's taking so long?"

"I'm thinking. Wait, when we were kids, you had to go to the hospital. You ate something. Mom told me it was your favorite, but you were highly allergic. What was it...had to use your hands..." He glanced down at his.

"You lose!"

"Lobster! That's it. You only put up with the consequences of eating it in private with your doctor present."

"Prove it."

"We can postpone this and go do so. I have Mother's journal hidden. She wrote about it, worried she almost lost you. We can go to the hospital and have your allergen tested."

"Forget it. You're right. Stop wasting my time."

"We're tied."

"Last question. The loser is a dead man. You," George said.

"What is on the top of the list for needed structures in Carasivia?"

George scoffed. "Highways. I haven't had the time to deal with it. Been busy with international relations. It will get done when I get to it."

"You've been busy inviting war. You're wrong. Highways are second. The people need hospitals more urgently. Numbers have shown that people have died from lack of enough hospitals, not great highways, though those do need to be built, after the hospitals."

"It's a matter of opinion."

"No, it's based on fact, based on lives. I spoke to engineers and city planners this morning in our brother's hideout. They put the figures online."

"The list of those to be executed grows, I see. Last question, *Cory*." He sneered. "Do my citizens enjoy lower prices since I took the throne?"

"The practical answer to that is no, Goran."

"I knew you'd say something slanderous like that. You're wrong. We could see by looking at any random price tag and comparing its equivalent that existed before I made my helpful policies for the people, and you'd see I was generous to them."

"You may have ordered prices to be lowered, but you hiked up taxes on everything. People may see lower price tags, but they're paying more for everything than they have in years. Standard of living has gone down. It's like our citizens live in an earlier century, in many ways. Lying in front of our people to make yourself look good. Stick to science. I'll stick to math."

They looked over at the guy behind the computer, the fact checker. George glared at him in warning.

He trembled and looked at both, pale. "I uh, I..."

"Speak!" George roared.

"Prince Corentin is correct."

"You're a dead man too," George said to him.

"I'll protect you," Cory told the man.

Jon approached. "Prince Corentin is the winner. Four to three. Congratulations!" He shoved his hand out. Cory shook it.

George turned to two guards behind him. "I grow weary of this charade." He faced Cory. "Just wanted to show you that I didn't fear facing you. Do you really think there was any way in hell I'd step down and let you take over? The questions are done. Time to do what I always intended." He looked at his guards. "Put him on the block."

Two guards seized Cory and pushed him to his knees. One shoved his head onto the chopping block.

~ * ~

Kat screamed and squeezed Gunther's arm. "Please God, no!"

Ten

Cory struggled against the holds of the guards. "I will repeal the repressive laws against women! I will clean up our cities and give you freedoms! I will fight to make this a great nation!" he screamed to the people.

The crowd burst onto the stage. Several men tore the guards away from Cory, and someone helped him stand. Men and women surrounded Cory.

Cory touched one man's shoulder. "Excuse me."

The man looked at him questioningly.

"It's okay. Thank you."

The man stepped aside.

Cory approached George.

"This place is set up for an electronic vote." A man on stage turned to the audience. "Vote for king. Prince Corentin or the tyrant."

"This isn't a democracy!" George yelled.

The guy behind the computer stood up. "Maybe not, but there is a precedent. Five hundred and seventy years ago, a king's younger son asked his indecisive father if the people could vote for their next king, since the prince's older brother was an evil man. The king agreed and signed it into law. The law is obscure, but it's on the books. The vote must be allowed *if* the king is unworthy."

"I will not allow it!" George yelled. "I have an army behind me."

Jon pulled a paper out of his pocket. Cory recognized it as the DNA results and whispered to Jon, "For Mother, don't make this public."

Jon showed it to George.

George paled. "Fine. Do the damn vote." He looked into the audience. "Remember, I lowered prices, I protected you. I'm a strong leader, and other countries fear us. This traitor to our country is weak, filled with values from another nation. He's not one of us!"

Cory leaned toward the microphone. "The values I picked up from that other country complement what my mother taught me about human kindness. Carasivians know the meaning of strength, and our neighbors will discover this, but not through bullying. Rather through merely watching us thrive and growing to admire us. Those who interfere with us in any way will discover how strong we are." He glared at George. "Not one of you? I beg to differ."

Calls and votes were coming in and being displayed on a large electronic bulletin board, being calculated.

After hours, it seemed, Cory won 94.47% of the vote. The guards seized George by the arms. One removed his crown.

Jon took it and put it on Cory's head, bowing. "Your Majesty."

"Kill Goran!" the people chanted.

Cory shook his head. "No. He's my brother."

"He was anxious to kill you," Jon said.

"I'm not the same kind of man as he is. Katarina would not want me kill him." He turned to George, balled his fist, and struck his jaw. The surprised George crumpled and fell. Cory sneered at him then looked at the guards. "He's banished."

~ * ~

Katarina's hand came to her mouth. She swiped away tears and knocked over a picture of Asher and his parents. Another two unframed photos under it fell to the floor. She picked them up, looking at the first. Gunther stepped closer.

The photo was of Asher holding a trophy, smiling next to his mother. Kat smiled and slipped the picture behind the other. Her heart froze. Brendan with his young sister on his hip.

Asher touched her shoulder. "That was the day she won a climbing contest. I had been giving her private lessons."

She went to the bed and punched a pillow, crying.

Sometimes Cory's a damn saint, and I admire him so much I could faint at his feet, but other times, he's...evil. He's going to save a nation, yet he killed his best friend.

When Cory called later, she picked up just to tell him to go to hell.

~ * ~

Cory held his grandmother's hand watching her as she rested, still in a coma. "I don't know if you can hear me, but I love you." He swallowed past the lump of sadness that had formed in his throat. "You've...meant so much to me. I know I've already told you this, but thank you again. When my father hurt me so many times, you and my mother gave me hope. You kept me from turning into something I didn't want to be. I only hope we can have more time together." He cleared his throat, stood, and kissed her forehead. "I will honor your values and love this country with all my heart."

~ * ~

Everyone was wearing black, being in mourning for the loss of Cory's grandmother who had passed away only days earlier. Cory stood with his brothers, Gunther, Asher, and Carasivia's council of ministers in his palace office. He glanced at Jon, imagining the looks on the faces of Gunther's uncle and aunt when the prince showed up at their house asking questions.

Jon had spoken to them in kind, protective tones, swearing to keep them safe, but they trembled with fear. Opening up to him was the right thing to do, and they knew it, he had told them. He'd tell George and the public that a retired clerk from Washington had the file, but he could still whisk Gunther's uncle and aunt to a hideaway if they wished. He even promised them a million dollars for their trouble. They broke down and gave him the file they had hidden for years, begging for forgiveness and begging him to keep their names out of the public eye. Jon promised.

In the palace, Cory glanced around the polished oval table at the stern faces of the men in the chamber. One minister gestured to Cory. He stood.

The minister tipped his head. "We have seen the evidence vindicating you. The file turned out not even to be necessary, but we have it for a matter of public record. Your name will be cleared publicly, and you will be crowned in a grand ceremony as soon as arrangements can be made to perform such a ceremony with all the due dignity of your station. However, the coronation is only for show. You are already our king." He bowed, and the others did so after him.

George glared at Cory.

"King Corentin, how do you wish to dispose of this tyrant?" He tossed a derisive glance at George.

Cory looked at George with regret. The familiar scent of beeswax penetrated the air. "First, I ask that no one speak of the true nature of his paternity." He glanced at each man.

Everyone nodded.

"Thank you."

The senior minister looked at Cory. "My King, if I may?"

The minister brought a threatening gaze to George. "Do not speak harshly against our king in public, or I'll have you arrested for treason for all the bad you've done, and oversee the punishment myself."

"Goran," Cory said. "I'm sorry it had to come to this. But he has a point. Spare our people the drama."

George just glowered.

The minister looked at Cory with admiration. "You're going to be great. Is there anything else, My King?"

"Not for now. I have things to think about." He glanced at each man. "Thank you, gentlemen. We'll meet up later. Your counsel will no longer be ignored. I will weigh your words and do what is best for our people."

"Very good." The councilor hesitated.

"What is it?" Cory asked.

"Will you be replacing those with any opposing views to you in your council?"

"No," Cory said. "A leader needs to hear all points of view, not just be told that everything he says is perfect. I will make sure the council contains men and women with varying ideas and ideologies."

The minister smiled. "Thank you."

"It's just wise. Please keep Goran in detainment in a comfortable room while I consider his options."

They nodded, several smiling, and left, guards escorting George out. Cory sank into a padded leather chair, putting his face in his hands.

"Brother." Jon touched his shoulder.

"Cool country. I saw some sweet machines on the road," Gunther said.

Cory lowered his hands.

"I'm surprised. I thought—no offense—that this would be a... backward nation."

Cory raised a brow.

Gunther shrugged. "Well, talking to your men on the plane over here, I discovered that not a single woman holds public office in this country."

"Those days are over."

"And no woman can inherit the crown."

"That will be the first law I change. If Katarina gives me a daughter first, our child will someday be the first ruling female monarch this country has ever had."

Gunther and Asher nodded their approval.

"You're kinda hoping your first is a girl," Asher said.

Cory's smile grew warm. "Yeah. What a great thought."

"It will be quite a change," Gunther added. "After all I've heard about the laws George passed, I'm surprised Carasivians have electricity and running water. I wondered what century we'd be walking into."

Cory sighed. "Time to bring us into the computer age—mentally as well as physically. Katarina could inspire the women here, bring them back to life, so to speak."

"We'll help you get through to her," Gunther said.

Asher nodded and looked toward the window. Cory followed his gaze and admired the familiar sight of a mountaintop.

"It's there, so I'm going to climb it," Asher said.

~ * ~

Cory sat in his office, staring at a picture of Katarina and himself. The raspberry air freshener he'd installed released a constant reminder of Katarina. In the photo, her arms were draped over his shoulders.

Cory's secretary tapped on his door. Cory slipped the picture into a drawer. The man handed him a stack of papers.

"What are these?"

"Several princesses want to marry you. Three of them are lovely. Might you choose one and give us a queen? We haven't had one since your beautiful mother, and the people would welcome a queen with cheer."

Cory regarded him. "I'll present you with a queen you can be proud of."

The secretary bowed and left.

Cory's personal cell phone rang, the one he'd had for ages, so the caller had to be someone close to him.

"Enjoying my crown?"

"Goran."

"Those guards you had watching me in my banishment are dead...you know, our country's finest. I oversaw their training. I knew their weaknesses."

Cory's hand curled into a fist. "You didn't have to kill them."

"Yes, I did. I'm free and have been promoted now that Grandmother has passed."

"Oh?"

"It's ironic really. As king, if I killed someone, it was just my prerogative. Now, I'm going to be famous for an assassination."

Click.

~ * ~

Kat focused on music to try to forget her broken heart. When her phone rang, she answered. She extended the cord and stretched out on her couch. "Hello?"

"Kat," said Asher. "Get to my place. Use the hidden key. Turn on my computer—"

"Where are you?"

"Go to the Carasivian home page. They're live streaming now, and English subtitles have been added to this site too."

She frowned. "Asher..."

"Do it!" He hung up.

Not long after, she found herself staring at Asher's computer screen since she was too poor to afford her own computer. With a trembling hand, she typed in the address.

She watched a scene unfold in an ornate room decorated with purple velvet, marble, and gilt-framed pictures. People in fancy clothes watched...the crowning. Kat held her breath. Cory wore velvet and silk clothes. Shivers of admiration coursed through her. Damn, Cory was handsome. She pressed her lips together, annoyed. Cory sat in a golden chair with upholstered armrests. A man in long white robes approached with a crown.

"Wait." Cory held up his hand. He got up from the throne, knelt before the large crowd and humbly bowed his head. The crowd watched with love and respect.

Kat's heart twinged.

The man in the robes crowned him. The look of adoration Cory had for his people knocked the wind out of Kat. No one could fake that kind of devotion. A smile curved her lips.

Cory sat back on the throne and glanced to the smaller but equally ornate chair to his right. The queen's empty throne. The sadness in his face shot pain in Kat's heart.

The camera panned to a commentator. "The king looks at the empty seat beside him with longing. Here's to him finding the woman of his dreams. God knows he deserves it, having already passed eight new laws giving Carasivians unprecedented freedoms. Perhaps His

Majesty thinks of the mysterious Katarina he named when he won his crown."

Cory looked at the camera. "I wish to instigate a national day of thanksgiving and charity." Then he named the date it would be celebrated: Kat's birthday.

She ran into the kitchen, slumping over Asher's counter. Pressing her hand to the cabinet, she pulled away and opened it, in search of something...hard. She found a bottle of vodka. In the fridge she found orange juice and made herself a tall drink, gulping it down. She made another and drank it in front of the computer. Staring for she knew not how long, tears rolled down her face.

You have the power to affect nations, Cory had told her.

Now she understood. She leaned near the end table and Asher's landline, not owning a cell phone. Her hand shook as she dialed Cory's cell phone, swaying from drunkenness.

Eleven

Cory sat in the audience chamber to welcome dignitaries who wished to offer their congratulations and gifts. Asher stood a few feet away, to his right, next to a guard, and held Cory's cell phone. Gunther stood next to him. Cory had told Asher that if anyone called—and only his American friends and George had that number—he was to take a message and Cory would return the call later...unless it were Katarina. He told Asher to give him the phone immediately if that occurred.

Cory graciously accepted happy greetings. Then, a certain man walked in. Cory gripped his armrests and sat up straighter. Gladomir bowed, the man who had killed Cory's best friend as a boy on the order of the former king, Cory's father. Cory still saw the face of his friend's mother when she got the news. Her boy was accused of slandering the king. He had denied it but wasn't given a chance to prove it. At least George had that over the previous king. George didn't kill children.

Cory trembled with anger. "What...do you want?"

Gladomir bowed again. "My King, I came to offer my apologies."

"He was only eleven years old!"

"I had to obey my king."

"My friend was innocent! You could have...left the country, got my friend out, I don't know, something ethical!"

"I...I," he stuttered.

Cory opened his mouth, about to have the man flogged before banishment. Then he'd appease his friend's mother with the knowledge.

When his phone buzzed, he heard the slight sound in Asher's jacket pocket and turned. His heart beat faster.

Asher stepped back and answered it in a soft voice. He looked at Cory and nodded.

Cory looked at Gladomir. "Wait here. I have an urgent call." He stepped down and accepted the phone from Asher then strode to a private office. He shut the door in the dim room. "Katarina, sweetheart, I'm so sorry. *Please*, forgive me."

"Cor...eeee," her voice was slurred. "I wanna say that I...oops." He heard stumbling sounds.

His mouth dropped open. "Are you...drunk?"

She sniffled, crying. "You aren't gonna hurt that man? Forgive him. Ah, yer look reeeeeely mad."

He gulped. Katarina was toasted. "Where are you? Are you safe?"

"Asher's house. Compuuuuter, watching streaming video."

"Can I come get you, my love? I'll leave right now."

"Don't kn...know why I...called. Maybe cuz I love you—"

She hung up. He slumped against the wall, closing his eyes. He walked back into the audience room and gave Gladomir his forgiveness.

~ * ~

Cory left love-filled messages on Kat's home machine. "Say the word, and I'll be there within hours," he'd end each message.

She ignored them and gave the many beautiful bouquets he sent to the widow next door, adding cheer to her life.

One night, the tragic way Cory said Katarina's name on the voicemail of her land line made her knees weak.

"Katarina, today—" His voice caught. "I created a children's foundation and named it after your sister Molly."

Who died in my arms as I tried to save her, climbing out a broken window to escape the fire. My blood was everywhere. The smoke. She wasn't breathing. Kat touched a gentle hand to her belly then her thighs where her many nasty scars reminded her of the ordeal.

Cory had looked at her as she stood nude on their wedding night as if she were the most beautiful woman in the world. When they were kids, he had been the one who had pulled her from despair. Without his intimate friendship all those years, she would have lost herself. It came rushing back in the pause between breaths: The times holding hands while she cried, leaning on his shoulder and sitting against whatever cold wall she collapsed in front of, opening up to him about her sister... He'd press her close, stroke her hair, calm her. *You're saving me, Cory,* she once told him. He tipped her face toward his with gentle fingers. *No, I'm giving you the sword to fight your own demons.*

Kat stared at her answering machine.

"Every child's life saved through this foundation will be on you," he continued. "You are a hero, my wife." His soft, harsh tone was her undoing, the last phrase being said through tears.

She sobbed.

~ * ~

Weeks later, after not receiving any more phone messages or flowers from Cory, Kat's heart sank. She cursed herself for missing his declarations of love and forced herself to remember why she was mad at him. She cursed herself again for almost not caring what he did and nearly calling him dozens of times.

The band's singer, the blonde Madison, approached Kat in a dressing room after a show. "Did you notice third row?"

"I never look anymore. My angry ex said that guys just gawk at me with raging lust."

Madison shrugged. "The dynamic guy in black was staring at you with his hand over his heart."

"Dark brown hair and intense blue eyes? Trim but muscular—"

"Yes. He looks *very* familiar."

Kat fell back into a chair, her hands trembling. "My husband."

"Whaaaaaaaaat?"

"I...eloped recently."

"*Damn*, he was good-looking."

Kat scoffed. "You should see his brother, Jon. You'll doubt your own vision."

"Oh?"

"Never mind. Jon's an archaeologist, totally hot, and yet manages to be a bore."

"Huh. Hey, now that I think about it, I've seen your husband before at our gigs and always pulling you aside, so we could never talk to him. His clothes and demeanor have changed drastically. He even combs his hair differently now. He looked poor before but not grief-filled. I almost didn't remember." Madison took a seat next to her. "Bodyguards surrounded him. Did he become famous or something?"

Kat brought her stinging eyes to meet her friend's gaze.

Madison touched her arm. "What happened?"

"I left him."

"Why?" Her eyes widened.

"He's a king of a small European country, but he murdered our best friend."

After several seconds, Madison stood, grinning. "We're going out for coffee. Wanna come?"

"You don't believe me."

"I love you, but no. Why does he really have guards?"

She shrugged. "His country is small and relatively unknown here. It's not one you've likely heard of. His crowning wasn't televised here. Go on the Internet. You'll find it."

Madison frowned. "What's really eating you?"

"Despite it all, I miss him." She imagined him standing there in his black and purple jacket. She had felt enveloped in his essence when wearing his prized possession. So loved. Her heart broke for the hundredth time that day.

"Whatever he did, just talk to him. You've obviously misunderstood something. The guy is deeply in love with you."

"I want to go home." Numbness seeped into her weary bones.

"You sure?"

"Yeah. Thanks."

"If you need me, call. We haven't hung out, outside of band practice, for weeks. I miss you at my place for movies. I promise lots of popcorn."

"Thanks. Soon."

At the next show, Madison cornered Kat again, behind stage. *Please don't bring up Cory.*

"He was staring onto the stage with his imploring eyes. Speak to the poor, sexy guy. Don't leave him to suffer like that. It's cruel."

Inhaling deeply, not wanting to take out her frustration on her friend, Kat spoke softly. "I just want to lose myself in the music."

"You can't continue to ignore the audience," Madison informed her. "If you don't talk to your husband, at least look at the fans."

"Okay," Kat said. She followed her upstage for the next set and slid her bass on, inhaling the beer-drenched air.

At the end of the first song, Madison nudged her. "He looks like some kind of prince. His clothes are not American. And his guards. Who the hell is he, really? A foreign movie star who finally made it in his own country? That would explain the sudden exotic improvement in his wardrobe and the men who accompany him."

"Maddy, please."

The guitarist, the red-haired Bernadette, approached. "Kat, that *hot*, spooky guy I've seen before, the one in the jacket…" she trailed off, mesmerized. "Some reporters were harassing him. He promised them an interview later if they'd leave, so they did. Now he's looking at you like he's going to die."

"Please pity me." A surge of love for Cory ripped through her, but she clamped down on it.

They started the next song. When she looked up from her bass and her gaze locked with Cory's, she stumbled. The power of her love for him and the love shining in his eyes swept over her in suffocating waves. He stood there in a wealthy man's clothes, sapphire cufflinks, and the diamond talon pendant of his country sparkling on his chest.

Just as the last notes of the song resonated, Cory approached the stage with tears in his eyes. "Please, I *can't* live without you."

Her bandmates gaped. The audience turned and stared at him, then at her, all in breathless anticipation.

Sudden rage froze Kat's soul. "Go away. I'll never forgive you for what you did."

"Katarina."

She set her bass into a stand and ran off the stage.

He grasped her hands and pressed them to his lips for an urgent kiss. "Please!"

She tore away from him and spat in his face, despising him, but biting back agonizing tears of love.

He gasped and wiped his face and then turned and strode out of the music hall, guards following after him. The crowd parted, staring.

In the parking lot, he approached her, but she shoved him away as his guards stepped forward. She watched, huffing, her fists at her sides.

He held up a hand. "Gentlemen, please give us some privacy. As you know, the world doesn't yet know about my elopement. I trust you to keep this private until Katarina and I work things out. Keep anyone far enough away not to hear our conversation."

His stockiest guard tipped his head. "Yes, My King. The press thinks she's a scorned girlfriend who no longer wants you."

"I will remedy that soon, if God is on my side."

They looked at him with caution but stepped away, surrounding him with vigilant awareness.

Cory grabbed Kat's arms, glancing at her hand. "Your ring…"

"Hidden until I have the time to pawn it." She'd not really pawn his mother's ring, but she wanted him to think so, to punish him.

He let her go. "Please, my love, don't. Keep the ring. It's *important*. My mother—"

She smirked. "Guess you'll have to find another ring that's centuries old."

"No, please. *Don't.*"

His desperate plea touched her heart.

"I'll give you the money you would have received for pawning it."

"Are you asking for it back now, after all?"

"No! Please wear it, own it, as queen of a country with a long and beautiful heritage. My mother would want you to wear it."

"It's mine now. I'll do with it as I wish, and I don't want your damn money." *Wow, that was bitchy of me.* But she didn't have the courage to take back the words. The pain she saw in his eyes... She was disparaging an ancient royal family and their familial symbol, and the head of that family, a man staring at her with heartbreaking love, but she was devastated, thinking of Brendan's murder.

"Katarina."

"You're still not wearing yours. Good."

He touched his chest. "It's on a chain around my neck, under my shirt. I keep it out of the public eye for now because I don't want my queen harassed. I'll keep our secret until you allow me to protect you."

"Don't even think about *protecting* me," she snapped. "Let me lead my life in peace. No guards or *anything*."

He closed his eyes briefly.

A drunken couple stumbled out of the music hall, laughing. A guard stepped in front of them, redirecting them away from Cory and Kat. They looked daggers at the beefy man but didn't argue, circling around cars. Kat waited until the couple entered a neighboring café. When others drew near, Cory asked Kat if they could finish this conversation in the limo. He promised he wouldn't try anything funny. She looked around at the gathering crowd and nodded.

In the limo, she scooted away from him. "Did I anger you? Are you going to hurt me now, or are you waiting for later?"

He looked at her with troubled eyes. "I love you. I would never hurt you. And I don't hurt people."

She scoffed. "Evil one moment, then sweet the next. Why? In order to lure me into your lair?"

He reached out a hand, but she rejected it. "I'm not a killer, and you don't have to fear for me anymore. As you can see, I have protection, and George doesn't have the power he used to. I'm sitting on the throne of my country."

"So go back."

He frowned. "Not without my queen! You must accompany me because you deserve to enjoy being a billionaire." He gestured with open palms, offering her the world, the jerk, in his ritzy clothes in his gleaming limo. As if that were going to impress her!

She trembled in anger. "I can't be bought. I don't give a damn about that stuff. You should know that."

"You don't want…" his voice faded, and he glanced at his feet before looking at her again. "God, I would give it *all* away just to live in a hovel…with you, but let me give you half my estate, so I don't have to see you suffer, but *please*, take me ba—"

"I married you for love, and *only* love! Stop trying to *buy* me!"

"I can't stand knowing how you live in poverty!"

"I did fine before. Especially when we…"

"When we what?"

"When we shared two-dollar meals."

"My love…"

"But now…I liked you so much better when you were poor. Keep your damn wealth!"

Kat slammed her hand against her thigh. *Brendan was going to study to be a doctor, and who knows, with the mask's amazing qualities, and the gifts it bestowed upon Brendan, he may actually have achieved his goal to someday find a cure for diabetes.*

"Please, come back and help me do good for the people!"

"It seems," she admitted, "that you are doing well with this yourself."

"Thank you. But you make me even better."

"Maybe your guilt over Brendan drives an insane need to help millions."

He frowned deeply. "Remember how I longed to help my country for years? This is nothing new!"

Her shoulders dropped. She nodded.

"Think of all these past years how I used to come over, and you and I would stretch out on your bed and talk for hours."

An image of this came to mind. Her heart was touched with tenderness, but disgust quashed it.

Cory continued with hope. "I would help you with math, and you would help me with science. We talked about everything except my past."

She scowled, hearing him out before she would put him into her past.

"Please, remember."

She hardened her jaw. Her hand came upon her quivering belly. He glanced at it.

"Thank God, I'm not pregnant."

A thoughtful look came over him. "I know."

"You're a liar, but at least you didn't lie to me on our wedding night when you used your second mask-given gift and said I wouldn't get pregnant yet."

"Of course not! I would never do that to you! A baby..." he dropped off. "A psychic palace maid told me that you and I were supposed to have six beautiful kids together, delightful children that would make a difference to humanity. Well," he added, "our youngest will do great things to help animals. That would please me."

She swallowed hard.

He shifted. "You and I did the most fun, craziest shit together growing up, as best friends." He wiped his hands over his thighs. "Remember the sexual tension between us. Remember our respect for each other and tell me it's not possible to spend our lives apart," he begged, straining it seemed, not to touch her. "Please, my love. What we have, I'll never find again."

She did remember those wonderful times but still questioned her feelings for him. She believed those feelings were based in misconceptions about the kind of man he was, a man capable of giving in to his darker, buried tendencies.

"You have no choice."

"*Was* your love for me true? Like you said it was? Like I thought it was making love to you on our wedding night?" he asked on a harsh whisper. "Don't..." he looked down then back into her eyes, "... lie to me."

His anguish reminded her that she wasn't a cruel person. She'd tell him the truth. "Yes. I would die for you. I love you, loved you a thousand times more than I ever loved Asher, Gunther, or Brendan. I love you for thousands of reasons, which I question now." *But I can't help loving you still.*

"If you mean that, prove it. Kiss me."

"No."

Then he looked at his hands in his lap. His overwhelming sadness washed over Kat.

"I see," he uttered.

She zipped across the seat, grabbed the back of his hair, and pressed her lips to his. He started then leaned into her, putting his hands on her back. The hard kiss turned soft. Her tears wet his cheeks. She pulled away.

His face glowed.

"It's over." Not one mention of the loss of their best friend. Cory was a wicked person who got away with it.

"Oh, God." He bent over. "I won't give up. Believe in me. I'm innocent."

This was torture. She had to end it. "If you approach me again, I'll disappear to hide from you."

"What?"

"Do not call, send letters, or show up for my gigs, or I'll hit the road with what money I have saved. And don't try to have me followed. I'm not stupid, and I'll know."

"I didn't kill Bren—"

"Save it!" She held her palm to him, in no mood for his lies. He was clever enough to come up with something good, since his money and position hadn't impressed her. "I wouldn't believe a word you said if you told me the sky was blue. You fooled me for years. I've heard enough."

"Please! Brendan's alive! I can feel his life—"
She turned and jumped out of the limo, running.
"Katarina!"
She was running so hard she had to gasp for air.

Twelve

A couple of months later, Katarina went to see Gunther at his apartment. They stood in his living room.

"He's a jerk." She blinked back tears as a fresh wave of grief hit her.

"How many times do I have to tell you, he didn't do it?" Gunther placed a comforting hand on her shoulder. "He's going crazy without you. He flies to the States every weekend and paces my carpet threadbare, begging me to help him. He wants to approach you but is terrified you'll disappear if he attempts it. He said he'd use his last dime to find you but worries you could get hurt out there. He's crazy in love with you! Seeing him suffer like this is very disturbing. For the first time, I witnessed him in tears!"

"I know things you don't."

"What things?"

"On mine and Cory's wedding night, Brendan implied he was going to kill Cory then get me into bed."

"Are you serious?" His eyes widened. "I heard him say he was going to try to take advantage of you, but kill Cory? He said that?"

She nodded. "I told Cory the mask must have messed with his mind, but Cory didn't care. He told Brendan his words were fatal, and Cory had a gun."

"Oh my God." Gunther fell onto his couch.

"He promised me he wouldn't use it, but what if he broke that promise or killed Brendan another way?"

"Cory admitted they had fought. That's why he returned that evening bloodied up. But, I can't, I *won't* believe he actually went through with killing him, even if he had considered it."

"Brendan is gone!"

"He's probably so mad at Cory for marrying you that he set him up. Remember when he said he wouldn't let you go with Cory? This could be how he's implementing his threat. I'm dying to hear Brendan try to justify this stunt when he returns."

"Brendan's dead! His mother went to his funeral!"

Gunther gasped. "What?"

"Yes!"

"How did they say it happened?"

"An accident, the police said. I don't believe that, and neither does Brendan's mother."

"When?"

"Very recently."

He shook his head. "I still don't believe Cory killed him."

"I never thought you could be so stupid."

"Kat! Powerful people hate Cory. Think about it. This smells like a set-up."

"Brendan's mother loves Cory and wouldn't be part of a set-up. Also, Cory looked at me like he was proud to have gotten away with executing Brendan. He tormented me with that look. He *told* me he did it."

"Probably to piss you off in the heat of your fight."

She scoffed. "Good alibi."

"There's a tragic misunderstanding at force here."

"You're an idiot."

"I will excuse that. Why the hell do you, someone who knows Cory well, believe he could do it?"

"That look he gave me froze my blood." Her lip quivered. "I want him, but I won't have him. I love him, *so much*."

"Good, so take him back!"

Her cheeks heated. "Please stop."

"For fuck's sake, believe in him. He didn't do it."

"You weren't there."

"Do you have evidence?"

"No, but he admitted it."

He slapped his hands to his sides. "Haven't you ever said things in anger, to hurt someone? Give him a break. He was snatched away from his home, his family, and his inheritance for years because everyone thought him capable of something he wouldn't do."

"Brendan's dead."

He looked at her with patient eyes. "Cory's grandmother recently died."

"I'm sorry to hear that."

"His life is in danger."

"All kings must deal with that."

"George put a bullet hole in Cory's arm."

Kat gasped.

"He's okay. It happened in his palace bedroom. George sneaked in through a secret passageway and shot him. Luckily, Cory swung mostly out of the way while reaching for a handgun by his bed. George fled through the secret way before Cory could recover. Cory only told Asher and me and not his citizens, knowing his people would kill George on sight. He swore his doctor to secrecy about the nature of his injury. He locked up that secret door."

Cory spared George, showing mercy? Kat wiped away a tear.

"Come here."

She did, and Gunther pulled her into a hug. "I love you, Kat."

"I love you too."

"I want your happiness as much as I want his," he said.

~ * ~

Katarina watched the Internet news and read the online paper daily on Asher's computer for any stories on Cory. When she saw a picture of Cory on the arm of a beautiful woman, she stumbled back. Asher caught her.

"Kat?"

"What the fuck? Who is that?"

"Again, you sound like Cory. Are you jealous? I thought you didn't want him anymore."

"That's not true!" She slapped her hand over her mouth.

Asher smiled. "You don't want him to move on?"

"I...uh...I..." She sat on his bed, shaking and putting a hand over her sick belly.

"That's Cory's first cousin, Arabella."

"They don't...date or marry their first cousins in his country, do they?"

Asher laughed. "Not in this century. He told me that he's to escort her down the aisle to her soon-to-be husband, since her parents are dead."

Kat swooned with relief.

"Your look brings me hope, and I'm not even your groom."

She picked up his pillow and smacked him with it.

"You miss your best friend, don't you?"

She looked at her hands in her lap and nodded sadly.

~ * ~

Katarina was closing up at work when the phone rang. She picked it up. "I'm sorry, we're closed." As was her habit, she traced an imaginary musical note on the counter with her finger.

"Katarina?"

"Dad? You're still in Europe?"

"Yes. An extra-long trip. It was desperately needed. Mom and I were feeling...sad about Molly. We've been visiting happier places. Glad to catch you at work. Guess where we are now."

"London?"

"Further east. Carasivia. Thought we'd pick up a newspaper for our son-in-law, and your mom wanted to take pictures of the royal residence."

"You're in Cara...sivia, at the royal palace?" Her breathing sped up.

"Yes, right outside. You sound stressed. Are you okay?"

"Y…yes."

"Are you sure? You haven't called us since you got married."

"Sorry." She gazed at the guitars hanging in rows in the shadows. The place was eerily silent.

"How's Cory?"

That nice kid who used to say things to your mother and me like, 'Yes, ma'am, can I help you with the dinner dishes?' and 'Yes, sir, let me get that for you,' she could practically hear him thinking.

"We're pleased you married him."

She swallowed past the lump in her throat.

"Wait. Mom wants pictures of the inside of the castle. I wonder if they'll let tourists inside."

"Dad—"

"She's asking a guard now. He speaks English! It's beautiful up here on this mountain, majestic. Romantic, your mother said, with the fog rolling in and the charming cottages dotting the hills. The happy village below."

She trembled. "T…tell the guard…your names and have him inform the king's secretary you're there."

"Why?"

"If Mom wants to see inside…"

"Fine. Hold on."

She waited while her father had a word with the guard. Her dad spoke into the phone again. "He sent his colleague inside."

"There's something I never told you."

"Sweetheart?"

She rubbed a sweaty hand over her thigh. "How do you like Carasivia?"

"It's nice. They seem to be celebrating. Mom and I have missed the news stories. The capital city had ribbons and bright signs everywhere. I couldn't read them, but people are partying like it's Mardi Gras. A new leader, perhaps."

"I'm glad they're happy."

"I've got to find out what the excitement is all about. Cory!" he cried out.

Kat gasped and listened.

"What are you doing here? Why are you holding your arm like that, son?" Her dad's voice sounded softer, as if the phone were no longer next to his face.

"I had an accident, but I'm fine. Mom, Dad," Cory said, "this is a real pleasure!"

"Good to see you, kid. Congratulations on marrying our girl. We always suspected you two would make a great match."

"Thank you," Cory said. "Are you staying long?"

Hearing him pinched Kat's heart with tenderness.

"Oh, about a week," Dad said. "Why are you dressed so well? Sell a million books finally?"

"I—"

"Maybe now you can buy my daughter a cell phone. She wouldn't let me," Dad interrupted.

"I'd like to buy her a phone made of gold," Cory said.

"Can you recommend a good hotel in the area?"

"Hotel? Nonsense! I won't have that," Cory said.

"Why isn't Katarina with you?" Dad asked.

Kat's mom interrupted. "Do you have a family home nearby? I'll make those hamburgers you like so much. And salty French fries— your favorite, and we'll pay for the food, buy you groceries for a week, though it looks like you got a break and may not need it now."

"First, can we come inside the palace?" Dad said. "Mom wants a thousand pictures. Do they let in foreign tourists?"

Kat shook her head, amused. Her parents often spoke so rapidly no one else could get a word in.

"You're staying in the palace, in my finest guest suites, and take all the pictures you'd like. I'll show you around. It will be the royal treatment for you!"

"What are you talking about? Do you work here? Why aren't you back home?" Mom said.

Kat's eyes stung with unshed tears.

"I do work here, for the people."

"What's going on? We haven't had the chance to talk to Katarina since she told us about your marriage," Dad said.

"I'm the king here. This is my palace."

"What?" Mom chuckled. "I see Katarina has succeeded in giving you a sense of humor. She told us it was her mission in life to do so. Good for her for succeeding."

"I'm being serious," Cory said.

"Dad!" Katarina shouted to get him to put the phone to his ear.

"I'm here."

"It's true. He was recently crowned. But don't tell anyone about our wedding. It's still a secret. I'll explain later. Let me talk to Mom."

"Wow. Okay." There was a pause.

"Hello?"

"Mom. Don't go public with the marriage yet. What Cory said is true. He's a prince, and we never knew it."

"You're serious."

"Yes."

"Sweetheart!" Dad shouted away from the phone before speaking into it. "She fainted. Here, take the phone, Cory. Speak to your wife."

Kat grasped the receiver.

"Katarina?" Cory said, breathlessly.

She bit her lip. "Is Mom okay?"

"Yes. Dad is holding her. I just nodded to a guard. He's escorting them inside."

Dad. He was Cory's dad too. And it felt right.

"I'll be right there," Cory shouted, away from the phone.

Speaking to him made her blood pound a dizzy spell into her head. "Cory?"

"I'm here."

"Y...you were shot. Are you okay? It scared the holy living hell out of me." *Please don't be indifferent to me.* She held her breath.

"Oh, God." He sucked in a breath. "I'm...okay. Thank you."

She let out the breath, relieved but irritated at herself, not for being happy and grateful he was okay, but rather for being thrilled he still cared about her, as was evident in his voice.

"Beloved...I'll show your parents a grand time. I could fly you here for a *dazzling* coronation. I'm *dying* to tell my people they have a queen they'll adore."

His anxious voice pulled buried love to the surface of her heart in torrents.

"We could renew our vows publicly," he continued. "Wouldn't your parents love that? They'd be there this time! Dad could give you away. Mom could fuss over you. Allow me to put that crown on your head while you still wear a beautiful wedding gown."

She splayed her hand by a register and hunched her shoulders, losing the battle. "Please, stop."

"My love—"

The clash of ire against passionate love put her in a frenzied state. She lowered to the floor, stretching the phone's cord. "Shut up."

He sighed.

Something exploded on his end.

Her heart skipped into a frantic rhythm. "Are you okay?"

"Yes."

"That sounded like a gunshot!"

"My troops are preparing for drills."

"From what my dad said, the people are happy to have you as a leader, but there are a lot of weirdos out there. Just...be safe."

"Thank you. I have top-tier guards."

"I couldn't...carry on if someone...killed you."

"Beloved..." Cory said.

"Hey, beautiful."

Kat jumped to her feet, startled, and turned to see her new manager, Mr. Jace, the one who had a crush on her.

"Mm, how nice to see you alone in the dark," Jace added with insinuation in his voice.

"Who the hell was that?" Cory yelled. "Where are you?"

"Uh...at w...work," she stuttered.

"And with whom?" Cory demanded. "Doing what?"

"My new manager, Mr. Jace. Just closing up."

"Hang up on him, gorgeous. We need to talk," Jace said, standing next to her.

She pulled the phone away, squinting as Cory went into an angry tirade. He took a breath.

"Who's the pissed off guy?" Jace asked. "I could hear him from here."

"Her husband!" Cory shouted. "Katarina," he said softer.

She put the phone to her ear.

"Do not..." He paused, overtaken. "...betray me."

"Go get my dad."

"I demand—"

She hung up.

"Ha!" Jace said. "What a temper."

Kat swiped up her purse and dashed out.

As soon as she got home, there was a message on her voice mail. She heard her dad's anxious voice and called him.

"What happened? Cory set us up in a magnificent room then told us he was going to see you and that he hoped to be back for tomorrow night's dinner. He ran out of here before we could say goodbye."

She braced herself. "I'm divorcing him."

"What?" he cried.

"It's a long story."

"Are you crazy?"

She held the phone away as he went through excited words of disbelief. When he paused, she brought the receiver back to her ear.

"You'd tell me if he hurt you, right? Is that why you're leaving him? I'd be shocked, but still..."

"It's not like that."

"How long have you two had problems? Why didn't you call me? I don't understand. He loves you."

She cringed. "We'll talk about it when you come home."

"How did he become king here? Did you know about that?"

"Not until after the wedding. I thought I was marrying a poverty-stricken orphan whose only prospects were his talents as a writer."

"And?"

"I'll explain later. Please enjoy his hospitality, and don't tell Mom about the divorce until after. Bye." She hung up, her heart heavy.

Thirteen

At work the next day, Katarina was putting up sheet music. Jace walked by and winked at her, brushing a hand through his blond hair. She shuddered.

"Kat," he began. "I'm getting transferred to the main branch. Follow me there. I'll give you a promotion and a raise."

"No, thanks." She turned away.

"Afraid of your angry husband?"

She spun to face him. "No, Mr. Jace, but, you really don't want to get on his bad side."

"You're not wearing a ring. You're getting a divorce..."

"Not...true." Cory's voice couldn't be colder or deadlier.

Kat and Mr. Jace turned toward him. Cory stood in an expensive suit, backed up by several stern-looking bodyguards.

Kat and Jace gaped, as did everyone within view.

"Who," Mr. Jace cleared his throat, "*are* you?"

"Seven million people call me *Your Majesty* as you should be calling *my wife!*"

People gasped and came closer to watch the scene. The back of Kat's hand came to her mouth, goosebumps zipping up her arms. Cory's energy was frightening. She dashed past him, grabbed her purse from under a counter, and ran out of the store. He followed. They faced off in the parking lot.

"Thanks a lot!"

"My love—"

"Uuuuuugh! You're out of control!"

"We belong together. Till death do us part, Katarina. I will give you *everything*! Do you hear me? Everything! Do you want my life? I'll give it to you!"

Several onlookers gasped. Several of his security guards frowned.

"I'm not..." She fisted her hands. "...fucking around with another man! And even if I were, it's too bad because we're no longer a couple!"

"I *beg* to differ!"

"Go away!"

His frown became an expression of such injury, it cut through her heart.

"I'm *never* going to stop being in love with you."

"Let me go," she said softly.

"Please!" He reached out to her. "Please, wife, my God!"

"I can't."

He turned and put his arm on top of his limo, resting his face on it. His guards shifted, nervously. Kat noticed that two of them were female and just as intimidating as the men. A spark of unwanted pride for Cory surfaced in her heart for his work on women's rights.

She walked away. One guard approached her and laid a gentle hand on her arm. "He's ruling with sadness, My Queen, and he's great. Our country *loves* him. Imagine what he could do if he were joyous. The man is a history maker."

Her lip trembled. She strode home and picked up the small wooden box which contained her savings. She had enough to at least talk to a divorce lawyer, she supposed, having worked extra hours. She ran her finger across the box's smooth surface. "I fight my love for you, Cory, so hard, but this is a battle I don't want to win."

She recalled the seventeen-year-old Cory handing the box to her with a smile.

"Open it," he had said, on their last day of high school.

"Didn't you make this box in shop class?"

"Yes."

She opened it and gasped. It was a roll of money with a note that read: For a brand-new bass guitar, amp, and patch chords.

She dropped the box onto a chair and embraced him. "How were you able to afford this?"

"My summer job."

"You hated that job..."

"Every moment I worked, knowing it was so that I could present you with this graduation gift, was a moment of happiness for me."

"Thank you."

"You like it?"

She squeezed him. "Yes. I have a gift for you too."

"What is it?"

"Come with me to the guitar store."

"Okay."

Once there, his face glowed when she slipped the bass on and played it.

She feathered her fingers across its glossy surface. "It's beautiful. How will I ever thank you enough?"

He smiled and rocked back on his heels. "You just did."

"I wrote this for you. This bass ballad is your gift." She touched her strings, and romantic, melodious notes filled the store. Patrons drifted over to listen.

"You're an angel. Did you...write a song for the others?"

"No." I love you so much, but if I ever give that away, my premonitions say you'll get hurt because of me. I can't risk it.

He leaned to kiss her.

She pressed a hand to his chest. "No."

He backed away, with sad eyes. Her heart broke.

She thought of that bass she still used and would forever use, even if she became a rock star. She left her apartment, clutching the box of money, and walked to a church. She approached a priest, holding out the box. "Here."

He took it. "Miss?"

"Wait." She opened it, pulled out the money, and gave her savings to him. "Please give this to those in need." She snatched up the empty box Cory had made and stormed away.

Back at home she crashed onto her bed. There was a knock at her door. She dashed to it and looked through the peephole. Asher and Gunther stood there. She let them in.

Both took out their wallets.

"What are you doing?" she asked.

They each tried to hand her all their money.

"No!" She stepped back. "What's this about?"

"We heard what happened," Gunther said. "You can't go back to work now."

"Fuck," Kat said.

"Please, take our money to live on until we help you think of something. We'll get you more," Asher said.

"Oh hell," Kat said, spinning around.

They went to face her.

Asher pulled her into a hug. "If you care about us, you'll not make good on your threat to Cory and disappear, like you said you would if he showed up again." He leaned away.

Both Asher and Gunther gave her desperate looks.

"You can't stay here. The media will swarm on you soon. You can't stay with one of us because we're..." Gunther dropped off.

"Men," she said. "The scandal. And my bandmembers. They'd check there next. I'm not close enough to my other girlfriends to ask."

"My cousin, Wendy, lives a mile and a half away," Asher said. "She'd love to have you. We have bags in the car and will help you pack, but we must hurry before anyone sees where we're taking you. This should buy you at least a little time until a permanent solution comes to us."

Kat trembled in anger. "I have no choice, do I? You two aren't going to let me just disappear."

Gunther gave her a look of disbelief.

"We love you," Asher added. "Come on."

"Cory was right not to try this himself," she mumbled.

"He's cursing his own stupidity and praying you won't be just as idiotic and hit the streets," Asher said.

Gunther sighed. "He'll go back home to the palace and entertain your parents only when we reassure him that you're safe."

"Fine!" Kat snapped.

"Promise you won't try to disappear from Wendy's," Asher said. He put his fingers under her chin to lift it gently, so their gazes met directly. She'd never seen him this deadly serious.

"You've never lied to me, Kat, to either of us," Asher said. "Don't change the nature of our friendship and do so now. If you say you won't try to disappear, we'll believe you."

She slumped her shoulders. "Okay, but you'd better warn him not to put security on me, or all bets are off."

Asher nodded and kissed her head. Gunther gave her hand a squeeze.

Later, situated in Wendy's guestroom, Kat cried herself to sleep, and again the next night. Cory appeared in her dreams this night, smiling. He pulled her into a hug. She collapsed into his embrace, snuggling into the safety of his arms.

"You know I'm innocent." He nudged her cheek.

Her eyes came open. She stared into the dark room. The integrity that always had come from him plumped the air around her, his essence somehow left behind from the dream.

"I need a sign."

The tall, red-headed Wendy knocked on her door. Kat smiled, wondering what she had in common with her cousin, Asher. She didn't seem to be a goofball like him. Maybe she had outdoor survival skills like he had.

"Come in."

She approached, holding out her phone. "It's your dad."

"Thanks." Kat took the phone, and Wendy left.

"Hello?"

"How are you?"

"I'm fine."

"You didn't call me. Please tell me what's happening with Cory."

She crashed back onto her pillow. "I'm wavering."

"That's great news. Whatever you argued about isn't worth breaking up your marriage over."

She rolled onto her side. "How do you know?"

"I've known that kid since he was a boy. He's a good person, and this should be obvious to you as well. Whatever happened was a misunderstanding."

"You really believe this."

"When he showed us around, every word he said was filled with love for you. He said your name thirty-two times. Mom counted. Then, to my amusement, he rattled off the periodic table of the elements, I think to impress your mom and me. Said you and he discussed someday giving us a grandchild that will come work with us in our chemistry lab. You taught him."

"Yes."

"He must have been at our house thousands of times. I observed you two often in unguarded moments, interacting with true affection, esteem, and respect for each other. He's filled with integrity. I don't know how I could have for a moment thought he had harmed you or would ever do anything intentionally to distress you."

She moaned.

"What's wrong?"

"I have so much to think about."

"I'll leave you to it."

"Thanks. Bye."

"Mom and I love you."

"Love you both too."

He hung up.

And now Cory had guards to keep him safe. She allowed herself a small smile in relief.

Fourteen

Asher wanted an evening of games at home. He had begged, so she'd go. She combed her hair, gazing in the bathroom mirror at her tired face.

Grabbing a jacket, she headed out. The coast was clear, her secret hideaway still undiscovered. She rushed to Asher's place. A breeze brought the scent of May's flowers. At Asher's apartment she pushed open the entrance door and walked down a carpeted corridor. Turning a corner, she gasped. Two muscular men looked at her, their arms crossed over their chests.

She stepped back. "You're bodyguards for King Corentin. Ones I've never seen. No media is around. He slipped here in disguise?" she asked the taller of the two.

He smiled.

"I'm Katarina Brodnik."

"Show us some I.D."

With a quivering hand, she withdrew her wallet from her purse and pulled out the new I.D. with her new name. She had gotten it changed on their wedding day, thrilled to be Cory's wife. The guard snatched up the I.D. and looked at it.

Bowing, he handed the card back to her. His partner bowed as well.

"My Queen," he said, then knocked on the door. "My apologies."

"Think nothing of it."

Asher pulled open the door and grabbed her hand as she stepped away.

"You didn't tell me he'd be here."

"Do this as a favor for me and for yourself. Face your fears."

She nodded and entered the apartment behind him. The sound of laughter came to her ears: Gunther's and Cory's. Asher shut the door. All curtains were drawn closed. The green mask lay in an open box near Asher's climbing shoes in the corner.

"Hi, Kat," Gunther said. "I told you, he comes every weekend."

She glanced at a wig and a blue jacket on the floor near Cory then looked at him. He met the look with sad love. Her breaths became shallow. Overcome, she spun on her heel and reached for the doorknob.

Asher touched her arm. "If you really couldn't stand to be here, fine, but we really want you to stay."

Gunther nodded.

"It's too bad Brendan couldn't join us." She turned around.

"He will again," Asher said. "Then we'll all hang out at the palace, like old times but with nicer surroundings, and mess around eating hamburgers and watching old American movies."

"When he returns," Gunther said.

"I didn't know people could return from the afterlife."

"He's not in the afterlife, sweetheart," Cory said. "I feel his presence on this plane. He's alive, I swear it." He looked into her eyes so intently she trembled.

She walked to the foldout table. A game board rested upon it, and she inched down into her chair.

"Katarina, my queen," Cory uttered. "Brendan will return, despite what I said before. I have people searching for him. I'll find out why his mother lied to you, but I have my suspicions."

That sounded and felt heartfelt.

His lips formed a sad smile. "Perhaps you'll beat me tonight."

"I never beat you. Don't let me win."

"I won't."

She shivered. *Fight to win me back. Overcome my defenses.*

I will.

She grasped the armrests, her lips parted in surprise. Did they just have a psychic exchange?

He tipped his head in astonishment, as if he were thinking the same thing. "Wow," he whispered.

"I know you said Jon, an excellent detective, being an archaeologist, couldn't find evidence of a connection between George and Brendan, but I pray anyway George didn't get hold of Brendan's mother and threaten her," Asher said.

Cory looked at him. "She seemed genuinely not to know what I was talking about when I brought up George's—Goran's—name. She promised to call me if she needed anything. I check in with her often, have her and her girls under protection."

Kat pondered his words. They had come out naturally, without artifice.

They played for hours. Asher and Gunther told jokes, and everyone laughed. Cory spelled out simple words such as "love," "forgive," "sorry," or "alive" the whole time, when he normally went for words like, "exequy" or "pyrrhic." His scores were low. His gaze pleaded with her. *I beg you, Katarina...*

She barely saw the game pieces in her hand as she placed them on the board. Silence hung in the air. She raised her gaze to her friends. Gunther stared under a raised brow, and Asher nodded. She brought her gaze to Cory's. He smiled and placed his fingertips gently under her chin. Pulses of electricity seemed to surge through her. She looked down at the words below her hovering hand.

Fight for me.

"Excuse me." She went to the bathroom, shutting the door and sitting on the floor with her face in her hands. Sometime later, she crept back into the living room. The guys chatted.

Kat sat in silence as Gunther talked about the evidence that helped prove Cory's innocence in the death of his father.

"My parents were in politics, working as advisers with a certain group in Washington," Gunther said.

Asher poured everyone a glass of wine. He looked at Cory. "Who was that guy who killed the king, your father?"

"A palace chef named Rendell poisoned the food. He didn't like seeing a child beaten so often. There were two other kitchen employees besides Mary and her boyfriend in the corner of the room who saw the servant put some powder in the king's food. They later asked him what it was, and he told them the king's favorite spice. The king was in bed with the flu at the time. He took a spoonful of soup, gasped and died. The maids approached Rendell and said they knew he had poisoned the king. Of course, Mary and her boyfriend, other employees, saw this as well, but no one knew until recently."

Kat held her wineglass, cold under her fingers.

"Jeez," Asher said.

"I know," Cory said. "Soon after it happened, I ran into the maids in the corridor, and they told me what they saw. I wrote down their words and had them sign the sworn testimony. I then went to Rendell and had him sign a confession, which he did when I pleaded with him, promising to beg leniency for him." Cory sat back, his eyes focused on the past.

"Rendell was kind. He told me he believed my father was going to kill me 'by accident' because the king couldn't tolerate his defiant son, 'the light and joy of my mother's world, the one she put before her own husband' or so my father thought. So, with the signed papers shoved deep in my pocket, I searched out George, prepared to speak for Rendell, asking mercy. I couldn't find him, so I put the evidence in a file and hid it in the walls of a guestroom—pulling a loose stone from the wall and jamming it in there."

"You were a child."

"Twelve years old."

"What of the servant?" Asher asked.

Kat watched, riveted.

"I told George that Rendell confessed to me of killing our father, and I had Rendell's written confession and testimony of witnesses in a file I hid in the agents' guestroom. George blew up, shaking his fist. He said everyone knew I did it, and it was reprehensible that I'd blame a servant. Later, while heading down the corridor to Rendell's quarters, paramedics rushed past us. We entered his room to find him dead. George turned to me with the biggest, ugliest smile and informed me that I was to be punished for killing the king."

"So what happened?" Asher asked.

"I ran to the guestroom, in search of the file."

Gunther shook his head. "My parents had already taken the evidence from the wall."

"Yes," Cory said. "They died on that plane that day. With the evidence gone and Rendell dead, George said my claim that Rendell did it was far too convenient. I had the strongest motive, the means, and the opportunity. He shipped me off to America to a rough neighborhood because he didn't execute children."

"It wasn't you who killed the king," Kat said, with lowered eyes. She brought her gaze to his.

Cory shook his head. "I could never murder anyone."

Her chest throbbed, her heart longing to believe him.

"Sweetheart, I've said threatening words in anger before, but I have rethought the wisdom of doing that and have promised myself to never do so again." He paused.

"The maids, I found out," Cory continued, "obeyed their new monarch's wishes to keep the secret of what they had witnessed when they told him what they saw. George set them up in luxury somewhere."

"That's surprising," Asher said.

Cory picked up some game pieces and rattled them in his hand. "Perhaps they were his lovers, but George spared them, convinced they would obey him. Within weeks of my arrival in that American foster home, George claimed a boy who had died here was..."

"You," Kat said.

"Yes," Cory answered. "I assume George paid my caretakers well for what they did. They approached me and told me I had a new last name, and they gave me paperwork to prove I was this new person they claimed me to be."

Cory looked down and shook his head. "George has always despised me. It was his way of banishing me from the family, of humiliating me. After all, he feels *he* was humiliated, being the firstborn and yet not the apple of our mother's eye. He tried hard to win her favor, out of seeming love for her, but also pride, to compete with his punk kid brother. He blamed me that he never succeeded at what he saw as his biggest challenge—being my mother's favorite—even though I asked our mother to be warmer with him. It seems she was so emotionally injured by his forced conception..."

Asher dropped his gaze. "How did she know George wasn't your father's? Did she get a test done in secret? Surely, she and your father had been together during that time if your father never suspected..."

Cory nodded. "Yes. However, Jon thought something was off, but didn't say anything. He told me recently that whenever he had seen George and the king together, he got the oddest feeling they were not connected. He once even joked with our mother, asking if she had traded babies in the hospital, Goran for her real son. She shushed him and made him swear never to say such a thing again. George looked like our mother, but he had zero in common with my father, except a selfish, nasty disposition—something he obviously inherited from a man capable of rape—or perhaps he got it from just being around my father. But George had none of the king's talents or better inclinations.

"Not long ago Jon searched for evidence to support his suspicions, and then found his opportunity when the royal family got a new doctor. Jon approached him to have him do a DNA test behind the king's back. They had a blood sample from a previous physical exam. The former doctor would never have agreed to that, but Jon caught the new one glaring behind George's back."

"Good thing your father's mother was still alive," Asher said.

Cory tipped his head. "There's a sample of my father's blood in the lab."

"You have an intelligent little brother, putting all these pieces together," Gunther said.

"Yes," Cory gestured, "and a short time ago, he found our mother's journal, written in her native French, which my father didn't speak. She hid the narrow book within the pages of a knitting book. She kept another journal in her dresser, the one she didn't mind him seeing."

Kat leaned closer.

"According to her journal, she suspected she didn't carry my father's child as soon as she discovered her pregnancy, a nagging feeling. It was confirmed when George was born. He has a red, c-shaped birthmark on his hand, the same as a visitor had—a dignitary who attended her funeral. Mom once told my father her uncle had a birthmark just like the one George had, but she wrote in her real journal that wasn't true. Jon remembered seeing it on the visiting dignitary's hand more than once as the man visited our country. Jon said recently if the bastard hadn't died of natural causes, he would have taken a group of men to the man's country to snatch him up and throw him into one of our prisons. The lie Mother carried around, George's paternity, tore away at her."

Kat inched her hand close to Cory's arm. He watched, his back straight. When she pulled away, he frowned.

"No abortion would have been possible had she known then," Gunther dared.

Cory gave him a steady look. "No. Abortion was against her religion. When she discovered her fears were true, she could never let my father know. He would have blamed her and executed her. Trust me. He was that kind of man. She never appeared beat up, and he wouldn't have believed her if she told him that she had been drugged and woke up in the midst of the vile act, her mouth gagged—I later discovered." He shot his gaze down.

"Oh God," Kat muttered.

Cory looked up, scowling. "Men who repress or harm women disgust me."

Kat pressed a hand over her heart.

"The new doctor who helped me recently said he looked at my mother's sealed medical records," Cory continued. "About nine months before George's birth, one of my mom's blood tests showed that drugs were present. Good thing for George that he looked like our mother and not his father. We don't do paternity tests normally. My beloved mother was virtuous, and everyone knew it."

Gunther shook his head. "My parents, knowing your language, read and then sent the file with your vindicating evidence to America immediately, as I recently discovered, to my uncle and aunt, asking them to hide it until they could decide what to do." He drank down his wine.

Asher glanced at Cory with a frown.

Cory tightened his jaw and moved his arm to stretch it, wincing.

Kat studied him. "D...does it hurt much?"

He smiled. "No, sweetheart."

"Good. Need any ice for it?"

His face glowed, but he shook his head.

"Let me see it."

"What?"

"I want to see it."

Cory slipped off his shirt. She stared at the bullet hole scar on his arm, reached a trembling hand forward, and touched it. Her hands curled into fists. She tore her gaze down. "That fucker!"

"Sweetheart?" Cory put his shirt back on.

"The bastard shot you!" She blinked back tears.

"My love," he uttered. "Thank you for caring so much."

"What else?" Gunther asked. "Please continue."

Cory glanced at him. "The maids told me later that George threatened to get them exiled or even killed if they said a word, but their continued silence guaranteed them a life of luxury. I couldn't break that silence until recently when I told them evidence, their signed documents, had been located. Jon sent the ladies to a trusted friend's house to hide until I could take the throne." Cory paused, and then continued. "Those women had told George they overheard the American couple say they found the evidence to prove my innocence, but they would obey their king and not say a word."

Gunther drew a deep breath. "George figured the file must have been in my parents' luggage."

Cory nodded. "He said in passing to a guard, 'I wish those Americans would die on that plane back. That the plane would crash in a fiery mess.'"

Gunther cringed.

Kat touched Gunther's arm. "The guard…"

"Took it as a personal request from his new king," Cory said. He turned briefly to Gunther. "I'm so sorry."

"Not your fault."

Cory looked at Kat. "I will neither rule with violence, nor live by it personally. On my honor. I was wrong before, but I've thought about it. I swear to think before I act, always. I'll do it for you until I'm doing it for me. Let me prove it. I'm going to have a white flower pin designed as a reminder, our sign of true love, a miracle that can overcome all anger and hatred, all poisonous influence."

Cory. She shook her head. *But you killed Brendan, or did you? If I knew for sure you hadn't, I'd throw myself into your arms for the sincere promises you just made.* She curled her fingers to prevent reaching up to cup his cheek. He glanced down then looked at each person in turn.

"Guys." He took a deep breath.

Everyone watched him.

"What is it?" Gunther asked.

"I have an admission and another vow to make," Cory said.

Kat took a steadying breath.

He looked into her eyes. "I did lie, but I'll never lie to you again."

She bit her bottom lip.

"About what?" Asher asked.

Cory tossed Asher a glance. "About the horrible things I said, in anger, which I regret." His gaze met hers again. "My wife knows to what I refer."

He grasped her hand. She didn't move. He slid his fingers from hers, his withdrawing heat leaving her skin cold.

"Will you ever forgive me?"

Sparks seemed to dance across her skin. *Yes. I will.* She didn't say it.

"I see it's a private matter between you two," Gunther said. When no one said a thing, he spoke again. "My uncle and aunt had the evidence all along but said nothing, afraid for their lives when they heard the news that my parents' plane had been tampered with."

"Why did they finally give you the file with the evidence?" Katarina asked.

Asher gazed at him and tipped his head as if he were also wondering. "Everyone had assumed it was on that plane and lost in the crash."

"Had I known before that they were *your* parents, I might have wondered if your uncle and aunt knew anything…" Cory trailed off.

"I never gave any of you a clue about the circumstances behind their death or what they did for a living," Gunther said. "And I didn't know who you really were," he reminded Cory.

Kat hung on his words.

Gunther continued. "Prince Jon went to see my uncle and aunt. They broke down and admitted they had the file. The guilt was eating away at them. You see, my mother had translated the gist of the file's contents and placed the translation within its pages." He paused, his hands crossed before him.

"Washington has a copy of it." Cory nodded to Gunther.

"Yes," he responded. "And they support you."

"My country will appreciate America under my rule."

"You are the rightful leader of Carasivia," Asher said.

"I'll be a good one," Cory said, solemnly.

Despite herself, pride hastened through Katarina, strong and pure like a mountain river. She took a sip of her fruity wine then relaxed back onto the pillow.

"I love my countries, both of them, and I'm honored. I'll always be grateful to you, Gunther."

Kat looked at her hands folded in her lap and sat back, lifting her chin to watch the others in silence.

Cory looked at her. "Do you believe me?" he said, referring to his earlier admission, she knew.

"I don't know." *Where is Brendan? He'd never pull a stunt that lasted for months. He'd never put his family through such agony intentionally. What about Jon's information that he could find no evidence that Goran had ever heard of Brendan, so it's doubtful he's behind this.*

Cory gave her a serious look. "You will have *much* say in matters, My Queen. Your heart and good sense will never lead me in the wrong direction. You bring out my peaceful side. My love has crushed my stupidity."

Kat reached for her glass. It spilled over the edge, from her trembling hand. She scooped up a napkin and dabbed at her shirt.

"Oh, of course," he continued, "when you're out with your band, I'll have to consult with you over the phone."

Have you really changed? Are you innocent? I do not get deceit from you.

"Well," Cory said, clapping his hands together. "Who's up for another game?"

The time came for the evening to end. Kat stood by the door. Cory went to her and touched her arm. "Believe me."

"Don't. I'm..." *afraid, conflicted, about to give in. I need to think about tonight and let it sink in. My heart tells me that you didn't do it, but...Brendan is gone. His mother said she went to his funeral and that she knew in her heart it wasn't an accident. You were the last one known to be with him alive, filled with rage and a hunger for revenge against him.*

"Please," Cory said. His fingers curled around her arm.

She pushed past him. *God help me.*

"Wait!" He turned her to face him.

"Leave me alone!"

"Katarina?"

Her heart rent in two. She hurried out, returning to her temporary home. She crashed onto her bed and stared at empty space.

"The way you look at me. I miss you. I need you. Ah!" She pressed her hands to her face.

Words echoed in her memory.

He didn't do it, Kat.

Believe in your husband.

She muttered, "Fight hard enough to overcome my doubts or at least make me not care anymore if you're guilty or innocent." She shuddered. *What kind of woman am I?*

She changed into her pajamas and crawled into bed, fantasizing he was innocent of hurting Brendan; then...*more* than half believing it, even though Brendan was gone. Maybe Brendan took a trip around the world or something, fell and hit his head and was wandering around with amnesia. But why would his mother say she attended his funeral? Goran a.k.a. George. Maybe, he *did* know Brendan and his mother, despite Jon's investigation. Did George hurt him? She twisted back and forth in the sheets.

~ * ~

In the morning, Katarina stared at the ceiling. *I've known Cory and Brendan almost half my life. Until recently, Cory has been more of a gentleman and nicer person than Brendan, temper and fighting or not.*

She kicked off the sheets, searching her heart and remembering Cory's pleading expression, his powerfully sincere energy. *Cory, if I allow myself to be honest about this, you'd only lie for a damn good reason. I made you lie, didn't I? With my cruel words, hurting you bad enough to do that. I'll listen to you now.*

She dressed and made her way into Wendy's kitchen to start some coffee then went and sat on the couch in the empty home. Wendy and her husband were at work. An envelope with Kat's name on it rested on the floor, near the front door where it had been slipped underneath. She hurried to pick it up, tore it open, and pulled out a note. It looked like Cory had written it in emotional haste.

My beloved Katarina,

I tell you on my honor that I DIDN'T DO IT. My angry words sent him packing, and I regret that. I just got a lead, and I intend to find Brendan and bring him back. My contact, Mr. Belford, has promised me useful information. I also put hidden protection on Brendan's family. I suspect, despite no evidence, that they were forced to lie.

She touched her mouth. *Oh, thank God. I believe you!* Freedom *at last...* She lowered her hand and continued to read.

I will always love you. PLEASE return to me!

Tears of relief stung her eyes.

I'm sorry I said those horrible things to you, my love. I was so angry and let that get the better of me. I did not mean those words. I'm sick inside over what I said to you. Please let me make it up to you. I will spend my life doing so.

She cleared her throat. *I'm the fool who owes you an apology.*

Brendan left that day after we fought. I gave him what money I had on me and told him to disappear. I think now he was coerced into his recent bad behavior, even without a single physical sign of George's involvement, and Brendan was probably kidnapped. I wanted you to believe I killed him because you hurt me so deeply. I can't say enough how sorry I am.
I was furious with Brendan. When my head cleared of its rage, I was able to think more clearly. Why would he leave on my order? Neither one of us was clear-headed that day, thinking without any logic or reason. I just wanted him out of my sight and acted on pure emotion. That kind of anger will never rule me again. I see now that it causes me to make bad decisions. Sweet love, I don't know where Brendan is, but I'm going to fix that.

She pressed the letter close to her heart. After a moment, she read again.

I believe he really sees me as his brother, and I feel the same about him. Please understand all this. I pray you do. With eternal love, your Cory.

She went to her room, opened the wall safe in the back of Wendy's closet, pulled out a small box, and with shaking fingers, lifted out her wedding band. She had previously kept it in a bank box, but when she came here, hearing about the safe, she brought it along with her. She slid it onto her finger.

It's beautiful, Cory. Thank you.
I'm honored and damn well relieved that the woman I'd die for will accept it.

"Why did I tell you that I'd pawn it? I'll never again act out or say things in anger." *It seems we have more in common than either of us ever dreamed.*

Throbbing began in her head. She brought her hands to it and went to bed as a migraine was coming on. Moaning, she didn't remember falling asleep.

In her dreams, she reached for Cory across a chasm. He stretched his arm to her.

The ground under his feet, on his side of the divide, shook, and he stumbled.

"Grab my hand, Cory."

He leaned forward, wiggling his fingers. The ground trembled. His image faded.

"I'm losing you!"

Fifteen

The duke's mansion, the day Brendan disappeared

Brendan gasped on the ground, coughing up blood, as Cory stood above him, gripping him by the collar. Cory sighed and dropped him, stumbling back. "I can't do it. Get the hell out of here. Never come back." He reached into his pocket, withdrew a few bills, and threw them at Brendan.

Brendan scooped up the money and pushed himself onto his feet with shaky arms.

"I'll have Jon deposit money into your account. Use your credit card somewhere and visit a friend, just get as far away from me as possible."

Brendan nodded. He walked off the duke's property, gazed around through swollen eyes and spotted a sturdy stick. He reached for it to help him walk. He made it to the main road then rested before going to the home of a co-worker.

Wide-eyed, Jack, who drove their ambulance at work, looked over Brendan's tattered appearance. Brendan told him he got into a bar fight, and he needed a break and was leaving town. Jack let him rest, fed him, and then wished him the best. Brendan purchased a bag of food items with his credit card then sat at a bus stop.

A black car with tinted windows pulled up. A door opened. "Get in." The accent was Carasivian.

Brendan entered and slid onto the seat next to a man he'd seen in a meeting of the king's employees a week earlier at a warehouse. George had first contacted Brendan months before, via one of his agents, shocking Brendan, and threatening him into cooperating with him. The scent of new car leather filled the vehicle.

Brendan looked at the expensively-dressed Carasivian.

Gruff words escaped the man's mouth. "Been watching you. Report."

Brendan didn't *want* to say a damn word. If he hadn't pushed his best friend, no his *brother*, to the point of murder, with horrible, untrue words, and then infuse the mask with hatred and poison Cory with it, Brendan's sisters and mother might not have been safe from George's thugs.

"I gave Corentin the beating of his life and the ugliest words I've ever uttered. He'll ponder those hateful things." Brendan cringed inside. "It'll weaken him, and he'll suffer. His wife will be disgusted with him for the angry way he'll carry on about me. He won't run away again and will be accessible to King Goran, so His Majesty can play with him as he sees fit. Goran will be pleased with how well I did."

The foreigner glanced down at his manicured hands then back at Brendan, his lip curling. "That will do. Let Corentin stew in misery until the king decides to take him out, sometime after the Dowager Queen has passed."

Brendan's breath caught. Cory, the one meant for greatness, the one who worked hardest to help him study and pass his paramedic exams, who had been the first to stand by him whenever anything had gone wrong in his life...

Finally, after a long while, the car stopped in front of a warehouse. They had arrived at their temporary headquarters.

Brendan sat on his cot looking up at the one-square-foot window. Golden, dusky light streamed in, cutting through a gray sky. While his bruises had faded into memory, the ache in his heart persisted. He'd been gone months and sent out a silent plea that his sisters and mother weren't worried past bearing about his disappearance. Hopefully, Cory told them something, having enough heart, despite their differences. Brendan leaned against the cold wall.

Yes, Cory told them something, so they wouldn't worry.

The door creaked open, and the man who brought him regular trays of food entered, covered platform in hand. He set it upon the stand at the cot's end. Steam escaped the cover's edges, bringing with it the scent of chicken and broccoli.

At least they feed me decent meals.

He scanned his guard's face. "Are they going to kill me?" he asked the well-built, dark-haired man.

"Perhaps, but we feel you might still be of some use. You never know." The guard slammed the door behind him on his way out.

Brendan slumped back.

An hour later, George walked in. Brendan would think of him as George, and not Goran, out of respect for Cory. George had mentioned to him with disgust that Cory liked the name.

George crossed his arms over his burgundy-clad chest. Diamonds sparkled at his left shoulder. "Guess what I did? I made it look as if Corentin murdered you. Ha! His wife loves that one. I convinced that ass, Corentin, and his punk kid brother that I didn't know you. Prince Pipsqueak almost kept his investigation from coming to my notice, but one of his female detectives fell in love with one of my men and told him what she knew. I was able to clear all evidence of yours and my connection."

Brendan watched him. "What do you intend to do?"

George smirked. "The fake king is on his way here now."

Brendan's back stiffened. *Cory's on his way?*

"I intend on getting rid of him, and then taking back my crown. The fool never went public with those DNA test results."

Brendan cleared his throat. "But...doesn't the prince have copies hidden in five countries? That's what one of your men said you had been told."

He shrugged, glanced around, and then his dark blue gaze landed on Brendan. "*Jon* and his men, under rigorous efforts, can be convinced to see things my way."

"I see." Sadness rippled through Brendan. Cory was going to die, and a tyrant would once again rule his country.

"Get up," George said. "I've been thinking. You have served me well. Maybe I was too harsh to lock you up. How would you like to come back to Carasivia, continue to serve me well, and be granted a dukedom? You see, as of late, I'm short on good men, most having chosen Corentin over me. I need to recruit more people and prove that I'm not such a bad guy, if you're on my good side." He stroked his chin. "It would be a shame to waste someone as devious as you. After all, you did fool that bastard who calls himself my brother."

Brendan didn't move. "B...but..."

"I sent my men to kill his guards. It seems others joined his two, so I had to send all five men I brought with me to this...*country* away for a few minutes. They're not far. We'll wait for the fake king to arrive."

Brendan nodded, his mind racing. Could he warn Cory?

"Come on." George gestured. "Let's go finish him off, and then you can celebrate with me. Hey, look at it this way, I'm sure that trash will want you dead anyway."

Brendan gulped and got up.

At the sound of gunshots, Brendan flinched, followed George out, and looked down upon a large room, straining to see in the dimness. Scaffolding stretched in many directions, layers of metal crisscrossing other layers. Boxes reached toward the ceiling. Crates rested everywhere. Dust tainted the air. He made out Cory's form then leaned over the railing, his fingers curling around metal. He turned to take a step. George stayed him with his hand. They looked down at an angle.

Cory stood under the yellowish light of a lantern that hung from a hook by the door. He gazed up at George, visibly shaken, and frowned. "Hello."

George sneered. "Hello, American trash."

Cory's shoulders drooped. "It seems it's just...us three. My guards and yours died fighting each other."

George leaned toward Brendan. "Damn. What a waste of good men. The trash killed my five best men! And I don't have many others yet," he muttered.

"I wish I had thought to do an inner check for my guards." Cory shifted his gaze to Brendan. "Hello."

Brendan took a step forward. *I'm sorry*, his heart called.

Cory considered George. "Goran, Mom would be heartbroken over your behavior."

George grasped the railing. "Mom was blind when it came to you. Such injustice that you'd steal my throne!"

"I stole nothing. I kept your bastardhood a secret. I spared you humiliation, and I didn't have you arrested or executed after you tried to kill me. I was more than fair."

"I had my man Mr. Belford invite you here, so I could finish the job. Too bad he and the others are dead. But at least he duped you into thinking he was on your side."

Brendan's heart pounded.

"How are we going to resolve this, brother?" Cory asked, sad eyes on George.

"Don't call me brother. And with your death, that's how."

Cory dragged his gaze to Brendan. "I came here to search you out after Belford led me here...to tell you that I still considered you my brother, despite all that's happened. I forgive you."

George reached under his jacket and pulled out a gun.

"No!" Brendan rammed into George's side and saw Cory leap behind a crate.

They tumbled. George cried out as his hand smashed against the steel grating of the scaffolding. The gun skittered five feet away. Brendan straddled him, pinning his arms down. Cory's footsteps thudded across the floor. His boots rang out with each hurried step up a narrow staircase, pausing four yards from them.

"Get off me! I offered you a dukedom, and this is how you repay me?"

Brendan scowled. "I stand by my best friend, my brother, and Carasivia's true king." He tossed a glance at Cory. "I always did."

Cory shot him a look of brotherly love. "I forgave you months ago, actually."

Brendan released George's arms, shifting to relieve a cramp in his back.

"Don't make me sick." George thrust up and banged his head against Brendan's.

Brendan fell back and held his head with both hands, moaning.

Through his haze, he saw George stand, look at the approaching Cory, and scramble for the gun. "Remember that move, *brother*," George mocked. "The king laughed when I used to do that to you as a child."

"I remember. Maybe that's why I'm not good at science," Cory said with a sneer. He strode closer, standing two yards behind George. He stopped, caution in his eyes.

George, with gun in hand, looked at Brendan, who was sprawled out on the floor. Brendan scooted to a seated position against the wall. When George aimed at Brendan, Cory ran and leapt toward George.

George swung around and captured him, wrapping his left arm around Cory's neck. With his right hand, he pressed the barrel of the gun to Cory's head.

"Why not fight me, man to man?" Cory offered. "Or how about if I give you a full pardon, millions, and let you live as a prince?"

"I could assassinate you."

"Under guard, of course."

"No thank you."

"I tried." Cory elbowed him in the gut and stomped on his foot.

George cried out, releasing Cory, and doubling over. Cory kneed him under the chin, sending him sprawling. George landed on his back with a thud, groaning. The gun flew over the railing and landed with a clank.

"I learned that while living in the rough foster home you dumped me in, you bastard." Cory glared at him. "As King of Carasivia, under law forty-eight section twelve, which states that an attack on the king, in any country, warrants punishment, the type to be determined at the king's pleasure, I place you under arrest and sentence you to a maximum security prison for—"

George stood up on unsteady feet, rubbing his chin. "That's what you think." He shoved Cory toward the railing.

Cory reached and grasped George, wavering, his back bent over the horizontal metal pole. He swung around, and they struggled. Cory shoved him, and George hit his back to the wall. George pushed off and charged, flying over the edge, but knocking Cory over as well. Brendan yelled and jumped to his feet. Cory clung to the scaffolding, his feet dangling twenty-five feet from the concrete floor. George hung, grasping a horizontal pole ten feet below him. He jumped down, looking up at Cory. "Oh, I'm going to have fun with you." He ran out the door, rattling it behind him.

~ * ~

The pounding at the door woke Kat. She stood and stumbled to open it, only to have Asher and Gunther rush in. She shut the door behind them.

"Cory's not answering his phone," Gunther said. "I have a strange feeling something's wrong."

"Oh God. You don't think George *killed* him?" She stepped back.

Gunther nodded gravely. "It's possible, Kat."

Her knees buckled, but Gunther and Asher caught her, reaching for her arms.

Asher studied her. "I'm glad you still love him."

She swallowed hard. "Yes. Even if he were guilty, which I no longer believe, I would never get over him. My love is unconditional."

"Well, I'm glad to hear it," Asher said and glanced at Gunther.

"Let's go to the apartment Cory keeps here," Gunther started.

"We can search for clues there," Asher said.

"Yes!" Kat said, nodding. "That's a good idea." She led them out the door and to Asher's car.

At Cory's apartment, Gunther unlocked the door, and the three friends entered. He glanced at the plants Cory had him water on a regular basis.

"I'll search the bedroom. You guys look around out here," Kat said.

She dashed to Cory's room. His velvet coat lay across his bed. She picked it up and pressed it to her cheek. *It smells like rain.*

The memory came to her. The night she slept in his arms and surrendered her heart to him, she had told him that the woodsy scent of rain would forever remind her of him. Then putting the coat on after they made love...

I can feel you.

She sighed in relief, sensing in her heart that he was alive.

I will find you and beg your forgiveness. She prayed then noticed a notepad on his nightstand. She drew closer, seeing the indentations left behind. A half-torn sheet of paper rested above the lines. Her heart sped up.

Contact...for info...just west of Fernanda's Hideaway on highway... She continued to read the directions.

I know where he is. "My cousin used to live near there." She turned to rush out with the news but reconsidered. She looked at her trembling hands.

Once again it was time to show the newfound courage she had discovered the day she took a chance and told Cory she loved him and wanted him to be her husband.

"I don't want Asher and Gunther there." She put the pad between the mattresses, walked out, and saw the guys searching everywhere for clues.

"Guys, I feel sick. I'm going to rest at Wendy's house. Can we meet up in a couple of hours?"

"Are you okay?" Asher asked.

She nodded. "I'm fine, just a lingering headache."

"Okay, we'll take you back."

"No, please. It would ease my mind if you'd stay here and continue looking."

"Are you sure?" Gunther asked.

"Come and get me in two hours."

She hugged them then rushed to the house, which was only a couple of miles away. She tried calling Cory from the land line without success. Finally, she left a note on the door with Gunther's and Asher's names on it, saying she had a friend emergency and had to leave, and that they shouldn't worry. She filled a bag with peanut butter sandwiches and bottles of water. She put her long black hair up under a floppy hat and wore large sunglasses. Then she hit the road, hitchhiking. She got a ride along the interstate highway with a friendly old farmer heading east. He dropped her off in the neighboring state. Around dinnertime, she found herself on a lonely stretch of road a hundred miles from her destination.

She walked, nibbling on a sandwich. Sometime later, a young man offered her a ride.

She hopped into his car. "Thanks."

"You're welcome. Say, Miss—"

"I'm meeting up with my husband."

"I see." He frowned and pulled back onto the road, driving without saying a word for fifty miles.

They pulled up to a gas station just as pinks mingled with navy blue and stretched across the sky. The moon glowed above her. She stepped out of the car and went to the restroom. When she came out, he was gone. She turned her head, searching. "No! My bag!" Trembling, she walked down the highway with no food, water, or money.

"Cory," she mumbled often. "I'll find you. I only have to walk fifty miles or so."

Five miles later, she eased up on her quick pace. "Slow down. Pace yourself."

She glanced to her side at a wheat field. Golden ripples danced under the wind. Continuing a few miles, she stopped and stretched her neck up. The stars painted the sky with their beauty. She shivered in the crisp air and hugged herself. Yawning, she stepped off the road, squinting under the moonlight. A patch of grass struggled for survival amongst the weedy area around it, the green an island in a yellow sea.

She shrugged. "Looks springy." She lay down and used her arm as a pillow. The bouncy green blades drew a shiver from her. She closed her eyes and thought of Cory, falling asleep with a smile, stroking her wedding ring.

Birds chirped. She opened her eyes, blinking against dawn's light. Her stomach rumbled, and she swallowed, parched. *Normally, Saturdays started out better...* She looked around and spotted a smooth pebble. She picked it up, rubbed it on her pants, and put it in her mouth to stimulate saliva flow then began her trek again. She tripped, and the wedding ring flew off her thinner hand. She put it in her pocket.

Hours later, her eyes went blurry, and her stomach growled. Two cars driven by women hurried by, but the drivers didn't stop when she hailed them. She dragged herself along the lonely road. "Cory. Only a few more miles to go, I think." Dazed, she ordered her feet to move forward.

She tripped and landed on her face. Staring at dirt, the tears flowed. She pushed herself up and continued on. The day grew warm, then hot. "Water."

A sign announced a gas station, and hallelujah, Fernanda's Hideaway, one mile away. She smiled, on the verge of collapse. With the sun beating down, she rolled up her shirt, exposing several inches of her belly and her scars. She didn't care and faltered along.

"One block. Eleven to go. Two blocks ten to go..." She stumbled again. "I'm...here." She swayed on her feet. "Cory, my love, where are you?" Blurry-eyed, she saw spots, then an outline of a person running toward her. Could it be Cory? She staggered, and her wrinkled shirt tumbled down again over her scarred belly.

The man drew close...sneering, or was that the imaginings of her dazed mind?

Oh my God. The thudding of her heart made her taste alarm. She'd seen his picture. The blond King Goran. Make that just plain George, handsome with his blue eyes like Cory's.

He approached with a smile. "Katarina. I was going to search you out. What a lucky coincidence."

Crinkles marred his brow. "You look unwell. Allow me." He offered his arm.

Don't fuck with him. "Wh...what can I do for you?"

"I'm taking you to a doctor. We can talk later."

She stiffened.

"Dear lady, please. I mean you no harm."

Don't you?

"The stories that have been going around about me are lies."

"You...shot Cory."

"He shot at me first! It was self-defense."

"I don't believe you." Nausea overcame her, and she doubled over.

He helped her stand with an arm around her waist, surprisingly gentle. "Let me help you."

She swayed and passed out in his arms, only to awake in a hospital room, with him holding her hand. And smiling.

"Welcome back. Dehydration and a bit of heat prostration, but you'll be fine. How do you feel?"

Confusion dashed through her.

"Better. Thanks."

He nodded. "Good."

She looked at the water to her side.

He handed her the glass, and she gulped the cool, refreshing liquid, having to still her trembling hand.

"Katarina." He sighed. "There's something you should know."

His pause sent tingles of fear racing down her spine. "Tell me. Then prove it." *I dared to say it.*

He couldn't hurt her here in a hospital, right?

He met her gaze. "Corentin is not the man you believe him to be. He killed your friend Brendan."

She turned away and stared at a white wall.

George's hand fell on her arm. "Please, look at me."

"I have no need of your lies."

"Look at these. I paid a professional to get his hands on these."

She turned her head. He held up photos. The front one was of a headstone with Brendan's name on it. She gasped then shook her head.

"A fake. An empty grave. The wrong person."

He flipped the photo to the back of the pile. The second was of Brendan's mother and sisters, all in black, crying, in front of the headstone. "They saw the body. You can call them and ask them yourself."

"Perhaps you made them lie with threats."

He flipped to the next picture. Cory held a bloody Brendan by the collar, bent over him. Brendan's swollen face lolled to the side. He had on the same shirt he was wearing the day he disappeared.

"He beat him to death. Jon paid the police to lie. Cost him a pretty penny." He pulled out a recorder from a bag. "This was taken from a security tape on the duke's property. Listen."

I can also give one hell of a beating. Say goodbye to this world, Brendan.

It was Cory's voice.

"Oh God." She bent over and vomited into her trash bin.

He handed her a towel and water. "I'm sorry."

She sobbed, devastated, disgusted, and furious. When she calmed, George stroked her hand.

"What do you want from me?" She drew back.

"For you to be okay."

"And?"

"There is something."

"I thought so."

"You are the queen of my country. Speak for me. Corentin set me up, and I only want to live my life in peace, quietly in one of our family homes."

Pity for the wronged George raced across her heart. "I'll do what I can, but I'll need more information first."

"I need to pick something up at a warehouse where I've held meetings with some of my colleagues, and then we can discuss this further," George said.

"What do you need to get?" she asked.

"I have money there, and further proof of my innocence and his treachery. I was going to go inside, but then I saw you. You needed my immediate attention."

"I'll go with you."

"Are you sure?"

Her bottom lip trembled, and she nodded.

Sixteen

Meanwhile, at the warehouse...

"Help me, Brendan." Cory huffed. "My arm is...not fully recovered from the gunshot."

"Hang on."

Brendan leaned over the railing and stretched his arm. Four feet separated them. "I can't reach you!" He glanced around for anything resembling rope. There was nothing. "Crap, let me go down there and grab a pipe. The boxes look too heavy for me to drag under you."

Cory glanced down. "I climbed tall trees as a boy. I can land properly and roll, if you'll clear the clutter from the floor. Hurry! I can't...hang on much longer. If I land on those, I'll break bones."

Brendan raced down the stairs to the area below Cory. He swept the space clean. "Clear!"

Cory let go. He landed on his feet, tucked and rolled. "Shit!" He winced and grabbed his wrist. "I think I broke it. My damn arm cramped, and I tucked it in wrong."

"Let me have a look." Brendan leaned over him and examined it. "Any other pain?"

Cory shook his head then glanced at the door. "My brother and I could have been friends."

"He doesn't deserve it. Why do your people think he allowed the vote?"

"Rumors say to prevent the spread of a scandalous secret. People suspected him of shady dealings, perhaps even treason. George would prefer they believed that than knowing he really was a bastard."

Brendan touched his shoulder. "I'm sorry for everything. For being such an asshole."

Cory nodded. "Your mom tried to tell me you were dead and that she and your sisters went to your funeral, but I promised her you were alive. I think she clung to her lie about your death under coercion."

"Is my family okay?"

"Yes. I've had them under protection for a while."

Brendan smiled and helped him up. "Thank you. We need to get you to a doctor."

Cory held his arm. They stepped out into the sunlight, squinting.

"Behind the building," Cory said sadly. "His men. My men." He rounded the building, Brendan following, and bowed his head in prayer. "My loyal employees deserve a decent burial and honors. Their families will be provided for."

"We'll call the authorities on the way to the hospital."

"During the firefight, one of my men shoved me down and covered me. I couldn't fight alongside them as much as I wanted to. I fell hard. Couldn't find my gun afterward."

Brendan nodded. "Let's look for it. Maybe it's in the weeds of this isolated place. There are animal holes in the ground."

A half-an-hour's search revealed the gun in a shallow prairie dog hole. Cory carried the weapon to the car, and they were off. During the ride, Cory called the police and told them the situation, agreeing to give a statement at the hospital.

After being patched up and talking to the police, Cory and Brendan weren't up for a long drive back to the apartment Cory kept, especially knowing they were going to return to the warehouse. They arrived at a motel. Cory made a quick call to the palace then both he and Brendan soon fell asleep, after their exhausting day.

They slept in, then had a leisurely lunch, Cory wearing his cast. Cory called his brother, Jon, and then back home to the palace, speaking at length with some of his employees. Brendan watched television and read the Saturday paper, waiting. Finally, Cory sat with Brendan in the car.

"*Why* did we come back here?" Brendan nodded toward the warehouse. "Without new guards?"

"They're on their way."

"The police have obviously come and gone. It might not be safe without them here."

"I need evidence to throw George in jail for life. As a former king, he might have sympathy from some. I want to avoid undue problems."

"The police probably took away any evidence."

"Knowing George and his ways, I can almost guarantee I'll find something the police wouldn't find significant in this situation." Cory handed Brendan his gun. "Take it inside just in case. I'm going to double check out here first."

"You're the king! You take it."

He shook his head. "No one's out here. I'll only be a second."

They got out and walked down a dirt path. Brendan entered the warehouse.

Cory gazed around.

The hum of an engine then the click of a car door caught his attention. He spun around and gasped. *Katarina! And George? What the hell?* He ran to her, stopping three feet away.

She glared at him.

"Katarina?" He reached toward her arm.

She stepped back. George smiled and crossed his arms over his broad chest.

"Sweetheart."

"Don't sweetheart me."

"What's going on?"

"I know the truth, Cory. I saw the pictures and heard the recording."

"What pictures? What recording?"

"The security tape. You told Brendan to say goodbye to this world."

His tongue wouldn't move at first.

"Do you deny this?" There was impossible hope in her eyes.

Nothing.

"Well?"

"I said it, but—"

"You disgust me." Disappointment made her shoulders drop.

"He's alive." He prepared to tell her to go see for herself but stopped. He wanted her to believe him over George, without evidence.

"Sure."

"Look at me."

"Yeah? I'm lookin'."

"We threw down, hard, and I said those words, but I *let him go* in the end!"

Her brow crinkled. "You did?"

She believed him—he dared to hope. "Yes. If you'd been shown the *whole* recording, you'd have seen and heard that part. You *know* I'm telling the truth."

Katarina studied him.

"Believe him or believe your husband."

George was staring him down.

"Cory!" She threw herself into his arms.

"What are you doing?" George cried.

Katarina ignored him.

Cory pressed her close, elated. "Brendan's inside the warehouse. We're friends again."

"Forgive me, Cory! I was so confused, but I've done a lot of soul searching." Her tears hit his cheek.

"He's a liar, Katarina," George said.

She tossed him a glare. "No, you are."

George scowled.

Cory ran a hand down her trembling back. "It's actually quite understandable that you'd be perplexed about the situation. Beloved, you're *finally* home, finally back in my arms."

She sobbed. "What happened to your arm?"

"I'll explain later." He looked at George. "Did you somehow discover I'd be here today?"

George scoffed. "I had no idea. It seems we both had the same idea."

"To gather evidence against the other," Cory said. "Or perhaps you thought to collect the evidence I'd find of your guilt."

George snarled. "I had to wait for the police to clear out."

Katarina leaned back, drying tears, and pulled her wedding ring from her pocket. "Please, Cory, put this on me."

Cory's breath caught, and George gasped. Cory smiled widely, thanking God for his wife's words, and did what he ached to do for months—slide the ring onto her finger. His hand trembled as he did so. She curled her hand closed around the ring.

Click.

"I've had enough," George said. "Step away from him."

She let out a soft, short scream.

"Please, sweetheart, get behind me," Cory urged her.

"No way, Cor. We're in this together."

"If you love me," he said on a harsh breath, "you'll please do as I ask."

She slid, keeping her arms around him, holding him from behind.

"Let him go, or I'll shoot him in the head," George demanded, waving the gun.

She stepped away. "Don't hurt him. I'll do whatever you say... anything."

Cory gave her a concerned glance, seeing her wring her hands together.

"Divorce him and marry me. I'll keep him prisoner until it's done," George said with a smug smile.

"What?" Cory screeched. "You can't be serious!"

"You'll let him go and never hurt him again?" she said in a defeated voice.

"Yes," George said, shrugging.

"Do you swear, on the...mother and the grandmother I've heard you so deeply adored?" Katarina studied him.

George sighed. "Yeah, yeah, I do. What's your answer?"

"This is not happening!" Cory shouted.

"I'll...do it," Katarina said.

"No!" Cory said. "You will not!"

George chuckled. "Just kidding. Damn. I've decided I'm not ready for marriage quite yet after all." He looked at Cory. "I love messing with you! It's very amusing watching you twist in discomfort!"

"What were you planning to do about your lies when Katarina saw Brendan alive?" Cory asked.

"Quite simply, I was planning to alter his situation before she did." He aimed at Cory's gut.

Screaming, Katarina bounded and shoved Cory aside. The shot went off, but thank God she wasn't fast enough. The bullet hit him in the side instead of the stomach, shocking him.

Cory fell to his knees, pressing his hand over the stinging hole. Blood dripped from under his fingertips. Katarina scrambled to see Cory's injury.

George lifted the weapon and aimed for Cory's chest.

Cory saw flashing spots as he felt the blood leaking from under his hand.

Katarina jumped in front of him, waving her arms protectively. "No, no, Goran! I won't let you do this!"

"Katar...ina..." Bile rose up Cory's throat. "Step..." he gasped for breath. "...away."

"No way, Cory!"

"I don't want to shoot you too because you're so damn attractive. Also, you're obviously not pregnant with his child, having been separated from him for so long, so that's not a concern." George looked at Katarina with actual admiration. "Give me that wedding ring on your finger."

She looked back at Cory, with a look that spoke of her feelings of being heartbroken and afraid, sliding off the ring. She hesitated only when her gaze met his.

Waves of pain radiated in Cory's side, but now, the thought of the ring being lost to George panicked him, and he was sure his involuntary reaction showed.

George sighed. "Do so willingly, and I'll not kill you," he said to Katarina. "Don't give it to me, and I'm afraid I'll take it from your dead body."

"Give it to him!" Cory blurted. "Please, Katarina!"

She nodded.

Suddenly, sirens squealed way down the road. Cory inwardly cheered, relieved. George darted to his car, got in, revved the engine, and tore out of there, scattering dirt.

"Cory!" Katarina fell beside him. "Hang in there. You'll be okay." She put her hand over his, offering more pressure over the wound.

Brendan came running out of the warehouse, gun in hand.

"Help him!" Katarina embraced Brendan briefly.

Brendan tucked the gun in his waistband and hovered over Cory, examining the shot. He applied pressure as the ambulance and police drew close. "I heard the shot, ran to a window on the second floor, and called nine-one-one! They were in the area. I'm not a good shot, especially at that distance, so I couldn't risk hitting you while aiming for him. I ran down to the first floor toward the door, preparing to order George to step down when I got closer, but then I heard the sirens and saw him leave when I stepped outside."

Katarina cupped Cory's cheek, gazing at him with love.

"Your hand is cold, sweetheart," he said.

"Shh, reserve your strength." She trembled and turned to Brendan. "I'm sooooo glad to see you! Where the *hell* were you?"

"I was kidnapped and wasting away in that warehouse. Good to see you too, Kat!"

She looked at Cory and wiped away tears from her cheeks.

"You're scared. Don't be, Katarina. I'll be okay," Cory said, with a weak voice.

"Of course, you will be." She swatted at more falling tears and kissed his forehead.

"Don't *ever*, do that again." Anger tinged Cory's voice. "You could have died!"

"I had no choice, Cor," she said. "I love you."

Brendan glanced over. "I agree with you, Cory, but...had she not shoved you, the bullet would surely have hit you in a worse place."

"That's not the point," Cory said, wincing. "It could have hit *her*."

"If being mad will strengthen you, then be furious." She pressed her face into his neck, nudging him.

His anger dissipated, as he felt her trembling with sadness and worry. He needed to comfort her now and forget his own agitation that she had risked her life for him.

Brendan looked at her in a matter-of-fact way. "You saved his life, twice now, possibly, if you count stopping that guy with a knife approaching him."

"But never do that again," Cory repeated, giving her hand a squeeze.

The ambulance pulled up, and Brendan dashed up to them.

~ * ~

Cory made calls from his hospital room and started a manhunt for George.

Later, after Cory insisted that Brendan leave and see to his family, Katarina dried her tear-swollen eyes.

Cory brushed a strand of hair from her brow. "I'm mad at you, you know."

She shivered. "Then why are you smiling?"

"You love me." He shook his head. "Please swear that you'll never pull such a stunt again. I watched my mother die that way."

She threw her arms around his shoulders. "I'm sorry, but I'm not sorry."

He kissed her. She released him and leaned back in her chair.

"I'll make you swear later then." He paused. "Guess what?"

"What?"

"I'm going to arrange a European tour for your band when we go back home. Would you like that?"

"Yes. My first and last-for a while-tour. Let's make it a great one. After that I'll come home and play locally, stay near you."

He smiled. "Do you think your band will follow you to Carasivia, or will you have to find a new one?"

"I'll ask them."

"The media is going to go berserk during your coronation and covering our story."

She propped pillows behind him. "Can we renew our vows?"

His lips parted, and he nodded with the light of joy in his eyes.

She smiled. "Good."

"Asher is going to come with us to be one of my advisers and live in the palace."

"Really?"

"Yes, and Gunther can come too if he wishes. And Brendan as well."

"Thank you!"

"Of course. I'll open a garage for Gunther to run his own business if he likes. We'll visit the States often."

She hugged him again, and his warmth seeped into her skin. A sense of safety for the first time in months came to her, making her realize in comparison how traumatized she had been.

"Sweetheart, with your inspiration to be good, Jon, Asher, and Gunther say I have the passion to lead my country to greatness. Do you think they're right? Power tempered with wisdom and love."

She squeezed him closer, feeling his heartbeat.

"You are so beautiful. I will have to swallow my jealousy when you're on the road. All those men..." Cory trailed off. He nodded, serious. "But I will control it." He pulled away and smiled.

Not a doubt plagued her. She touched the ring on her finger. "I will never betray you. My wedding ring is never coming off. Well, it will when I give it to your child someday and honor your mother's tradition."

He looked at her hand, at her ring, with a sad smile.

"Hon?"

"The ring, sweetheart. I never told you the full story."

"Only that your mother gave it to you and told you to give it to your future wife. I'm sorry I threatened to sell it. I could never have done it. Tell me the story about the ring."

"On her deathbed in the palace hospital...she," he said and cleared his throat. "She...uh, took off her ring, gave it to me, and whispered her wishes to me. My...father found me moments after I ran from him, sitting in my room, crying in the corner. He pulled me up by the arm and tossed me several feet. 'The ring, boy! I demand to have it!' I tore out of the room and hid the ring in a crevice in the wall. He caught up to me around a corner and when I refused to give him the ring, he beat me until I was unconscious. He was puzzled as to where it could have gone." Cory looked down. "He beat me into a coma—I woke up in the care of a doctor—but there was no way I was going to dishonor my mother's *dying* wish to me."

Tears rolled down her cheeks. "I'm so sorry you went through that."

"It's okay now." He paused. "I'll miss you when you leave with your band."

"Do you not want me to go? I'll stay home with you if it will keep you sane and happy."

He gave her hand a squeeze.

"You're the most important thing in the world to me."

"You're going on that tour."

"And if a fan gets out of line?" She grinned.

"I'll trust you to put him in his place. Your band will be provided with bodyguards though, to keep you ladies safe. You are a queen, after all. Just promise me that you'll come home for the epic Christmas celebration I'll throw in your honor."

"I wouldn't miss it."

"Good. Would you be willing to play live, before our country? On television? Christmas music?"

"A...whole country?"

"It will be fun! I'll have a string section add fullness to your sound. It will be outstanding."

"Wow. Just the thought." She shivered.

"We can sell copies of the recording and give the money to charity."

She chuckled. "Now I have to do it!"

She gazed at his hand and the ten-dollar wedding ring.

He followed her gaze. "I couldn't take it anymore. I had to wear it again. I wanted to put it on so much earlier."

He brushed his fingers across her jaw. "Sweetheart, I don't blame you for thinking what you did, but I did stop from killing Brendan then. It seems you and I were both right and both wrong in ways." He shrugged. "My anger, well, it won't make me a good leader. There will be no more rashness. I have strength without my rage. I don't need it anymore, and you and our best friends have taught me to see the humor in things.

"I will strive to be a peaceful man who doesn't jump the gun." He grinned. "I have the mask, and I want you to put it on. Just a feeling."

She nodded, and he pulled the thing from a backpack and handed it to her. She put the green artifact to her face. Tingles danced across her cheeks and forehead. The images spilled forth in her mind...

"Brendan, in a way, you have helped me," Cory informed him.

"Really?"

"Yes, you pushed me so hard that I faced my darkest feelings only to finally find my redemption."

"I'm sorry, forgive me," Brendan said. "I hated myself for what I had to do to you. Your enemies threatened my family."

Cory nodded. "I figured that out."

"I had to infuse the mask with angry thoughts and then touch it to you, receiving and sending out the poison. It took concentration and focus to overcome that ugliness."

Cory tipped his head once.

Kat looked over at him, filled with elation. She let go of Brendan, whom she had hugged, went over to Cory and slid into his arms. He held her and kissed the top of her head.

Cory turned to Brendan. "Are we friends again?"

"We never stopped being so."

"Good. Brendan, there's a great medical school twenty miles from the palace and an extra room in my home for you. Would you be interested? I'll pay for your medical degree personally."

"What?" Brendan said.

"Of course, if you don't want to…"

"Are you kidding me?"

"No. I'll have a copy of all your books, your syllabi, every school material you'll need, translated into English if there aren't already English copies. I'll hire an interpreter to go to class with you or send you to any school of your choice in the world that you can get accepted into."

"Thank you, Cory, I accept!"

"No problem. Which school are you thinking about attending?"

"The one near the palace. Is it hard to get into?"

"Yes. But I hear you got into your top choice in the States. That impresses me sufficiently enough to go to the head of our best medical school and give the dean my personal reference for you."

"I'll test first to see if I'm good enough."

"I've checked already, Brendan. The American school you chose and got accepted into has standards just as high as ours."

Brendan smiled and nodded.

"Will you stay in Carasivia after that and work in one of our hospitals?"

"Yes."

"I'll build a new wing dedicated to diabetes research with the finest equipment and lab money can buy. And you can run it."

Brendan stared at him with profound gratitude. "I don't know how to thank you."

Cory smiled. "Throw your heart into your work."

"Done."

"And maybe, if we need you at the palace, consult with our doctors at least, with your expertise?"

"Yes. Or how about if you set up that lab in the palace hospital or at least near it?"

"It would be my pleasure." Cory paused. "We have some beautiful women you can meet in my country too. One of them won the title of Miss Universe a few years back." He scoffed. "She would have been runner-up if my Katarina were in the contest."

Brendan grinned knowingly. "Thank you."

Cory shook his hand.

Katarina leaned and whispered hotly into her husband's ear. "I love you."

Katarina lowered the mask, knowing in her gut that this vision was going to come to pass.

~ * ~

Cory and Katarina lay on their bed. He wrapped the uncasted arm around her, pulling her against his chest. Her long, black waves feathered over the arm she draped over him.

Damn, her light raspberry scent was a turn-on. He wanted to see her silky hair spread over his pillow.

"We have happy preparations to make." He curled a strand of her hair around his finger.

"What type?" She traced a bass clef on his chest with her finger.

"For the public renewal of our vows and your coronation."

She squeezed him. "Please help me to be a good queen. I wish to honor you."

"I wish for your eternal happiness."

"I love you *so* much. What you did for Brendan, for George... you truly are a good man. It's wonderful that you put protection on Brendan's family until you're sure they're safe. You proved your honor and sincerity, and I'm a jerk for ever doubting you."

He took her hand in his. "No, now enough of that."

"Cor?"

"Yes, my love?"

"What if we have all girls?"

"What if we do? I hope our daughters look like you."

"I hope they look like you. I'd like to see if the female version of you is just as good looking as the male."

He smirked.

"Can a woman inherit the throne?"

"Not in George's reign, but in mine, yes. I've already changed the law. There are going to be a lot of changes that are good for the people now that I'm in charge."

"I'm proud of you."

His heart leapt. "Well, I'm pretty proud of you too."

"Cor?"

"Yes?"

"Do I have to bow before your royal presence now?" she teased.

He chuckled and kissed her knuckles. "And call me *Majesty*. Don't forget that."

"Are you *serious*? Is that a...thing there?"

He gave a mock sigh. "You'll just have to try me. Maybe I'll put you in the stocks for displeasing me."

She hit him with a pillow. "Cor—ee! Tell me!"

He chuckled. "Kiss it out of me."

"If it takes all night."

"It will," he said, breathlessly.

Seventeen

Cory had a bad feeling. His fingertips tingled, and his heart pounded in warning the way that happens seconds before life says, *Fuck you. Surprise!* He paced the private yellow parlor in the cathedral and bumped into the polished oval table. A red candle wobbled, spilling hot wax. With a curse, he jumped back, barely avoiding having his white wedding suit stained.

He tore the gloves from his hands and raked his fingers through his hair. *He's going to ruin this big day. I can feel him.* The place was loaded with security. Cory let out a slow, deep breath.

Jon tapped on the open door and entered. "Your unbelievably beautiful bride awaits you. It's time." His smile melted. "What's wrong?"

"George is here."

Jon shook his head. "How? He couldn't get in."

"As a writer, I can imagine him killing one of the dignitaries and stealing his I.D. and then disguising himself."

Jon scoffed. "Brother, it's just your nerves. Relax."

"All right. I'll worry about this later." He followed Jon into the corridor.

"Don't let Kat see your anxiety. She'll either misunderstand, or you'll upset her."

"You're right. She told me the thought of all those people and cameras was enough to make her nauseous."

"She's crazy about you. You're a lucky man."

"I know." He went within himself mentally, using his gift and searching. She wouldn't die this day, but...something was *really* wrong.

~ * ~

Katarina stood at the end of the aisle in Carasivia's grand cathedral, at her father's arm.

"This is unbelievable." He looked around. "Cory's court—Am I still allowed to call him Cory?"

"Call him *son*, as before."

He smiled. "Have you ever seen such extravagance?"

Jewel-bedecked kings and queens, princes and princesses, and a sea of dignitaries sat amongst regular folks. White flowers ringed the room. Kat's mom sat up front near Brendan, Gunther, and Asher. Kat's bandmates stood as her maids of honor. They had agreed to follow her to this country rather than find a new bassist. After all, her husband would soon be financing their brilliant European tour and would be allowing them to live in the palace.

Jasmine-scented incense floated from silver holders. Royal knights stood in purple and silver livery, their sabers sparkling in the light of hundreds of candles at the periphery of the echoing room. Cameramen stood respectfully in the corners, near the altar.

"When Cory and I got married before a judge, he was wearing jeans and his nicest button-up shirt. I was wearing my best dress, a five-dollar thing from a discount store." She ran her hand over her belly, glancing at it. Hundreds of tiny diamonds sparkled from the silver-lined white silk. "Believe it or not, this ceremony is a toned-down version of what he wanted to do. He wanted this outside with a big procession, historic style, even tried to get me to wear a gown that cost ten times what this elegant dress cost."

"Really?"

"Really. *This* dress. I'll save it for your granddaughter to wear. Or maybe I'll sell it and give the money to charity. Also, he did not use taxpayers' money for any of this. He paid for it himself." She poked a toe out from under the luxuriously soft folds of the material. The diamonds on her shoes sparkled. "Cor didn't have to do any of this for me. I'd have lived in a shack with him." She looked at her smiling dad.

As the music started, strains from an organ filled the air, and all eyes turned toward her and her father.

She trembled. "I'm scared."

He gave her arm a squeeze. "He's your husband."

"All these people and the people watching on television, here and in America."

"You should be used to being watched—on a stage," he muttered under his breath. "You're a musician."

Was that acceptance of her music? Hallelujah.

"But this is different!" She felt the weight of everyone's stares and heard their gasps as she passed. She inhaled the Jasmine scent. "Will I be a good queen?"

"Yes. Just focus on your love for him. Not this opulence, and not the crown."

"I love you. You're right. Thanks."

"I love you too."

She brought her gaze to Cory and gasped. Could he be more handsome? His gorgeous brother stood near his side, but Jon paled next to Cory, her love, in his jewel-encrusted, white ensemble, a suit of a king. His gaze met hers—she saw through her sheer veil—and he stumbled. Jon offered his arm. Cory held up his hand.

She flashed back to their first wedding, so small and private. His smile had filled the room with light. Now, his adoring blue eyes and parted lips spoke volumes of his feelings here too. She smiled as a wicked thrill rushed her. Pretty enough to keep all those princesses away from his bed—but he'd never cheat on her anyway.

He mouthed, "I love you."

Her heart clenched. People's eyes, the heat of the packed room, the cameras...

Oh, God, I married the love of my life, my best friend. Now I'm marrying a king.

She paused.

"Katarina," her dad whispered. "What's wrong?"

"I'm scared."

"He loves you. It will be okay."

Tears sprang to her eyes, and she pressed her cheek to his shoulder. He embraced her. She pulled away, sucking in a breath. Cory stood fifteen feet away and stepped down from the altar.

He strode in her direction. "Katarina, I love you."

The weight of a thousand stares made her stomach quiver. "I love you too."

"Then please, marry me again."

"Are you sure...you want me? You're a king. I'm not exactly a princess. This has made it hit home. I'm not good enough for you."

He took her hand in his. "You have that backward. And you're more than a princess. You're a queen."

"Run while you can. Annul our marriage and hook up with someone better than me, someone worthy of you."

"Katarina," her father muttered in warning.

"Annul our...marriage?" Pain etched Cory's features.

She darted a glance around. All stared. Her attention came back to the king before her.

"Don't you love me?" His voice escaped in a harsh whisper.

She swallowed a sob and stretched her collar down, so he could see the cornstarch pearl necklace he had made her when they were on the run. "So much."

"You wore it?" He looked at her, amazed.

"It's my prized possession." She cupped his cheek and dragged her fingers along his jaw, finally pressing her palm over his heart.

"So why do you ask me to run and hook up with someone else? I'd be certifiably crazy."

"I don't want you to! I want you."

"Thank God. There is no one better for me than you. A poor slob like me is blessed to have you." He dropped to one knee with a look of reverence.

There was a collective gasp.

"Please, marry me."

She drew a raspy breath. "Get up. They're staring."

"Only if you agree to marry me again."

Embarrassment washed over her. She flushed—so hot—and nodded.

He closed his eyes a second then stood, looking at her again. "Good."

She reached and gave his forearm a squeeze. "I'm sorry."

"You're my best friend. You're forgiven." His warm smile sent shivers of adoration across her skin. He retook his place at the altar.

Her dad tapped her arm. "I've always liked that kid."

She smiled and approached Cory.

The ceremony was formal. An American priest stood by a Carasivian one in long white and purple robes. Each spoke in their language, performing the ceremony together. Cory said his vows with reverence, as she did hers. He lifted her shear veil with shaky hands and kissed her tenderly. He drew back, looking into her eyes.

"I'm so in love with you," she whispered.

Cory kissed her. After he pulled away, both priests blessed them. She gazed at the room, all the charmed faces: hands pressed over hearts, smiles...

Her cheeks heated.

Smiling, Cory took her arm, and they faced forward as they were announced as husband and wife.

"My good people," he began first in his native language then in English. "Thank you for joining us this day as my beautiful bride and I renewed our vows. Normally, I'd save this next part for another day, but I really want to do this now, since I've been dying to do so for months. I wish to crown our queen."

Katarina pressed a hand over her chest, trying to catch her breath. Cory laid a gentle hand on her arm with a smile that flooded her heart with memories of them growing up together. He'd given her that look so many times, in his ragged jeans and T-shirts. *We're in this together*, he often said.

Yes, everything would be okay.

Jon approached with a gold crown, which sparkled with diamonds, sapphires, and thousands of tiny pearls. It was a man's crown.

Cory took it from his brother's hands, turned to Kat, and touched her head with it. "I share my crown with you, my love." He placed the crown on his own head. The head of his church had already placed it on his head at his formal crowning ceremony and so now just stood and watched.

A maid helped Katarina remove her veil and took it.

Jon leaned close. "Now you must kneel before your king."

Her eyes widened. Cory had left this part out. She glanced around the room. The only time an American knelt like that was in prayer. American wives did *not* bow down before their husbands. No one moved. Everyone stared. Such extraordinary circumstances... Time to adjust. She did respect the dignity of Cory's station and his traditions. With shaky legs, she bent her knees.

"Stop," Cory said, pressing his hand on her shoulder. He turned to Jon. "I told you, this was not to be part of the ceremony."

"My King, the tradition has been carried out for centuries, since the beginning. Our mother did this before our father."

"I'm king now, so this country will *finally* know women's equality on a first-hand basis."

Jon turned to Kat with pleading eyes while all the world watched, it seemed.

"No, I won't have it," Cory whispered, harshly.

Would Cory's people think less of him if she broke a tradition that had occurred since the founding of their country? Should she make this public gesture? She gazed into his loving eyes.

"Don't do it, my love. I respect your culture as well."

Her heart lurched. She could do this. She fell to her knees and lowered her head in respect.

Cory grasped her wrist and urged her up. She stayed her ground.

Jon leaned toward her ear. "Remember, publicly swear fealty to your king."

"I pledge my loyalty and love to My King."

Cory urged her up by her hand and leaned toward her ear. "My darling, promise me that you'll never bow before me on your knees again, unless it's in the bedroom." He'd said the last part even softer and gave her a fleeting, seductive look. "But thank you for the public gesture."

"I promise, but I owed you." A smile tipped her lips.

"*Never* think that, sweetheart."

Jon handed him a smaller crown then, similar in its design to the bigger one with diamonds, sapphires, and pearls. Cory took it and placed it on her head, as he had earlier arranged it to be done.

"With great joy and honor I crown you queen of Carasivia, and I pledge my love and loyalty to you not only as your husband but because you are my queen." Cory bowed over her hand and kissed it.

"That last part is new, those words... He just came up with that," Jon muttered.

The archbishop placed his hands a few inches over her head and gave her a blessing. He lowered his hands and nodded to Cory. "It is done."

"Long live the queen!" Cory shouted joyfully then took the diamond-topped scepter and the orb from Jon's hands and gave them to Kat. "Rule with me over our people with love and tender care."

"I swear it," she said.

She was given another blessing before the room exploded with cheers as people stood. A footman took the orb and scepter from Kat. Cory took Kat's hand, kissed it, and bowed over it. After a few moments, he held up his hand. The room hushed, and everyone retook their seats.

Cory whispered in Kat's ear. "Please, say something. It's tradition."

"You could have told me this sooner," she muttered.

"Tradition demands that it be spontaneous."

She cleared her throat, looking around, and then drew in a deep breath and smiled. "I'm honored and thank everyone for being here.

I will try my best to live up to your expectations. If I falter, I'll turn to our king to help me."

A translator spoke after her in Carasivian.

Cory muttered, "Very nice. They want more, I'm sure. Go ahead, be yourself. That's what I advise."

"More, really?"

"Yes, sweetheart."

"My, my, now that you're a king, you're demanding," she teased. "I'll get you later for this."

He chuckled lightly. "I can't wait."

She took another deep breath and looked ahead, preparing to speak in a louder voice that carried. "Women of Carasivia, I urge you to go to college, run for office, get the best jobs you can, and have all the fun you want to! Men, you be happy too. Just...be happy." Was this really happening?

The translator again spoke, repeating her words.

"You heard our queen!" Cory clapped.

The audience stood and applauded. Moments later, Cory nodded to Jon, and he took their crowns, placing them on velvet pillows held by footmen.

Cory took Kat's hand to lead her through a door in the back. They pushed it open and stepped into a narrow passage.

"Cor? Shouldn't we be walking past the people, down the aisle, out to the car?"

"Not today, my love." He suspected George was in the crowd, waiting to do something devastating. "We'll meet everyone at the reception center for the party, but we're going the back way. My guards have been informed. They'll meet us right outside." He had a search going on for George.

An elderly foreign dignitary with white hair and a red jacket approached from the other end of the passage, looking around as if confused.

"Who's that?" Kat asked Cory.

"His uniform tells me he's from two countries over," he joked, "but I don't think I've ever met him. I wonder how the old guy stumbled upon the door."

"Maybe he accidently fell and knocked it open."

The dignitary's face lit with happy recognition. "Your Majesties, what a pleasant surprise! I lost my way."

"How did you get past the guards?"

"Guards? There were no guards."

Cory tensed next to Kat. The stranger looked at her and smiled.

"Oh, you're sweet," she said.

He shuffled one step to her, his shoulders hunched.

"Step back!" Cory ordered the man, draping his arm across Kat's chest protectively.

"Don't be silly, hon." Kat turned to the old one. "Here, let me help you." She grabbed the hand he held out.

"Thank you, Your Majesty."

Cory looked into his face. "Don't move, Katarina."

Cold alarm waved through her. "Why? What's wrong?"

"It's George," he whispered.

Her mouth dropped open. She trembled and pulled her hand away, but he held it in a grip.

Cory looked at George, first his hand and the slightly discolored fingertip of his index finger lifted away from her skin, and then his face. "Remember in my third novel, Katarina."

"Oh my God. Poison," she said, under her breath. She continued softly. "He has protection on his index fingertip and poison over it. The tiny needle attached... All he has to do is touch me with that finger." She swayed on her feet.

George steadied her. "You're right. I killed that stupid old dignitary and made myself look like him. Waited patiently for the right moment. I killed the guards to this entrance too. I was going to brush by you near the cathedral's great aisle and nick you with the poison, but you went through this quiet corridor, but this place will do." He looked at Cory. "I need a word with you."

"Fine. What do you want?"

"Make a choice."

"Go on."

"She dies, right here, right now, or you do."

"Me," he blurted.

"No way!" Kat screamed. "Don't you two know by now I won't allow it?"

Cory tensed, looking at George. "Let her go, and fight me."

"All I have to do is touch you, and you're dead."

Cory shook his head. "You're such a wuss. Afraid of my fists to go to such measures."

George's brow rose. "Hardly."

"Let. Her. Go," he said, through gritted teeth.

"Since I doubt she'll leave your side, I swear on the grandmother we both loved—though it turned out she wasn't my grandmother— that I'll give your wife a running start after I kill you. On one condition."

"Name it."

"Cory, no!"

"Please, Katarina."

George scoffed. "Tell me the most important family secret our mother told you that she didn't tell me."

"I don't know which you mean."

George's jaw tensed. "I'm sure, because there were many. You'd better impress me. If it's not mind-blowing, I won't release your wife."

"Uncle Lothar can't have children," Cory blurted under emotional duress.

"Elaborate."

"Mother told me he someday intended on secretly adopting while keeping his future wife from the public's view, so he could tell everyone she was pregnant. He intended on taking this adopted child and making him his heir."

"You wouldn't lie about this?"

"I would not."

"On your honor? That actually means something to...well, everyone," George said with a scoff.

"On my honor," Cory said.

"Uncle Lothar's much younger wife is in confinement now, with child."

"Not really," Cory admitted, looking at George's hold on Katarina. Anxiety raced through him.

"This means—"

"Yes, Goran. Being Mom's oldest son, you're her brother's closest living relative, next in line for his throne."

"Huh," he said in satisfied tones. He released Katarina's hand. He looked at her with evil intent. "Run."

"Not without Cory!"

George reached his hand toward her.

Cory lunged and punched George in the face. George stumbled back; then Cory grasped Katarina's hand and pulled her the other direction, running hard. He rushed her outside to the waiting limo. Inside, he turned to her. Anger mixed with great relief in his eyes. He opened his mouth. Kat thought to tell her a thing or two. Instead, he drew her into an embrace.

"Forgive me." She pulled away.

He shook his head. "You're unbelievable."

"You're not mad I wouldn't leave without you?"

"I'm furious." He smiled and kissed her nose. "But I understand."

"You can yell at me now. I'll understand."

"No, my love. You bring out my forgiving, peaceful side. I intend on making your life beautiful."

She snuggled against him.

"They'll find him," Cory said.

~ * ~

At the periphery of the ballroom, Asher strode over with the mask in his hand. "I put it on and got a vision."

Cory and Katarina looked at him.

"I suppose you want to know what it was."

"If you wouldn't mind," Cory said. He told Asher what had happened with George.

"My mask vision makes sense now," Asher said. "George is on the run, and you and Katarina are safe for the time being."

"Thank you," Cory and Katarina said to him.

Asher nodded. Cory took Katarina's hand, led her across the floor, and swept her up in a dance, gliding across the royal ballroom. The elegant classical notes stopped and faded. Cory took her hand, bowed over it, and kissed her fingertips.

He nodded to the musicians. "This is the time."

They started up again, with an orchestral form of the song Katarina had written for him while they were on the run, the song she called, *I Love Cory*. She looked at him with surprise. He smiled.

"Cor, that's *beautiful* set to strings like that. It gives me chills."

"It's going to be a hit. The orchestra leader congratulated me on finding a woman who loves me so much. Powerful music." He took his darling wife in his arms, moving across the ballroom as everyone watched. Love filled her eyes as he swept her to the rhythm of the romantic music.

They passed under the brilliant light of a chandelier then lifted their arms, palms touching, and slowly lowered them, pulling their hands away. Others took the signal and joined them on the dance floor.

"You're so good for this country," she said.

"Where did you hear that?"

"Jon told me about a newspaper headline saying, 'A tribute to the best monarch in Carasivia's history.'"

The music ended. They walked to the edge of the dance floor.

Asher approached them again. "Oh, forgot to tell you. I saw you, Cory, speaking to a huge crowd in French."

Cory dropped his gaze. "My mother's brother is the king of a French-speaking nation."

"Does he have an heir?"

"No. Well, George. Then me, after him, if he fathers no legitimate children."

Asher shook his head. "There's going to be serious trouble."

Cory shifted from foot to foot. "I know."

"If you win the war your brother will bring," Asher said, "you're going to bring peace to a wide region under the protection of your two crowns, and it will last a century after you're gone." He paused.

"If you lose, war will spread to the continental and possibly global level. The mask showed me both options."

Kat gave him a look of concern.

"I'll be careful, sweetheart." He felt terrible. This was his fault. He told George that the crown had to pass to him. George would never have known otherwise, and his uncle's country would have someday been passed to his secretly adopted son instead of to the tyrant George. But then again, if Cory had kept his mouth shut, Katarina would be dead.

She pulled him into a hug. "I'm scared. George is—"

"I know." He lifted his arms and encircled her, mentally preparing for the biggest battle of his life.

Eighteen

Cory looked up from his mahogany desk to gaze at the photo of Katarina, his queen. She was in Paris—touring with her heavy metal band and surrounded by his best bodyguards. He often used his mask-given gift to sense death or impending death, to assure himself of her safety. The moment he got a bad message, he'd bring Katarina back to be under his personal protection.

She still played the $200 bass he bought her on their last day of high school. He could afford to buy her a bass made of gold. He touched the small black braid by the picture, the one she cut from her hair for him.

Suddenly, voices sounded outside his office door. He opened it, and his queen rushed into the room, guards apologizing to him. He went to her, arms outstretched. Embracing her, he inhaled deeply. The faint scent of raspberries reached him, coming from her soft locks. The two guards bowed before him and offered their apologies again.

"Why do you apologize?" Cory asked them, his eyes closed. He nuzzled Katarina's cheek with his and opened his eyes, stepping back. He let his hands linger at his beloved's waist.

"Hi, Cor," she said, looking into his eyes.

"Majesty," the first guard said. "Forgive me for letting her storm into your office. You know I worked for your father, and well, a trusted servant poisoned him. We will be more meticulous in our duties."

Cory frowned and placed one arm around his wife's waist, pulling her to his side. "Do you forget this is our queen, gentlemen, my beloved wife?" He brought a hand to her cheek and looked into her eyes. "You'd never hurt me…" He grinned.

She shook her head. A soft smile covered her lips.

"Of course, Majesty," the guard offered. "My mistake."

"Thank you. You may leave now, good sirs, and allow our queen free access to my office or anywhere in the palace for that matter, at any time, day or night and without having to consult with me." He nodded, keeping in mind that this nation had only recently gotten a new queen. The last one had been his mother, whom a visitor killed in an attempt to murder his father when Cory was a child. That may be why the guards were a bit touchy about the matter of new people in the palace.

They bowed and left, shutting the door behind them with a click. Cory held Katarina close. Waves of smoldering heat coursed through him. A moan fell from his lips as he trailed kisses down her neck.

"Mmmm, Cory…" She pulled away, leaving cold air between them and went to the doors, clicking the lock. Slinking back to him, her ebony tresses dusted her leather-covered breasts. She made her way to his desk and stacked his paperwork neatly aside.

He watched, amused. "Beautiful one?"

She lay atop his desk, dragging her fingers down her neck and sides. "I missed you. While the girls were trying to get drunk, I paced my hotel room stone-cold sober, wishing you were in my bed."

He smiled and gazed at her from her glorious brown eyes to her little leather boots then strode across the marble floor to her.

"Please, make love to me."

Aroused, he wrapped her hand in his. Tingles rushed him. "Come with me, sweetheart."

"Here, handsome." She turned her face and gave him *the* look. Her hair tumbled off the edge of his workstation, and her beautiful eyes sent such a rush of powerful love to him that his mouth went dry.

"In my...office?" He cleared his throat.

"Mm-hmm," she purred. "How about on your furry throw rug? I want you to have wild memories of us...in here, when I'm on tour. I want flashes of our passion to disturb your work." She bit her bottom lip. "I want to ruin you for other women."

"That was done years ago."

She eased up to a sitting position and dangled her legs off the desk. He glanced at her crossed ankles. Up came her fingers, to trace his jaw.

He let out a desire-filled breath and dragged a finger across her lower lip. "Those years waiting for you...were *worth* it."

"Go rough, love. I plan on it."

He tore open her shirt. Buttons went flying off the bodice, clinking onto the floor.

~ * ~

They sat on the floor with their backs against the wall, breathing heavily and holding hands. His shirt remained open as did the top button of his pants. They looked into each other's faces. He brushed aside a strand that was sticking to her cheek.

She lowered her lids, and the corner of her lips curved up.

He slid his hand across his thigh growling suggestively. "That was..." he breathed out, "...magni...ficent."

She sighed happily. He let go of her hand and skipped it up her nape, grasping her black waves between his fingers.

"Mmm, Cory, your essence lingers on me..."

He wrenched her close and gave her a deep kiss. When he pulled away, he hooked his arm around her shoulders and lowered her head onto his lap, gazing at her with love. "I adore you."

"Well, I think you're kinda cool yourself."

He touched the tip of her nose. "That's all?" His brow lifted.

"You told me you adored me on our wedding night."

"It's still true, but more so now."

"I'm mad about you, Cor."

"Good."

She rubbed her thighs together.

"Stop, you're making me hard again."

"Oh? You like what you see? Perhaps I can entice you into another round?"

He reached for her thigh and scraped his fingers over it. "I love what I see. Your scars are a ribbon on a gift of perfection."

"I'm glad you like them."

He bent and kissed her forehead. "I don't like that you got them—the pain you went through, but...beautiful because they are a part of you, and for my eyes only. I'm privileged to see them."

"You're so...protective about them. I used to hide them out of shame, but you made me feel beautiful. I'd be willing to even wear shorts now in public, or shorter skirts than the ones that go past my knees."

"Please, hon, no."

She dragged her fingers down his neck.

He kissed her hand. "The day I first saw them by accident from several feet away, when you were crying and trying to cover them, something happened in me."

"Tell me again. I like hearing it."

"I liked you, respected you, was entranced by you." He stretched a long black curl leisurely by her face. "Then I saw you so vulnerable and injured and...love knocked the shit out of me. Protective, powerful love. I connect your scars to intense, intimate feelings for you. I don't want some asshole to see something on you that changed the direction of my life in such a personal, profound way."

"What if I weren't physically...attractive to you?"

"Impossible."

"But what if?"

"Suppose I'd keep you around, you know, cuz I'm kinda in love with you."

She looked up as he grinned and winked.

He swiped up her hand. "I'd better get back to work."

"Kay. For now."

He helped her up.

"I'll get the jacket you have in your thinking room to cover up my torn shirt, go change in our chambers, and then return." She slipped through a private door and into a narrow corridor, which led to one of the rooms where she could grab the jacket.

Cory buttoned up his shirt and pants, his body tingling all over.

Jon knocked on his office door, announcing himself. "I just wanted to say hello."

"Hold on. It's locked."

"I have your spare key."

"Use it."

There was a click before the door sprang open.

Jon walked in wearing his impeccable velvet jacket and tailored slacks and stopped on a dime. He offered a curt bow. "What happened to you? You're sweating."

Cory grinned...widely.

"Why didn't you work out in our gym? And your clothes..."

The cloud of sexual satisfaction still whirled around Cory's head. He took a step and stumbled.

Jon frowned. "Are you okay? Don't tell me someone attempted to hurt you! But...how..."

"Katarina..." He took a breath. "...paid me a visit."

Jon gaped.

Cory tapped his shoulder, smiling. "Why do you look so surprised? You're the absurdly handsome one in the family. Surely, women have torn *your* clothes off."

Jon cleared his throat. "A few." He straightened his collar. "In my bedroom...in private."

"The damn door was locked, so don't give me any crap."

Jon nodded. "It was probably needed after turning away so many women, ladies who wished to keep you company in the queen's absence. I'm happy for our queen. She deserves your fidelity."

"Damn right, she does."

"You don't worry about her on the road, surrounded by so many men?"

Cory's brow came up. "Katarina would never do that to me."

"I need to tell you something. George called me today. He's been living on money from a secret account."

Cory frowned. "Go on."

"He's livid with you but has sick new respect for you too, calling you the only worthy archenemy the world could have given him, obsessed with you. It's scary, in a psycho kind of way."

Cory swiped a hand over his face. "And?"

"He's beyond mere longing for revenge. He intends to..." Jon looked down.

Cory touched his shoulder. "What is it?"

Jon brought worried eyes to meet Cory's gaze. Katarina came back into the room.

"Later," Cory said, to Jon.

Cory smiled at Katarina who wore a loose-fitting white shirt with a high collar and a long blue skirt that hovered five inches above her feet. She was a modest dresser unless on stage with her band, in which case she wore leather and lace. Though she never showed much skin. Her slippered feet padded across the shiny floor.

She reached up and pinned a stray curl into her upswept hair. "Hey, Jon, what's up?"

He blinked, staring, and then turned away. "Forgive me." He faced her again and bent to bow.

"No prob. And remember, don't bow. I'm American."

"You're my queen."

"And you're the best damn looking prince in Europe."

He blushed. Cory's brow lifted again.

"But Cory's the one who does it for me." She approached Cory, grabbed his ass, and then bit down gently on his earlobe. "I take that back about your brother, Cor. You are gorgeous and make that beautiful man look ugly. You're fun, exciting, courageous, heroic, inventive. He's, well...not." She smirked. "If you can get away from your duties, *My King,* come see me play tomorrow night in Paris. We'll spend the night in such a way that you'll never see France in the same way again. Every time you fly over it, you'll need to excuse yourself to be alone."

Cory gaped. "Please. Do that to me."

"American women," Jon muttered. "Grabbing in front of others. And musicians...the way they talk."

"What did you say about my wife?" Cory gave him an authoritative look, crossing his arms over his chest.

She made her way past Cory, brushing her hand through the air. "He and I are friends. He can express his true opinion to me, even in a disrespectable way if he wants."

"No, he can't," Cory said.

"Please forgive me!" Jon said.

She smiled. "Of course!" She turned to Cory. "You've given me more political power than any Carasivian queen has ever had."

"You're my co-leader," Cory said. "Not my consort."

"That kind of power is unnecessary."

"But you have heart like my mother had, and that's good for the nation. If my father would have made her a co-leader, Carasivia would have been better off."

"Thanks, honey, but no thanks. It's not that I don't appreciate it, though."

"Just keep me in line, then." He winked at her.

She kissed him. Raspberries and sex wafted toward him. His chest tightened with stirrings of arousal again.

"I like to put you on a pedestal—every given chance. Call it gratitude and respect."

"She belongs there," Jon said. He turned to her. "Again, forgive me. I'm just so used to the last repressive reign and how women especially didn't have freedom. Your American expression takes some getting used to."

"It's cool." She turned to kiss Cory before taking a step to leave his office.

Jon smiled. "Wait, My Queen, before you leave. I'd like to discuss Corentin's birthday with you. What do people in America do for their twenty-fourth?"

"Not sure." She put her arm around Jon's shoulders for a quick squeeze.

"I'll...talk to you later, Corentin," Jon said, and shifted, nervous.

"Call me Majesty."

"I...uh," Jon stuttered. "My *deepest* pardon, Majesty." He attempted a bow.

Cory chuckled and passed a hand through the air. "I'm just shittin' ya."

"You've lived in America too long." Jon stiffened, regret clear on his face. "I'm sorry. I'm out of line." He shifted his weight.

"Ease up, we're brothers and close friends. I love you. Don't forget that."

Jon smiled. "I love you too."

Katarina grinned. "I don't know any other men that would openly admit that to each other, that aren't, you know, in a relationship."

Jon raised his brow in surprise. "Not even brothers?"

"Well, brothers, maybe," she said. "I've just never seen it. The brothers I've known, even the close ones, have always called each other names like *dickhead* or *douchebag* and then punched each other even if they hugged each other too."

"What an odd culture you come from!" Jon's cheeks flushed.

"What an odd statement coming from an archaeologist," she responded.

"I am deservedly criticized and corrected. I'm sorry."

She nodded on a smile.

Cory shrugged. "I wouldn't say such endearing words to Brendan."

She laughed.

"Being back here makes you so focused on protocol, Jon. Remember how we interacted in America and how...confident you were," Cory said.

"It's the palace. What a fascinating thing," Jon said. "Americans are more informal than we are and yet hold back certain feelings they have for their fellow men."

"You gotta love us," Katarina said.

"Corentin, since our queen is here, I'd like to steal her for a moment."

"Uh-huh," Cory said, smirking. "Don't run away with her, or I'll have you caught and executed. I chased her for ten years before she gave in to me. Imagine the lengths I'd go to to keep her."

"Cor—" His fearful expression melted into a smile when Cory grinned again.

"Don't mess with him so much. You're freaking him out," Katarina said.

"I was joking, but I meant every word," Cory said.

"Ease up a little." She smiled.

"As you wish."

"And Jon?"

"Yes?"

"You have my permission to mess with him back, please." She spun to face Cory. "Remember that."

He nodded. "Of course, but I thought he knew he could do that, even in the palace. Because I know he wouldn't be blatantly disrespectful."

"You haven't been king for long," Jon began, "and the last two before you would have had me whipped for merely speaking up to them."

"You know I'm different."

"Yes. Of course. Old habits."

"Come on." Katarina tapped Jon's arm. "Let's go look up that info on the Internet."

Just then, a palace servant, the mask keeper, appeared, holding the mask, the green alien artifact. He dusted the sleeve of his royal purple livery and bowed.

"What are you doing with the mask?" Jon asked.

"While cleaning it, a message came to me that I should bring it to His Majesty." He turned toward Cory. "Majesty, it advised me that you should keep this close from now on."

Cory sat at the edge of his desk.

The mask keeper suddenly pressed the mask to Katarina's face. Cory jumped up and stormed to him. Before he made it, Katarina stumbled back.

She touched her chest. "Oh...my."

"Are you okay? That thing has powers!" Cory asked.

"I'm good," she said dreamily and took the mask, handing it to Cory. "Here, *quick*, put it to your face. And hold my hand."

He did so without question. Tingles raced through him, and then elation lifted him. He tripped back. "Wow." He lowered the mask.

"I know," Katarina said. "It feels like my neural pathways were manipulated. In a good way."

"Mine too. And linked us in a new way." Cory faced the mask keeper.

"I feel you'll be thanking me later," he said to Cory.

Katarina leaned close to Cory's ear. "Sweetheart, I believe the mask just gifted us with greatly enhanced...well, our lovemaking will be taken to new realms." She leaned back.

He gave her a sexy look. "A new level of heaven."

Cory looked at the mask keeper again. "Have you discovered how it determines what it's going to bestow upon someone or how it will affect them?"

"I've confirmed in my parents' lab that it's composed of extraterrestrial elements," Katarina reminded them.

"I took the queen's research and went further in my investigations. A person's intentions can inspire it, such as when it acts as a medium of communication. The brain's electro-magnetic waves are involved. But it doesn't always...catch."

"Yes, sometimes that stubborn thing seems to be asleep," Cory said. "It can affect a person's mood—one can charge it with emotion and impart that energy upon another—or cause them to admit the truth about something. It can make a person drop all pretense and show what they're really feeling. It can also give one the power to manipulate others, to get them what they want, some kind of... irresistible pull."

"The extraterrestrial elements affect humans in sometimes strange or unpredictable ways," the mask keeper added. "It sometimes seems to have a will of its own, such as when it imparts a gift."

"How can we explain that?" Cory asked.

"I have a theory," Katarina said. "The extraterrestrials had advanced technology, and there's some kind of a...computer chip, a program, in there made differently than ours and not easily detected. It could be triggered by a person's chemistry when it makes contact with their skin or triggered by brain or heart waves."

"Gunther admitted that once it tempted him, offering him the power to do something immoral," Cory said. "We found out later it was testing his integrity."

"That's just wild. It must be reading our minds," Katarina said. "Yep, there's got to be software in there making decisions based on many things."

"How did this alien mask find its way to me?" Cory shook his head.

Jon looked at him. "Remember, brother, that my archeological society found it, and—"

"I know," Cory said. "But why does it seem proprietary?" He turned to Katarina. "What do you think, sweetheart?" Cory brushed his thumb over her fingers.

"Maybe the extraterrestrials had contact with your ancestors? Spoke to a king in your line when they visited. Perhaps your family did them a favor, and the aliens chose to reward them and their descendants and so gave them the powerful mask."

He kissed her cheek. "Your theories blow me away with their brilliance."

"And who knows how the mask ended up in the dirt for Jon's group to find," she added. "But to guess, I'd say, among your ancestors, a younger brother, perhaps, was jealous of his older sibling, a king, and hid the mask from him in the ground, punishing him by separating him from the strange gifts the mask imparts on people."

~ * ~

When Jon entered Cory's office, Cory gestured for him to take a seat across from him at his large desk. The scent of jasmine drifted in after him from the corridor.

"Hey." Cory tipped his head. He tapped his fingers on the polished surface of his desk and smelled beeswax. "What do you know about asshole?"

"I wish that were all George was." He gave Cory a direct look. "Quite frankly, I'm...freaked out."

Cory leaned closer. "What did he say to you?"

Jon straightened his tailored collar. "I don't like to use such vile ideas in my speech."

"I have to know. Just say it."

Jon let out a breath and poured himself a glass of mint water from a sparkling pitcher on Cory's desk. Cory waited patiently for Jon to take a sip and put his glass down.

Jon cleared his throat. "He's disgusting. He said that what he has planned for you is so sexy the story should be made into porn. You're going to be his...bitch."

Cory's eyes widened. "Now I'm freaked out." He reached for the water.

"You did him a favor, and he tried to kill you, first just hating you then being driven by revenge, convinced you stole his crown. He's... disturbed. Sometimes he's in the mood to kill you, and at other times he wants you alive so he can play psychological games with you."

"Yeah."

"He also resents *me* for choosing you over him. I wonder if he'll decide to punish me as well." He paused. "You are a gracious leader and brother, though. I can see you're open, after all this, to be his friend." He waved an elegant hand in front of him. "You were my hero growing up. When you were shipped off to America as a boy, I missed you."

"I missed your dumb ass too." Cory shifted, feeling how exquisitely comfortable his clothes were. This suit cost more than a year's wages he had earned as a pauper writer living in America.

"Nice suit," Jon said.

"Thanks. Katarina liked it." He straightened his collar, hot, thinking of her slamming him against a wall in it and pressing against him, giving him hungry kisses while undoing his belt with anxious hands.

Jon smiled. "Women talk about how handsome you are. I've heard it when I go out in disguise to mingle with the people."

Cory grinned. "That must hurt your ego to hear that. You've always been vain, knowing the sick truth about those damn looks of yours."

"But *Katarina* didn't fall in love with me. She's beautiful. And kind-hearted. Sorry."

"Don't apologize for the truth. She's also as good at science as Mother was..." He rubbed the back of his neck.

"One of my contacts saw George in Paris."

"Paris? Katarina will be back there!"

"Don't worry. The bodyguards you have following her and her band will protect her with their lives. George is biding his time until our uncle dies, leaving him the throne of his country."

"In a weird way, George won that crown, by threatening Katarina's life and getting me to tell him our uncle's secret. Our ill uncle may pass soon. Mother would not have approved of George inheriting her brother's crown. This is my fault." He tore his gaze down.

"No. As you've said, you told George in order to save Katarina's life, and I know you can't regret that."

"I don't."

"Also, George would have found out anyway. I spoke to Uncle Lothar. The guilt was eating away at him. He was going to come clean and tell George himself."

"Seriously?"

"Yes."

Guilt and shame slid away from Cory, making him lighter, but he braced himself for the confrontation that would occur when such an angry, arrogant man as George took the throne. Cory prayed for those people, hoping against hope that George would remember their good mother and respect her ways.

"George longs for that day he's a king again, so he can declare war on Carasivia."

Cory rubbed his brow. "On me. I'll never trust him, but I'll still attempt to make things right between us as best as I can under the circumstances."

"I hope he doesn't try to assassinate Uncle Lothar to get his throne sooner."

"I doubt it. It would look too bad, and the people wouldn't accept him."

Jon nodded. "You're a gracious man and king. Our country is crazy about you."

"And our queen," Cory said.

Jon nodded. "They say on the street that you two make a beautiful, blessed couple. Morale has gone through the roof since George stepped down and you took over."

Cory smiled. "I'm glad. Our countrywomen are starting to emulate Katarina and American fashion. Let them express themselves however they see fit. Let them enjoy freedom!"

"Certainly. Our queen," Jon began carefully, "when she's not on stage, dresses conservatively for an American but in their style. It's interesting to see such different sides of her expression. She never even wore a miniskirt, not even in America."

Cory studied him. "There's a personal reason for that. It's her choice. Now she does it for me too, but not for the reason you think."

"What reason is that?"

"Don't want to talk about it. It's a personal, husband and wife matter." Cory glanced at his watch. "Katarina's gig is tomorrow. I could see it and talk with the contact about George. I'll be back in a flash. Will you hold down the fort while I'm gone?"

"I hate acting as regent. I have my archeology organization to think about."

"But you love me and our country, and it will only be for a day. If any tough decisions come up, just call me."

"And I respect my king. Of course, I will *hold down the fort,* Corentin. Or should I call you Majesty?"

Cory smiled and stood, came around, and clapped him on the shoulder. "Thanks. Corentin is fine. You're a good sport."

"I'm learning. Father and George were tyrants. I didn't dare *displease* those kings. I'm still getting used to your progressive ways...and not being threatened just for breathing wrong."

"You're a good prince to our people, looking out for them, I want you to know."

"Thank you."

"No, thank *you*."

Jon tipped his head.

"I'm sorry for startling you with my jokes. Sometimes I forget how shell-shocked you are because of the tyrant kings before me. I just try to be funny."

Jon smiled. "You are most amusing at times. I'll gather a dozen bodyguards to go with you."

Cory scoffed. "Five, the best we have here, including my favorite, Stu."

"Bring more. You were an *American* for so long and don't always realize the danger—"

"Stop. The top five guards I have here will be sufficient. Besides, I want to enjoy Paris. I want it to look like I'm just one of the guys hanging out."

"Of course." He stood and bowed.

"You don't have to do that. We're brothers, and I don't absolutely require it from my citizens."

"I'm honored to follow tradition. Besides, you're a worthy king."

Nineteen

Cory visited with Asher, Gunther, and Brendan in a small parlor drinking American beer, waiting for Katarina to join them. Cory clapped Gunther on the shoulder. "Thanks for fixing my motorcycle. You always do great work."

"Welcome. Thanks for buying me my own shop."

"And paying for my medical school," Brendan added.

"And making me your American ambassador and giving me beautiful mountains to climb, so I can continue rock climbing," Asher said.

Cory chuckled. "They were already there."

"Close enough."

Cory faced his friends. "How you guys liking it here?"

Gunther grinned. "Now that you've brought this place into the twenty-first century, it's great. Damn, you repealed some astonishingly repressive laws. Your Bill of Rights makes an American proud."

Cory gave a mock bow. "I believe in it but did it in honor of Katarina. You know what else I did for her when she returned to me and turned me from a depressed man into one celebrating how awesome life is?"

"Allow me," Asher said.

Brendan scoffed.

"Shut up, douchebag."

"Okay, Cinderella."

"Women like my hair better than yours. They run their fingers through my soft blond locks," Asher said to Brendan, glancing at his shaggy reddish-blond hair. "And have more to grab onto while I'm doing more for them than you ever could."

"Point goes to Asher," Gunther said.

Brendan laughed.

"Cory put out an olive branch to an ancient adversary of this country and brokered peace after a five-hundred-year cold war," Asher said.

"Fuck, dude, that's great!" Gunther said.

"I'm impressed," Brendan added.

"It was a *challenge*, but heaven has been visited upon me. What can I say?" Cory stroked his wedding ring, smiling.

"People have gone from calling you a history maker to a miracle worker after that one," Asher said. "Kat has an amazing effect on you. I can't wait to see what you do next in her name."

"It will be big," Cory said. "I'm going to bust my ass fighting for reconciliation among other enemies nearby. I'm going for *regional* peace."

His friends looked at him with great respect.

"I love the way you and Kat dance across your ballroom," Asher added.

"Goofball," Brendan mocked then glanced at Cory. "But it is pretty cool, dude. You guys really live it up."

Asher nodded. "Thanks for having palace staff speak English to us while we struggle to learn your language."

"I did that for my queen, a marvelous musician and scientist, but a weak language learner. Actually, back when I was poor, Jon paid English tutors to give people free lessons because in my heart I knew Katarina would someday be mine. My family already spoke English, though, as a second language, for diplomatic and political reasons."

"We have an American influence on you," Brendan said.

Cory shrugged. "Haven't had any complaints about *that* yet. My people find American culture exotic and progressive."

"Cool," Brendan said. "What if people did complain?"

"I get complaints often."

"But the people here are thrilled you're their leader," Gunther said.

"But people disagree with each other. I get polar opposite petitions, and when I don't give each party exactly what they want, they voice their displeasure to me."

"I'll bet they didn't do that with George or your father," Asher said.

Cory scoffed. "Not if they knew what was good for them."

"You give them freedom to express their opinions, and they beat you over the head with it," Gunther said.

Cory shrugged again. "Better than to give them a hint of my father's or my brother's reigns. It's worth it."

"But it tests you at times," Asher added. He turned to Gunther and Brendan. "You don't see it, not consulting with Cory about politics as often as I do, but some days, after Cory has been working long and hard to help them, he'll be exhausted then have some citizen tell him they want him to do yet another project differently. They don't care to give a guy a break."

"They're worth it," Cory said. "They suffered from enforced silence for too long. That day when George was still king and put my head on the chopping block, I made promises to the people that I intend to keep."

"You call on us if you ever need anything," Gunther added.

"We'll work for their well-being," Asher added. "Even when they write demanding, unreasonable letters to their king."

Cory looked at him in surprise. "Being my ambassador has given you a tough streak. You used to be so mellow, a rock-climbing hippie."

Asher opened his mouth to respond, but Cory held up his hand. "You've done an excellent job. I'm pleased with your service and wasn't implying otherwise. I'm just amused to see this side of you. You're so protective of me."

"You're my best friend. Have been since we were boys."

"That goes for us too," Gunther said. "As well as to Katarina."

"Yep," Brendan added.

Cory glanced at his friends. "You heathens may not share blood with me, but you're family."

They held up their beers in a toast.

"I got the looks in the family," Brendan joked, looking at Cory. "Fuck, you're ugly, dude. Katarina must have to down a six-pack before bedding you."

Cory scoffed. "Stop thinking about my wife. And sex, in the same sentence."

"Want me to face punch him for you?" Gunther asked Cory, chuckling.

"Might make him prettier and more tolerable to the ladies," Cory said.

Brendan chucked Cory's shoulder. Cory hit him back in a friendly way.

Katarina walked into the room laughing. "So, this is how you guys talk when I'm not around! I heard you from the corridor."

The guys gave her a group hug.

"Oh, by the way, Brend," she started, "Cory is such a stud that my clothes fall off whenever he enters a room I'm in alone."

The guys chuckled. She pulled Cory into a kiss then leaned away, turning to look at hers and Cory's closest friends. "I'm glad you guys came to live with us here." She rested her head on Cory's shoulder. "I go back to Paris soon, but I'd love for the five of us to watch a movie tonight in the palace theater and snack on junk food. Get a little drunk. Laugh our asses off. You know, our usual stuff we used to do."

"Great idea," Cory said.

"Thanks! This is wonderful, but the highlight of my life," she said to the others, "was Cory's and my honeymoon. Even the danger couldn't dampen how beautiful it was being with him."

He looked at her with love. "Our honeymoon was *memorable*." Then he whispered into her ear, huskily, "The constant delicious sex made me loopy in the head. Let's do it again soon—make love for days on end."

She drew in a sharp breath and grasped her thighs.

"Fuck, dude," Brendan started. "Whatever you just said to her—"

"Say it. I dare you," Cory challenged him.

Brendan chuckled. "Never mind. I'm just...awed by how you can bring such a beauty to her knees with only words."

"Shut up, now," Cory said.

"Our honeymoon, running..." Katarina began.

"George failed to kill us."

"No thanks to me inspiring you to defy your king's command to marry a shrewish stranger to make your life hell instead of—"

"Marrying the love of my life."

She pressed her forehead to his.

"Don't ever again attempt jumping in front of a bullet for me like you did when—"

"Try and stop me."

"Katarina! Don't torture me!"

She kissed him and headed for the door. "Who wants nachos? After the movie, if we're all inebriated, how about a word game? It's hilarious to see the words you all spell in a certain condition. It's the only time Cory, the word genius, doesn't win!"

~ * ~

Cory walked with his bodyguards along the Seine. He stopped. "Well, gentlemen, I have enough cash now that I can make the French government a respectful offer."

"For what, Majesty?" a muscular guard asked.

"The Eiffel Tower!" Cory smiled.

Two of the guards scoffed playfully. Cory's lifting partner, Stu, laughed. All had been given permission to be casual with him in private. They had been hesitant until he made them feel like friends.

"For my wife. Do you think Katarina would like it? What say you, Stu?" Cory joked.

"I think she'd prefer a new bass amp. The Eiffel Tower would be an honor but is too big to carry around."

Cory laughed. "Yes, and I was just joking."

The men snickered.

Stu regarded him. "You're nothing like your father or older brother."

"Thank God. Thanks for saying so."

"You're...approachable. Your father wasn't. *George* wasn't."

Cory tipped his head. Even though he called his half-brother *George* behind his back, Cory called him by his given name *Goran* to his face in order to prevent the oppressor from getting in a bad mood and hurting someone.

"We'll go see our enchanting queen play, I'll spend some... private time with her, and then I'll contact a man I need to see about George." Cory stopped a passing man in a suit and asked in fluent French if he would mind taking their picture. The gentleman complied. Cory stood with guards on both sides and made a happy face, arms spread out mischievously, celebrating life. The guards chuckled in the picture. Cory sent them each the joyful photo from his phone.

~ * ~

After the show, Cory took Katarina by the hand to her hotel room. Stu and the others followed.

Inside the suite, Cory turned to them with a grave look. "Men, if I'm not out in one hour, call a doctor." He pushed open the door to the adjoining room, pulled the queen inside laughing, and slammed the door.

~ * ~

In the morning, Cory creaked open the door. He was enchanted with the gift the mask had bestowed on him and Katarina. Their sex life was great before, but now their heads buzzed with the added depth and intensity they enjoyed. His body still rang with pleasure, and his mind floated in a cloud.

His men greeted him.

Cory offered a smile. "Who's hungry?"

They nodded.

"Wherever you guys want to eat. We'll find something good here in Paris!" he said cheerfully.

He practically danced down the hall with the men following after him.

Walking toward the restaurant, Cory said, "We'll dine here in this fine city of lights then fly back to my...what did Brendan once call it? Oh yes, a dark, mysterious castle on a foggy mountainside, or something like that."

Vlad said seriously, "Sire, that's what it is."

Cory put his arm around Katarina's shoulders. She nudged him with affection.

"I like this country. Perhaps we'll vacation here?" Cory asked.

"I'd like that, sweetheart. But come. We should eat."

"Shall I call for a limo?" Stu asked.

"No, let's continue to walk. The weather is fine," Cory said. "Unless you guys aren't up for that?"

"It's fine, Sire." Stu and the others followed Cory and Katarina as they walked along the Parisian streets.

When they arrived at a charming, family-owned restaurant, they were seated in a private dining room.

Cory looked around the table at his guards. "Order whatever you want. You men do a damn good job, and I intend to show my appreciation often."

"Your father..." Vlad shook his head. "Pardon me, My King, but it's truly remarkable. My father worked for him and came home unhappy every night. He said the king—"

"I give you leave."

"...was a despot. And what he did to you—"

Cory shook his head. "Almost killed me, numerous times, beating me."

Stu looked at him with eyes of affection. "You are a good man not to have turned rotten to the core for having sustained that, and you are so...down to earth, even to us, your servants."

"Gentlemen, you're not my servants. You're my respected colleagues."

"Majesty," Stu said, "is that the American influence coming out of you?"

"Perhaps."

Katarina gave a happy sigh. "Thanks for having them speak English in front of me. I'm learning, but your language is hard to learn. Give me time." She tapped his hand. "Excuse me. Gotta use the ladies' room."

Stu stood to escort her.

"It's okay, Stuart. I don't need an escort."

"My Queen—"

"Please. I'd be embarrassed." She gave Cory a falsely criticizing look. "I intend to inspire the women of your country to come out of their shells and be strong and independent. They were discouraged for far too long under your father's reign, then George's."

Cory grinned and nodded his respect. "I hope you succeed, my love. But still, maybe Stu should escort you while we're here. Or me? Since you are a queen."

She rolled her eyes. "I can make it the thirty feet to the bathroom myself. But I love you. Thank you anyway." She kissed her fingers, held her hand in Cory's direction, and pranced off, out the private dining room and into the larger room filled with people.

Stu shook his head but watched her.

"What is it?" Cory asked.

He looked at Cory. "Your brother, George, repressed women, and you give our queen, our women such respect. You've brought women's rights to our country, making it stronger. There's far less internal strife now. People feel…safer, more confident—"

Katarina came back, and breakfast arrived moments later. They had a nice morning before heading for the private airport. Cory made his call and discovered that George had disappeared. Katarina kissed Cory then pulled away, clinging to his hands, and looked at him as if it were her last day on earth.

He wrenched her into another kiss before boarding the plane, his heart aching. Damn, he missed her already. From the window of his jet, he watched the limo driving her back to her band.

That night, Cory picked at his food. Gunther, Brendan, and Asher as usual ate at a different time due to their schedules.

"Brother," Jon began, sipping his wine. "What troubles you?"

"I hate that Katarina is always gone, but I support her dreams."

"You could insist that as our queen, she must be here fulltime to fulfill her social duties."

"It's against my personal philosophy to order a woman around, and it might feel like repression to her." *It would give her doubts in my unconditional love. A man with that supported his woman's lifelong dream, whatever the heartache to himself might be.*

"You're good to Katarina."

"Call her *Kat*. She decided years ago that only *I* shall call her *Katarina*. That is one privilege you couldn't pry out of me." Cory was the only one who called her Katarina...except her parents. "The exception is in choosing to use her title, *Queen Katarina*."

Jon nodded. "You are demonstrating true love for her."

Cory smirked. He couldn't talk this way with his friends—well, Asher, yes. He looked up and met his brother's gaze. "It's what I feel." When Katarina was there for more than a day, she did civic duties. Abroad, she was an ambassador for their country. She slipped in charitable activities in the name of Carasivia.

"She gives inspirational messages to our women," Jon said.

Cory shoved his plate away. "I can't eat."

"Our queen would reprimand you for that. Thanks to her advice and example, our citizens now aspire to eat healthier, adding more vegetables to their meals on her urging. And you, of course, have filled this need by importing and growing more. Eat, for her sake."

Cory dragged his plate closer and took a bite of salad. When drinking water, his phone rang. He set his glass down and looked at the surface of his phone and smiled. "Katarina." He touched the screen and pressed it to his ear. "Hello, my love. Miss me as much as I miss you?"

"C...Cory?" her voice came out in a harsh whisper. "Help me."

Cory sat up straighter. "Sweetheart, what's wrong?"

She sucked in a breath. "Oh, God."

He bounded to his feet. "Where you are. What's happening?"

He glanced at a frowning Jon, who was standing now.

"Bernadette and I went to her friend's house. Mandy Devereaux." Her terrified whisper alarmed him.

"And?" He gripped his phone.

"I'm hiding in a shower."

"What? Why?"

"Her friend had a really beautiful guitar to give her..." she sobbed silently.

Cory swallowed hard and listened, walking.

"I went into the bathroom, and then I heard Bernadette scream." Her words came pouring out. "Then gunshots went off! I think Bernadette and the guards are dead! Someone shouted, 'Find the queen!' Cory, my poor friend! Mandy. Your guards! What if I never see you again? I wanted to have your children, and now it's too late. They're going to find me. I can't escape."

Cory strode in the direction of his airfield. "I love you. I'm on my way. I will *never* give up. I'll find you!"

Jon followed him. They entered another corridor, and Cory gestured harshly to a guard. The man rushed over.

"See to getting the jet ready."

He nodded and rushed to do Cory's bidding.

"Footsteps are coming closer. I love—" Her words were cut off by her scream.

"Katarina!"

The phone went dead.

"Katarina!" He ran straight for his jet, dialing Paris police on the way.

~ * ~

Once in Paris, Jon took charge of the search. Cory was needed back home to run their country. After an impassioned argument, he finally relented, as long as someone called him every fifteen minutes with an update. He called Asher who was just returning from a mission in Germany.

"Cory, no! Don't despair. They'll find her. I'll join the efforts."

"Please. You love her too, Ash, like your sister. Find her."

"I swear, I'll never give up. I'll call Gunther and Brendan."

"Thank...you. I'll...consult the mask." Cory ended the call and leaned back in his chair, closing his eyes.

That night, he sat in his office, on the phone with Stu. The mask had been unusually quiet, and he had put it in a desk drawer, wanting to try later.

"Sire, we split up. Prince Jaromír—Jon—headed north on a whim."

"Thanks for the update. Call back. Fifteen minutes to the second," Cory responded.

"Yes. We notified the queen's band. We won't give up. And—"

"What is it, Stu?"

"She's safe out there, somewhere, Your Majesty. I feel it in my bones, and I've been at my job in security for a long time."

"Thank you. I feel she's alive too, but she could be hurt. She could be alone, afraid...shivering in some black pit, lost, away from me...forever."

Someone spoke to Stu.

"Stu, news?" Cory asked.

"Your Majesty, I have some good news."

Cory leaned forward. "Yes?"

"Bernadette made it through surgery."

"Thank God."

"But it's in God's hands now."

"I see. Have all her medical bills sent to me, and get her family out here on my jet, as soon as possible. All expenses on me."

"Will do. Sadly, Mandy died. Two of the queen's guards have hope of recovering, but they are still in bad shape. I've contacted their families."

"Thank you. Keep me posted."

"I'll call back."

Cory hung up and pressed his forehead to his folded arms on his desk.

When Cory got Stu's call two hours later, Cory shuddered with a bad feeling. "You have something bad to report."

"Sire, I'm sorry to report that the prince is missing, and his guards were found unconscious."

Cory closed his eyes and utilized his gift as he'd been doing for Katarina. He focused inwardly. "I sense my brother is still alive."

"Yes, Sire, me too. This could be George's work."

Cory nodded. "It's possible."

"The guards are going to pull through."

"Thank you. Call back. Fifteen minutes."

At three in the morning, Cory was jolted awake by the sound of his phone. He lifted his head off his desk and pressed the phone to his ear. "Hello?"

"Your brother has wanted your wife since he first laid eyes on her."

"Who is this?" He pushed to his feet.

Click.

The next day, pacing, Cory's head swam with fatigue. He fell onto a lush couch in a parlor and leaned his head back. Tears burned his eyes. "Beloved, where are you? Think of me. Send me your whereabouts."

Nothing.

The gentle touch of a secretary's hand woke him.

"Majesty. You're exhausted. You haven't eaten in over twenty-four hours. Please, for our queen's sake, eat."

He managed a light meal.

~ * ~

Jon came to and rubbed his aching head. "Ohhhhh," he moaned, blinked, and pressed his hands to the cold dirt-packed floor of the shack. His eyes adjusted to the light, and he saw Katarina sprawled out on the ground. Her eyes closed, and then her head rolled to the side. She lay motionless. Jon heard people scrambling outside but ignored them. He sprang to his feet and went to Kat, checking her pulse. Nothing. He gasped and began CPR.

Twenty

Cory paced in his office with fisted hands. Brendan was due any minute, and they could talk about strategy.

"I've got to go look for her myself!" Cory sighed and plopped down into his chair, closing his eyes to draw on the first gift the mask had ever given him. When he went within and searched for his beloved's life energy, nothingness greeted him. His heart paused. He gulped and did it again. Nothing.

He shook his head. *A mistake.*

He drew a deep breath, with shaking hands, and tried again, sending his senses across space to feel for her life force.

Nothing.

He swayed in shock and tried again.

Nothing. Cold, dead, nothing. Gasping, he checked the life force of a guard he had seen earlier to test his skill. He felt his life energy on this plane. The truth about Katarina leveled him. He sprang to his feet and yelled out then fell to his knees, crying. Two guards burst through the door and ran to him with Brendan rushing in behind them.

"My King?" one asked.

"She's dead, she's dead, she's dead!"

"No!" Brendan urged. "You used your gift. Use it again!"

He looked at Brendan through tear-blurred eyes. "I did it four times!"

"Take it from me, and try again!" Brendan begged, grasping his shoulders.

Cory rubbed his forearm over his wet eyes and nodded, closing his eyes and going within. He sent his mental feelers out there, and this time, they tingled. He reached further with his consciousness, and her life force zapped him. He jumped to his feet. "She's not dead! But..." his voice came out rough. He looked at Brendan in desperation. "How?"

The guards were gaping.

Brendan studied him. "What did I do for a living before getting accepted into medical school?"

He crinkled his brow. "Paramedic."

"Think, Cory. What did I do often with my hands?"

"I...uh," he said in a daze.

"CPR. Many people came back."

Cory drew in a shaky breath. "You don't think..."

"Whoever she is with was successful at that technique or another to bring her back."

Cory pulled Brendan into an embrace. "Thank you."

"I'm not the one who saved her."

"No, but you just saved me." He turned to his guards. "Gentlemen, you just discovered that I have a...gift, which I can also use to predict those to die in the near future. Please do not tell another single person about this. Not even your wives. It's a private matter. I trust you. That's why you're my personal guards."

"Of course," both said.

After that, Cory checked for her life force many times a day. His council convinced him not to leave immediately to search for her himself.

~ * ~

Katarina came to and struggled to focus in the dim light. She lay on cold, hard earth, aching all over, and moaned.

"My...Queen?" came a voice from close.

"Jon? Is that you? You just..."

"Pulled you from the afterworld."

"Oh my God. How can I ever thank you."

"Not necessary. You're my queen. My brother's wife, my sister, my friend..."

"Where are we?" She pressed her hands to the ground, but pain tore through her, and she collapsed, yelling out as she hit the ground.

"Are you...okay, My Queen?"

She took uneven breaths. She closed her eyes then felt the pressure of his hand on her forehead and looked at him. A quivering grin came to her lips. "You're gorgeous. I just can't get over how much so, but right now, you look a mess." Her eyes roved over his ragged appearance. "Like you've been dragged through the mud. But you make the mud look good."

"You're burning up, My Qu...Katarina."

She shivered. "Just Kat. Only my parents and Cory call me Katarina."

He darted glances around and frowned. "Sorry. I forgot. Kat. Not much for coverings." He touched his head, squinting. "I've a splitting headache."

She shifted. "What happened? I think I was drugged then hit over the head when dropped off here."

"At about two a.m. Paris time, a strange feeling overcame me. I separated from the group and headed north. I turned a corner, and someone hit me over the head. I'm pretty sure I was drugged too. I woke up here."

"Where's here?"

"Allow me to go look around."

She smiled. "You don't have to ask my permission for anything."

"You're my—"

"And if you frickin say 'You're my queen,' I'll wring your neck." He chuckled softly.

"Now that's a sound I like, your laughter."

"I shall endeavor to do so more often, then, in your presence."

"Go explore...if you want to."

"Yes, My Qu...Kat."

"Thank you!"

He stood and pushed open the door of the shack, leaving.

She closed her eyes. "Cory," she muttered, concentrating on his face. "I'll come back to you, my love. I'm okay. Don't worry." She tried to send him this message with her heart and mind.

Sometime later, Jon shook her gently. "Your fever is broken. Thank God."

"Huh!" Her eyes snapped open. "Sorry. I fell asleep." She shivered.

He lay beside her and hesitated to put his arm around her.

"It's okay. I'm not going to violate you," she said.

He encircled her with his arms. "I didn't explore long enough to find decent coverings for warmth, so I hope this helps."

"Thanks. I'm freezing."

He rubbed her back rapidly.

"So, t...tell me about you and Cory. Did you ever toss a ball around as boys? Did you hop fences together before he got shipped off to America? Tell me about my mother-in-law."

"My goodness. Mom was great. Intelligent. She had a doctorate degree in biology and always did well for the people. Very caring. And Corentin. I admire how well read he is in all three of his languages. Has read on more subjects than anyone I know. One of his favorite topics to discuss with me is international politics. He knows a lot about a lot just by talking to experts and reading."

"He did many interviews as a writer."

"Yes. And he was my hero. Whenever our father beat him, Corentin would hobble to his feet and look our father in the eyes. Then he'd turn and stumble to his room. I'd find him there expecting to see hatred broiling in his eyes, but I never did. He said Mom's and Grandmother's love was enough to sustain his belief in humanity and the good in the world, and that his people deserved a good prince in him."

"Nice. But did you often climb trees together—things like that?"

"Many tall ones. We hiked the mountain our castle resides on, numerous times. Cory and I would wrestle and play rough and tumble as boys do. I'd ask him a million questions, and he'd tell me the answers with patience and ask what I thought about things."

"Nice brother."

"The best."

"What were his...issues as a boy?"

"Our father beat him humble, so arrogance was never an issue with him, that and living in America made sure of that. But if I had a complaint, I'd say I was jealous because he occupied most of our mother's attention."

"You, jealous of him? Your looks alone... As handsome as my husband is—and he rocks my world—in physical looks, yours are so outstanding that you should undergo tests in a lab. But don't get me wrong. The whole package deal makes him more attractive to me than you could ever be, so to me he's better looking."

He laughed. "The scientist comes out in you often."

"Can't help it. My dad wanted me to follow in his footsteps and be a chemist like him and my mother. They taught me everything they know about chemistry. My world was surrounded with it as I grew up. I knew the periodic table before I was in middle school. I have the equivalent of a graduate degree from my home study. Believe me, my parents gave me *rigorous* training. I worked in their lab almost every day. They drilled me heavily, all my life, made me read college text books...

"Dad was upset when I told him I wasn't going to college. I told him I didn't need to because I could hold intelligent conversations with professionals in the field. He said I needed that piece of paper." She paused. "Enough about me. So, you were jealous of Cory. Wow."

"I was just a second spare to the heir, not nearly as important."

"That wasn't his fault."

"No, but I don't think he did anything to make Mom pay more attention to either me or George. George really hates that name. Says it's too American. He wants to be called Goran, but Corentin and I love calling him George—our version of his name."

"Cory was abused, by George, yes, but more so by your father. You weren't, not in comparison. Cory had to cling to something to stay sane. He needed his mother's attention. After what your father did to him."

"Good point. Corentin was hospitalized a few times. I thought he was going to die, bringing me one step closer to the throne I did not want and still don't want."

She fiddled with a small twig in front of her. "Why didn't you want the throne? It's about freedom, isn't it?"

"Corentin always did brag about your brains."

"What else did he say about me?"

"That you were so damn beautiful he thought he'd go crazy and was so deeply in love with you. Said your looks were a bonus but completely unnecessary. He said you filled up empty spots in him, and your sweet nature humbled him more than our father's fists ever did."

"Cory..." She shivered and swiped a tear from her cheek.

Jon hugged her close. "We'll get you back to him."

"Which reminds me, *where* are we?" She dropped the twig.

"It looks like a deserted island."

"An island? How long were we out?"

"That's what I'd like to know. Well, it's not blazing hot out there. We must be above a certain latitude. Also, we're alone."

"You brought me here to seduce me. Fess up."

He sat up. "My Queen, no!"

"I'm kidding, sheesh! I'm in love with Cory, and I know you'd never hurt him, or we'd be enemies. Lie down. I'm freezing."

He laid back down. "I'd give my life for him."

"As a brother or because he's your king?"

"Both. And friendship. He took a beating for me once."

"When?"

"I let a palace servant out one of the secret hideaways in the palace when my father was searching for him. The servant escaped to his car. I didn't know yet why he was running. I just...opened a door. I don't know how he knew the door was there."

"What did he do?"

"I found out that he stole one of the tapestries hanging in the palace because it was worth a fortune, and his son needed heart surgery."

She faced him. "Go on."

"Corentin had run up next to me, panting, having been looking for the servant when he heard Father was looking for him. Our father saw the two of us standing there, saw the open door, and saw the servant's cap lying on the floor at our feet. Corentin picked up the cap, looked the king in the eyes, lifted his chin and smirked. He told our father the man was long gone and that he was proud the man had gone to such lengths to save his son. Father grabbed a handful of Corentin's shirt in his clenched fist and dragged Corentin, who was choking and scratching at his neck, tumbling out the room. I found my brother in a crumpled heap in a shadowy palace corner, fearing he was dead. I approached, shaking, and shook his shoulder. He didn't move. I threw my face against his chest and cried like a baby. Corentin gasped and opened his eyes. He smiled and told me to man up. He was eleven. I was ten. I went and got some ice for his swollen eyes. If that had been me under Father's fist, I'd have died. Corentin somehow knew that."

Kat closed her gaping mouth. "Wow. Okay, could you tell me about George? He's handsome too, like the two of you, but he's the only blond one, like your mother."

"Too bad he didn't get her sense of honor."

"Yeah, after what he did to Cory..." She cleared her throat. "A counselor taught me how I could forgive George because the anger was tearing me up. I finally did forgive him and became freer."

"I haven't yet. I don't like talking about him."

"There's hope for him."

"Huh."

"Some of your mother had to seep into him."

He tapped her arm. "Your husband is the kind of man that doesn't give up. If he did all I told you about for a servant, what would he do for you?"

She snuggled into his arms, shivering. "He did that for you."

"His love for you is twice what it is for me. I think that kind of love trumps brotherly love."

"Not always."

"In your case, it does. He has the real thing for you."

She smiled. "I know. It's been developing for a long time. All those looks when he thought I wasn't looking. Those smiles…"

He shivered. "It's actually kind of a thrill to witness. Makes me want to fall in love. It's really kind of sexy. You have the real thing for him too."

"Yes. Jon? You're admitting that you have those kinds of thoughts about the subject? You? Mr. Straight-laced?"

"Every so often," he said with a serious tone.

"Hm. You're not as warm as Cory. He's *smoking* hot. Someday I want to give him children that will love him."

"Nothing would make him happier."

She drifted to sleep. Later she woke up, and the flickering flames of a small fire cast warmth from two feet away.

"Where'd you learn to do that?"

"I am an archaeologist." He chuckled. "But…when I was younger, I learned in Carasivia's version of the boy scouts."

"Ah. Hunt us up some food, please. Or dig us up some food."

Damn you're good-looking.

"I already did. Plucked it, actually."

"Whatcha get?"

He brought a piece of yellow fruit to her and put a chunk into her mouth.

"Mm, thanks. Juicy. What is it?"

"I'm not sure, but I tried it first. It's safe."

"Very considerate of you. You didn't have to do that."

"Of course, I did." He looked into her face. "You really are beautiful." He looked away.

"Thanks. Cory once told me the same thing, but he wasn't looking at my face. He was looking at my soul."

He cleared his throat. "You are kind, and…easy-going, good to people."

"Would you have pursued me if Cory didn't love me?"

His eyes met hers.

"As your queen, I demand an honest answer," she teased.

"Yes," he muttered.

Her brow rose to reflect her surprise.

"Would you have considered me?" he asked. "If you weren't so enamored of him?"

"Okay, now I'm really surprised."

"Forgive me. I was out of line. It's this place." He looked around the dim hut then back at her.

"It's okay. When I saw you at that costume party Cory and I attended before he and I were a couple, I stared at you, and Cory gave you a murderous look. I told him while still looking at you that my babies would be *gorgeous*."

Jon turned red. "Oh my God, it's a miracle I'm still standing."

Her stomach rumbled. "Please, give me more of that fruit. Id'a gone for you if I had never known him."

He handed her a tree-bark platter, and she ate, watching him with a mirthful heart.

"But, Jon…"

"Yes?"

"I'd not have loved you with the depth I do him. It's just not possible."

He grinned. "I know. You married him when he was an impoverished nobody and while knowing me, a wealthy prince that women go crazy over."

Her brow came up. "How come you're not married?"

"I have never fallen in love."

"Lots of sex though, right?"

She could see how hard he swallowed as he looked down.

"Please look at me."

He did. "I'm sorry, My Queen, Kat."

"Only answer if you want to."

"You are my sister. Fine. Yes, I've had 'lots of sex.' Americans."

"Don't let Cory ever catch you saying 'Americans' in that tone."

"I'm sorry. I didn't mean to imply anything."

"So, are you a secret womanizer?"

He coughed. "Um...no."

"Don't...secretly prefer men?"

His mouth dropped open.

"Men who prefer men would kill for you. Women would too."

"I prefer women. My closest friend apart from Corentin, though, doesn't. He's currently working in Asia. Corentin loves the guy, financed his project, thinking he's a genius. I'm discreet with women. I don't want my escapades plastered all over the media." He gazed down.

"Don't be embarrassed. This is the twenty-first century. Men and women can discuss these things without sleeping together."

"Of...course. You are wise, My Queen."

She shook his shoulders. "I'm your sister!" She lowered her hands, chuckling.

"I see you've regained your strength."

"You have robbed me of it." She paused with a sudden smile.

"Your face glows."

"I'm thinking of Cory again, the most superb human being I've ever had the honor of knowing. He's just so damn dynamic and heroic, and the way he's always looked at me was quite a turn on. Like he was tortured not being able to express his love for me."

"His strong feelings didn't scare you?"

"No. His restrained ardor was tempered with *gigantic* respect. He's treated me like a lady since the day we met. We'd waltz in my room with the door open when we were teenagers. My parents were stunned at the deeply sincere gentlemanly treatment he has always given me. Little did we know that he was a royal prince, but I could have guessed that, looking back at the situation now."

"He likes your—"

She smirked. "My what? My legs?"

"Don't you know this already?"

"Yeah, but I want to know what he said to you!"

He let out a hard breath. "That green shirt you used to wear."

"Green's his favorite color, so why not? That shirt cost three dollars."

"Maybe, but he said he knew you would wear it because he liked the color so much. It mattered to him that you did that."

"Good."

"And when you complimented him for wearing dark blue—"

"Mm, makes his eyes look bluer."

"He likes you in his black, purple-cuffed jacket with your hair mussed up. He told me that after a night drinking, actually. A cousin's wedding celebration."

"Mm." She touched her neck. Heat flushed her cheeks.

Jon grinned. "What did he tell you about *me*?"

She tilted her head. "Do you want to hear the good or the bad?"

"Both."

"Cory said you were intelligent. He could trust you, and that meant something to him. He once admitted..."

"Admitted what, Kat?"

"That he'd die to save your life."

Brotherly love filled his expression. "I believe that."

"Yep," she said. "You're his baby brother."

He smiled. "What bad things did he say?"

She smiled. "He admitted to me you're boring and uptight at times. Even pissed him off now and again, like the time the three of us got mugged in America, a guy had a weapon pressed to me, and you wouldn't give him your wallet."

"I deeply regret that."

"I forgave you. Even with all that, Cory said he wouldn't trade you in."

He chuckled.

"Did he complain to you about me, Jon?"

He sighed. "Yes. Besides the stuff you know..."

"Tell me."

"You dating other guys occasionally in high school and after drove him to have meaningless sex with casual girlfriends. You tortured him, keeping him intimately close to you and rejecting him.

You occasionally praised other men in front of him. He thought you were kind but had a mean streak. But he wouldn't trade you in."

Embarrassed, she changed the subject. "You don't have a Masters' degree yet."

"I've signed up for grad school next semester. Corentin has considered college, but can you imagine him in a class? It's bad enough with me in class, so I have to take as many online classes as possible. I think it would be too intimidating to his classmates for him to be there. Perhaps at a later date he could work out some full-time online deal with the university."

"I'd encourage it. Cory was always working his ass off, poor to the point where he felt a two-dollar loss, but richer than me," Kat said. "When we weren't talking about literature, music, or more mundane things, we got onto more serious topics. He, like me, enjoyed becoming self-educated outside of high school. He'd listen to me rattle off my chemistry this or that, and I'd listen as he got books on international relations and political science and read to me passages that stood out to him. He'd ask me theoretical questions. He'd get excited and go on and on about his ideas."

"He mentioned that to me. He loved discussing those things with you. He saw the two of you as a tiny example of international relations in action."

She smiled. "He really impressed me one day when he compared the ideas of America's forefathers with those of your country."

Jon nodded. They talked for a few more minutes, and she fell asleep again.

~ * ~

After a week in a hellish daze, one of Cory's ministers came rushing into his office, holding out his cell phone. "Sire, I don't know how they got my number."

Cory ripped the phone from his hand. "This is Corentin."

"You're never going to see her again. Your brother wanted her, and now he has her."

"You son-of-a—"

"At least she's alive."

"Tell Goran—"

"Goran? I meant your *younger* brother."

Cory stumbled back. "No."

"Afraid so."

"Who...is this?"

"One of his servants. Stop looking. You'll never find her. *You* know, like everyone else, that the prince is an exceptionally handsome man. Like you, but even better. It's only a matter of time before he seduces your wife."

"It will never happen."

"He has some heart. He wanted you to know that she's in safe hands, and at least, unlike Goran, he doesn't believe in rape. He'll be good to her. Resign yourself to never seeing her again, but if by a miracle you do, by that time, it will be too late. He'll comfort her, be there for her, slowly make her his because she doesn't know he's behind this. Or maybe, this is what she secretly wanted...in her heart."

Click.

Cory stared at the phone in his trembling hand then gave it to his minister who left.

Jon? No. He is being set up. Cory and Jon were close. Jon loved him, his big brother, his hero, he had said.

He had called her a beautiful woman.

Cory shook his head. Everyone thought Katarina was beautiful. He slapped his hands to his face. Would Jon have him killed? He was next in line for the throne. He always hated the thought of being on the throne. Was it an act?

Cory lowered his hands. He sent his closest friends, his American friends, to different continents with unlimited funds to search the world for her.

His minister came back and said the call had come from the American east coast.

The next day, a maid entered his office showing him a ruby ring she had found in Jon's chambers, on a table. She bowed. "Majesty. I picked this up to dust and happened to see something...interesting."

"Thank you, Marta." He took the ring, and she left.

He read an inscription inside. *"Katarina, I love you. Be mine. –J."*

Cory gulped. That night, he had nightmares of Katarina crying on Jon's shoulder. He'd tip her chin up, look into her eyes, and kiss her. She'd resist at first. She'd resist for a long time. But what if...she felt hopeless? Cory woke with a start and punched his pillow. "Don't you dare abuse my sweet wife that way!"

A month later and twenty pounds lighter, Cory tried to sign a state paper with a shaky hand. He had to still his hand and try again. He slapped the pen down and leaned back in his leather chair. Two more calls had come in during the last month about Katarina when Cory's and her friends were gone searching for her. One call was traced to Russia, and the other to Argentina, probably to throw him off track. Cory rubbed his eyes. Brendan had called to report from New York that he had no news. Asher called from China to tell him the same, and Gunther called from Australia to repeat the heartbreaking news that he could find no trace of her.

Weeks later, someone knocked on Cory's office door. He sat up and gazed at the door hard. "Enter." One of his older guards came in, a man who had worked for his father.

Cory narrowed his brow. "Dimitri, what is it? News of my wife?" He held his breath.

Dimitri pulled out a weapon from under his half-cloak, and Cory gasped and reached for the pistol under his desk.

~ * ~

Katarina and Jon cleaned up their hut, brought in and stored all the fruit they could find, and talked into the night, growing closer. Sometimes on a warm day, they'd swim or lie on the beach, silent, or hike, or take some of their fruit and picnic on the sand. They devised a trap made out of reeds and sticks and caught fish, cooking it over the fire. They sang over the campfire and laughed.

One day, while on a hike once again looking for anything that might help them get off the island, like they did daily, she lost her footing on a hill. He reached for her, and they tumbled downward, landing with a thump, him with his body covering hers.

"You...okay?" she coughed.

"Y...yes. And you?"

"Fine. Jon?"

"Yes?"

She looked into his mortified face. "Don't be embarrassed. It's a natural guy reaction. Men can get...aroused without even thinking about it."

He leaned and brought his lips an inch from hers, pausing. He closed his eyes, cursed in his native language, and rolled off her.

"How can I make up for this grave offense, my queen?"

She smiled. "Hey, it's cool, if I didn't love Cory, I'd tear your clothes off."

"Oh God."

"But I'm not hitting on you! I love Cory."

"So do I."

"With all my heart. You're just my very sexy brother-in-law. I'd no more sleep with you than I would anyone else on the planet except your...dreamy brother. You're a great person, but Cory is great, as in he's making history." She glanced up. "I miss you." Tears rolled down her cheeks.

Jon rolled to his side and faced her, smiling. "You're sweet. No wonder he loves you so much. You made a tragically uncomfortable situation bearable, true queen material. My greatest respect to you, and just so you know, I'm sorry. I'd never touch my brother's wife. I was stupefied by the moment."

She wiped away her tears and sat up, offering her hand. "Come on. Let's get more water from the spring."

Katarina sang a song she had written for Cory. Jon complimented her.

"Hey, tell me the best joke you know from your country," she asked. "Cory started to tell me a good one on our wedding night..." she paused and sighed with the memory, shaking her head to dispel the incredible sexual shivers that were coursing through her with the thought of making love to her husband.

Jon rattled off a joke and made her laugh.

By the time they reached the spring, they were laughing again. In front of a tree, they stopped short. Kat gasped and covered her mouth with her hand. Carved in the trunk, it read: *Corentin is dead, and you're never getting off this island.* On a twig, Cory's ring, the Royal violet family crest ring, dangled. Next to it was his wedding ring, the inexpensive one Kat bought him that symbolized epic love, the one Cory told her would only come off over his dead body. *He was murdered.* She collapsed into Jon's arms.

Jon pulled Kat to the ground. She pressed against him and sobbed. When exhausted from crying, she gasped, little breaths. He squeezed her. She looked into his face and saw anger.

"I will avenge my brother, I promise you."

Twenty-one

Late at night, soft sobs filled Katarina and Jon's hut.
He cuddled next to her, holding her. "I'll kill them," he spat.
"Was it...George, do you think?"
"He's the most likely."
"Why not kill us too?"
"I don't know, but I'll find out. I'll torture those who robbed my country of our greatest king, and me of the brother I worshipped. You of your beloved husband."
"Wouldn't...George fear the truth about him being a bastard getting out?"
"Unless he found the evidence and destroyed it."
She cried herself to sleep.

~ * ~

Weeks passed. Jon had to urge her to eat, but she still lost weight. He offered her fish one night, and she shook her head. "Not hungry."
He placed a gentle hand on her arm. "Please, My Queen, for me."
She nodded and took a bite.
"Another please."
"Fine." She swiped it up, then another.
"Thank you."

She ate then collapsed on a reedy mat she and Jon had made together. For another week, she mostly slept, depressed. He tinkered around the hut, making it homier. He put together two crude chairs made from branches, and a simple table. Next came a couple of shelves. One morning she awoke and found a bright pink flower on the shelf.

"Thought it might add a little cheer."

"Thank you," she squeaked out, and then fell back asleep. She awoke and found the place filled with many brightly colored flowers.

"Jon..."

"Do you like it?"

"Yes."

"Please smile. I need to see that," he said. "Corentin would beg me to make you smile."

"For him." She managed a small one, and he returned it.

"Jon?"

"Yes?"

"Aren't you...devastated at losing your brother?"

His expression fell somber. She touched his hand.

"I," he began, and swallowed hard, "I can't focus on it, or I start to feel like my control is lost to me. I dared to let it out while you were sleeping. I ran. I shouted, I cried, I collapsed. I have a grip now. I have to."

"Oh."

"I have a surprise for tonight's dinner."

"Hmm," she moaned, sad.

"I found some plants that resembled vegetables and tried them. They're good."

"I appreciate it, so much, but I can't eat much. My life is ruined. I don't have a grip. I'm slipping away."

He sat beside her and took her hand. "I'm sorry I judged you before. Corentin was right. Being back in the palace made me uptight and formal, but I've seen a deeper side to things. I need to tell you something."

"What is it?" Her hand was limp in his.

"What my people thought of their new queen. I walked about town. I sat in council, and I talked to many people. You added cheer, light, and hope and just good leadership with your regular words of love and inspiration to our nation. You're a damn good queen."

"I'm no longer a queen," she said in monotone. "Cory called me his co-leader as opposed to only his consort, but I never officially accepted the honor, and now it's too late. I miss him so much. I wish he'd walk right in here and take me away, anywhere. Back to America to live in that shitty neighborhood in obscurity."

He drew in a deep breath and rubbed her hand. "I've been thinking."

"About what?"

"The women of our country love you. You have already started to make a difference. They wear brighter clothes, and more laughter can be heard in the streets."

"That's Cory's doing. He brought women's rights to the country."

"Indeed. But you are part of the reason for their cheer. Our colleges received tons of applications from women after your coronation speech to our people. We're due to have an unprecedented number of women doctors and scientists since that day of your advice to the nation."

"Glad my short life meant something."

"Short life?"

"I have no reason to live."

"The music that is your driving force."

"Without Cory, I don't give a damn."

"What if..."

"What if what?"

"What if...you could stay a queen? Or rather, become a queen again?"

She pulled away. "What are you saying?"

"We're getting out of here, one way or the other. My first matter as king will be to hunt down Corentin's killers. Then I'll make a grand memorial for my brother. I'll make his birthday a national holiday and commission books and movies about him. I'll celebrate his life and...keep his queen on the throne."

"Are you...asking me to...marry you?"

"Yes."

"I can't. I want to die."

"Corentin would want you to live."

"I want to join him."

"It's not what he'd want, trust me. Live because you love him, and continue to help our country."

"But...I married him for love. It's all I'm capable of doing."

"I don't expect that any man could ever replace him, so the best you could hope for is a distant second."

"You...deserve better."

"I'm not a romantic kind of man."

"But you did romantic things, like bring flowers into this hut."

"To make you happy, not to seduce you. I discovered you have every quality in a woman that I respect, and I want you to live and thrive."

"I'm a romantic. Cory was a romantic." Her bottom lip quivered.

"I'll learn."

"Why are you doing this?"

"Corentin would want you looked after, and he trusts no one more than he trusts me. I'd see to it that your life was filled with meaningful experiences. I want to honor my brother's memory by helping you. You could do so much more as a queen. Do great things in my country in his name. And maybe after a decent length of time, you could learn to live with me...as your husband. I know it could take years, though, but I'd be faithful to you while I waited during our grieving time and always after."

"Sounds like self-sacrifice on your part."

"Not at all."

"You don't love me."

"I very well could if we go down this path. I respect you and Corentin, and I'm trying to show you that. But if you must know, I find you intriguing, intelligent, and kind-hearted. I enjoy your companionship."

"I don't love you. Not that way." She rolled over. "I'm tired and need to sleep. It's cold. Please put more sticks on the fire if you will."

"Think about what I said."

She closed her eyes and slept. Sometime during the night, wind crept in and blew out the fire. Her teeth chattered. Jon held her close to keep her warm.

The first light appeared under the door. Kat rolled over and put her arms around Jon, sleepily. "Cory, my love," she muttered.

Jon pulled her against his chest. "Shh, it's okay. I'll avenge him."

The door opened, and Kat heard a gasp. She and Jon sat up. She blinked, adjusting to the dim light.

"Cory!" she screamed, jumped up, and ran to him, slamming against him and squeezing him. Tears ran down her face. She held him as her dizzy spell passed.

"Corentin, thank God!" Jon said.

Cory trembled, took her by the arms, and leaned away. He took off his long jacket and wrapped it around her. Kat looked into his tense face. Her insides went from soaring joy to the heaviness of fear. Something was terribly wrong. Surely he knew she was happy to see him. Was he happy to see her?

Guards walked in behind Cory.

"Take him outside," Cory said, flatly.

Two of the guards seized Jon by the arms.

"What are you doing?" Kat asked.

"And shoot him on my command."

She gasped as they pushed Jon out of the hut.

"Please, Corentin!" Jon yelled.

Cory strode out, and Kat followed, her eyes adjusting to the bright light.

Kat took Cory by the arms. "Oh, my love! Cory, I *love* you! Please, hear me out. You promised me you'd always hear me out." She clasped her hands together and dropped to her knees before him in supplication.

The guards shoved Jon against a tree and lowered their guns, pointing at his chest. They watched Cory.

Cory held up his hand. "Wait."

They nodded.

Cory turned to Kat, tears in his eyes. "He kidnapped you! Se... seduced you while you were vulnerable, my poor wife. You...were sleeping in his arms, the way you sleep in mine, but this is not your fault. He...must..." He looked down before gazing at her again with tragic eyes. "...pay, then you and I, we can seek marriage counseling. However long it takes. I'll do whatever it takes to win back your exclusive—"

She sprang to her feet shaking her head. "No marriage counseling."

"*Please*...I know he played with your mind, drew you closer to him with manipulation, but—"

"We don't need it because I'm in love with you—only you—and am so grateful to see you. Are you...upset with me?"

"No. You were his victim."

She shook her head again. "No. When he held me as we slept, it was not the same as it is with you. In fact, it was *vastly* different. I hold you for love, for life. He held me to keep me from freezing, and he did not take me. Someone abducted both of us and put us here for whatever reason."

"Corentin, whoever kidnapped *us* wrote in a tree trunk that you were dead," Jon said. "I swear it to you, brother."

Cory turned his fiery gaze upon Jon. "And you saw your opportunity to *comfort* my wife? Is that what you're saying?"

Kat wrinkled his sleeve between her fingers. "No, sweetheart! I'd need a lot longer than that to mourn you! I wanted to die! I was crying and freezing in there. The fire went out. Jon only lay next to me for warmth, I swear it. He was a gentleman."

Cory's eyes sparkled. "I wish I could believe you, but you looked manipulated, seduced...lying there in his arms. Sweetheart, I don't blame *you*."

"You're a good husband. A damn fine one. Now please, be yourself further and be a good brother."

Suddenly, an old man in a wheelchair approached from the distance. Cory gasped and stumbled back, becoming ghost white.

Jon narrowed his brow; then his eyes went wide. The man stopped a few feet away. He said something Kat didn't understand. The guards bowed.

Cory glanced at Kat then back at the old man, trembling. "In English, please...Father."

The old man said something else in his language.

Cory snapped at him in the same language. Kat turned her gaze from the old man to Cory.

"Fine," Cory's father said. "Whatever." He sneered.

"Father," Jon said, curling his lip in disgust.

"I..." the old king gasped. "...suppose you want an explanation."

"Please," Cory said.

"I'm dying, Corentin."

"But you...died years ago."

"Obviously not."

"I don't understand."

"After that criminal servant poisoned me, I woke up in a small village, in another country, not knowing who I was, and permanently crippled from that damn neuro something or other drug I was given. The drug should have killed me. It didn't.

"Then recently, the old hag who had fed me all these years told me the truth. She had worked in the morgue. Everyone thought I was dead. She was alone, getting ready to do an autopsy. She detected a faint sign of life and saw a chance to win over a man she'd always lusted for. She stole me out of there, filling out her report for cause of death as poisoning. She later reported she took the presumption of burying me and wouldn't tell others where."

"She was fired and fled the country," Cory muttered.

"She took me away and cared for me. Later I woke up, confused. After years, I was diagnosed...and given three months to live. That was five months ago." He gasped for a breath, holding his chest and wincing as if it hurt. "She had given me a drug to erase my memory, but very recently in a flash of compassion, she administered one returning it, admitting what she had done. I then immediately set upon my goals."

"What do you want?" Cory asked.

He looked at the guards nearest Jon. "I remember you two. You worked for me."

Both nodded.

"You will lower your weapons aimed at the prince. Someone in my line needs to be king. In a moment, you will execute Corentin, on my command." He winced in pain again.

They bowed but stole nervous glances to each other, lowering their guns.

Kat turned and stood in front of Cory, arms out now. "No! You'll have to kill me to get to him!"

Cory took her firmly by the arms and set her behind him. She tried to go in front of him again, but he was stronger. "Katarina! If you love me, you will not put me through this again!"

"All right!" She wrapped her arms around his waist from behind, pressing close. "If they shoot you," she said, "it will go through me too. I can't live without you."

He tried to shake her loose, but she had him in a death grip.

"I won't stand for it, Father!" Jon shouted. "Leave Corentin alone! If you kill him, I'll defy you and become a monk. The crown can go to the devil."

Cory tossed a surprised look at Jon.

His father sneered. "You'll have no choice, son."

"Then imprison me for defying you," Jon said. "I will not reward you for harming my brother."

"Jon," Cory said sadly. He turned and looked at the old king. "I... deserve to know. Tell me."

"You don't deserve shit, but when I found out your mother gave birth to a child that wasn't mine, that Goran—"

"You found out?" Jon asked.

"She was raped!" Cory said.

"Irrelevant." The old man lowered his head, grasping his chest. He looked at Cory with hatred. "I had that *visitor* shoot her. Called him to the palace seconds after my servant reported the news of your mother's treachery. He walked in with my blessing. How else do you think he got a gun past my guards? He pretended to aim at me. Damn, your mother was predictable. I knew she'd jump in front of me. Stupid woman."

Cory lurched and lifted him by his lapels.

"Calm down. I'm...on death's door." He coughed.

Cory dropped him. Tears streamed down Kat's cheeks.

"You're behind all this," Cory said.

"Yes."

"Why?"

"I hate you. My wife loved you more than she ever loved me."

"Mother tried her level best to be a good wife to you. Your standards were unreachable. As for me, she was just being the best mother she could be. She was kind and attentive, and you wanted her strict attention. You wanted her to ignore her children and serve your every need."

"Nevertheless, she loved you more than me."

"You beat me numerous times as a reminder."

"She loved you even more than she did your brother or that bastard Goran she pushed into this world."

"She did not love me more than my brothers! You didn't beat Jaromír the way you did me or a tenth as often or Goran at all. Mother's heart reached out to me in a motherly way, you sick bastard."

"Enough! You were always her favorite. She burned with pride over your...*heroism,* she said. She informed me you'd make a better king than me or Goran, something about your temperament."

"Compassion!" Kat said.

The old man scoffed. "Weakness." He looked at Cory. "You disgusted me. I had to smack you around."

"Weak, Father?" Cory said, wretchedly.

"Whenever a pathetic palace pet got injured, and Goran prepared to kill it—" His breath caught.

"Viciously!" Jon said.

His father sneered. "Corentin would rescue it, hide it, and nurse it like a woman."

"He saved many animals that didn't have to die!" Jon added.

"Then," his father continued in disgusted tones, "it carried over to people. I'd try to dismiss servants who were injured or sick and could no longer fulfill their duties."

"You," Cory began dejectedly, "would put whole families on the street. I'd have had them treated by a doctor and given time to recover or given them a pension for service well done."

"Paid! I got sick and tired of you nagging. A child, telling me what to do!" He shoved his finger Cory's way. "Then giving them food to take with them, behind my back! Weak and disgusting. You were a traitor to defy your king." He grasped the sides of his wheelchair in pain.

"I wished I'd had the guts to stand up for him." Jon turned to Cory. "I'm sorry I did nothing."

"You were young."

"Only a year younger than Cory," Kat said to Jon. She pressed her cheek against Cory's back briefly. "You're heroic."

Cory's father gave her an ugly smile. He looked at Cory. "That servant poisoned me before I could arrange Goran the bastard's *accident*, so he escaped unpunished. When I found out recently who I am and why I'd been poisoned—for your sake—I knew I'd make you suffer something worse than death. I agonized in that village for years, and I wanted to see you suffer for what moments I had left to me. How else but through your beloved, cheating wife. It's embarrassing that all of Europe knows you're whipped!"

Cory trembled. "If being whipped…" he hissed in anger, "… means being so happy and so grateful for being with the woman who does that to me, then *hallelujah*! I'm one of the lucky ones!"

"I'd never cheat on him!" Kat yelled. "And I'm the one who's… under *his* spell. I'd do anything for him." She swung around, looking into Cory's face. She brought a hand to his cheek. "Believe me, my love. There's nothing romantic between Jon and me."

"Believe her, Corentin! On my honor. I am your servant. I have only respected you both."

Cory tipped his head toward Jon and said, "I do. I'm sorry I didn't moments before. A...reaction that had been festering. You'd never do that to me." He looked back at Kat.

"Never," she uttered.

"I have recalled my senses." He glanced at Jon again. "You know what she means to me. Forgive me for doubting you."

The old man spoke again. "Well, you certainly suffered after she was kidnapped. All I had to do was find a couple of servants still loyal to me and swear them to secrecy. They arranged everything."

"A guard..." Cory began tensely, "...came into my office with a weapon. He hit me with a dart that knocked me out. I awoke, and my rings were gone. My wedding ring gone."

His father smirked. "If I weren't so close to death, I'd have reclaimed my throne and publicly executed you. Being this sick, I don't have the strength to go through all that public mumbo jumbo."

Cory's shoulders lowered.

Kat reached for and clasped his hand. She looked the old king in the eyes. "You're insane."

"He is," Cory said under his breath.

She continued, in a strained voice. "The people wouldn't have stood for it. They'd have executed *you*! They love Cory. He's a great king and an even greater man."

"Shut up, American girl. You're too pretty to have a brain in your head."

Cory drew in a deep breath. "I don't care who you are. You will *not* speak to my wife that way."

"At least you chose someone *I'd* take to bed. I'd romp with her until—"

Cory lurched again.

"Guards, shoot the bastard," his father said in a strained voice.

Twenty-two

Cory went stiff. His father had just ordered his execution.

"Wait!" Jon held his hands up. "He's not moving, Corentin."

"Check his damn pulse."

Jon bowed and obeyed. "He's dead."

Cory looked at the guards.

They gazed at each other and then him. One spoke. "We see no bastards here, Majesty."

"You're the best king we or our ancestors ever had," his partner said, looking at Cory with respect.

"Yes," the first agreed.

Cory rubbed his face then fell to the ground. The guards went to assist him. He held up a hand. Kat curled up in his lap, and he kissed her head.

"Thanks for keeping your promise to hear me out," she said.

"Thanks for loving me."

"Thanks for believing me."

He squeezed her and turned to look at Jon. "Thanks for keeping her safe and *not* seducing her."

Two of Cory's guards stumbled forth from behind a patch of trees. Their clothing was torn, and their hair ruffled. They panted and looked at Cory, bowing.

One spoke. "Sire, while looking around the island as you commanded, we saw the old king's guards escorting him. We asked his intentions. He told us. Then his guards attacked us. While fighting, the old king wheeled away. We barely got away with our lives, unlike them, and I'm sure I speak for us both, we're deeply grateful you are unharmed."

"Thank you, men." Cory turned his focus to Kat.

She kissed him and pressed her ear over his heart. "You've saved me. Thank you. I was dying in that hut without you."

"I've been going crazy without you."

"How did you find me?"

"I spent half of our personal wealth in doing so, Katarina. Not that that matters now that I've found you. I would have given my last dime."

Jon gazed at him. "Thank you. I'll pay you back, since I'm now richer than you are."

"Keep your money. Damn mask is on vacation or something," he said as an afterthought.

"It told you nothing?" Kat asked.

He shook his head. "Asher's returning from Asia about now, Gunther from Australia, and Brendan from America. I called them off their searches as soon as I got the lead that sent me to this island. I had to pay one man alone almost five hundred million dollars—after I spent millions elsewhere sending people all over the planet searching for you—to give me the name of this island."

"How...did you find him?"

"He came to me wanting great wealth. And he told me—"

"You really thought I kidnapped her?" Jon asked.

Cory gazed at him. "You disappeared shortly after she did. In your room a maid found something interesting."

"What was it?"

"A ring engraved, *Katarina, I love you. Be mine –J.*"

Jon shook his head and scowled. "Father was a sick son-of-a-bitch."

"Twisted," Cory added. "The man I paid for information admitted that his boss was an immediate family member of mine. That's all I could get out of him."

"I'd think I did it too," Jon said.

"You called me gracious before, but Jon, that applies to you."

Jon smiled. "You would have stopped the guards from shooting me, even if Kat hadn't asked you?" He waited in seeming breathless anticipation for the answer.

Cory didn't move but finally nodded once. "I would have stopped them. I only wanted to scare you to teach you a lesson, but you would have rotted in prison."

"And I would have deserved to had I been guilty."

"Cory..."

Jon turned to Kat teasingly with a smile. "You didn't jump in front of me when guns were pointed at me."

Her cheeks heated. "No. Sorry."

"Don't be embarrassed, Kat," Jon said. "I'm not Cory."

Cory smiled. "Everyone knows you're better looking than me, hell, better looking than any man born in three decades, I'm sure. Father must have assumed it would be plausible for Katarina to betray me for you."

"He was wrong," Kat snapped.

He kissed her, and she snuggled closer to him. "Please, don't ever let me go."

"I'd die first."

"I wonder how long he's been here, watching Jon and me."

"Probably didn't think I'd find you, that I'd spend the rest of the short days he planned for me grieving over my *cheating* wife, making it look like Jon took you away."

"But I was kidnapped by your father's men. It's not like I ran away from you with Jon."

"It's not like my mother asked to be raped, yet he gave her the death penalty. In his eyes, the victim is the villain. The kidnapped woman is a cheating bitch."

Jon spoke. "I suppose he would have given us a way off this island as soon as he thought you suffered long enough and had you killed. He wanted me on the throne."

"Yes, and when I did find you, that suited his purposes as well. Or perhaps he told his man to tell me, so I'd find my wife in your arms." He glanced down.

She shivered with sadness. "Damn cold. That's probably why he chose this island. The nights are chilly, and there's little in the way of covering material."

"He wasn't stupid." Cory's voice carried the edge of death in it. Something in him had died over this ordeal.

She put her hand to his cheek. "Cory," she breathed out.

"When you look at me that way, wife, my soul lightens."

She pulled him into a deep kiss and cuddled against him again.

"You hold onto me as if for dear life." Cory dragged his fingers down her arm.

"I do. Is Bernadette...all right?"

"Yes."

"Thank God. And the others?"

"We'll talk about that on the plane." He stroked her hair. "Sweetheart, you're shaking. Why?"

"I don't want to lose you."

"No, never. You know, if I didn't love you so damn much, I'd insist that you give up music forever and just stay by my side."

She nuzzled his ear, whispering, "Heal me, love. With lots and lots of lovemaking."

"Until I drop dead. Thank you, sweetheart," he said.

"For what?"

"For giving me back life."

She closed her eyes.

"My wedding ring is missing."

"I have it in the hut. I slept with it under my leafy pillow every night."

He sighed in relief. "I can't wait to put it back on."

When Cory brought her home to the palace, she leaned against his side. They passed through the main corridor to a cheering, applauding crowd. He took her to their private chambers and stopped at the door. Cory told the guards that they weren't to be disturbed. They'd ring for food later.

Katarina was undressing near the bedroom's bathroom when Cory's phone rang. It was an unknown number.

He answered. "Hello?"

"Your father was so stupid, he didn't realize those men he had doing his dirty work were my men. He approached his old employees, swearing them to secrecy, but they approached me anyway."

George.

"I don't believe you."

"Believe me. Those men in your employ that did this—my men—actually weren't thrilled with your epic work in women's rights."

"Damn, of course, there would be some such assholes left. At least they got weeded out, died on that island, though it's too bad they had to *die.*"

"I was there. I got off watching Katarina and Prince Pipsqueak fucking like rabbits on the beach day and night. Ooh," he said gleefully.

Cory could hear him rubbing his hands together.

"You gave me nearly five hundred million dollars, which I can use to dream up some wonderful drama to star you in. I only had to give the guy one million, some petty criminal, to play his part. I can't wait for what happens next!" George hung up.

Cory dropped the phone from his shaking hand. He was at a loss, incapable of dealing with an evil of a higher magnitude than he had ever before known. He shoved the images of Katarina and Jon from his mind.

He and Katarina took a hot shower together, doing nothing but giving each other sad, tired kisses before going to bed. He pulled back the covers. She slipped under them, and he joined her, holding her close. She nestled against him and fell asleep in his arms.

~ * ~

Having passionate dreams, Katarina awoke to a dark room. Cory's slow, even breathing told her he was asleep. Filled with desire, she slid her hand down his side onto his thigh and up. Her lips parted in a smile when she made contact with his arousal. She kissed his neck, and he sighed her name.

"Mm, yes," he added.

She straddled him, lowering onto his erection. His soft moan brought a quickening to her stomach, and she rocked her hips, slowly at first. His hands came to her thighs then slid to her back. He arched up, and she rocked faster, her breaths filling the air.

"Katarina," he called out, shuddering.

She fell atop him, kissing his neck and face. His soft touch down her spine brought shivers coursing through her.

She rolled off him and fell asleep just as he tugged her close and held her possessively.

They slept late the next day. When she opened her eyes, he was lying awake, watching her.

"Sweetheart." He traced her jaw with his fingertips. "I missed you so much. It was pure hell."

Tears stung her eyes. She grasped his hand. "My heart ached for you. You're too thin, Cory. You've lost weight."

"So have you."

"I've been living off fruit, wild roots, and the occasional fish."

"Katarina..."

"Don't fret it, hon. It was okay. Your brother made the roots taste good by cooking them in a soup. Said he learned to do that stuff from your country's version of the boy scouts. It was fortunate I was trapped with an archaeologist, though. He knows a lot about how people of less technologically advanced cultures survived, and that came in handy."

He glanced down.

"You didn't eat much while I was gone, Cor. I'm disappointed."

He brought pain-filled eyes to hers.

She kissed him and sat up. "I expect you to eat better now."

He sat up. "You too. I instructed our chef to create deliciously fattening foods...with healthy side salads."

She swung her legs over the side of the bed. He didn't move.

"What is it?"

"You...were on that island alone with a man you find devastatingly attractive."

She drew back. "Not this again." A quick flash of irritation dashed through her, quickly crushed by the agony in his eyes.

"You swear you and Jon didn't...not even once? I'll forgive you. Just, please, I have to know."

"Look into my eyes, husband. Not even once."

His shoulders dropped. "But he saved your life. Surely you were grateful. If even half as grateful as me—"

"The only man I've ever slept with is you. The only man I will ever sleep with is you." She pulled him into an embrace. "Don't you understand? I must have driven him crazy talking about how much I missed you."

"You did that?"

"Day and night, but the thing is, he constantly talked about you too. Your brother loves you. You and I have something precious and irreplaceable. It's not possible for me to ever find love this profound with anyone but you."

A sad smile tipped his lips. "But how long would you have waited, after believing me dead?"

"To go to him in that way?"

"Yes."

She paused before answering. "If at all, years."

He looked down.

"Oh, hon, I probably would have died young."

"No."

"Yes. I love *you*, not him. Please, believe that...in me, in us."

"I do."

"Thank you. I don't want your brother. He's nothing next to you. I thought that even when you were an impoverished writer."

"Yes, but what about when you looked at him at that party before we were together and told me that your babies would be gorgeous?"

"You know I was in love with you at that time, but I was terrified to tell you or even admit it to myself. In denial, I made that comment. Yeah, the guy is good-looking, but so are you, and—"

He scoffed.

"I wanted you, not him, even then. You and I have a beautiful connection based on enduring love and respect."

"That's true."

"I made that stupid comment, but at that party, did I flirt with him, or did I stay by your side?"

"Good point."

"And when I proposed marriage? Was I dreaming of your brother?"

"No. Greatest moment of my life. Until the second we were pronounced husband and wife." He sighed happily.

"Remember that." She paused. "You didn't...find comfort in your grief when I was gone...in the arms of another—"

"Fuck no!" He seized her hands. "I knew you were still alive, and I will never cheat on you! And even if you had been dead, I would not have wanted another woman."

"Thank God." She paused again. "Your greatness as a man enhances your handsome looks a hundred-fold. When I told you once that Jon was average, I meant it. He's a good guy, but he's nothing special. You would have changed the world for the better even without your crown."

His gaze darkened.

"Besides," she said and swept a strand of hair from his brow, "your eyes are bluer than his and have a depth in them his can't match. Your lips..." She dragged her finger across them and nudged her cheek against his. "...are so much more welcoming. You're passionate and hot. He's sometimes standoffish and not the romantic type, I hear. I like the romantic type."

"Me? Romantic?"

She kissed him. "Yes. Remember dancing in the park?"

"To the music of those street musicians? I pictured you in a wedding gown as I swept you around in my arms."

"Cory…" She pushed him back onto the mattress, kissing him.

Later, they left the room to eat breakfast. Cory wanted to speak to the cook. To Kat's surprise, Bernadette rushed into the kitchen. She dashed to Kat and embraced her.

"I'm so sorry."

"It's not your fault, Kat."

"I'm glad you're okay. I feel like I'm responsible. They were after me, and you got caught in the crossfire."

"Please, don't blame yourself, but you can ease my trauma."

"How? Anything."

"I'm absolutely desperate to get back to work. Immediately. We must get our band out there again."

"Bernadette, she just got home."

She looked at Cory. "I know, I'm sorry, but Kat said anything."

"I did. All right, I'll pack."

Cory took Kat's arm. "What? No. It's too soon!"

Kat faced him. "Hon, she almost died…because of me. I have to go."

"No!"

Bernadette looked at him with regret. "I am deeply grateful for all you did for me and my family, but…I can't explain. I just have to go out there and do this. I'm anxious."

"No, Bernadette, not yet."

"I'm sorry, sweetheart, yes," Katarina said to him.

"Do you want this?"

She nodded.

"But I thought you wanted to be with me."

She touched his arm. "I do. So much, but… We'll be together a lot after a tour."

"You're sure, really?"

"Yes."

He sighed loudly and stepped back, frowning. "Fine." He strode out of the kitchen.

~ * ~

Once in his office, Cory's personal line rang. "Hello?"

"Oh, that delicious wife of yours. Damn, she's too gorgeous for words."

George. Cory cringed.

"She's leaving you again, so soon, isn't she?"

"How did you know that?" *Shit.*

"You just told me. I'd want to get away from you too, and I'm sure brother Pipsqueak, that sissy-ass, pretty boy coward, is hoping to bag her again while she's on tour."

"Shut. Up." Anger shot through Cory's veins.

"Someday, I'm going to have a taste of that exquisite woman, I promise you."

"Meet me man to man, Goran."

George laughed. "Naw, I'll just wage war on your ass as soon as Old Unc dies."

"Why involve the people, you sick fuck?"

"To make you suffer."

Cory clenched the phone. George hung up.

Katarina was just going to have to put up with having so much security, it would probably be embarrassing. She'd have no choice in the matter.

Twenty-three

That night, Cory picked at his food, thinking of his wife. Why did she want to leave him so soon? Fears he had shoved deep down spiraled up.

"I'm glad you put extra security detail on her," Jon said. "I know you didn't want to let her go, were adamantly against it, but you love her."

"Is it that obvious?" Cory said sarcastically.

"We're all going to miss her," Jon responded quietly.

Cory put down his fork and looked at his brother. He propped his elbows on the table and clasped his hands together. "Indeed."

"I got to know her even better, Corentin. She's a wonderful person, not just stunningly beautiful."

Cory's brow rose. "You think so?"

"Yes."

"You...saved her life, and for that, you have my undying gratitude. I could *never* convey—"

"Happy to do it." Jon smiled.

"I owe you big. A favor. Anytime you want to cash in, just ask. But no favor could possibly repay you."

"It's not necessary."

"It is. However," Cory paused and slid a hand through his hair.

"What is it?"

He studied him, haunted. "Her...extensive bodily scars didn't bother you?"

Jon shifted. "They don't diminish her beauty, but I had no right to see those. However, our clothes became ragged. Her scars became evident. Your poor wife, to have suffered such physical injury as a child."

"You're right. You should not have seen those scars. I consider those intimate."

"They'd be visible with shorts, a miniskirt, or a half shirt."

Cory slammed his hand down. Jon jumped.

"When have you ever seen Katarina wear any of those things without dark stockings or an undershirt? She used to cover them up for herself, out of shame, but when I made it clear that I thought they were beautiful because—"

Jon smiled. "Yes, a reflection of her inner beauty—"

"When my thoughts upon the matter became clear," he interrupted tersely.

Jon stiffened his back.

"She covered them up so that only I could see them in the privacy of our own bedroom. Do you understand me?"

"I, uh—"

"Our best friends don't even know about them. Only two men knew of them before that island—me, and her father. *He* has never even seen those scars—only the original injuries. *I* have only ever seen them. And now you."

"I'm sorry. But it was not my fault."

"You couldn't have...found something, anything, on that island to preserve her modesty when she started to show places of her body that she had always covered up?"

"I'm sorry, Corentin."

He sighed loudly. "I fell in love with her the day I first saw her scars by accident when that older girl hurt her. I turned a corner and saw. I was shocked by Katarina's vulnerability as tears streamed down her face, as she gathered the torn edges of her clothes, her strength shining through as she battled her agony with courage, her..." he dropped off. "Love hit me *hard*. I had never known it before that."

"How did you come to see that scene?"

"On the school yard, moments after a bully had attacked her. What I saw seized me. Katarina and I became connected after that in a way I can't explain."

"You married a great woman. She told me how she almost died as a child, trying to save her sister, how badly she got cut up in that broken window while escaping the fire with her dead sister in her arms."

Cory looked at his brother, searching for more behind the words. "Just how great of a woman is she, Jon?"

"What do you mean by that?"

"What do you think I mean?"

Jon shrugged. "I'm not sure. I was paying you a compliment. That's all."

"Really now?"

"I'm not sure you understand. Your tone—"

Cory let his hand drop, rattling the dishes. "I will use whatever tone I wish with you."

"Er...y...yes, of course, My King."

Cory pushed his chair out with a screech, stood up, and strode out of the room.

Relations with his brother grew more strained over the oncoming weeks. Jon became formal with him, and Cory didn't care. Nightmares plagued him. He dreamt many a night of his wife lying beneath his brother on that island. Had Jon fallen in love with her, struck just as hard as *he* had been when he saw a physical manifestation of her true heroic nature in her scars?

Cory's secretary entered his office and handed him a paper.

"What's this?"

The secretary offered a curt bow. "Sire, a rather attractive woman..." He tugged at his collar, uncomfortable.

"Just say what's on your mind."

"You are, Majesty, if you don't mind me saying, tense since the queen has been away. Perhaps, this young lady—"

Cory tore up the paper, looking his secretary in the eyes. "I would not dishonor my wife by engaging in meaningless dalliances."

He bowed again. "Of course. My apologies."

"In the future, when a woman gives you a private note to hand to me, and you sense her intentions to be like this one, tear the note up. I'm not interested in betraying my lovely wife."

~ * ~

Three months after Katarina left, mumbling and grumbling, Cory swept a stack of papers off his desk, got up, and paced, something he had done a lot of since going through the trauma of Katarina's disappearance and then having her leave the day after he got her back. He hadn't been able to tear away from work to visit her. George made things worse. He sent Cory threats of inevitable war, and he most recently sent Cory a clock, telling him the countdown had begun; Uncle Lothar was sicker. Cory's nerves were raw. Asher had just left him to go to work. He had been there as a friend, trying to calm Cory's obsessive thoughts. Gunther had tried as well, several times, without success. Even Brendan, with his medical knowledge, couldn't help. Thoughts of Katarina raced through Cory's mind. Had Jon been able to look him in the face all this time out of fear for his life?

The floor vibrated, and Cory stopped pacing. Was that a bass line? He looked at the door. Another melodic line in a low register filtered through the floor, and then came a fast, jazzy-metal bass line. He tore open the doors.

Katarina greeted him with a huge open-mouthed smile. "Hi, hon!"

"You're back!" He strode to her and chuckled, hugging her over her bass guitar and kissing her. He leaned back and helped her off with it. "Damn, it's good to see you."

The guards were smiling.

She handed her bass to the liveried guard on the left. "Would you mind please putting this in our practice room, Mr. Stephanov?"

"Not at all, My Queen!" he said cheerfully.

"Thank you!"

His face turned serious, and he looked at Cory. "Majesty, you don't mind if I leave my post a moment?"

Cory smiled. "Please, if you will, honor Her Majesty's wishes."

Mr. Stephanov bowed, touching his chest, and picked up Katarina's amplifier.

Katarina faced Cory. "Thought that bass playing would grab your attention."

"Sweetheart, come into my office." He took her hand and pulled her inside.

She kissed him and shut the door behind them. "Let's sit down. I have something important to tell you and flew back to do so."

"I was dying to see you. I love how you surprise me."

She took a seat on a sofa, and he joined her, taking her hand in his.

She gazed into his eyes. "How do I...tell you this?"

"Tell me...what?"

"It's serious." She gazed down.

He braced himself. "You're scaring me."

"Your life is about to change."

He sucked in a breath. "Go on."

"You didn't use your gift. You never checked for this."

"My...gift? You mean to check for...your death? Don't. You're not going to die anytime soon!"

"Not that gift." She looked into his eyes, took his hand, and placed it on her belly. "The other, the one you almost never use."

He gasped. "You're...going to have a...baby."

Just then, there was a knock.

"Yes?" Cory said.

The door opened, and Jon swept into the room. "Corentin, let's talk." He looked at Katarina's and Cory's hands on her belly and shut the door. A smile lit up his face. "My Queen, you're—?"

She smiled. "Yes."

"That's wonderful!" Jon exclaimed.

She and Cory stood. "I'm three months along, as you could guess."

Cory gazed at Jon. Jon's expression showed true happiness. Sudden dread overcame Cory. His stomach dropped and pushed acid up his throat. *No...* Was Jon now going to take his wife from him?

Cory stumbled back, sick. Katarina took his arm, and Jon came to his side.

"Sweetheart?" Katarina squeezed Cory's arm.

"Are you all right?" Jon touched his shoulder.

Cory tore away from Jon and glared at him.

Katarina lowered her hand, slowly. "What's wrong?"

Cory's heart raced. "How do I..."

"Just say what's on your mind," Katarina said.

Cory paced then stopped, letting out a harsh breath. "Imagine for a moment that there's a woman more beautiful than you. I know it's a stretch but play along."

She crossed her arms over her chest and raised a brow. "What's this about?"

"Please, humor me."

"Fine," she said.

"Imagine that I'm friends with her, that I respect her and like her, even have platonic love for her."

"Okay."

"Picture that she and I are alone on an island for months."

"Cory—"

"In this scenario, imagine that we get news of your death. I'm devastated because I don't have my gift and don't know otherwise."

She frowned and lowered her arms.

"It's cold there at night. The woman and I sleep in the same bed for warmth. She holds me in my agony, comforts me in my loss. We share body heat. Do you think it's possible that our lips might meet in a kiss?"

"Cory, we never—"

"Is it possible?"

"Sure, but—"

"And that kissing leads to more. She's beautiful. I respect her. I like her. I'm a widower… I'm in desperate need of comfort, and… things happen."

"Cor—"

"Then, picture that to my shock, you appear, alive and well. I'm overjoyed. But…now I have this…thing on my conscience. I'm afraid to lose you. I'm afraid you might explode and lash out at the woman, maybe even hurt her, so I lie, not out of dishonor and a dishonest nature, but to protect another, perhaps from being executed. Could this happen? Might I lie not because I'm not trustworthy but rather because I think I'm saving the life of another human being? In this situation I would live with the lie, bury it deep, let it eat at me, haunt me, hurt me, ruin my peace…because I'm…a deeply unselfish, good and loving person, who despite this lie deserves a person's undying trust and devotion?"

She lowered her shoulders and strode to him, "We never even kissed, as I've said."

"Swear to me. Swear it to high heaven, but I won't jail or hurt Jon if…something happened back on that island. You and I can get therapy to fix anything broken. On my sacred honor, due to the extreme circumstances. I'll even put it in writing if you wish. If you can't swear it, and the child…is not mine…I'll still treat him or her well, with love, give the baby a good life—raise him or her if you want me to play the part of dad—if Jon doesn't stand in my way—but not adopt the child. It must be my child, our child that I prepare for the throne. Your second child if need be. Just…please, for the love of God, tell me everything that happened, and if it's what I fear, convince me that it's over between you two. Please, end my torment. If you don't think I'm worthy, know that the punishment you dole out will be a life sentence. This is not the kind of love a man gets over." His shoulders slumped.

She pulled away and stepped back, giving Jon a quick smile before looking at Cory. "Okay. After what happened to your mother, I get it, though thank God you know your brother could never *rape* me." She glanced at Jon. "Well, Jon, it's time for the moment of truth."

Jon paled.

Ice slithered through Cory's veins. "Oh, God. Sorry." He drew a deep breath and stilled his trembling hands. "I promise. There will be no repercussions. Do not fear to tell me. I just...long to sleep at night again. Get out the truth. I'll get intense therapy. I've got to have peace."

She looked at Cory. "He is wealthy, and you know how important that is to me." She rolled her eyes. "A royal prince, and more handsome than you, you've always said—I don't see it."

"You're the only woman ever to think me the better looking of the two, or at least to say it. Thank you."

She nodded and touched her chest. "Here goes nothing. It was a rather nice day."

"Go...on." His breathing became shallow.

"We were walking near a short cliff, and I slipped. He tried to catch me, but we tumbled. He landed on top of me, facing me."

"And?" Cory croaked out.

"He had an automatic male response. I felt it through our clothes."

"You felt...*that*?"

She sighed. "I didn't touch him, Cor."

"Go on."

"He leaned to kiss me but stopped short."

Cory closed his eyes. "And?"

"Cor, look at me. Jon rolled off me swearing and begging forgiveness because I didn't want the kiss, and he didn't really want to give it. We started talking about you. I cried. Jon said he'd never betray you, and he was grievously sorry for getting caught up in the moment for even half a second."

Cory glanced at Jon.

"I'm sorry," Jon said.

"I understand," Cory responded. He looked back at Katarina.

"The circumstances...led to nothing. *I swear it,*" she said. "Not at any time before or after."

"Was that before you thought me dead?"

"Yes. Afterward, I was suicidal."

Cory gasped. "Sweetheart..."

She expelled a small sigh. "Jon tried to help me with kind words, said it was what you would want."

Cory glanced at him. "It is." He paused. "Thank you," he said to him.

Jon nodded.

Cory returned his gaze to Katarina.

"I thought my life was meaningless. Jon told me I inspired the women of your country."

"You do."

"He wanted me to continue doing so. I told him my life was over. I was trying to decide if I was going to jump off a cliff or stab myself with a—"

Cory shook his head. "Katarina, no..."

"Jon told me I could do things in your honor, as a queen. He'd make me one again since I hadn't officially accepted the honor of being your co-leader."

"What?" Cory's pitch rose.

Katarina touched his arm. "He wasn't hitting on me. He suggested waiting years for...certain things, while we mourned you. He was unromantic about it and was concerned for my welfare and honoring your memory and what he thought you'd want—me looked after and having a fulfilling, meaningful life. I suspect he knew about my suicidal thoughts and was trying to save me."

"I see. Did you...accept his offer?"

"No."

He let out a breath he'd been holding.

"He's not...exciting enough for me. *You,* on the other hand... I get a rush just looking at you. He's saved one person—me—and I'm grateful for that, but you've saved many, and at risk to yourself. Ever since I've known you, you've stuck your neck out for others and have suffered injury doing so. You are a *hero.*" Her truth filled the room.

"In that shitty neighborhood we used to live in back in America, there was the time you got broken ribs saving a woman from rape—"

"You know about *that*?" Cory's eyes widened. "I'm going kill Asher for telling you."

She chuckled. "No, I overheard you talking on your deck. I could go on, if you have all day. The man you saved who was being mugged for his rent money, people whose lives you improved by your intervention, not to mention the millions of lives you bettered here with your new policies, freedoms and laws—"

"Sweetheart—"

"Why the hell would I set myself up for such disappointment after experiencing being *your* lover? I mean, damn. You're fantastic."

He grinned. "You inspire me."

"And why would I go to another man when I'm so in love with you that I tried to jump in front of a gun to save you?"

"Perhaps you thought you would never see me again."

"Cor, before we thought you dead, I swore I'd find a way to get back to you. After we thought you dead, I pondered the route I would take to join you." Tears sparkled in her brown eyes.

He dashed to her and held her close. "Thank God."

"You believe me."

"Yes."

"For good this time."

"Yes. Er...not thank God you were pondering suicide—"

"I get it."

"I am going to sleep well tonight!" He chuckled.

"Good."

"My wife loves me! Only me!"

"You big idiot. Of course! God knows why."

He grasped her hands, looking at her with joy. "God does know why. I don't deserve you." He pulled her close and pressed his forehead to hers then moved to whisper into her ear. "*Nothing* means more to me than you do." He leaned away.

She glanced down briefly then gave him a penetrating look. "Maybe we do have a marriage based on love and trust."

He nuzzled her. "We do. Forgive me. I am so sorry."

"You're my best friend. I forgive you."

"Thank you. You have lifted the biggest burden of my life from me."

She kissed him.

Jon looked at Cory with respect. "You're so much better than Father was. He never would have heard Mother out."

"Thank you," Cory said. "I'm sincerely sorry."

"I accept your apology," Jon said.

"I appreciate that." He turned toward Katarina. "By the way, Katarina, you don't have to officially accept anything at this point. You are my co-leader. If I die, you lead. I recently made it law. Every future monarch will have the same choice. They will decide, based on the worthiness of their partner."

They gasped.

"What happens if she gives me an opposing request to yours?" Jon asked.

"Obey your queen. She won't make it a habit to request the opposite that I do." He said that to mean he knew his wife and he agreed on most things, and she was not trying to have a power contest with him, as he was not with her.

Katarina smiled to confirm this knowledge.

Jon left.

"Thank you for your trust in me, Cor. I know we're here to improve their lives. That's all."

He tipped his head and gave her a smile. "I let my emotions get the best of me. You pointed out during our honeymoon that that was something I should be aware of, and I do know better. Thank you for keeping me on track."

"That's what I'm here for."

He dragged his fingertips down her jaw. "How did winning your such exquisite love happen?"

She shivered. "We've had a connection for many long years."

"You had a connection with Asher, Gunther, and Brendan as well. You could have fallen for one of them."

She shook her head. "No, you idiot. It wasn't the same. I love you so much I put up with your immense crap." She took his hand, and they sat on his couch.

He kissed her hand. "I promise to make it up to you. Trust me, on my honor as your husband and as king of this country. You make me a better leader."

She leaned away and slid her fingers under his hair, drawing him into a sensual kiss. She leaned against his ear. "I'm *so* in love with you, you insecure—"

He twisted his head to look into her face. "Insecure? I make decisions daily that affect millions of people, and I do it with confidence."

"And you do it with love. I meant with us."

"Because I'd rather lose my crown than you. I did lose you before. I never want to suffer that way again."

She pulled him into a hug.

"I'd better go talk to Jon and apologize again, tell him that I'll make it up to him. He's wealthier than me now, but maybe I could build him something...perhaps something for his archaeological work? What would make him really happy?"

"Do it later. I just want to be with you."

"I'm *so* happy we're having a baby." He tipped her chin up. "This is, my God, the greatest thing to have ever happened to me. I'm *beyond* thrilled."

She swallowed visibly.

"Aren't you happy too?"

"I'm awestruck to be carrying your child, hon, but I'm in the middle of a tour."

"Cancel your tour."

"No."

"The band can hire someone to fill in for you then."

"No!"

"Yes, my love."

"No."

"Yes, or postpone it."

"I must do this while my baby is still inside of me. After his or her birth, I'll be home for a while. Who knows when I'll be able to go out again with the band."

He grasped her arms. "You're not going back pregnant. It's too risky."

"Many women work until their water breaks. I'll be careful, I promise. I'm going."

"No."

"On my honor, I will take it easy. I'll baby myself. You have nothing to worry about."

"Are you kidding me?"

"No. Your guards have never been more diligent. The girls in my band will make sure I don't overdo anything. I won't load heavy equipment. I'll even put up with you hiring a servant to come along and pamper me, if it will ease your mind."

"You're not going back."

She tried to pull away from him, but he held on.

"Is that an order from my husband or my king?"

"It's a strong request from the man who loves you."

Twenty-four

Katarina ripped from Cory's grasp, and this time he let her go. "Don't be a sexist tyrant."

"You know I'm neither! I brought women's rights to this country!"

She sighed and nodded. "I do know that. Sorry."

"I love you, sweetheart. Please, don't do this."

The desperation in his eyes tugged at her heart. "I have signed contracts."

"I'll buy them out."

"No!"

"The matter is settled." His voice came out shaky.

She jumped to her feet, and so did he.

"Are you going to hold me as a prisoner here, against my will?"

"What?"

"Well, are you? Keep me behind locked doors?"

He frowned. "I'd never treat you that way!"

"You'd have to in order to keep me from going, but if you do, our marriage will suffer deeply."

"Is it so bad here...with me?"

"No! I love it here. I love *you*! I just need a few months. Then I'll be back."

"You force my hand then. I'll make some calls, and not a single club manager in Europe will let your band through the doors!"

"What?" she cried.

"Try me."

"You'd do that to me?"

"I'm desperate. I'll build you a fine studio here like I always planned. Hell, I'll build you a record company and hire the best advertising and promotions company out there. Tour our fine city. Travel to the neighboring cities. Just stay here in the country you and I preside over while you carry our child! You can pick up the international route again in a couple of years. Bring a nanny on the road with you and our little one. Or I'll care for our baby at home. Or, we can split up the time or—"

"We must finish this tour. Now. It's important to the girls, and me, but if you make those phone calls, you'll force *my* hand. I'll go back to America and do shows with my band there!"

"You're queen of Carasivia! You belong *here*!"

"I have to go."

He stumbled back. "You're...leaving me? After all this?"

"No, but we'll have a long-distance relationship."

"We have one now," he muttered sadly.

"I'll call every night from America if you'll still allow me access to our bank account even after defying you. I might not make enough for phone services otherwise."

He took her hand. "Don't leave me."

"I'm not *leaving* you. I'll be faithful as always, honey."

He sucked in sharply. "Of course, you'd have full...access to our account in America. I don't have the power to take that from you, but please, reconsider goin—"

She grasped his arms. "I love you! I'll come back before the birth."

"*Please*, don't go. Remember how I once told you that when you carried our children, I'd take thousands of pictures?"

"Yes?"

"It's important to me to be there as you grow. I *must* be with you. You don't understand what this means to me."

"You have a country to run. You can't come with me."

He rubbed his face. "Hold on. I have an idea that I think we can both live with."

"What is it?"

"Wait here?"

"Where are you going? Wait for how long?"

"Ten minutes. I have to talk to my council of ministers, and they're around now. Will you wait?"

She nodded stiffly. "Ten minutes."

He kissed her quickly and dashed out the door.

Eleven minutes later, glancing at his watch, he came tearing into the office. She lowered her arms from across her chest. "Well?"

He encircled her waist with his arms and kissed her nose. "You're going back on a fully-funded tour. In Europe."

"Thank you. You do love me. But...I know there's a but."

"I'm going with you, and I'm going to take thousands of pictures of my pregnant and growing wife. And I'm going to baby and protect you."

She grinned. "You come from such an old-fashioned culture. It's charming. Protection. I'm a woman of the twenty-first century. Wanna join me there?"

"I'm a realist. You're a queen. You're beautiful. You're a musician. You're pregnant. You were kidnapped, could've been killed. Jeez, after what you went through, and what I went through...You. Need. Protection. Even independent American women realize that."

"My band has bodyguards, and you have a country to run. I'll send you pictures of me."

"I will run the country, and I will take those treasured pictures myself. Video conferencing. Online. Documents will be faxed to me or emailed. I'll sign them and send them back. Jon will keep his eye on things here. I'll fly back for an hour if I have to. I wish I would have thought of that when you were missing. I'd have found you sooner.

Now I'll get my thousands of pictures of you carrying our firstborn. I will *be there.* I will feel when he or she is kicking your belly. I will place my hand on your belly and kindly ask our child to get off your bladder. I will rub your aching feet and back. I will fill you up with whatever weird foods you crave. I'll remind you of how beautiful you are. I will tie your shoes when you no longer can. I will help you get out of chairs when you need the help—" He sighed. "Fatherhood. Finally. Finally." He glowed. "I'm so excited I could blow. *You* are having my baby!"

She pulled him close. "Breathe, Cory! Take a breath!"

He chuckled. "Are you as excited as me?"

"You make me even more excited about parenthood than I already was," she said. "Thank you."

"No," he said, "thank *you.*"

"You'll have to disguise yourself. You'll draw too much attention otherwise. As it is, my band draws much attention, luring people who want to see a queen on stage. Good thing the girls get a kick out of that, or I'd have been booted out by now."

"I'll be your new roadie. Should I dye my hair red? Make my eyes brown or green? Should I attempt an accent?"

"How will you explain your absence here?"

"I'll say I'm travelling on diplomatic business. It's only for a few months. The people will put up with Jon as Regent if they know I'll be back soon, but he won't be truly leading. I'll talk with him every day. He has no longing to be the decision maker. He'll respect my wishes."

"Okay," she said.

"Hon, once you're big, how will you handle your bass?"

"Duh, the same as if I weighed two hundred pounds."

"You'll be awkward. Your balance will be off."

"I'll manage."

"You'll be full term when your contracts are fulfilled?"

"Yes. The last gigs are here."

"Good, because our child should be born here."

"Yes."

He hugged her from behind and rubbed her belly.

"You sure you want to waddle on stage and play when you're that size?"

"Knock it off. I'll sit and play then. I'll wear loose clothes and not go under the spotlights. I'll ask to be shadowed. I'll take naps and rest when I need to."

"If it's what you truly want…" He swept her hair aside and kissed her neck. She shivered.

"God, you're beautiful."

"Not too bad yourself, handsome."

"We can still have lots of sex, right?"

"Constantly."

"My beautiful pain in the ass."

"Fuck you." She chuckled. "You're the pain in the ass."

"Mmm. But I'm worth it."

"Yeah, surprisingly," she joked. "But don't push me."

"Lovemaking should be an adventure when you're big."

"Let's get started now."

"Yes. Then before we leave, I'll get people started on that palace studio, so you have somewhere great to practice at home."

~ * ~

Months later, back in Carasivia, Cory and Katarina sat in their hotel room after a gig. They were within a mile of a hospital, as Cory had arranged regularly for the past two months. Katarina rolled onto her side, and he rubbed her lower back.

"Ah, that hits the spot. Thanks."

He trailed kisses down her spine.

She shivered. "Take off your pants, handsome. I'd do it, but I can't even tie my own shoes now. I'll admit handling the bass was tricky. I liked your idea a couple of months back to replace it with a standup bass."

He dragged his fingertips down her back, placing kisses in various spots. "You're due in three days."

"Let me pleasure you."

"Sweetheart, you've been doing that the entire time. I think we've had sex more times than gigs you've played."

"Mmm." She tilted her head back. "Was it enough?"

"It's never enough. I'm voracious when it comes to you."

"And yet, you're incredibly giving in the sack. Let's do it now."

"Relax, sweetheart, and let me rub away your aches and pains. After the birth and you've recovered fully, prepare to spend a lot of time lovemaking. I'm going to keep you tied to the bed—"

"With what?"

"Hot looks."

She shivered. "I want you."

His phone rang. He pulled it from his pocket. "Fuck."

She sat up. "Who is it?"

"George."

She gasped, and he answered the phone.

"Let's talk. Meet me tomorrow night," George said.

"Why, so you can make another attempt on my life?"

"Look, our uncle is old and expected to die soon, and then his crown will be mine."

Cory gripped the phone. "I know, and then you intend to wage war on me, on Carasivia."

"Maybe, we can avoid that. I've been doing some serious soul searching."

Cory didn't say a word. He didn't trust him.

"Corentin?"

"I'm here."

Katarina pressed his arm. "Give him a chance."

"I heard her. She's right. Give me a chance."

"All right. Seven o'clock. Tomorrow night."

"I'll call with a place nearby." He hung up.

"This time, I'm going armed, and I'm wearing a vest, but I'll do this for the sake of international relations."

Katarina hugged him. "Call Brendan. I want him near you now."

"The mask."

"Yes. It predicted that Brendan would be your saving grace right before I had our first child. It may not be George who causes your trouble. But I am sure you'll be okay if Brendan's with you." She shivered.

After Cory called Brendan, he sent his jet to retrieve him, and when he arrived, he got him a room nearby so Katarina could sleep easier.

~ * ~

That night she dreamt that Cory held their little bundles. She woke up with a smile. When George called, Cory hesitated to leave Katarina so close to her due date. She urged him to go, telling him all would be okay. Brendan would go with him. Fifteen minutes after Cory left, Katarina's water broke. She picked up the phone to call him but decided not to because he'd not meet up with his brother to try to patch things up, and this could be trouble at a later date, perhaps even war. She went to the hospital with the ladies in her band and accompanied by guards.

Cory didn't call her. She grew worried during her labor. He should have been done by now. When she was wheeled out of the birthing room, Brendan greeted her, limping, and with a frown, accompanied by her worried-looking bandmates. Guards hovered in the background. One whispered to another who shook his head.

~ * ~

Cory paced in front of the brick wall of a building wearing a bulletproof vest and carrying a gun. Brendan, also armed, leaned against the perpendicular wall. A few guards stood at the side, watching for George's arrival.

"Where is he?" Cory asked.

Brendan shrugged. "You excited about fatherhood?"

Cory felt his face light up. "Katarina's the mom. What do you think?"

Brendan nodded. "Those are going to be some good-looking kids. Kat's a beauty."

"With her as a mom, I know they'll be good people as well."

"I'll be a good uncle."

Cory gave him a quick smile. "Thank you."

"And I'm American. I don't see rank with us."

"I don't either. And how can I not love Americans. My wife and best friends are American. My children will be half-American. You're more of a brother to me than George, despite the mother he and I share. You can teach my kids some of your American ways, just not your questionable ones." He chuckled.

Brendan grinned. "Thanks, man."

"Katarina's pregnancy has been the happiest time of my life but also the scariest."

"Why scariest?"

"If anything had happened to her…"

"Not a chance," Brendan said. "Kat is so *damn* gorgeous."

Cory scoffed. "*Don't* think about my wife that way, asshole," he joked.

Brendan chucked his arm. "I'm not. Not since you and I worked through our differences. I respect her like a beautiful stepsister. Like my best friend's, no, my brother's wife, but also as one of my best friends in her own right."

"Hmm."

"But why did she choose you over me? Back in America, you were a poor kid from a bad part of town, and I was a successful paramedic."

Cory shoved him back, smirking. "Don't mess with me," he said in the I'm-joking-but-I-meant-every-word way he was famous for.

Brendan held up his hands, chuckling. "Kat's my best friend, got it."

"Siiiiiiiiiiiiiiiiiisteeeeeeeeeeer." Cory dragged out the word sarcastically. "People don't think of their sisters that way, but they sometimes fantasize about their beautiful friends. So, she's your *sister*."

"But—"

"Stop or I'll adopt her to you legally as your sister."

Brendan looked at him in awe. "You're serious. I had no idea you held such power. I mean, you did give your people a bill of rights… the freedoms and liberties you made law."

"And those rights do not allow the sovereign to hurt citizens or those living permanently in this country. I don't see making Katarina your sister—with her permission of course—as hurting you or her. In fact, it would have been financially, socially, historically, and legally beneficial."

"You don't want to do that. You don't have *my* permission."

"Why?"

"I'm your brother, right?"

"Yeah," Cory said.

"So, if you made Kat my sister, and you're my brother, that would mean you knocked up your sister."

"You are a true douchebag."

"Ha! This round goes to Brendan!"

Cory twirled his wrist and bowed in mock reverence. A couple of the guards snickered.

"But seriously, man, you have the legal power to do anything you want as long as you don't hurt the people."

"Yes. I made sure protecting them is iron clad."

"The kings before you didn't give a damn."

Cory frowned. "I couldn't tolerate it. When George, the tyrant, was king, and I was yet under suspicion for a crime that would have barred me from succession, I was prepared to help Jon gather support and usurp that bastard. Every day, I ponder how I can make the people's lives better."

"Thank you, Sire," the guard closest to him said.

"It's my honor," Cory responded.

"Do you think you'll ever turn that council of yours into a legislative body?" Brendan asked.

Cory shrugged and leaned back against the red brick wall. "You never know. If it will make my country a better place."

"It's good that you listen to the voice of the people. Not all future monarchs will be as good or as trustworthy as you."

"My child will be. I'll make sure of it."

"But later descendants," Brendan said.

"Perhaps. But the laws I've created to protect my people will only become more entrenched. My citizens are growing used to them and won't tolerate a disruption."

"True."

Suddenly, a car's tires squealed, its driver intending to crush Cory against the wall. Guards rushed toward Cory. One aimed his weapon at the driver and fired, but the windshield was apparently bullet-proof. Brendan was closest to Cory and shoved him, getting nicked in the leg by the car. Cory hit his head against the perpendicular wall and fell, unconscious. Brendan's arms smashed into the wall above him. The car, with George behind the wheel, hit the back wall. George pulled the dented car out and rushed away. Guards attended to Cory, stood, and then fired their weapons at the disappearing vehicle.

Twenty-five

At the hospital, Cory sat up in bed with a bandaged head when a nurse wheeled Katarina into his room with a baby in each arm. He gasped. Katarina rose from the chair and sat on his bed.

"Meet our son and daughter."

Tears stung his eyes. "Oh my God."

"Are you able to hold them? You're not too dizzy?"

"I'm good." He reached for his children.

She handed them over. He looked into their faces then at Katarina and cleared his throat. "These are *our* children. *You* had my babies!"

She smiled. "I did, I'm very happy to say. It was thrilling to hand you your children."

"How are you, sweetheart?"

"Fine. Just tired."

"I'm sorry I wasn't there for the labor."

"I wanted you to try to patch things up with your brother. Are you okay?" She touched his head.

"Great. I love you so much."

"I love you too. Why are there tears in your eyes?"

"I'm a father..." he dropped off. "And they're yours." He kissed the babies' foreheads. "Who came first?"

"Our daughter."

"The future queen of Carasivia. She'll be the first female ruling sovereign of our country," he said with a serene smile.

"Thanks to you changing the law, even against the opposition."

He gazed on his girl and stroked her downy cheek. "Looking into her face, I'm pleased I did so. She'll make a *great* queen. I can feel it."

Katarina smiled.

"Our babies are beautiful," he said.

"Intensely. She looks like you. Look at the shape of her eyes, her lips. Her nose. Even her little chin is European." She tickled her daughter's chin. "I'm glad. Better than her looking like me."

"Why do you say that?"

"Because every time I look at her, I think of you, and my heart swells with gratitude that you fell in love with me."

His lips parted. "Our son looks like you. Very good looking." He grinned. "That black hair. Those eyes are going to be expressive someday, daring someone to mess with him." He touched the tip of his son's nose. "You're full of your mother's spunk. Aren't you, son? And you'll have your mother's heart. I'm glad you look like her. She'll inspire you." He kissed the baby's cheek. Then his daughter's. "My little princess. You're going to make history."

"That's good luck, Cor, for them to look like their opposite sex parents."

"His face will remind me that I'm the lucky bastard to have won your heart."

"Thanks!"

"Are they as gorgeous as if..." *as if my brother would have been their father?*

"I know what you're thinking, and I could smack you for that, but I'll excuse you due to the head injury. They're more gorgeous, Cory."

"I'm sorry."

"Don't be. I regret the day I ever made that unfortunate comment at that strange party."

"Of the names we discussed, which are your favorites? I knew you wanted to look into their faces before we made a final decision. For our girl, how about Zahra, after your mother?"

"Thank you. Mom deserves such an honor, but I've been thinking, Cor. I want to name her Mérane after *your* mother. We can call her Merry for short. She looks like a Merry. Mérane Zahra Brodnik."

"Yes. Thank you. And our son? Please don't say Jakab, after my father."

"It's a good name, but... You make the final decision from our choices."

"Liam, after your father."

"Perfect. Liam Corentin Brodnik?"

He smiled. "Love it. Our kids will have such international names. Maybe we can give Merry a second middle name: Katarina. And our son a second middle name: Jaromír?"

"Nice idea, but let's save those names for our future children."

He kissed her.

She touched her side. "I'm heavier than before."

He bent close to her ear and growled suggestively. "Gives me more of you to ravish." He pulled her into a kiss over their sleeping babies. He leaned back and gave her a serious look. "I'm absolutely under your spell, woman."

~ * ~

Later in her hospital room, Kat heard Cory's voice in the hallway. "Katarina had my babies!" He cheered.

People in the hall laughed.

The next day, in the palace, Asher paid her a visit in her studio, right after her nap. He was chuckling.

"What is it, Ash?"

He shook his head, smiling. "Cory is going around with a huge grin telling everyone that you had his babies. Everyone laughs, delighted by his absolute elated amazement. He's bringing light everywhere he goes."

She smiled. "That reminds me, I have to go get our little ones for feeding time."

"I passed Cory in the corridor while you were sleeping. He had a baby in each arm, trying to balance two bottles with his chin. He was just showing the kitchen staff your beautiful children, and when he informed them that 'Katarina had his babies' they gave him hearty congratulations! When he went into a main hall, he looked about and yelled out, 'I love Katarina!' Ten people in the vicinity heard, cheered, and clapped, delighted that their king is spreading joy throughout the palace. He's promising celebrations wherever he goes. Colorful balloons are popping up everywhere. Wait till you see all the happy faces! I saw a banner that said, 'Thank you, Queen Katarina, for bringing heaven to this mountaintop palace. We love you.' It was in Carasivian and English. Your husband is the most excited father I've ever seen, and he can't fathom how blessed he is that you're the mother." He shook his head. "It's out of this world, outrageously joyful to watch, and it's spreading, down to the cities and countryside."

~ * ~

Cory took a sip of coffee from a mug that said, 'Got twins. Need caffeine.' He glanced on his desk at the silver-framed picture of Katarina, the babies, and him and smiled. He stood and exited his office, intending on heading down the corridor toward the nursery. He ran into Jon.

Jon greeted him. "I was just going to seek you out."

"What's up?"

"I wanted to invite you to an archaeological talk I'm giving later tonight."

"Oh? What about?"

"It's a surprise."

He touched Jon's shoulder. "I look forward to it."

"Thank you! Going to see the babies?"

Cory nodded. "Yes. I think Katarina is in band practice now."

They headed for the nursery.

Jon glanced at Cory. "I heard the latest talk. Women are throwing parties to celebrate the future ascension of Carasivia's first ruling queen."

Cory chuckled.

"But," Jon continued, "they are making it clear that they are in no hurry to see that happen. Many are in love with you."

Cory shook his head with a smile.

"Men are calling you brilliant, giving them the happiest women they've ever seen. They're benefitting, I assure you."

Cory chuckled again. Once at the nursery, Cory gestured for Jon to enter first. "Come see your niece and nephew."

A young maid saw them, blushed, and curtsied.

"Hello, Lanya," Cory said.

"Your Majesty." She glanced at Jon. "Your Highness." She took her leave.

"I wish she weren't so nervous around us," Cory said.

Marina, the head nanny, looked up from her chair where she was reading, and greeted them. Cory gestured for her to stay seated.

Marina grinned.

Cory gave her a curious look. "Marina?"

"Sire, you two intimidate her."

"But...we don't act like the previous leaders here."

"That's not the issue. It's both of you, Your Majesty. You have an extraordinary effect on women. One alone is bad enough, but both... I hear lots of giggling from palace maids when the two of you pass by together."

Cory shook his head, amused.

Jon smiled and clapped Cory on the arm. "Liam's the better looking of the two children," he teased, looking down at the cribs.

Cory frowned, suddenly annoyed and defensive of his girl. "Why would you say that?"

"He looks like Katarina, and Merry looks like you!" he said, jovially.

"I can't beat that logic," Cory said, good-naturedly.

"You know I'm messing with you, right? Like our queen asked me to," Jon said. "Merry is lovely."

Cory grinned. "That's my girl. She's surprisingly pretty for *looking like me!*" He put his hand into the crib.

Merry stirred.

"Sweetheart," Cory said, stroking her little hand.

Merry grabbed his finger but kept her eyes closed. A rush of love surged through Cory. Merry moved her lips in a sucking motion. Cory kissed her head and withdrew his hand. Jon put his hand next to Merry's. She did not grab his finger.

Jon smirked. "She's a Daddy's girl. You're a lucky man to have such wonderful children."

Cory looked at his daughter. "Yes. I love you, Merry, so much." He gazed at Liam. "And I love you, son, so much." He laid a gentle hand on Liam's back and leaned to kiss him. Liam sucked in air and shivered. Love tore a path through Cory. He withdrew his hand.

Jon smiled. "What's it like being a father?"

"Indescribable. My life has changed for the better. You'll know fatherhood someday."

"As great as it seems, I'm in no rush."

"Why? You'd take your responsibilities well."

"Perhaps. I need to love a woman first."

Cory grinned. "Dating anyone?"

"A lady in my archaeology club."

"Why didn't you tell me?"

Jon shrugged.

"Think it might get serious?"

The two brothers left the nursery.

"I doubt it. We just...you know."

"Sleep together." Cory gave a soft chuckle. "Don't be so uptight."

Jon nodded.

Cory heard Katarina's laughter, and his insides warmed up. Katarina turned a corner, chatting with a young woman. Katarina's gaze landed on Cory, and her face glowed. She went to him and pressed a loving kiss to his lips. Jon gave the woman she was with a happy smile. Katarina's friend kissed Jon.

Cory's brow rose. He glanced at Jon. "Please, introduce us!"

Jon introduced Cory to his casual girlfriend, Natalia. She curtsied, and Cory told her it was nice to meet her.

He turned to Katarina. "You know Jon's...*girlfriend*?"

"After a show, you know the one you had to miss, she came up to me and said she was our biggest fan. We got to talking, and I found out she was a new archaeologist. Oh, I had to introduce her to Jon when I heard that!"

Natalia squeezed Jon's hand. Cory watched her. She seemed really into Jon, but Jon wasn't ready for anything serious yet. He was not even actively searching for *the one*, but only having fun at this point. Still, Cory was happy his brother was dating a lovely, intelligent woman. Katarina pulled Cory into the nursery to gaze upon their sleeping babies together, and Jon and Natalia turned down the hall.

~ * ~

Cory's secretary entered his office. He glanced at the papers in the man's hand as he approached.

"What are those?"

His secretary set them onto the desk with a bow. "Your Majesty. I took the liberty of having this done because of a rumor."

"What rumor?"

"Well, your wife and brother were on that island alone for months. Your blood is in the medical lab. My brother is in charge there and so complied with my request."

He swiped up the papers without looking at them. "These were completely unnecessary! My wife told me nothing happened between her and my brother!"

"Please," the secretary urged. "Look at them."

Cory tore the paper in half, glaring without looking at it. Before he knew what happened, his secretary picked up the pieces and held them before Cory's eyes. Cory grabbed the papers, seeing the test results, gasping. He drew in a deep breath and stood. He threw the offensive documents onto the floor.

"This is a mistake! It says that Liam is mine but Merry isn't."

"That would make Liam the heir to the throne."

"No, it wouldn't, because I trust my wife, and she assured me that she and the prince were never together. My brother also swore it. They're just friends and siblings! And they're both honorable, trustworthy, and have integrity."

The secretary shifted, nervous. "Majesty, forgive me."

"Do you doubt my judgment?" Cory asked tensely.

"Majesty, no. But the test showed that you are Merry's uncle."

"This is garbage! Don't see a problem here? Merry is mine, and I don't care what those tests say!"

"My King...no."

Cory gritted his teeth. "She. Is. Mine! It is physically impossible for her not to be. The test is at fault, or the people behind it."

"I'm so sorry, but—"

Cory picked up the papers then tore them up before tossing them down. He gestured harshly and strode toward the door. "Follow me. We're going to the lab to prove that a mistake has been made, or perhaps a conspiracy by sexist assholes trying to push my Merry out of succession. You'd better hope you weren't behind this."

Twenty-six

Katarina trembled and inched the back door to the office open past the crack once Cory had left the room. She had been about to surprise him and knew he didn't hear her there because he had kept working when she had initially pushed open the door. She wiped her tears away then strode across the room, heading for the lab.

When she entered the lab, Cory was rolling his sleeve down over the blue tape holding a cotton square in place. He started. "This isn't what you think!" He curled his hands around hers.

She kissed him. "I know."

He turned to the doctor. Katarina frowned. This was not the palace doctor she knew. The doctor greeted her, nodded, and then left.

"Cor? Who is he? Where is the other doctor?"

"You mean the one who falsified genetic tests to 'avoid changing history?'"

"You have proof of that?"

"It's the only explanation. My people will find the proof quickly, I'm sure." He paused.

"What is it?" she asked with a frown.

"There is another explanation—"

She sank back as her heart fell to her feet. "Cory..." She shook her head.

"Maybe Jon knocked up a woman, and they switched his baby for ours." He gave her a serious look.

Her brow came up. His lips formed into a smile.

He touched her nose playfully. "But I'm attached to Merry now," he began, "so Jon can't have her back."

She gasped.

"I'm kidding!" He chuckled, kissed her, and put his arms around her waist. "I trust you." He pulled away and gave her a tender look. "But I'm quite attached to Merry. That part wasn't a joke."

"I hope you love Liam just as much," she teased.

He cupped her cheek. "Yes."

"I wish the doctor who proved your eligibility to the throne were still around. I wish he wouldn't have been in that accident a while back."

"Me too. This new one I recruited today is from the university. He was actually in the palace visiting a friend when I called. I trust him. He's Brendan's mentor."

He looked at the doctor when the man reentered the room. "Thank you for making this a priority."

"Of course, Majesty. I'll push it through as fast as technology allows. We must prove the queen's integrity at once!"

Cory put his arm around Katarina's waist and pulled her close again. "I'm angry that someone dared to do this to us."

"It will be remedied right away."

When the doctor left the room again with some papers, Cory pulled Katarina into an embrace. "I wouldn't have bothered to prove the previous doctor a fraud, just dismissed him, but he may have released the sham results to the media, and I don't want people to suspect you. I wish, my darling, that my word alone would suffice."

"I understand, but to me all that matters is that *you* believe me."

~ * ~

The DNA results came back, and the doctor approached Katarina and Cory in Cory's office, holding out a document.

Cory shook his head. "I don't need to see those personally. I already know the truth. Never show them to me."

"Very well, Majesty."

Katarina snatched up the results, not looking at them, and approached Cory. "Here, sweetheart."

"I don't need those."

She held them up to his face. His averted his eyes.

"Look."

"Don't need to."

"What would you say if this said she wasn't yours?"

He frowned, and his brow crinkled. "I'd still take your word for it. I *trust* you!"

"Over science?"

"Because of science."

"Huh?"

"After everything we've been through. Physics supports my faith in you."

She laughed. "You were anti-science when I told you about my pregnancy."

"I was a complete dumb ass."

"Yep," she said on a chuckle.

"There would be an authentic explanation for test results like that. Any baby that wasn't mine wouldn't be yours either."

"Look. I insist."

He sighed and looked. "Yep, as I knew. Damn, I haven't been this angry in some time. Someone tried to wrong our Merry."

She grabbed his hand. "Assholes."

"We don't have to show this to the media," the doctor said. "The last doctor's treachery never got out. But we'll keep this on hand just in case something slipped through. Majesty, there's something else."

"What is it?" Cory asked.

"I found evidence that your half-brother, Goran, was involved with the falsification of the first tests."

Cory bit back an answer and nodded sharply. *Psychological and historical warfare. That's how he's playing it. Until he decides to spill blood.* Cory curled his hands into fists then released them.

The doctor bowed and left.

Katarina gave Cory an earnest look.

"What is it, sweetheart?" he said.

"This was an elaborate scam, wasn't it, to get your tests."

He gasped and stepped back, his expression of shock and horror screaming his innocence.

She smiled and pointed at him. "Just messing with you for when you doubted me about whose baby I was carrying."

He let out a breath and ran a hand through his hair. "Good one, dear, and deserved. Consider your revenge effective and accepted due to its justification for treating you that way."

"Not true revenge because I already forgave you. Just a joke."

He wrapped his arm around her and kissed her head. "We're growing old together."

"Good."

He glanced at his watch. "I have a meeting with my council. See you at dinner. Love you."

"I love you too."

~ * ~

Three days later, Cory found her in the nursery. He watched from the door.

She kissed the babies. "I love you, little sweethearts. Be just like your father. I'll always speak English to you, and Daddy will speak Carasivian and French."

Cory cleared his throat.

She turned around and hugged him. "Take the rest of the day off."

"Already cleared it. We won't be disturbed. I'll work hard tomorrow to catch up if I have to."

"Unless I wear you out."

He threw his head back. "Thank you, God."

~ * ~

Cory texted Jon and asked him to come to his office. Jon arrived and took a seat across from Cory at his desk.

"You want to talk?" Jon asked.

Cory slid a book across his polished desk. "Take it. It's for you."

Jon picked it up. "What is this?"

Cory smiled. "My latest novel. I don't have the free time I used to to write my novels, but this book is special. I made the time. Open it and turn to the dedication page."

Jon gasped. "To my brother Jaromír, my friend and inspiration, without whom I would never have found my place in this world, without whom I might never have married the woman of my dreams. Thank you. Much love and gratitude, your brother, Corentin," Jon read. He looked at Cory with great emotion. "Corentin, I could never thank you enough..." his voice dropped off. He cleared his throat. "I'm honored beyond words."

Cory leaned forward and clasped his hands together on his desk. "It's fiction, but the main character is based on you and your archaeological adventures. Quite a change in genre for me, but I thought I'd give it a try. The lead character is very much like you... intellectual, a bit of a personal bore, but someone people can admire."

Jon chuckled softly. "I...I don't know what to say. I'm...touched."

Cory leaned back. "Glad to make you happy."

Jon stood and went around the desk to face Cory. Cory gave him a curious look. Jon bent down and hugged him. Cory returned the hug with a soft chuckle.

Jon stood and strode away. "I'm going to start reading this immediately."

~ * ~

Marina walked into Cory's office with his son who was wearing a little blue hat. Black hair peeked out from under it. His daughter had brown hair that matched his own. Cory greeted Marina and stood. Marina handed him Liam who cooed in his arms.

"Hi, Marina. How are you today? How's my boy?"

"Good, on both accounts. Thank you. And you, My King?"

He kissed Liam's forehead and sat down. "Grateful for life's goodness. Where's Merry?"

"She's sleeping. There's something I need to tell you."

"What is it?"

"I have a gift."

He smiled. "Oh?"

"The queen brought the mask to the babies and me."

"The mask? Why?"

"She felt the urge to give it to me to try on. Then she placed it gently over the babies' faces."

"She...did?"

"Then mine while I held their hands. Now the babies and I have a telepathic link. But more importantly, they have a strong link with each other. We can read each other's minds!"

"That's outstanding! Must be strange for you, though, considering their extreme youth."

"I heard Liam fussing, so I fed him. I looked into his face and felt that he wanted his daddy. Your face flashed in his mind. The sound of your heartbeat thumped in his ears. He told me in his own infant way to bring him to you. He wants to hear your heartbeat."

Cory smiled. "Excellent. Thank you, Marina."

"My pleasure. A moment, please, Sire." She held up a hand briefly. "Liam's getting something in his head from his twin." She smiled. "Merry wants you too!" She chuckled. "If I may."

Cory nodded then spoke lovingly to his boy as Marina left.

Moments later, Jon came in, holding Merry and giving her kisses on her cheeks, making her coo. "How's my little niece?"

More happy cooing.

Jon looked at Cory with a big smile. "I ran into Marina in the hall and couldn't resist taking Merry from her. I sent Marina on to the kitchen for more bottles. Your girl is the sweetest little thing! She makes everyone smile. What a great temperament. Kat told me it was all the love you gave her belly when she was pregnant."

Cory smiled and tipped his head toward his daughter. Jon handed her over.

"Your son has a nice temperament too, but Merry is exceptionally happy.

"See you at dinner. Oh, by the way, your book is remarkably realistic. It's obvious you were listening when I told you about my work. It reminds me why I've always felt close to you." Jon looked at the babies, kissed his niece and nephew then left.

Cory held a baby in each arm while they cooed. Merry batted his cheek.

"My sweet," he said and kissed his daughter. He turned to Liam and kissed him. "Sweet children. I love you so much. Your daddy is honored that you wanted to see him." He cleared his throat, choked up.

Cory looked up.

Katarina approached him with her phone. "Got the picture. That was the most amazing thing I've ever seen. You holding a baby in each arm, looking at them so tenderly. I'm sure they feel it. Damn, Cory, beautiful. I'm sending that picture to the magazines. Oh, I got the video of you telling them that too. They're going to see this someday."

The picture of the loving father went viral.

~ * ~

Katarina found Jon in his office. "You're coming with me today."

"My Queen?"

"Call me Kat."

"Okay. What's going on?"

"I want to surprise Cory. You know how much I love to do things for him. I'm going shopping in the village, and I would appreciate your insights."

"Wouldn't you be happy bringing your girlfriends shopping?"

"I need an expert on Carasivia. Come along and help me pick out a *just because* gift that speaks volumes about the respect I have for your heritage. And..."

"What is it?" He touched her arm.

"I just need a friend today, someone close to Cory."

"I'm honored you chose me."

"That fucker George called me."

"What?"

"I picked up only because it's dangerous to mess with him."

"What...did he say to you?"

"Something disgusting and sexual. If I told Cory about this, he'd hunt him down just to beat the shit out of him."

"Okay. Let's go. Don't ruin Corentin's day with news of that call."

"I won't, but I'm changing my number and getting a new phone. That one's been raped."

They headed out. Going down a steep, rocky section, he offered her his arm, and she took it.

~ * ~

Cory stood up from his desk and stretched. He walked out of his office to take a break and strolled down the corridor. He paused in front of a large window to appreciate the mountaintop view and saw Katarina and Jon. She had her arm hooked in his as they started downhill. Two guards followed closely. Cory frowned, but then he realized he was being foolish. Katarina and Jon were friends, so of course they'd spend some time alone—relatively speaking—together. Cory headed to the nursery to peek in on his kids. He'd not even mention the fact later that he had seen her.

~ * ~

In a trinket shop, Katarina and Jon browsed. Jon kept shaking his head. The two guards stood back, grinning.

"There's got to be something good here. This is a heritage shop." Katarina turned a corner. Jon followed her.

She sighed.

"What's wrong?" he asked.

"I'm so in love with Cory. And I want to find a gift that matches my intentions, but..." She placed her hand on Jon's arm. "I just want to show him how much I respect him and this country. How he always was, is now, and always will be the only man for me."

Jon smiled.

"Why are you smiling?" she asked.

"Because my brother is a great man and king who puts the people first, and I am grateful he married the woman of his dreams, a woman who loves him the same way."

"I'm the grateful one. I will never take my husband for granted. Thanks for being a real friend. To both of us. Remember how on the

283

island I drove you crazy pining after him. Talking your ear off about how much I loved him and missed him."

"I never minded because I also missed and loved him. I admire my brother. I've always liked him as a person and respected him."

"Listen to us, going on about Cory as usual."

"Come on. We'll find something. It can be simple but it can say worlds. I think I saw a row of items that can only be found in this country."

~ * ~

Cory picked up a stack of papers that his new secretary had just dropped off. He flipped through them without much thought when something caught his eye. He read over it, then with curiosity turned toward his computer, going online. He typed in what the paper noted: *I caught Queen Katarina and was disappointed.*

Cory sat forward and watched a video uploaded from a phone. Carasivian subtitles appeared over the picture. A man whispered into his phone saying, "I followed the queen and the prince. Sh, they're having a conversation around the corner. Perhaps I'll hear something juicy." Then he moved the phone, tipping it around the corner.

Cory watched the recorded scene between Katarina and Jon in the shop, and tears stung his eyes.

The video showed the owner of the phone facing it on himself once again. "Well," the man said, "that was disappointing. I thought I'd have something controversial." He shrugged.

Another man came to his side. "You're an asshole. Everyone knows the queen has integrity. Otherwise our king wouldn't think so highly of her. And thank God for our queen's good nature because the king deserves that kind of happiness!" He shoved his friend aside, and the video ended.

Cory's phone rang.

"Hello," George said.

"What do you want?" Cory sighed.

"Time draws near but isn't quite here yet. Then the real games will begin. I'm not going to kill you yet, but rather rid you of someone you love." He hung up.

Cory closed his eyes and said a prayer.

Minutes later, Katarina entered his office with a saucy grin. Cory sprang to his feet, strode to her, and pulled her into a passionate kiss.

When they leaned away, she looked at him dazed. "Wow. I love being married to you."

He hugged her.

"Mm, sweetheart," she purred. "I have something for you."

"How is it that every time I see you, I'm shocked that I love you even more?"

She squeezed him tighter. "I feel the same way."

He leaned back with his hands on her hips and gazed at her adoringly.

She tilted her head with a serene smile. "The way you look at me...it's so intense." She cleared her throat, stepping back and reaching into her pocket, and then held a fist out to him.

"The last time you offered me something in your fisted hand, my life changed dramatically for the better," he said.

"When I proposed and gave you that very special ring."

"Yes."

"Here."

He held out his hand. She put her palm to his. He didn't retract his hand but looked at his under hers.

"Take it, Cor."

"Wait. I'm enjoying the moment."

She chuckled. "You're making me nervous."

He curled his fingers over the object in her hand. She pulled hers away; then he uncurled his fingers. He stared at the heart-shaped stone in his hand, made from a mineral only found in his country. He swallowed hard. The simplest little object said the most profound words to him. He pulled her into another hug and closed his eyes.

"You approve." Her voice came out muffled against his shoulder.

He stepped back and took her hand. "I'm going have a hole drilled into it and have it attached to a leather band, so I can wear it as a bracelet."

"Very cool!"

"Come on, sweetheart. I couldn't possibly focus on work now. Let's just...spend the day together."

"Really?" she said happily.

"And we'll stay inside today. I want to show you the archives. There are some fascinating things down there."

"Awesome. Want to get our babies?"

"Just what I was thinking!" He retrieved his gun from his desk and holstered it at his side. Her brow lifted, and damn, it was sexy.

Twenty-seven

Katarina strolled down the main palace corridor looking every which way at the magical Christmas décor Cory had arranged. He once promised her that when he took the throne, he'd make the palace look like a cozy Victorian Christmas, charming beyond her dreams. He kept that promise. She shivered, looking at the sparkling lights, holly, red bows, silver bells, and so much more. Soft carols emanated from speakers on the walls. Smiling people passed her with curtsies and cheerful well wishes, complimenting her and the king on making the palace so hauntingly beautiful. She stopped before the huge Christmas tree, looking for the donation box, and couldn't see it. She turned toward a palace guard standing nearby. He wasn't familiar to her.

She held out her hand. He shook it with hesitation.

"Hello, I'm Katarina. You're new? What's your name?"

"Uh..." he stuttered. "My Queen, I'm Ivan Stanwich," he said in English.

"Nice to meet you."

"The honor is mine."

"You speak English, or I was going to have to attempt my poor Carasivian."

"I took advantage of those free language classes the prince provided."

"Are you having a nice time? You're free to help yourself to the buffet while on duty."

"This is the best Christmas I remember in the palace. I'm enjoying the festive atmosphere greatly!"

"Fantastic! So you're not new then."

"Majesty, I started as part of the cleaning crew years ago and had no hope of moving up because of my family background, despite my talent as a fighter, until your husband took the throne. He opened up opportunities. I applied. He interviewed me last week, and here I am."

"Well, I'm delighted!"

"Thank you. I like the respect that comes along with it and the perks. I like this job very much."

Katarina gave him a nod with her smile. "By the way, do you know where the donation box is?"

He smiled and pointed over his shoulder.

"Thank you so much, and Merry Christmas!"

"Merry Christmas to you!"

She shook his hand again and went to the box. She slipped a large bill into it. She and Cory were going to use the money collected nationwide to buy gifts and food for poor families. No Carasivian family would have a bleak Christmas. Anything not covered by donations they would pay for themselves.

She was excited about the show she was going to perform with her band on national television. They would perform a Christmas concert for hers and Cory's gift charity. Her pretty blonde singer, Madison, didn't speak the language, but the words would be translated on a screen.

Katarina glanced at her watch. "I'm late!" She dashed down the hall toward the audience chamber, her long white dress swishing as she went. She paused at the door where a line of children and their parents awaited. She pulled up the hood lined with fluffy white feathers as she made her way toward Cory. Her black hair stood in stark contrast to her hood and dress.

Cory rose from his large chair and stared at her. "And you married *me*."

She smiled, curious as she drew near. "Cor?"

He shook his head. "It's sometimes so hard to believe my fortune in being your husband."

She squeezed his hand. "You never let me forget how much I mean to you."

"You have no idea."

She took a seat next to him. Cory kissed her hand before beckoning the next child over. A little rosy-cheeked girl stood before him. She curtsied and said something.

Cory leaned and whispered to Kat. "She said, 'Your Majesty, thank you for seeing me.' I'm going to ask her name."

He turned to the girl and spoke in Carasivian. She bounced on her feet and spoke. His secretary held up a paper to him then gave him a set of headphones. Cory pressed a button and listened to something. He nodded, impressed. He spoke to the child. She wrapped her little arms around his neck. He chuckled. From what Kat could tell from her body language and tone, her mother seemed to apologize. Cory said something, and the mother smiled, curtsied and replied, and then took her girl away.

"What was that all about?" Kat asked. She knew that the way they celebrated Christmas didn't include Santa Claus, but every citizen could enter a lottery, and the winners had the right to ask a reasonable request of their king as a Christmas gift. This was a new tradition, started by Cory. They had left their names and contact information for him ahead of time, and his secretary was sitting nearby taking notes. Cory did have the right to refuse, but apparently, he had said "yes" to the little girl. Had he said no, he'd have offered her a consolation gift.

He leaned toward Kat. "She asked for a recommendation to a prestigious music school. She had been told she had talent but was on the cusp of acceptance. She needs something exceptional to put her over the top. My secretary showed me her scores on the practical test, and her playing impressed me adequately. The girl was good but borderline for such an important school. I could see she had heart, though, and that convinced me."

"So you're going to give her a recommendation. You made her day." Kat put her hand over his. "Maybe someday she'll be a court musician for Queen Merry."

"That would be cool," he said.

"What if you couldn't have given her that recommendation?"

"Besides the consolation gift, I'd have advised her to practice hard, and then show me another recording in three months."

"Sounds fair."

Several more people had their turn. Cory shifted, somewhat uncomfortable.

"Sweetheart?" Kat asked.

He leaned toward her ear. "You look so damn beautiful. It's difficult to rein in my desire to kiss you like I mean it."

She rubbed her thumb over his hand. By the time the last person had approached them, Kat was drooping. The hour was late when Cory escorted her to their bedroom. She stripped out of her dress, fell face first onto their bed, and closed her eyes. She felt his hands slide up her calves. She rolled over and looked at him.

He stared at her with raw desire. "I've waited all *night* for you."

She yawned. "Sorry. Oh, hon, I'm exhausted. Please, let's postpone this."

He nodded, leaned, and kissed her. "Okay, sweetheart." He turned around.

"Where are you going?"

"To take a cold shower," he said over his shoulder. "A long one. Love you."

"Love you too."

"Get some sleep, my love."

She heard him turn on the water and closed her eyes.

~ * ~

The next night, in festive traditional clothes, Cory led Katarina down the mountain path to the lit-up village below. Katarina's bandmates followed as did guards. Katarina gasped when she, Cory, and the girls drew close.

"It's magical," Katarina said.

"I knew you'd like it. Come on!" He pulled her toward the town center where villagers had gathered to play upbeat, cheerful Christmas music.

"You'll like our carols," Cory said. "They're a bit different than you're used to, though."

Katarina and her friends stood listening, nodding, and tapping feet.

"Very nice, hon," Katarina said. "Kinda like gypsy music with an Eastern European, heart-filled emotion behind it. There's a real love of life, a gratitude feel to the music."

Cory looked at her and the others. "Yeah, these are new carols."

"I'll bet the gratitude comes from getting you as a leader," Katarina said.

He pulled her close by her waist, looked into her eyes, and kissed her.

The girls cat-called.

"That's the sweetest thing to say, but I can't take the credit. They're grateful Christ was born."

"Of course, but still," Katarina said.

Cory smiled. "Would you ladies be willing to learn all the traditional stuff and be official court musicians in addition to the classical orchestra we already have, playing for social functions? I'd give you a respectable salary."

Katarina talked it over with her friends and turned to Cory. "We agree. Thanks!" She kissed him. "But I won't personally take a salary. They can have theirs and split mine or give mine to charity."

~ * ~

At the car, Cory kissed Kat and said, "The tour of our cities should be fun. I want our people to see you and you to see them. And don't worry. I'll have extra men and women *especially* on the lookout for George. Maybe we can trap him."

Cory stood at the podium set up in a town center and greeted the citizens. As he finished speaking to a crowd, they stood and applauded. When they sat down, he thanked them and then asked for questions and told them ideas he had, getting their input. Certain people had been assigned ahead of time to ask questions that concerned the town. When near the end of the session, he brought Katarina to greet the cheering people, grasping her hand.

Cory and Katarina visited several cities as they planned to do every other year to meet face-to-face with people all around the country. At night, he and Katarina would fall exhausted but happy onto their hotel room beds. Marina and the babies always stayed in a room attached to the suites.

Twice, attempts were made to harm Cory. Both times, his security took down gunmen and arrested them before anyone could be hurt. Once back home, Cory received a call from George.

"What the fuck do you want, asshole?" Cory said, on a tired sigh.

"Damn, you're recklessly brave, going on a tour. Too bad you didn't receive the full benefit of my nice, warm, brotherly welcome."

"I refuse to let a psychopath keep me from running this country far better than you ever did."

"Yep. Brave." He hung up.

Katarina and Jon walked into Cory's office. Jon was carrying a fat scrapbook under each arm. He set them on Cory's desk.

"What's up, Prince Boring?" Cory asked him.

Katarina scoffed.

"Nothing much, King Not As Good Looking As Me."

Katarina's hand came to her mouth to stifle a laugh. She lowered her hand. "Good ones! I'm impressed!"

Jon took a bow.

"But Cory's better looking," she said.

Cory smiled. "You're just jealous, Jon, because you'll never have a wife as beautiful as I have."

"*You're* just jealous because I still get to dig in sand boxes, and you're stuck in an office."

"My wife makes it up to me in the bedroom."

Katarina laughed. "You two brothers, ah," she said and shook her head. "Your banter is strange, but I love it."

Cory carried her hand to his lips for a kiss. "Goddess of my dreams."

"Brother, Kat, my collection of articles grows." Jon opened the books. "Look at all these stories about you two!"

"Show me a negative one," Kat asked.

Jon pulled out a folded piece of paper.

Katarina snatched it up and read it out loud. "King Corentin has failed to address the issue of municipal repairs in my town in a timely matter..." She scoffed.

"It's okay, sweetheart. Freedom of the press," Cory said. "He has a right to his opinion. I can't do everything all at once. I talked with my advisors and mayors and had to prioritize things. It's not possible to do otherwise. This citizen has a right to be annoyed. He doesn't see the bigger picture."

"Still," Katarina said.

He wrapped his arm around her waist and kissed her temple. "I got a personal letter last week from someone who was disappointed in me for not fathering more children yet."

"Hmm." She folded her arms over her chest.

"I get angry letters more than you'd think from citizens demanding opposite things."

"How do you handle that?"

"My mother taught me to follow my conscience. I listen to my advisors then clear my head, never making a decision while emotionally charged—as you taught me—and do what my heart tells me is right."

~ * ~

Goran sat on the throne he inherited from his mother's brother only that day, in a nearby country. The stubborn bastard, Uncle Lothar, had taken his sweet time dying.

Sneering, Goran held the famous picture of Cory and his babies. It was an old picture, for the babes were turning a year old tomorrow.

He crumpled it up and looked at his cousin who was groveling before him. "It's time to put our special plan into action. Prepare to be awarded beyond your dreams. That should erase any qualms you have for what you're about to do."

Landrick bowed. "My King."

Twenty-eight

Lightning startled Cory, and he looked up from some state papers at a high-positioned window. "Hmm. Storm coming in. Merry likes the sound of rain." He thought of the last rainfall, the day Katarina had gotten the kids cute bunny costumes to wear at an Easter function. She had brought Merry in wearing her rabbit ears, and he was surprised anew at how even more she resembled him as she got older and yet was still so incredibly cute. Katarina joked that they should have named her Corinne or Cory junior or Corentina. Katarina would often hand him their daughter, calling her by one of those names or simply "Daddy Junior."

"This is what you would have looked like if you had been a girl," she told Cory, as Merry sucked on her fingers. "Who knew the female version of you would be so pretty!"

Cory smirked. "Well then, my wife, how do you explain that our son, who resembles you, is not pretty when you are so unbelievably so?"

She frowned. "He's not?"

"No, he's manly."

They chuckled.

Cory looked back at his papers.

Katarina came tearing into his office crying. He stood and went to her. "Katarina?"

She didn't answer but only pulled him by the arm out the hallway and down toward the nursery.

"Our babies. What's going on?"

She ran faster, and he kept up, his heart pounding. They arrived at the nursery and saw Marina sobbing as she sat near the changing table.

"What's going on?" Cory demanded.

Marina stood up and wiped her eyes. She curtsied on shaky feet. "My King, your cousin Landrick came by. Everyone knows him, of course, though he's from your mother's side of the family. He was... friendly, as usual, and so I, I let him in to see the babies. He..."

Cory touched her arm. "Please..."

"He said he was going to bring his little cousins to see you and surprise you. I thought nothing of it!"

"And?" Cory got out roughly.

"When I approached your office, I asked your guards if Landrick was still there. They said he never showed up. You weren't there either at that time and didn't respond to my text. I found the queen, and she raced back to your office looking for you."

"I couldn't get out the words!" Katarina cried.

Cory stumbled, "N...no. It's okay." He drew a deep breath. "Probably took a wrong turn. How long ago?"

"Twenty minutes."

Katarina threw herself against his chest. "Guards can't find them! I told them to text me when they did. Everyone's searching."

"I went to my man cave to meditate about a political problem and had only been at my desk a few minutes when you came in."

"You left your phone somewhere—"

"Damn it. I think it's in the kitchen. I dropped by there earlier for a snack. Felt like talking to the cook about his latest creation. Twenty minutes? Landrick knows where my office is. Why didn't anyone else tell me before now?"

"I'm sorry, My King! The chaos!"

"This isn't your fault, Marina. He's probably just—"

"Just…what?" Katarina said. "He knows the palace."

Cory drew in a deep breath. "We shouldn't jump to conclusions. He's family. Think. Marina, do you sense anything through your link with the babies?"

She closed her eyes a moment then looked at Cory. "He took them outside."

"Let's go." He took Katarina's cold hand and hurried out with her.

"Does he know about the secret hiding places?" Katarina asked, rushing beside him.

"Yes, sweetheart. We played in them as boys, but why—" He stopped jogging in front of a tapestry. "Oh God."

"What is it?"

"George got his throne today. Landrick is one of his subjects. Would he…sink so low? Landrick and I have always been friends. But George…Goran—"

Katarina covered her mouth.

A guard approached them and bowed. "Majesties. Outside. Come with me, please." They jogged toward the door. The guard spoke as they went. "A village boy saw your cousin get into a car with the babies. Landrick came out a back door to an isolated area and drove away. Baby seats were in the car."

"Let's get the car," Cory said.

Katarina was crying as rain started the moment they stepped outside. They rushed toward the garage.

Cory looked at the ground. "I can still see tracks. We'll follow them before they wash away." He squeezed Katarina's hand.

Cory and Katarina got into the car, Cory driving. A farmer pointed northeast, the little village boy having just run up to his side telling him something. Cory drove in that direction. They went past the village to miles of farmland.

"Shit, shit, shit!" Cory banged his fist against the steering wheel.

Katarina pointed, gasping. The car the boy had described was crunched up against a tree. Cory and Katarina got out of the car and ran up to the damaged car, looking into the window. The baby seats were empty. They looked down the dirt road at fields on both sides and saw a barn. They got into their car and drove toward it. When they drew close, they saw Landrick running with the babies in his arms. Cory got out of the car and ran with Katarina following. Cory blocked him in front, and Katarina from the back.

The babies were crying as the rain came down harder.

Cory held up his hands. "Please, we're family."

"So is Goran!" Landrick shouted.

Cory nodded. "Yes. Those babies are his niece and nephew. They share his blood, and yours as well. You wouldn't hurt innocent babies? Your own family? No amount of money he offered you could be worth that? Please hand them over. They're scared, cold, and wet. I can feel their terror." He swallowed down a tight throat.

"I need them to get away. You'll never let me off now."

"Give me back my babies!" Katarina screamed, taking a step.

Cory held up his hand, and she froze on the spot.

"Landrick," he urged, "hand them over, carefully, and I swear on my honor I'll let you go. You can take the car."

"You're known internationally for your honor. You absolutely swear, on your mother's name?"

"I do."

"And how about paying me what Goran would have. Ten million and a high title. Lands."

"Don't press your luck."

"But he'll...execute me for failing. I have no choice, Corentin."

"Fine. I'll give you one million. Start somewhere new."

"Okay. I trust you far more than I do him to do the right thing."

"Wise decision. There was no way I was going to let you get ten feet farther with my babies. You accepting my offer without hurting them any more prevents me from beating the living crap out of you once they're safely in their mother's arms."

"I could kill them with a squeeze of my hands if you got near me!"

"No!" Katarina darted closer.

"Katarina!" Cory begged.

She stopped again, pale and trembling.

Landrick shook with fear. "I'll take your deal, Corentin, because I know by that famous picture alone that if I did take them hostage and got away, you'd go to the ends of the earth to hunt me down. You'd even manage to get at me on Goran's turf, I'd bet. I was a stupid fool, and I'm sorry. Goran ordered this, but I didn't focus on the depth of your devotion to your family. I was just…terrified to defy him."

"Fine. Now….Give. Me. Back. My. Babies," he enunciated.

"Y…you'll really give me the money?"

"Yes! If you refrain from additional harm. Do *not* squeeze them! I'll wire the money to whatever account you tell me, and I'd better never see you again!" He went to Landrick, as did Katarina. Each took a child.

Landrick ran to the car. "I'll be in touch. Soon!" He drove away.

Katarina kissed her babies. She and Cory hurried into the barn and did their best to warm their shivering, crying children. Sometime later, the barn door opened, and several guards ran in.

~ * ~

Cory paced the hospital waiting room, and Katarina sat in a chair, hugging her knees, silent tears running down her cheeks. Both children had fevers, and Merry had bruises on her head. Katarina jumped up and threw herself into Cory's arms.

"Tell me again. Use your gift. They're not going to die!" she whispered into his ear.

"They're not going to die but…" He bit his tongue.

She grasped his shirt. "But what?"

"I see…cloudiness around Merry's head. And that isn't part of my gift, as you know, but only my father's instinct."

"What does that cloudiness mean?"

"She's not going to die, sweetheart. I promise you, or I'd not be capable of keeping this calm voice."

"What's wrong with her?"

His eyes stung with tears. "I don't know."

Suddenly, Cory's head secretary came into the room and looked about at various palace employees. Many had their heads bent in prayer.

The secretary bowed. "Majesties, any news?"

"Not yet, Olaf. You have some news to impart?"

"Your council is bracing itself. Did Goran declare war?"

"Yes." Cory drew in a deep breath and sank into a chair, holding Katarina's hand. She sat next to him, clinging to his hand.

"By taking my children and putting them in harm's way, he declared war officially on me. Then he declared it on the country."

"The former king. What's next?"

Cory rubbed his brow. "Damn it! My children are ill right now!"

"I'm sorry, Majesty."

"No, you need to know. Everyone needs to know what's going on." He closed his eyes briefly. "Goran called me and told me what he is planning to do. He's livid with me because he thinks I stole his crown. He's mad that the country voted him out because this isn't a democracy. He thinks I'm American trash leading a treacherous country. He's hungry for revenge. He might succeed, if we let him ten feet near our border, because his land troops are stronger than ours. We can keep him at bay in the air because we have a better air force. He was a tyrant before, but if he comes back here to rule, bloody from battle, he will be an absolute monster. My babies—" his voice broke.

Katarina wrapped her arms around him.

He looked at his shaking hands. "A moment, please." He took more deep breaths, collecting himself. "Tell the council we need to prepare for attack. I'm afraid there is no way around this as much as I want us to remain at peace."

The man bowed and left.

The doctor walked into the room, and everyone hushed.

Cory and Katarina stood, still. "Doctor?"

"Shall we go somewhere private?"

Katarina gasped. "Tell us now!"

"Their fevers have broken."

Katarina squealed in relief.

"But..."

"But what?" She touched his arm.

"Your daughter sustained a serious injury."

They gasped. "What kind?" Cory asked. "Her...head."

"It seems they weren't strapped into their baby seats when that car hit the tree. Your daughter has lost her hearing."

Katarina cried out.

Cory grabbed the doctor's arms. "Do something!"

"I have the finest expert in this country's opinion on this matter. There's no hope."

Brendan came into the room, talking heatedly with the nurses. He was in medical school, and Katarina rushed to him expectantly. Brendan was a medical genius, gifted by the mask to be a prodigy.

Katarina looked at him in desperation. He hugged her. "They explained everything. I'm sorry."

Her knees gave out. Brendan supported her. Cory took her from him and sat her on his lap, tears running down his face.

~ * ~

A week later, Cory walked into his bedroom where Katarina lay in bed, surrounded by her bandmates who were trying to comfort her. "Ladies," he greeted them. He bent to kiss his wife's cheek. "Sweetheart. I did it. It's law now."

She pushed herself up into a sitting position. "What's law?"

"We are officially a bilingual country. Carasivian and Sign Language. Every school and even the homeschoolers have one year to prepare to meet the first of our new standards. Every child must learn sign language from the age of five. We're to start our own classes soon with our babies. I will recruit as many teachers as possible over the next year to teach every citizen not in school. I will give those teachers lucrative paychecks to inspire them to volunteer in hordes. I will advertise across Europe. We'll have our best teachers give free lessons to huge classes of students and record lessons, giving them out for free. I'll create a panel that tests every citizen every three years. After all, the future Queen Merry will appreciate that every person in the kingdom will be able to talk to her. She'll still read in Carasivian, French, and English of course. And when she's older, we'll get her lip-reading classes. I'm attacking this from all angles."

Katarina embraced him. "Thank you. I need to know what's happening with the war."

Cory sat on the bed. The ladies watched him.

"It's head to head now. Too many losses on both sides. I hate this shit. But if we don't fight—"

"Yeah, I know." Katarina trembled.

He ran his hand up and down her arm. "Remember that Marina is connected telepathically to our children."

"She is, isn't she? It had...slipped my mind."

"She can communicate with our babies, especially Liam, far better than we can at this stage. Merry can speak to us intimately through her and Liam, even before we learn our first word of baby sign language."

Katarina smiled, inspiring the same reaction in Cory.

"Oh, and our twins actually do that with each other, as you've heard in rumors. I caught them for the first time, and it was great. Merry gazed at her brother in their high chairs with intensity. He turned to Marina and stared at her hard. She jumped up and filled Merry's sippy cup with chocolate milk. I leaned against the counter, watching with the biggest grin as this went down. Our girl drank down her chocolate milk so fast rivulets of it streamed down her cheeks. Imagine that! Also I discovered when I put Merry's hand on my throat while I talk to her, she smiles! She also likes it when I put her hand over my heart and send her Daddy's love. She'll giggle with glee, muttering, 'Da, Da, Da!' She is one happy girl, my love. Don't let your sadness cloud your knowledge of that. You've been so sad this week. The accident has had a strange effect on her. She's twice as giggly as she was before. It's amazing! Everyone in her presence smiles now!"

"I think I'm ready to face the world again."

Her friends gasped in happiness.

"Cor, could we start those sign language lessons tonight?"

He kissed her hand. "Anything you wish." He paused. "We'll bring our babies. Get ready to laugh when you see our happy girl's face."

"I can't wait!"

"When we win this war...you know that I'm next in line for that throne, and their law is written in stone, or else my uncle never would have left the kingdom to that bastard older brother of mine. Guess what I plan to do when our kingdom is twice as big?" He chuckled. "You may be surprised. I expect to make history."

"You really think we're going to win, even though they have a stronger military?"

His phone rang. He looked at the surface, kept a straight face, kissed Katarina's forehead, and excused himself, going into the hall.

"Goran," he said into the phone. "Were you really going to harm my children? You've never executed a child, only adults. You have those standards, at least."

"Do you have any conception of how much I hate you?"

"Please. I have to know about my babies."

"I was going to tell you they died and raise them as mine and turn them against you. They were going to grow up hating you and adoring me. Then I was going to send them to you as adults to murder you in the dungeon you'd have been lingering in all those years."

Cory drew a deep breath. "No."

"That plan has failed, but happily, I came up with a better one."

"What the hell is wrong with you?"

"Prepare for misery before you die."

"You loved our mother. Goran, I'm begging you. Let's end this. Let's forget the past and make peace. We are political equals. Let's work together for everyone's good. Let me be your brother. Please, find it in your heart—"

George hung up.

Cory stared at the phone. It rang again, and he picked up. It was Asher, who gave him great news about a diplomatic project he had been working on. Cory hung up, smiling. When Brendan called just to tell Cory something funny that happened in medical school, Cory was greatly amused. When he hung up, he was laughing as Katarina approached.

He took her hand. "Why is it that every time you walk into a room to greet me, I didn't know how bad my day sucked before you arrived?"

"You were laughing!"

"Yes, but, beautiful wife of mine, it almost freaks me out how lucky I am to be yours. I'm dangerously lucky."

She put her hand behind his head and drew him close, turning toward his ear and speaking in a husky voice. "Do you have any conception of how deeply I love you?" She pulled him into passionate kissing.

He leaned back, dazed. "Let's go get Liam and Merry and learn some sign language."

"You mean, Liam and Corentina!"

They went into the nursery where Cory headed straight for Merry's crib. She was holding onto the railing and cooing. Cory picked her up, held her close, and sucked in a sharp breath. Katarina went to him.

"You're infusing her with love. I can feel it from here," she said.

"I'm so grateful our babies are okay," he said.

She looked at Liam. He was wagging little fingers. "Ma ma ma. Daaaaaaaaaaady!" He squealed with joy.

Cory chuckled, handed Merry to Katarina, and picked up his son, kissing his cheek. He gazed at him with pride and joy.

Katarina had a lifted brow.

"Sweetheart?" Cory asked.

"You are clearly their favorite. What magic is this that you work, Daddy?"

"No. I'm sorry, I..." he stuttered.

She chuckled. "I'm just thrilled that my babies adore their father. I fantasized about asking you to marry me when we were eighteen."

"*Really*?" he asked, amazed.

"Yes. I started daydreaming about life with you when we were sixteen...younger." She looked at him adoringly.

His heart warmed, bringing him a measure of peace.

"There's something else."

"Darling?" he asked.

"I was talking to the girls in the band."

Merry cooed and laid her head on Katarina's chest, playing with a strand of her hair.

"About what?"

"They think you're awesome, letting them live in the palace, so because of you, I can get them to agree to almost anything!"

A smile tugged at his lips. "What can I do for you, My Queen?"

"What makes you think I want something?"

"Oh," he chuckled. "You do."

She clucked her tongue. "I've been thinking about something. No more international tours, or at least those will be limited. We'll concentrate on Carasivia, make a career here. Make records here, tour here. I'll be home almost every night from now on and into the far future."

He gasped, happily.

"How far, in terms of driving time, is it to our farthest border?"

"About five hours."

"Then I'll never be more than five hours away from you. If I use your jet, it will be much faster."

"That's great! Thanks!"

"There's another reason for that."

"Oh?"

"I want more children with you."

He dropped into a chair, holding Liam, and his mouth fell open on a happy sigh.

"Lots of children. I want to fill your palace with our beautiful, happy babies."

"*Our* palace."

"I heard your ancestors built this place with their own money. Then some of their descendants kept building upon it. The state doesn't own it, but you are the actual owner."

"*We* are the actual owners. Father had left it to Jon to snub Goran and me. He made this change to his will from Goran to Jon shortly before his so-called death because he had just found out that Goran was a bastard. He planned on Goran having an *accident* but *died* before it could be arranged. Goran assumed he had inherited the palace, and no one dared to tell him otherwise. My honorable little brother found out when I was crowned and handed the palace over to me, saying tradition demands that it belong to the rightful king."

"Wow. Jon is amazing."

"Yes, I know. And when you came back to me, I put it in writing that you and I equally share ownership of this place."

"I'm...stunned."

"I'm in love."

"So am I." She cleared her throat. "So, if I wanted to decorate with a musical theme, I could?"

He chuckled softly. "That brings up funny memories of when you used to leave musical symbols wherever you went." He paused. "My favorite was when you arranged balls in the shape of a treble clef on a pool table. Then took a bow."

She laughed.

"Or no, when you used lip gloss to draw a heart with a bass clef on my bathroom mirror. I still have that picture on my phone. So yes, sweetheart, have your way here. You don't even have to ask."

She passed her hand through the air. "Nothing dramatic. I might hang up a picture or something."

"How about some glass musical note-shaped pieces in the windows along the main corridor to catch the light?"

"Great idea!"

He tipped his head.

"After we win this war, keep me in the bedroom until we make a baby."

He was speechless.

"Ooh, I just came up with a good idea," she said.

He smiled widely, and he couldn't find any words.

"I'll aim for a multiple birth, less pregnancies."

He laughed.

"What?" she asked sweetly. "You're not the one who has to go through morning sickness or gaining weight or labor!"

"You'll *aim* for a multiple birth!"

She laughed. "Mind over matter! Or maybe *you* should aim for a multiple birth!" She winked and then gave him a suggestive look.

"Oh, I'll aim all right," he answered just as suggestively.

"Mmm," she purred.

"It will be hard finding nannies as good as Marina to help with all those bottles, but we'll search!"

"And all will learn baby sign language."

"They can sign, 'Feed me. Feed me now.'"

"Or, 'I love you, Daddy,'" she said. She kissed Merry's head.

"I'm glad I do regular dad stuff like change a few diapers every day and do at least one feeding a day and take time to play with them."

"You're the best."

"Thanks, sweetheart."

"They like it when you take them into the gardens to play. Your babies adore you."

"That means the world to me," Cory said.

"Marina gives me a look whenever I change diapers. She tries to shoo me away, and I promise her she can have the next heavy one."

He chuckled and considered her. "You have no idea the happiness you give me."

Liam curled little fingers around Cory's thumb. Cory kissed his son's hand.

"Will you build me a palace *chemistry* lab as good as that of my parents? We promised Mom and Dad a grandchild who would be a scientist."

"The day we end the war, it will be first on my agenda. I'm still getting royalty checks from my days as a full-time writer."

"That's funny how, back in those days, your checks were barely enough to keep you alive, but since you've gotten crowned, your stories have sold in the millions!"

"I'll use those royalties to build your lab. It would be my pleasure."

"*You're* amazing." She smiled, and then it fell. "You can't talk George into peace."

"No. He's evil."

She looked down before looking back up at Cory, tilting her head as if she were up to something.

"I know that look, wife. Ask away."

She chuckled. "You always think I want something. I just love you."

"I love you too. Now ask."

"Perhaps I could talk some sense into him. Send me—"

He sprang to his feet, and Liam squealed.

"No!" He put his son into his crib, gently took his daughter, and put her into her crib. He took Katarina by the arms.

"Cory—"

"*Fuck*...no."

"Cor—"

"No!"

"But—"

"No!"

"I could talk to him on the phone!"

"No!"

"I invoke my privilege of co-leadership."

"You don't get it. He. Is. Evil."

"You're being dramatic."

"I wish I were," he said sadly. "How can you wonder otherwise when he shot me twice, and he's the reason Merry is deaf?"

"Hope. You share a good mother. One filled with love."

"Not for him. She favored me, as you know. He's hated me all my life."

"I just thought some good genes must have sneaked in there."

"He's all his rapist father. And my father, before he found out George wasn't his, taught George how to torture animals. He thought cruelty made a man a man."

"George is killing our soldiers. We've got to stop this war!"

Cory rubbed his face. "I'm trying to find a way. But the moment I hesitate, he'll blow us to kingdom come. I can't let up. But be reassured, we're only defending, not harming."

She took his hands. "He can't be completely evil."

"You have no idea how much he abhors me. And he's mad at this country for kicking him off the throne."

"Ask the mask."

"I have."

"What did it say, Cor?"

"I got a creepy feeling and went into prayer."

She shivered. "That stupid mask is asleep or something."

He hugged her. "I have to handle this war with delicacy. We've riled up a wild animal." He kissed her temple. "We'll figure out a way. Don't worry."

"I'm not going to win this argument, am I? You won't let me speak to him."

"No," he said, firmly. "He's too dangerous."

The babies stood up, holding the bars of their cribs, so Cory and Katarina picked them up and then entered the corridor, each holding a baby.

A guard approached and offered a bow. "Majesties."

"What's up?" Cory asked.

The guard smiled and glanced at the window. "There's a nice sprinkling rain now, and Princess Merry loves the sound of rain."

Katarina frowned. "How can you say that since—"

Cory held up his hand. "It's okay, sweetheart. Come on, I'll show you. You've been in such a fog lately." Cory thanked his guard and led Katarina toward the window.

When there, he said, "Watch. Her accident enhanced something." He took Merry's hand and pressed it to the windowpane as raindrops hit it.

Merry smiled.

"You've been spending *a lot* of time with them," Katarina said.

"I let them rest on my lap often this week, while you were depressed. I hum, and they fall into blissful sleep. Merry clings to my chest. She taps my shirt chanting, 'Da, Da.' I give her kisses and blow raspberries on her cheeks, and she giggles."

"And Liam?"

"Plays with my buttons. He tore two off my shirt, picking at them as I sang to him. He looks up at me with those big brown eyes he inherited from you and leaves me speechless."

"Being a daddy hits you hard."

"Yes."

"I'd love to see them sleeping or playing on your lap. Almost every time I go to them, Marina is with them. I was lucky to catch you holding them in your chair. I took them to see the dairy farmer recently when you were so swamped with work I didn't want to disturb you. They stared at the cow. Liam called it a doggy, and Merry called it a big kitty. I just forgot to tell you. It was funny."

"I'll bet." Cory reached for the bottom of the window and opened it, letting in the smell of moist air. He gently stretched Merry's arm out so that raindrops hit her hand. She giggled.

Cory smiled. "See? As a bass player, this should make sense to you. Your instrument allows people to feel music so profoundly. We'll fill Merry's and Liam's existence with the music of life."

"Do you predict he'll take after one of us and be a musician, scientist, or author?" She lifted her free hand and held Cory's head close for a moment.

"Mmm, perhaps, but I have a feeling our little guy will hang out with his Uncle Jaromír in his archaeology digs, the way he enjoys playing in the garden."

"Who the hell is Jaromír? Do you have another brother hidden away?" she teased.

Cory pulled away. "You didn't think my parents gave my brother the name Jon, did you?"

~ * ~

Katarina tossed and turned, having had a look earlier at the latest report from Cory's generals. George was starting to win the war. She looked at Cory's sleeping face and whispered her love. *I've got to do something only I can do.* She tiptoed out of the bedroom with the key to Cory's desk and put her finger to her lips when the guards acknowledged her.

"I'm going to try on the mask."

"My Queen." The guards bowed.

She rushed down the corridor and into Cory's office where the mask rested in his desk. She sat in his chair and pressed the green artifact to her face. Streaks of light flashed before her eyes, and a powerful energy pressed her into the chair. The message zoomed over her consciousness.

She dropped the mask into her lap. "No." She swiped tears away. "That's the only way? No wonder you didn't tell Cory, you stupid mask!" She cursed under her breath. "Fine. For my love of Cory. For the country. I'll do it. To save my family." With a trembling hand, she picked up Cory's landline and called George, having looked up the number in Cory's black book. She glanced around the empty office.

"Well hello, beautiful," George said when he heard her voice. "To what do I owe the pleasure?"

"Goran," she said through gritted teeth. "I've been doing some soul searching."

"Oh, tell me more."

"I'd like to discuss closing this war. Not a surrender, just peace. Would you be willing to hear *me* out, if not Cory?"

"On one condition."

"Yes?"

"Get away tonight. Without him knowing. Sneak away and meet me. I'll hear you out and consider what you have to say. But it has to be in person."

"Why, when you hate him so much?"

"I don't hate you. I think you're a fine woman who's too good for him."

"You won't...hurt me."

"I promise on the mother I loved."

"You were going to hurt my children."

"I was certainly not, and I'm deeply sorry to hear about your daughter's condition. You have my most sincere apology for that. I was going to take great care of them and then barter with your husband."

"For what?"

"A formal, public apology. I wanted him to grovel for it at my feet. I wanted to humiliate him, and he would have turned down my offer, I'm sure, but I would have tried. I would have then given you back your babies."

"You're a liar." She stopped herself, thinking of the mask's message.

"If you think so, why did you call?"

"I'm sorry. I just want this war to end."

"If you truly do then meet me."

"Okay."

"Remember, sneak out."

"Got it."

They talked details, and she hung up. "The mask said he wouldn't kill me and that I could end the war. I'll do it." She rose on shaky feet, went to the wall, and pushed a secret spot leading into a hidden corridor where she and Cory had often made love. From there, she made her way outside the palace and into the dark, brisk air. She retrieved her car and drove to Carasivia's border.

Twenty-nine

Cory woke up and rolled over to an empty bed. He thought nothing of it. She was probably with the children. By lunch, when Marina asked about Katarina, saying the children wanted her, Cory became concerned. When no one could find her and she didn't answer her cell phone, he became alarmed and alerted the palace staff to her absence. His guard of the chambers told him that last night, the queen had gone to his office, something about the mask. Cory went there and looked around. He sat in his chair and noticed the drawer with the mask was open. The mask was turned a different way. He touched it. Tingles ran up his arm, warning him of trouble. He put it to his face. He got an urge to call the phone company and trace the last call made from his landline. When he found out that a call had been made there the previous night to George, he sprang to his feet.

"Oh, God." He swiped his face. "Oh, God, no."

He called George. "Goran!"

"Looking for something? Took you long enough." George hung up, laughing.

Cory called back. "Wait! Don't hang up! What...do you want? Me? Fine. Just...let her go."

"Would you like to talk to her?"

"What?"

"Katarina, he wants to say hi."

Cory sucked in a breath.

"Cory," she said.

"Are you okay?" He ran a hand through his hair.

"I'm fine."

"Did he hurt you?"

"No," she said on a chuckle.

Cory sagged back. "Oh, thank God. How—"

"We're talking terms. He's going to end this war. Not a surrender, just a stop to the fighting."

"What?" Cory froze.

"Yes."

"How?"

"I'm persuasive."

"Katarina," he said with alarm. "Knock him over the head or something and get out of there! I'm coming for you!"

"No! We want this war to end, so I'm ending it."

"At what price?" he asked frantically. "What the hell does he want from you?"

"What do you mean? Don't you think I'm smart enough to talk sense into him?"

That was a loaded question. "Of course, but he's not reasonable."

"I've got to go." She sighed.

"Wait, sweetheart."

"Don't insult me further, Cor." She hung up.

He crinkled his brow. What the hell just happened? He called back.

George answered. "What the fuck do you want? We're trying to have a nice meal over some fine champagne. Diamond-studded glasses—"

"Let me speak to my wife," he said tensely.

"Whatever. It's amazing you got that beauty to marry you. What did you do? Threaten her? Drug her?"

"Please, just put her on."

"Yeah, yeah."

"Hello?" Katarina said.

"What the hell is going on? Your children want you! I'm coming for you!" He paced.

"Don't use my children against me."

"Enough already!" He paused as coldness seeped into him. "Are you...under coercion?"

"No."

"Please, let me talk to George."

"Yeah?" George said, a moment later. "Your wife is very diverting. Who knew that essence of loveliness was so damn intelligent. Who knew that feature would be so damn sexy. I'm completely shocked by that last discovery."

George could slit her throat if Cory weren't cautious. "Goran, I'm glad you see that Katarina is wonderful. I'm grateful she has talked you into making peace. Let this be the beginning of friendship between you and me. I'd even allow you and her to be friends."

"You'd allow us?" he asked mockingly.

"I'm sorry. I phrased that wrong."

"I should say so!"

"I meant to say, I'd encourage your friendship. Look, Goran, I'll bring the paperwork for peace—"

"Tell you what. I'll trade you...peace for your wife."

"What?" Cory stepped back, shocked, even though George had *joked* about this once before.

"I want her."

"You can't have her!"

"What if she wants me?"

"She doesn't! She loves me!"

George laughed. "You sure about that?"

"Yes!"

"I *love* fucking with you. You can have that damn peace agreement."

Cory's breath caught. "Why now? I've tried several times to get you to sign."

"Eh, I'm bored. I think I'll play with you in new ways now."

Cory was temporarily overtaken. He was dealing with a mad man. Finally, he said, "Thank you for peace. Please allow me to come to you, sign the papers, and then I'll take my wife home."

"I'll meet you just outside my border in the neutral territory between our two countries in that excellent five-star hotel Grandmother liked so much. Twelve hours from now."

"Why, if I may ask, are you...allowing Katarina to return to me safely?" He squeezed his free hand into a fist.

"I won't say I didn't try to seduce her away from you. I think I came close to doing so since I'm better looking than you and more of a man. Hell, I think she's wavering now. I also can be very persuasive." He hung up.

~ * ~

Cory showed up with soldiers and guards and saw that just a few of George's bodyguards stood in the distance in the hotel lobby, so close to George's border.

"Katarina," Cory strode to her.

George grabbed her and kissed her. She didn't fight him.

Cory stopped on a dime. "Katarina, sweetheart, I know what you're doing. I'm not mad. I'm grateful you love our country so much."

George pulled away but held her by the waist and laughed. "Good one, Corentin."

"I know my wife."

"So do I now." He smirked and looked at her. "Go now, comely one."

She looked between him and Cory with hesitation and stepped back, closer to George.

"My love, step away from him," Cory said, stretching his arms out to her.

She shook her head. George hugged her to his side.

Cory stepped closer, staring George down. "Whatever threats you have given my wife, I'm informing you now that enough is enough. I'm taking her home."

He laughed. "Against her will?"

"Not against her will." He swiped up Katarina's hand. She pulled away and pressed it to George's arm.

"Ah," Cory said, glancing at the fancy floor tiles. "So this is how it's going to go down." He reached into his jacket and pulled out a gun. He pointed it to George's forehead.

Katarina gasped. George's bodyguards aimed their guns at Cory. George ordered them to put them away, and they did.

"Get behind me, wife."

"No."

"That wasn't a request." Click.

"You're really going to shoot your brother? I thought you were above revenge."

Cory glanced at his men who held their guns in the direction of George's guards. "If they lift a hand again, shoot."

"Cory!" she gasped. "I didn't think you had this in you! This is murder!"

She pushed George's arm away and glared at Cory. "Fine. I'd like some time apart from you, though. He came here personally unarmed, trusting in you and your famous honor. Go on. Cuff me if you like, and drag me home."

"You're not fooling me, sweetheart." He grabbed her wrist gently, knowing this was an act.

"Let go and give me my dignity."

He released her.

She stepped back. "Leave. I'm mad at you right now."

"If you think I'm leaving without you, you're delusional," Cory said.

"I want some space."

"Uh-huh, sure you do. Stop with the bullshit now and come home with me. You can walk out, or I'll carry you out."

"Give me a second. I have something to say to Goran."

"No."

"Is this the kind of marriage we have now? You order me around? And I obey without question?"

"Katarina—"

"Just a moment!" She went to George and whispered something to him. He frowned. She grabbed his arm briefly and gestured with her other hand. He nodded.

Katarina approached Cory. He wrapped his arm around her waist. "What did you say to him?"

"I don't wish to say."

"I demand to know."

She shoved him away. "Fuck you."

He gripped her hand and led her stumbling to a car with guards following after them. "Tell me, for your own safety."

"Not happening."

In the car, Cory apologized. He had only been terrified for her and had to show strength in front of George. She stared out the window at the passing countryside.

Within five minutes, she pointed out the window. "I have to use the restroom. Stop at that gas station."

Cory gestured to the driver. They pulled over in front of the station. Katarina got out of the car. Cory did too, following her to the door.

She pressed a hand to his chest. "I don't think so."

"Sorry, you have no choice."

"What the fuck? Why are you treating me this way?"

"I don't trust George."

"That makes no sense! He's not here!"

"Exactly. He's not looking, so please relax." He kissed her cheek, but she drew away.

He grinned. "I know you're putting on an act, my love, though I can't figure out why you're still doing it. Do you fear spies?"

She scoffed.

"Never again will I fall for it," he said. "Why are you even trying?" He chuckled. "I fell for it twice, and the second time only barely because of your hysterics and threats to have me arrested. You left me to save my life when George was chasing us. You pretended to no longer love me in your terror because he was trying to kill me. Never again will I believe that you don't love me anymore or want to be with me. Never. Again."

"You didn't even formally accept his peace terms!"

"He made no offer when I was standing there. I believe he pulled all this crap just to play with me. If he threatened you, beloved, please tell me, or I'll assume he did." He traced her jaw with the back of his fingers.

She shook her head.

"Don't put me at a disadvantage. You've got to tell me how he threatened you."

"Let me go to the ladies' room in peace."

"Sweetheart, I've made passionate love to you for days at a time. As long as no other women are in there, I'll wait in there to protect you."

"No. I insist."

"Fine. I'll wait for you right outside."

"I know the way. I stopped and used this toilet on the way here." She strode to the back of the rather large interior, past rows of food, maps, and traveling supplies. He followed.

She pushed open the door to the ladies' room. He stopped and waited. Having waited for Katarina many times over the years, he grew uneasy. She didn't usually take this long. He waited one more minute. He cracked open the door without looking in. "Katarina?"

No answer.

"Is anyone here?" Emptiness echoed. "I'm coming in," he shouted in warning, and then pushed open the door widely.

He strode by the stalls and shoved open the doors. When he got to the last one, a cool breeze from an open window grasped his attention. He saw a peace agreement from George stuck to the wall. He snatched it up, curling it in his fist.

~ * ~

Katarina and George sat in his car, driving away. She sat pressed as far away from him as she could manage.

"Good job, Queenie. You actually did it. A good thing, too, because I was about to go medieval on Carasivia."

"Fuck and you."

He laughed and sped them away. "It's obvious Corentin values you even more than the crown, so this jewel of an idea is brilliant."

"He'll get over me eventually."

"No," George said.

"Yes, he will. He probably only values me for my looks anyway," she lied.

"That's plausible. You do make mirrors happy."

"Then where will you be when he forgets me?"

"No, where will *you* be? Maybe you and I—"

She scoffed.

"Why'd you actually do it then? Not for the country. You're American. Not for his dumb ass. I just couldn't believe that."

"My children." It was all of the above.

"Ah. That I can believe. You probably saved their lives. War is dangerous, even for children. Bombs don't distinguish."

She swallowed hard.

"I've got to know," he started, "why did someone with your crazy-good looks marry that loser, and when he was a pauper?"

She considered her answer, studying his arrogant expression. He'd never believe the truth about enduring friendship and true love. She couldn't compliment Cory in any way. "He…" She couldn't think of a good enough false answer. She shrugged. "He was always there for me hanging around."

"Like a desperate, lost gutter puppy playing on your woman's sympathy for a pathetic creature with the biggest set of balls an impertinent fuck-up can have." He broke out in a loud laugh. "Maybe his stupid, reckless courage is what did it for you?"

"Fuck off."

"Perhaps I will, with you."

She sucked in a breath, turned around, and pressed her face against her arm resting on the window, trembling.

Thirty

Cory held the signed peace agreement in his fisted hand just outside of the ladies' room. He stood staring at the floor, not moving. He didn't remember the guards guiding him into the car. He snapped out of it. They headed for the border of George's country.

Once there, Cory got out of the car and faced the border officers. "Move aside. I have a queen to bring home."

The officers gave each other nervous looks. One cleared his throat and drew a breath. "King Corentin, we do not mean to provoke you, but please, let this go. If we let you pass, and you approach our king, the peace agreement is voided. Do you wish for the war to start up again? No one over here wants that."

Cory rubbed a hand over his face. "I don't want that. I respect your people as well as mine. Your people are my cousins. I wish you only good." He slumped against his car. "Please understand we were only defending ourselves."

"By the humane tactics your generals use, that's obvious."

One of Cory's guards approached. "Sire, we'll figure something out. Let's go home."

He nodded stiffly, got into the car, and slammed back against the seat, closing his eyes.

He sat in his office stupefied all night, staring into the darkness. He tried to reach out to Katarina mentally and with his heart, but felt nothing come back to him. When he stumbled out of his office the next morning, the cheering crowd holding up banners of peace suddenly silenced. They let him pass. He went into his room and dropped onto his bed, staring at the ceiling, going through every detail in his mind, searching for the smallest clue Katarina might have given him. The mask hadn't helped when he tried it on earlier. He prayed. He meditated.

Sighing angrily, he sat up, needing to burn off some emotional steam. He called Asher, Brendan, and Gunther to join him in the boxing gym. Asher handed him a newspaper from George's country with a story praising Cory. It seemed the border officials slipped the story to the papers, telling them that the common belief that Cory was an honorable man was indeed true. Cory feared for those men now. Surely George would punish them. If they came to Cory, he'd give them refuge.

Wearing gloves, Cory sparred with Brendan.

After some rough practice, Brendan held up his arms. "Whoa, Cory, wait." He took off his gloves, and so did Cory.

Brendan studied him. "I can't blame you for being upset. We're all upset. We love her too."

Cory bent over and grasped his knees, fighting the sting of tears. He drew a deep breath and stood, muttering.

"What?" Asher said from the other side of the rope.

Cory muttered again.

"Sorry, Cor, we didn't hear you," Gunther, standing near to Asher, said.

Cory put his hands around his mouth and shouted, "I said, Katarina sacrificed herself for all of us!"

Everyone in the gym stopped working out and stared. Cory repeated his shout in Carasivian. Then he swooped under the ropes and stormed out of the gym as all eyes in the room watched him. He heard the explosion of conversation from the hall.

Cory went back to his bedroom and paced. "He can't have you!" He stopped before the wall and pounded it in anger. He'd give his palace for her. He'd take his children, his wife, and live in obscurity... he'd give his crown...except, to do so would put the country in grave danger, and he could not do that to seven million people.

Katarina loved Cory so much and put herself in the hands of a rapist—

Oh, God... Cory touched his gut and closed his eyes. His darling woman. He picked up her framed picture and stared at it.

"I have to get you out of there! But if I do, George will call on the war again..." He collapsed onto the bed, sick to his stomach.

He stared at her image again.

Start building that lab for me and the children. I'll be home. He imagined her words. She didn't want to be there, his mind screamed. He reached for the mask on his end table and put it to his face. "Give me something." The mask had acted as a medium in the past, giving him a connection to his mother. "Connect me to Katarina," he begged. "She and I have linked before, briefly, without you."

Tingling started on his skin. He felt linked to Katarina's heart in a more tangible way now. *Finally.*

Cory, thank God. I'm meditating in my room.

Are you okay?

For the moment.

Do I have to assassinate my brother to end this?

No.

I don't see another way.

I have to go. He'll be here soon.

Wait! I want you home! Now! He slammed his fist onto the mattress.

Cory, I love you. Please tell our babies I love them. You must let me go, for the sake of seven million people, unless I can think of something. You must not make a move! Oh no, he's here! No, please, Goran, don't!

He sensed that she turned from him and was urging his brother to have mercy.

The link broke. He gasped. His heart raced. He got up and paced again then dashed off to his jet to go get his wife and bring her home and away from George. The word *rapist* kept echoing in his mind, and his heart pounded in terror for her. Three members of his council ran onto the field and approached him as he prepared to step aboard.

They gave curt bows.

"My King," the head councilor began, "you're...going to rush over there and demand to have her back—"

"You're wasting my time." He adjusted the gun holster at his side.

"Majesty," said the second, "please, hear us out."

Cory wagged his wrist in a gesture to speak.

"We all love her. You know that. But if you do this, he could have you killed, and then she would be trapped there. Then he would declare war again and kill many of our citizens and try to take over here. Let's face it. If you die, the prince is not strong enough to lead us to success. Goran would probably kill your children. Let's think this through, for the queen's sake as well as for our nation's, improve our chances of success at getting our queen back."

Cory studied him then at length nodded. He saw all three visibly relax.

~ * ~

Gifts came into Cory's office from all parts of the country. His people were trying to offer comfort. The word had gotten out that Katarina had gone away to save them. Cory had stacks of homemade gifts, and many thousands of kindly-worded cards. He gazed around at his room of gifts one day. He went onto television and thanked his people for their loving consideration.

He'd spend his evenings with Marina feeding one baby and then the other, and they always traded off. As his child slept soon after, crooked in his arm, he'd read the kind letters from his people. He also made sure the babies spent a lot more time in his presence. He had the bassinettes moved into his office, and Marina cared for them while he worked, interrupting occasionally, so he could give his children loving attention.

Many times a day he considered ways to get Katarina home without declaring war and, using his gift, checked to make sure she wouldn't die there. Was she devising a way home? Every time he called George to offer brotherly friendship, George hung up on him. The mask wouldn't link Cory up with Katarina.

When finally one day Cory felt the link, his heart rejoiced. He told her he loved her and if she were in danger, tell him, and he'd go there immediately. He asked what he could do to speed up the process of getting her home, but she was silent.

He wiped his cheek, but it was dry. They were her tears he was feeling. His eyes began to burn with unshed tears of his own. The link broke.

When next he made contact with her through the mask, he was jolted with sexual, romantic energy.

I miss your touch, and I'm working on a way to get back to you...

He sat up, smiling. She must be unmolested. He sank back in relief.

He and Katarina sent loving messages to each other that way over the next few weeks. What was she up to? She never said. When could he bring her home? Would she remain safe? Those thoughts were forever on his mind. Dozens of times a day, he nearly risked starting up the war again to go get her.

George thought he was having his sweet revenge. Cory had finally called him up, angry and agonized. He really felt it, but not for the reason George thought. It was driven by worry for Katarina's continued safety and impatience to have her back. He knew by George's reactions to his words that he believed Cory's tortured words were driven by a deep tragic sense of losing his wife forever. But Cory's heart told him he'd have his wife back.

Perhaps she was trying to find some evidence or something she could use to keep George in line. He didn't know, but he believed in her. When a month went by without contact with her through the mask, he worried something on Katarina's end had fallen through, and he began to formulate a serious rescue mission. Ready to snap, he spoke with his advisors about possible ways to prevent war despite George's threats.

Then an odd message came through the mask. "I'm coming back to you in a new form. Will you still love me?"

He fell into his chair, stunned.

~ * ~

Kat entered the dark bedroom and tiptoed toward the bed sometime around one a.m. She could hear Cory's even breathing. He was asleep. *Good.* She eased her way closer and gently, slowly, lifted a corner of the blanket. Inch by inch, she slipped under the blanket and lay there, still. Cory moaned and rolled over. His hand landed on her thigh.

In a sleep daze, he moaned sexually. "Katarina." His hand slid up.

He sat up suddenly, running his hand up her body, her neck, her shaved head, and gasped. He jumped off the opposite side of the bed, landing on his feet, and retrieving his gun nearby.

"Who are you?" he said in the dark, but Katarina could make out outlines.

"It's me," Katarina said.

"Katarina!" He set the gun down on the nightstand, jumped onto the bed, and embraced her emerging form as his eyes adjusted to the darkness, she knew. His arms were spread out wider than normal. She had gained a lot of weight.

"I'm so damn glad you're home!" He chuckled. "Let me get the light."

"No!"

"Why not?"

She hesitated. "I'm not the same. Things happened."

"What do you mean you're not the same? So you put on a few pounds. Who cares."

"A few, Cory, really? You felt me just now."

"I don't give a shit. You're home!" He laughed in joy.

"My hair is cut very short."

"I don't *give* a shit."

"I...he scarred my cheek."

She heard him draw in a deep breath.

"He...hurt you?" he said tensely.

"Not badly."

"Son of a bitch!" He went for the lamp.

"Don't you dare touch that light!"

"How badly did he hurt you? Let me see!"

"No!"

"Katarina, I don't care what *form* you've changed into. You're my wife, and I'm *crazy* about you."

"When I turned down his sex, he got angry and slashed my cheek with a knife. Oddly, he still wanted me, so I had to turn him off. I shaved my head and gained weight. That actually worked. He wished me good riddance, promising we could still have peace when I asked, and I got into my car and raced home, crying."

He embraced her. "Thank God. Damn you're smart, woman. Are you *okay*?"

She started crying. He rocked her in his arms then turned her face to his, kissing her tenderly. "Sweetheart..."

"I'm okay. I'm crying because I'm glad to be home."

"Besides..." he said tensely, "...daring to put a knife to your face, did he harm you further? Violate you?"

"N...no," she lied. She didn't want to incite his fury toward George further and so kept the knowledge of the rape to herself...to keep the peace.

"Oh, sweetheart, are you sure you're okay?"

"Now I am."

"I want to go there and lay down the punishment."

"No! I missed you. I fantasized about your touch. Will you give it to me?"

"Mmm." He nuzzled her cheek.

"Keep the lights out while you touch me."

He sighed. "Okay, but then I want to see you. I love you."

"If you see me, you won't."

"Wanna bet?" He reached for the light and clicked it on.

She cried out and held her hands over her face. He gently pulled her hands down by her wrists and examined her cheek. He traced a finger over the slash and gulped sadly.

"Don't." She pulled his hand away.

"I'm sorry."

"Don't be. Just please, be patient with me."

He kissed her lovingly, urging her mouth open into deep kissing. She leaned her head back. Then he made his way to her neck and trailed hot kisses there.

"My love," he said, with a question in his voice. "Are you sure? After what you've just been through?"

"Please, yes. You don't want me?"

"Are you kidding me?" He made tender love to her.

As he held her, silent, hot tears hit his hand. "Why are you crying? Are you thinking of our time apart?"

"I'm ugly. Ugly scarred body, and now an ugly scarred face to match. You're going to lose interest. I'm going to lose you."

He rolled on top of her but held himself above her, looking into her eyes. "Not possible."

"You probably just made love to me now because you haven't had sex in a while."

"That's not the reason! The very thought of you arouses me. I'm crazy in love with you!" He traced the back of his fingers along her jaw. She shivered.

"And, nothing has changed. You're still so damn beautiful I can't believe you want to be with *me*! You're also a genius. You got the world's greatest asshole off your case, and you got me my wife back. You saved our country. I'm in awe of you."

"My scar is never going away."

He shook his head. "I don't care except that you had to sustain it. I have you back." He placed soft kisses on her lips.

"No one's ever going to call me beautiful again. They'll laugh at you for keeping me."

"Not true! They love you."

"They'll turn away in disgust."

"*Stop* it, sweetheart."

"How are you not turned off by me? Your brother was."

He moaned and rubbed his hips against hers. "I have my beautiful wife back."

When she started to disagree again, he nudged her knees apart with his. "May I?"

"If you're crazy enough to want to."

He rammed into her, and she called out in pleasure, as did he.

"Do you know how in love with you I am?" He held her hands above her head driving into her with as much vigorous abandon as when she was at her physical best. He called out, "I love you!" then collapsed onto her, squeezing her close. "I have my wife back," he said in amazement and leaned away.

She touched his lips. "I don't know which is better."

"Don't know...what is better?" he said with a dreamy smile.

"The intense pleasure you give me or watching you, hearing and seeing the intense pleasure I give you. That was beautiful."

"It's how we are together." He held her close and fell asleep smiling.

In the morning she pulled the blanket up to her chin. "Don't look at me."

He tore the covers from her and stared at her with desire. "Care for another round or two? Let's make our next baby."

She couldn't help it. A smile spread across her lips. She wiggled her fingers in welcome. He chuckled and ravished her.

Afterward, he held her, stroking her cheek. "I have my wife back."

She chuckled. "You keep saying that."

"I'm in heaven. Katarina?"

"Hmm?"

"Please, for the love of God, don't make me suffer from such a long separation from you again. I've gone through more than a husband should."

She snuggled closer. "Thank you for knowing I was faking wanting to stay with that...that man. I had no choice."

"You sacrificed yourself for our country," he said, and kissed her head, holding her close.

~ * ~

Cleaned up and dressed, he reached for her hand. "Come on, sweetheart, time for breakfast."

She stood her ground. "Our babies won't know me. They'll shriek in fear. Your palace guards will go wide-eyed and try to hide their disgust. Your night guards treated me well, with no restrained disgust, but that could have been a fluke. I'm not leaving this room. Please bring me my food."

He pulled her forward. "I'm going to have to prove to you the kind of stuff my people are made of. In that regard, I'm ashamed to say, they have a superior attitude to Americans who put so much stock in looks alone. Not that yours aren't as exquisite as ever."

"You must have true love to think that."

"You know I do."

"How?" She gestured over her body. "Look at me."

"You know how the process works, right? Your love actually has to be without conditions to be unconditional."

She smirked.

"But what does that type of love have to do with it?"

She paused. "George was born and raised in this country, and he told me with a snarl that I was revolting now."

"George is a bad person and doesn't represent us. Something is seriously wrong with him. He should get his eyesight checked and then see a psychiatrist."

"You're serious. You're not just saying that because you love me."

He gave her a look that proved that and pulled her toward the door.

"I can't!"

He swept her up and stumbled under her weight. "Guards!" he shouted. "Open...the...door!" he struggled to say.

"Put me down!"

He did, and the door flew open.

Pleasure lit up the two guards' faces. They bowed.

"My Queen!" one said. "What an honor to have you back!"

The other turned to Cory. "Sire, this calls for a celebration, does it not?"

"Indeed, it does. I'm going to alert the kitchen staff and have them order catering out. Tonight all palace personnel are invited to a feast to join me in my rejoicing! We'll have it in the great hall, so even those guards on duty can participate in the fun."

The guards looked at Katarina. "Your Majesty, how did you escape?"

She touched her cheek, over the slash.

Cory looked at his men. "Long story. My wife was traumatized."

"I understand," one replied after the other. "Sire, the war—"

"Do not worry. Our queen was able to get him to let her go with continued peace terms and a good riddance, thank God for all of us."

"Yes!" one guard said, and the other nodded.

Cory led Katarina to the nursery. Both babies clamored for her with their arms out. She picked them both up at the same time and kissed their heads as they squealed. Jon came whirling into the room.

"I heard you were back!"

Cory took the babies and put them in their cribs. Jon strode up to Katarina with his arms out but gave Cory a nervous glance.

"Go ahead. Give her a heartfelt hug. Just don't grab her ass," he joked and laughed lightly.

Jon hugged her and even kissed her cheek. "This day just got better. Thank God you're okay! The prayer services worked. I'd take walks at night and found people holding candle-lit vigils for you. Corentin told them you sacrificed yourself for them. You, My Queen, are our most beloved citizen. I'm glad you finally became one." He pulled away.

"I had to. I'd die for Cory. I'm not going anywhere."

Jon smiled. "How did you get away?"

Cory shook his head, telling him to drop it for now.

"You're not grossed out by me either?" Katarina asked Jon.

Jon's eyes got wide. "What do you mean?"

"Ah, come on, guys. Look at me."

Both threw arms around her and hugged her. A rumble started in her gut, and she laughed. Then the babies laughed, and then the guys. Marina came in and squealed. She shoved the men aside and embraced Katarina. Then she pulled away and apologized to her king and prince. They excused her cheerfully.

After breakfast, Katarina told Cory she needed bigger clothes. The only outfit she could wear was the one she had on, one a compassionate servant of George's had given her.

"Let's go to the village," he suggested. "There are some nice women's clothing shops there, and we can get some fresh air."

"No, just have a secretary pick them up for me."

He gave her a raised-brow look. "Doesn't sound much like my *American*-Carasivian wife."

"Ah, come on, Cor. You don't really want to be seen walking around town with me!"

He picked up her hand and kissed it. Holding her hand, he led her outside, against her grumblings. They paused at the overlook of the mountain pass.

"It's beautiful," she said, looking down at the village nestled between pines and aspens.

"I've always liked it. When I was a kid, I'd come out here and dream that I lived down in that village, with a dad who loved me."

Katarina turned to face him, as sadness zipped through her. "I'm so sorry you had to go through that." She stepped back. "Cor—"

"Sweetheart, what's wrong?"

"You didn't really...consider that—"

"Consider what?"

"I got a rush of emotion from your boyhood, such sad frustration. You once considered jumping off this mountain. Was it after a particularly bad beating?"

He gaped. "How did you... I considered it after awaking from that coma my father had put me in with his fists. Right after my mother died and days before he was *murdered*."

She hugged him.

He pressed her close then pulled away. "No worries. My dreams came true. I crowned you my queen. Though growing up, I only hoped to make you my princess—that was before I found out that my older brother was only a half-brother."

"Come on. Let's go pick me out something flattering."

He nodded to the guards who had been keeping their distance. They approached and followed. Cory led the way down the twisting path to the village. People greeted them with smiles, speaking rapidly and excitedly in Carasivian then slowing down and uttering elementary English phrases. Katarina would hug them. One lady pulled Katarina into a hug first, thanking her for her sacrifice. By the time Katarina and Cory arrived at the small clothing shop, Katarina was smiling.

Cory carried her packages. "Great choices, sweetheart."

"You helped. Can we go to a pet shelter?"

"Sure. There's a little one about a block from here. You want a palace pet?"

"A family pet."

When they arrived, Katarina looked around. "They don't have any kittens left."

"Why didn't you tell me you wanted one? Maybe we can find one in the city."

"Come on, let's go home."

~ * ~

Katarina and Cory entered the palace, and Asher, Gunther, and Brendan welcomed them, shoving each other aside to hug her. She gave them kisses on the cheeks, and Cory told them they could discuss the bad part later, in private, the things she went through.

"Cory texted that you were back!" Asher said.

Brendan took her by the upper arms, frankly admiring her.

"Damn, Kat, even fat and scarred and with short hair you're still hot enough to make me feel guilty for my thoughts. I'm shocked!"

Katarina and Cory gaped.

Cory scowled at Brendan. "Skinny chicks aren't necessarily more attractive. And different hair styles suit different women. Also, as for scars, don't—"

"I know that," Brendan said.

"Good," Cory replied. "Now leave my goddess alone."

Katarina sighed on a wide smile.

"But I think I'm into fat chicks now," Brendan added.

Cory shoved him back by the chest, making him stumble. "Ease your shit, asshole. She's *mine*."

"Your sex appeal just does not stop," Brendan said to Katarina.

"Say one more thing about my wife, and I'll punch you in the mouth."

Brendan grinned and looked at Katarina again. "If he stops treating you well, you know where to find me!"

Katarina smirked and grasped Cory's hands to keep him from lifting them. "You can't be serious," she said to Brendan.

Gunther looked at her. "Oh, he's serious."

Cory kissed her hand. Seeing the glow on his wife's face relaxed him. Brendan gave his wife's self-esteem a boost, and that was more important than Cory's jealousy. Though he couldn't grasp why her self-image suffered at all. She was the most beautiful woman he had ever encountered. The fact that his son looked like the woman of his dreams thrilled him.

Cory looked at Gunther then Asher. "So, I suppose if I screwed up, you two would step in as well?"

"Don't screw up," Gunther said with a smile. "I could compete with these assholes," he joked, looking at Asher and Brendan.

They all laughed.

~ * ~

The next day, Cory walked into Katarina's studio with his hands behind his back. She put down her bass. He brought his hands around, smiling.

Meow.

She gasped and took the kitten from him, a little orange fluffball with a baby blue ribbon around his neck.

"Oh, hon, he's adorable! How did you get him so fast?"

"I saw the look in your eyes. I worked fast."

She kissed him. "Thank you!"

"My pleasure. What do you want to name him?"

"Meowser."

~ * ~

In bed that night, Katarina looked into Cory's face with wonder. His smile wouldn't die.

"You really want more babies with me?"

"Dozens. I've always *loved* you, Katarina." He smothered her mouth with a kiss, rubbing his heated body against hers.

Eight weeks later, in his office, when she told him she was pregnant, he wrenched her into a passionate kiss. Then she clapped her hands together in grateful delight.

"Triplets this time. I'm about eight weeks along."

"Woo-hoo! Triplets!" After swinging her around in a dance of joy, he ran through the palace cheering.

People laughed, watching his excitement, and clapped.

Thirty-one

Months later, Katarina walked into Cory's office.

He went to her, taking her hands. "Sweetheart, you're done with band practice? You want to work with me on something?"

"Yes."

"On what? Something social, political—"

"I miss dancing with you."

He looked at his watch.

She took his hand. "Now, unless you have pressing work to do."

"Let me ask the boss." He grinned, looking at her.

"You can go." She winked.

Once in the ballroom, he took off his jacket and rolled up his sleeves. She looked down at her feet. "I can still see my toes. Not my whole feet."

"Your balance will be off." He took her hands. "Close your eyes and take a deep breath."

She did so.

"Now," he said hypnotically. "Listen to my voice. I want you to visualize gliding across the room with me. Don't think of the steps. Just clear your mind and let it happen. Feel the pressure of my hands and float with me. Allow me to worry about the technical stuff."

She opened her eyes. "You're a natural. You don't think about it anymore."

"Perhaps not, but I'll be compensating for your shifted center of balance. Trust me. Relax into it."

"Okay."

He pressed buttons on the music player built into the wall, and a waltz began. Katarina took his hands and lowered her shoulders. He swept her around the room.

"You're doing great, sweetheart," he said.

"I'm completely at ease in your arms. My shifted balance means nothing with your expertise."

The music stopped.

"Damn," he said.

"What is it?"

He shook his head. "I'm astonished," he said softly.

"At what?" She brushed hair from his brow.

"I just love you so much."

She looked into his face. He was serious. She kissed him.

~ * ~

That evening, Cory's new secretary entered his office as he was working. He offered a quick bow. "My King, you must see something." He flipped on a flat screen television on the wall.

Cory dropped a paper and watched George talking with an arrogant smirk. As George rambled on, Cory pressed his fisted hands to his thighs, trembling with rage. He stood up and strode to his bedchambers where he knew Katarina was napping.

He gazed upon her sleeping form and made his way to the bed, sitting beside her and putting a gentle hand on her arm. He watched her, not wanting to disturb her, as much as his heart was racing, and his head throbbing.

She moaned. "Mmm, Cory." Her eyes came open. "What's going on?"

"I..." He cleared his throat. "I'm sorry to disturb you. I'll come back later."

She touched his trembling hand and frowned, sitting up. "What's wrong?"

He hesitated. "George was on television, telling people something very ugly about you and him, the babies..."

She gasped.

Cory took both her hands in his. "Tell me it was all lies, tell me again that he didn't...do the unthinkable and touch you...that way. Did he violate y..." He couldn't finish the phrase.

Tears plumped onto her cheeks. She cast her gaze down.

"You told me he didn't harm you further, and you wanted me to make love to you. He told everyone on television that you and he... had an affair, while you were...still somewhat pretty—his words, not mine." He closed his eyes briefly then looked at her. "That the babies you carry are his. Please, tell me he didn't rape you!"

She wiped away more tears.

He took her upper arms. "Talk to me. Tell me. My God, tell me."

"I..." She sucked in a sharp breath. "I turned him down when he tried to seduce me, of course, and he got angry. Terrified, in my guest chamber that night, I cut off all my hair."

"Wait, you did that...first? I thought—"

"Let me finish. When he saw me in the morning, he hit me across the face for my attempt to dissuade him."

Cory held her arms in a grip, breathing hard as he listened. "Go on." He loosened his grip.

"He played mind games with me, would pin me down in my lavish prison, a gilded bedroom, and lift my skirt, stop short and laugh, telling me that our glorious time was coming. Since I was *your* wife, he wanted to play this out and make it last. He said my scars were bizarre but hypnotizing. He was mesmerized by me, he said, the woman his archenemy would die for. He wouldn't let me admit to anyone I was his prisoner, though. He threatened to start up the war again if I did."

Cory dropped his gaze, attempting to rein in his whirling emotions. He looked at her again.

"So I started eating constantly, ordering fattening food sent to my room—he didn't monitor that. I didn't move much and gained weight fast. He had left town on business for a few weeks. When he returned and saw how heavy I was, I noticed a change in the way he looked at me. His mind games slowed down, not as often and not as physical. Then one night..." She stopped.

Cory held his breath. "What—"

She wiped away more tears. "He came into my room angry and said, 'Your weight gain is the best attempt yet at dissuasion, but I will have that bastard's wife. I thought you were intelligent and would come to me of your own accord, which would have been phenomenal to tell that prick, Corentin, about, but apparently, you really are stupid. So time's up. I'll remember you as you were and fuck you before you're huge.' He threw me down and—" Her hands came to her face.

Cory sprang to his feet, his hands fisted at his sides, yelling out curses. He punched the wall yelling out. "I'm gonna kill him!"

She cried.

He embraced Katarina. "I'm sorry. Are you okay, sweetheart?"

"I'm working it out with my counselor. I'm sorry I didn't tell you, fearing you'd start the war again, even inadvertently. I had to tell someone."

"Can I do *anything* to get you through this!"

"Don't start the war again!"

"I want to go there right now, point a gun to him, and rid the earth of his evil presence."

"Please! Don't do anything *rash*."

He held her close, rocking her. "How many times?"

"One."

He was silent.

"Love me. Just love me."

"I do!" He pulled away to look into her eyes. "Oh, God, I...uh... after your trauma...we made love. I didn't know—"

"Your beautiful, loving touch gave me hope. Gave me a measure of healing. I wanted you. I needed you. Still do."

His eyes stung with tears.

"Let me tell you the rest. He was going to starve me to get me back to an agreeable weight and told me so, so that night, I slashed my own face."

"Katarina—"

"I'm sorry I lied about that, about all of it."

He cupped her cheek.

"When he saw me, he was *angry*. He ignored me for a while and finally came in one day and said, 'Let that trash have his ugly wife. You're free to go. I will laugh my ass off when he divorces the so-called love of his life. I will mock his name across Europe for being a fake. True love, my ass.' I asked him about the war. 'Eh,' he said. 'Don't need it anymore. It bores me.' I personally think he finally accepted the truth that even if he won, our people would never take him back, and his people would not support him."

Cory was bewildered. He kissed her gently on the lips and swiped his own tears away.

"And Cor, I never told you, but I kept my wedding ring in my shoe while with him, knowing how much he wanted it. That fucker was not going to take my ring! After your mother gave it to you on her death bed, you ran with it through the halls of the palace with your father chasing after you demanding it, you hiding it then having your father beat you into a coma for it, there was no way on earth I would have let it fall into George's hands. Your mother wanted you to have it. I told George I had removed it in Carasivia to have it cleaned."

Cory kissed her again. When he had gone to retrieve her from George, she had been wearing gloves.

"I love you so much." He walked out of the room. He went to his man cave and collapsed on the floor, his back to the wall, and his hands over his face in grief. Then he recalled her pregnancy, and panic raced through him. He jumped up and ran straight to Katarina. She was crying on the bed. He climbed onto the bed and wrapped his arms around her, pressing her face to his chest.

"Sweetheart, I love you unconditionally." He kissed her head then took her hand and kissed each of her fingers.

"I love you too."

"It devastates me that he hurt you."

She snuggled closer. He stroked the hair at her brow.

"This situation I'm about to discuss is different than when you were on that island alone with Jon. I need to know if those babies you are carrying are in the succession. If not, I'll adopt them in secret. I'll be their dad, and I'll love them. My mother taught me a powerful lesson."

Katarina drew back in alarm. "You think—"

"You were raped. It's a possibility."

"You wouldn't have adopted Jon's baby when you thought he and I slept together, but you'd adopt George's."

He kissed her temple. "Because I know Jon. Jon would want to be their dad, and even if that had been the situation, and I used all my talent to convince him to let me raise them, he'd still have competed with me for their love. It would have further damaged his and my relationship, the love of those babies, so I wouldn't have adopted them. Even when I believed that a terrible fate might have brought you two temporarily together, I came to discover that deep down I knew I'd have forgiven him eventually. I also knew he'd never actually let me adopt them had they been his."

"You're the king. You could have done anything you wanted."

"Only a tyrant would have used his power that way."

"Good point. But a rapist...your bastard older brother...does not have rights."

"Damn right he doesn't."

"And Jon—"

"Jon saved your life. That means something beyond what I could ever express."

"You made it sound as if only a biological child of yours could inherit the throne, my 'second' child."

"In that hypothetical situation, I couldn't have skipped over my own biological child to leave Jon's the throne. Not without overturning the law the way I did to make women eligible, but I don't think the people would have liked me to do that with the succession law and kids that weren't mine. If I have to...adopt the triplets...I'll figure out something about the succession. But then again, I won't have to. *Nothing* will get in the way of Merry ruling someday."

"If George thought I carried his babies, he'd want them for ugly reasons."

"I know. I'd have to do something I never even considered and deceive my people. I didn't think I was capable. We'd *have* to keep it a secret though."

"Or risk disaster. He'd never leave the babies or me alone if they were his. He'd make an international incident of it to use them for evil purposes."

"Do you think they're his?" he asked tenderly.

"Would you still love me?"

"Of course."

"The same as always?"

"Yes," he said softly.

"And the triplets?"

"Yes."

"Why?"

"Many reasons. They're yours, they're my mother's grandbabies, and I saw what it did to George when our mother held it against him that he was the product of a rape. Well, she wasn't close to him anyway because he was cruel like my father turned out to be. But the biggest reason of all, I'd love them just because they'd be mine, even if they weren't."

"They are."

He narrowed his eyes. "How can you know for sure?"

"I know."

"Is this a woman thing? You just sense it?"

She chuckled. "As a matter of fact, I do feel your energy growing inside of me, but back then I was terrified and when I got to Carasivia, I went to my doctor. He was kind and helpful as always. I got tests done. No diseases and no pregnancy. Besides, the number of weeks pregnant I am. The rape didn't occur right before I left. It had been a little while. Trust me, Cory, the gap of time alone is enough to ease my mind even if I hadn't gotten those tests. He couldn't be the father. My doctor here could tell when I got pregnant. It was here, with you."

Cory let out a breath. She looked into his face. Relief was tangible there.

"I'm sorry to say, but I'm glad," he said.

"Me too."

"You could have told me what he did to you."

"I'm sorry. I was afraid. Especially after your reaction to my first pregnancy."

He traced fingertips down her arms. "I didn't blame you when I thought you and Jon had become lovers."

"But you—"

"That was entirely different, and I can't say enough how sorry and stupid I was. Never again fear the man who loves you so completely."

"Okay." She cuddled against him. "Here, kitty kitty!" she called.

Meowser came scrambling across the floor and jumped, clawing his way up the bed. Katarina chuckled, and the kitten curled up on her legs. Katarina played with the bass clef symbol hanging from Meowser's collar. "Even looking at Meowser reminds me of how lucky I am to be married to you. A guard told me that you personally went to thirteen pet shelters during your work day to find my little puff ball."

He moaned and shifted underneath her. "It was okay. I saw some pretty cute puppies too, so the day was an extra good one! We may have to go back and get Meowser a canine foster brother."

She gave a fleeting smile. "Cor?"

"Yes?"

"I anticipated the secret of the rape getting out, so I did something."

"What would that be?"

"Could you reach into the drawer of the nightstand on my side of the bed and retrieve my journal?"

"You keep a journal?"

"Yes. Lately I've found the need to express myself this way."

He got her journal and gave it to her. "What's this about?"

She opened it and pulled out a folded sheet of paper. "Here."

He took it and opened it, staring at the page. His hand fell upon her arm lightly. "I believed you."

"But others might not. Please do a press release and show these test results to the people, so they don't doubt that I carry their princes or princesses. And please—I am the victim so have no shame about his crime against me—make it clear that to your utter horror, the only encounter was violent, ugly, and unwanted, and that you didn't know until now."

He wiped his face and nodded. "Only because I don't want the slightest smear on your impeccable reputation. Otherwise, I couldn't bear to. This is intolerable. I need to put him out of his misery."

"Don't provoke that monster!"

He gazed at her with love. "I won't." He kissed her then left.

~ * ~

After the press release, Cory got so many inquiries from his people about the possibility of starting the war again to avenge his wife that he went back on television to assure the nation that the vicious crime against the queen would not be repaid in that way, but in a more personal way that did not involve the people.

A journalist had approached him while on television and offered a bow. "Majesty, with all the respect due to your dignified person and station and that of Her Majesty, just to clarify, I humbly ask for your forgiveness..."

"Here." Cory shoved the DNA test results into his hand.

The man read them out loud with a look of relief on his face.

"Don't think I don't trust my wife. She knew the babies were mine but anticipated doubt among the people so had these done. I had no part of that, trusting her word when she told me the ugly encounter was spaced far enough apart from when she and I were together again that there could be no doubt." Cory left the set abruptly.

Katarina grew her hair out again but kept on much of the weight, her pregnancy counteracting pounds she managed to lose. Cory continued to treat her with adoration. She received many letters of sympathy concerning the rape, asking her to not return to America after all she had gone through for their country. She went on television, gripping Cory's hand, to tell them she loved them and this country, and most of all she loved and adored their king, and she was here to stay.

George called and told Cory it wasn't over. In disgust, Cory hung up then shuddered with regret. *I should never have done that.*

Thirty-two

Cory got up from his desk chair and stretched. He strode across his office and pushed open his doors. A crew was busy removing the antique palace pictures lining the wall outside of his office. He approached the man who was giving orders to other workers.

"What are you doing? These have been up for over a century," Cory said.

The man offered a curt bow, shifting his gray cap. "Majesty, Her Majesty wanted this. Are you reversing her orders?"

Cory tipped his head, confused. "Our queen ordered this?"

"Yes."

"Carry on."

"Yes, Your Majesty."

Cory smiled and tried to text Katarina, asking where she was. She didn't answer, so Cory approached a guard. "Pardon me, have you seen the queen?"

"She's practicing with her band, Your Majesty."

"Early. Thank you." Cory turned toward the palace studio.

When he entered the studio, the band had just finished their song. He greeted the ladies and approached Katarina. Her face lit with happiness. She put down her bass and went to him, kissing him. They sat on a cushioned bench. He rubbed her shoulders.

"Hon," she began, "we were going to surprise you. We're getting ready to do another benefit concert."

"How delightful! Let me know if you ladies need anything. And thank you."

Katarina turned and brushed her fingertips across his brow. He closed his eyes as her touch made his face tingle with unworldly love.

He took her hand. "Sweetheart, I'm curious, what's going on with the pictures?"

"Oh, I'm sorry. I forgot to tell you."

Maddy touched her shoulder. "We're going to the kitchen. Need anything?"

"I can't eat yet. Give me an hour."

"Okay." Maddy looked at Cory. "Want anything?"

"No, thanks. You're very thoughtful."

She clucked her tongue. "You're so gentlemanly with us, but please feel free to let loose and be American with us any time. We appreciate how you treat our girl so well... and us, so be a slob once in a while. Eat fries and ketchup in a T-shirt and sweatpants and laugh with us."

"I love how you ladies often give me a dash of American culture."

"It's our pleasure!" Maddy said. She left with Kat's other band members.

Katarina looked at Cory. "A village lady approached me. She and her husband own a small shop specializing in frames. Simple but elegant frames that to me represent Carasivia's beautiful culture, made out of wood from local trees with the national flower carved into the frames. I thought I'd order a bunch from a small businesswoman like her and reframe those pictures near your office. Those current frames look expensive, but they are lacking something, cultural charm. They were shipped here from some other country, weren't they?"

He nodded.

"I hope you don't mind what I did."

He swept hair from her temple and smiled. "Not at all. Good idea. You really class up the joint." He gave her an earnest look, sending the appreciation in his heart to her. Every damn day his heart sang with gratitude that he had won the devotion of the great love of his life. Not for one second did he take her for granted.

"Oh, crap. I just thought of something," she said.

"What is it?"

"What happens if every small business person in the land wants me to do the same thing?"

He smiled. "If things get that intense, we'll have competitions or something. Don't worry. It will work out."

"I did something else too."

He traced her bottom lip with his thumb and pulled down on it. "What did you do?" he asked huskily.

"Made another executive order."

"You are the queen."

She shifted. "You weren't around, were in the village that day your cell phone battery died, so I made the decision."

He took her hand. "What decision?"

"That law you were pondering...well, the head of the council couldn't locate you, and I ran into him. He gave me a look—one filled with respect—and told me that a timetable got moved up, and they had to know your decision about something. I asked what it was, and when he told me, I told him to go ahead and pass it, thinking that was best, and that you'd agree with me. I signed the paper right then and there. He thanked me, knowing you had given me the power to do this."

"To which law do you refer?"

She smiled. "The one about changing the tax structure of—"

He stood up. "I was going to reject that one."

She gasped. "What? Why? It was sound."

He ran a hand through his hair. "I'm the one good with numbers, not you, and I did the numbers!"

She frowned. Her lips parted. "I...I'm sorry!"

He sighed and sat down, taking her hand. "No, I am, sweetheart. I didn't mean to offend you. Why did you pass it, though?"

"Your councilor made a good case. He showed me long term projections."

"A risk."

"Yes, but my instinct said it would work out. And for some reason, my instinct is extra sharp when I'm pregnant."

He smiled. "Indeed it is." He started rubbing her shoulders again.

"Mmm, thank you."

"My pleasure."

"Feel free to override my actions."

"Why would I venture there? We're co-leaders, and you were the first to make such an order. You wouldn't attempt to override mine."

"No. Next time, sweetheart, I'll make them wait and discuss the issue with you first."

He looked at her with love. "If this had been something I *seriously* disagreed with, my policy would have been to argue my point to you in private and try to convince you to reverse your decision. If I couldn't change your mind, your decision would stand, since it was implemented first."

~ * ~

Kat's bandmembers ambled toward the studio with food.

"Don't get crumbs on my guitar," Bernadette said to Maddy, flipping a red braid out of her own eyes.

"No way, dude, you're the one who clogged up my equipment last time with your damn chip crumbs."

Their drummer, the blonde, wavy-haired Treena, grinned. "Cory is such a stud."

"I agree," Maddy said.

"Yep, and a real gentleman," Bernadette added. "He paid all my medical bills and even offered to move my family here to be near me after the shooting. He paid every dime of their expenses to see me when I was in the hospital."

"Did they try to get more money from him since you got shot because of Kat?" Treena asked.

"Take that back! My family is not that dishonorable, and I didn't get shot because of Kat! I got shot because a psychopath felt the need to mow down people in his way. Neither Kat nor Cory had anything to do with that!"

"I'm sorry. I take that back. I'm being a douche bag."

"Fine. Cory's so good to all of us. Don't you admire him the way we do?" Bernadette asked Treena. "And not just for his sex appeal?"

"Yes. I really meant nothing by it. Besides, how could I think poorly of a hottie like that?"

Bernadette smirked. "That he is, but that's not why Kat loves him. The way Cory treats Kat brings tears to my eyes. I want a man like that."

Maddy smiled. "Then you'll have to find a man madly, deeply, passionately in love with you."

Bernadette sighed dreamily. "They looked great gliding across the ballroom floor together, but the other day, I caught them watching a movie together, in their T-shirts and jeans, throwing popcorn at the screen, chuckling, and booing one of the characters. The playful banter between them is amazing. They're best friends. Friends who pull each other into passionate kisses."

"What about that hot brother of his?" Maddy asked.

Bernadette looked at her. "Hot he is. Fuck. But Kat was right. He's boring, even in his digs, I hear. Who the hell can make archaeology boring? Cory is so dynamic compared to him. Kat deserves a man like that."

"Jon is jaw-dropping, deliciously good looking, but there's just something about the almost-as-good-looking Cory that has nothing to do with him being a king. If I had never seen Jon, I'd think Cory was the hottest guy I had ever seen." Treena reached for the door. It flew open.

Cory and Kat greeted them. "Are you all up for movies and booze tonight in my private theater?" he asked.

"Uh...hm..." Treena tapped her chin with one finger. "Yes."

"Great! Meet Katarina and me there at seven. I'll have all your favorite comfort foods waiting and a bartender to make your favorite drinks."

"Virgin drinks for Kat," Bernadette said.

"Yes, and infused with vitamins and minerals. Thanks, ladies!" Cory led Kat chuckling down the corridor. They stopped a few yards down.

Kat gazed at him intently. He shoved his fingers up her nape. She gasped happily. He wrenched her into a passionate kiss, and then leaned away. Kat swayed, an open-mouthed smile complementing the happily dazed look in her eyes. Kat grasped his hand, and they continued down the corridor.

"Did you see that?" Treena whispered behind her hand to her friends.

Three passing guards looked after the royal couple with warm looks saying how happy they were for them, who were always smiling, chuckling, and holding hands, and how happy they were to have their king in such good spirits again brightening up the place. How refreshing it was to have a leader openly desire only his wife as opposed to the dishonorable ones who cheated on their wives behind closed doors. They felt the king was making a strong statement about love and commitment, and many appreciated his integrity.

Maddy spoke to her friends. "It's our turn next to find some sexy Carasivian men."

"What about Kat and Cory's closest American friends?" Bernadette asked.

"Asher's cute," Treena said. "I haven't approached him, though. He's a fricken ambassador. You know he used to be a rock climber instructor and climbs the mountains here? Explains his fine physique."

"I like Brendan better. Not as cute, but manlier, and a future doctor," Maddy said. "He could examine me any time." She giggled.

Bernadette laughed. "I don't know. Gunther and his silent strength. He's pretty hot sitting on his motorcycle, covered in grease from his work at the mechanic shop. And once, I caught him and

Cory talking in code. It was confusing, amusing, and intriguing. Kat wouldn't tell me what that was all about. She just shrugged and told me that Cory and Gunther had been doing that for years. Cory knows three languages—working on four if you count sign language, can speak in code, has serious street fighting skills, and God knows what else. Is he secretly a spy?" she joked.

"Maybe Gunther is," Treena responded.

"Maybe you are!" Maddy teased.

They went into the studio.

"I dare you to seduce Gunther," Treena said to Bernadette. "I think he likes redheads."

She shook her head. "It's not a game, Tree. He and Kat and Cory have been like family since middle school. Same with the other two. I would only approach Gunther with the utmost respect. For to do otherwise would hurt and offend Kat and Cory."

"Hmm," Treena said. "You're making too much of it. Maybe I'll do it and see if he's a spy. He's a mysterious guy. His parents had been involved with the American government, I heard. They were corresponding with Cory's family here in the palace, and their plane crashed on the way back to America on orders because of their secrets. That's all I could ever get out of Kat."

"Leave this alone," Bernadette said. "I don't like your attitude today. If you continue to be such a jerk after all Kat and Cory have done for you, maybe we'll find a new drummer."

Treena's eyes widened. She looked at Maddy.

"I agree with Bernadette. Back off."

Treena held up her hands. "Fine. I surrender."

~ * ~

Cory laughed at Katarina's joke as her bandmates entered the private theater. He turned. "Welcome, ladies."

"Thanks," they said.

Treena curled a strand of blond hair around her finger. "Like the shirt?"

"Green. Nice," he said simply.

"Your favorite color, I hear," Treena said.

"Yes, my wife looks great in it." He turned to Katarina.

"Hon, feel." Katarina placed his hand on her belly.

He smiled. "My children are moving around."

Bernadette and Maddy came over and felt her belly. Treena just watched.

Later, the girls were tipsy, except for Katarina, drinking her juice. Cory sipped the same beer, despite Katarina's friends' urging him to drink more.

He looked at them. "It's not as fun when she can't join me in my drinking."

"You're really attached to her," Treena said.

"You think?"

Treena gazed away then downed another beer.

Later again, drunk now, Katarina's friends laughed and tried to get Cory and Katarina to do so with wild tales.

Treena looked at Cory. "What's it like being a king?"

He crossed an ankle over his knee. "An honor, but a lot of work."

"You do work hard," she said.

"He does," Katarina said with pride. "But look at the difference he's making."

The others agreed.

"He's changing the world," Katarina said.

He kissed her hand, gazing into her eyes. "For the joy of being the one you love."

"And do I," Katarina whispered.

"Holy shit, you two," Treena said. "You could slack off, Cory."

He shook his head. "Only when my family needs me."

"Kat comes first," Treena said.

"Yes," Cory answered.

"But what if that conflicts with your duties?" she continued.

He studied her before answering. "Katarina is my co-leader for several reasons. She'd never have me compromise the good of the people. If I put something off for her account, it would be with her blessing, knowing she would not hurt them."

Maddy smiled, and Bernadette sighed happily.

"What is it with you two?" Treena said.

"What do you mean?" Cory asked.

"You're closer than most."

"I can't stand how much I love her," Cory said harshly.

Treena's eyes widened. "What's so special about her?"

"Her entirety."

"What do you mean?" Treena asked.

"Why do you like food, besides for the taste?"

"It keeps me alive."

"There you go," Cory said.

"What?" She chuckled. "Wow. You can't be serious."

He drew in a slow breath and sat up straighter. "I am."

Treena frowned. "Damn, dude."

Katarina looked at Treena. "Don't disrespect my husband. Cory and I have history. We've suffered and celebrated together, sacrificed and rejoiced, experienced the little things and the big, like getting shot. He has me...entranced."

He kissed Katarina's hand again, setting it in his lap.

"But Kat is fat now," Treena said. "And has a scarred face."

Bernadette and Maddy glared at her.

Cory tensed. "Don't disrespect my wife with your impertinent tone and implications."

Katarina tapped his hand and looked at Treena. "I have too much class to respond to you as you deserve, and we've been friends for years. You're also the best drummer I've ever met and make the band that much better, so, I'll only say this: Cory and I *love* each other. I hope someday you are lucky enough to know what that feels like."

"She won't," Bernadette said. "The kind of love you two have makes it into the history books."

Maddy grinned.

Treena sat on a sofa and blew hair out of her eyes. "That must make for some epic sex."

"You have no idea." Kat slapped her hand over her mouth then turned to Cory. "Sorry, hon."

He gazed at her under lowered lids.

"But how's that possible?" Treena said. "Look at her."

Cory sprang to his feet and helped Katarina up. "Excuse me. I think I'm going to go make love to my *beautiful* wife, if she'll have me."

"Oh, I will," Katarina said.

He looked at the other ladies who were gaping. "Evening, ladies." He pulled Katarina from the room without looking back, seeing her smirk from the corner of his eye.

Thirty-three

Katarina tapped on the door of Cory's man cave. "It's me."

"Come in." He stood and helped her to sit on a cushioned chair. He stood behind her rubbing her shoulders.

"How do you feel?" he asked.

"Fine. I don't mean to bother you in here. Trying to work out something tricky?"

"Just the regular tricky things. I'm trying to be as efficient and fair as possible."

"Maybe I can help."

"Can we discuss it over dinner? I need to shift gears, need a break."

"Sure. Just give me an idea."

"Well, I always have a panel of psychologists and sociologists investigate the long-term projections of the happiness levels of the local residents before starting an important project in their area."

"Wow," Katarina said. "Good! We'll talk more about it later."

He gave a fleeting smile. "Thank you. I could use your ideas."

"I...need to tell you something."

His hands froze. "Oh?" Whenever she had started sentences like that in the past, it had been a big deal. He came around and squatted in front of her, taking her hands.

"You're so attentive," she said with a smile. It melted.

"What is it?"

"I was propositioned by one of your...our subjects earlier. He wanted to start a secret affair with me, saying I was an exciting woman. He said, 'How many other women can end a war by herself?' I told him it was more complicated than that, that our soldiers deserve the real credit."

"Who the hell would dare approach you for an indiscretion? I mean you're beautiful, but what the fuck? You're married! Who would dare risk his king's anger in such a way!" He stood, upset.

"I've been hit on before, many times as a musician."

"I've never liked that—at all—but I accepted that it was going to happen. I just assumed that because you are a queen, men, *our citizens*, would have the respect necessary not to cross that line and approach you for an actual liaison!"

"I ordered him to leave me alone and never step foot in the palace again."

"Who?" he said, agitated.

"I'm overweight and scarred. He couldn't have been serious."

"Nonsense! I'm going to call him into my audience chamber and have a serious word with him."

She shook her head. "His queen handled it."

"Fine, but you'd better tell me if he bothers you again."

She gave him a raised-brow look. "I'd better?"

"Don't punish me this way. A husband has the right to scare off an unwanted suitor sniffing around the love of his life."

She smiled and held her hand out. "Very well. You win. Help me up."

He did, and she pulled him into a hug.

The next day, she entered his office as he was working and locked the door. He grinned knowingly and went to stand. She held up her hand, and he sat back down. She made her way to him.

"Scoot back a little."

He did, watching her. She moved his paperwork aside and sat on the edge of his desk, facing him.

"Sweetheart?" he asked.

She parted her knees and slid her skirt up her thighs, searing him with a sexual gaze. His mouth went dry. Then she slipped off her panties, and his lips parted. She grasped him by the lapels and urged him forward, putting her hand on his head, lowering him to the level of her thighs.

"What do you want, My Queen?" he teased, glancing up at her.

Her brow came up, sarcastically. She leaned forward and down and traced her tongue up his neck, stopping to suck his earlobe. She leaned back. He splayed his hands on her thighs and gave her what she wanted. Her head fell back, and her heavy breaths filled the air. Soon, she was grasping handfuls of his hair and called out, trembling. He leaned back with a smirk.

"Mmmm," he said. "Delicious."

He stood, and she hurriedly unbuttoned his pants. He slid them down. She spun around and placed her hands on his desk. He eased into her. Blinding pleasure seared him, and he once again silently thanked the mask for enhancing their already great sex life. For every degree he loved her, the mask's gift matched it with pleasure during sex. He smiled, grateful he had uncommon love for her. He knew she got the same pleasure and thrilled for it. Their calls mingled, and he pushed harder. He grasped her shoulders, and then...white light exploded, and his mind blanked, hearing her call out as he did. His spasms finally stilled, and he swayed. He pulled up his pants and fell back into his chair, staring at her with an open mouth. She spun around and smirked and leaned forward, placing her hand on the side of his head. She kissed his forehead then slipped her panties back on. Glowing satisfaction overwhelmed him, and he couldn't find any words.

Finally, he muttered, "I love you."

"Oh," she said huskily under lowered lids, "it's mutual."

"You know one of the many things I love about our lovemaking?" he asked.

"Mmm, tell me," she said, touching her bottom lip.

"You not only call out in pleasure, you also call out in joy. It's uplifting."

"For both of us, my love." She turned and left him there, staring after her.

At length, he looked back at his paperwork and smiled. He was in a superb frame of mind and tackled his work in utter serenity. Later, his ministers praised him once again for his unusual clarity and foresight. One man called him gifted and handed him reports from mayors all over the country, reporting improvements in a dozen areas of interest due to Cory's policies.

Cory faced his advisers. "Ladies, gentlemen, do not underestimate the influence of a marriage made *in heaven*. I'm so often in a great place in my head that I'm sure divine inspiration just flows right to me. Thank God for Katarina."

"Long live Queen Katarina!"

"Hear, hear!"

The next day, Katarina paid him another visit, repeating the day before. She left Cory with a grin on his face. He glanced at his work happily.

~ * ~

Another day Katarina entered Cory's office. He set a paper down and ran his fingers through his hair. He smiled and prepared to stand.

"No, it's okay. Sit down." She came around and kissed him. "You look frazzled."

"I'm buried in work."

"I wanted to say hi before going to the village. My belly is growing fast. I need a new coat and some exercise."

"I'll go with you, sweetheart."

"Naw, it's only a short walk, and you look busy."

"Are the girls going with you?"

"No. They decided to go to the pub."

"Can Jon accompany you?"

"He's on a dig, and our American friends are busy."

"I don't mind going with you."

"No, sweetheart, really."

"Why not just stay then?"

"I need fresh air, and walking is good for my back."

"Okay, but don't forget your guards, several of them."

She grinned and put her hands on her hips.

"Don't give me that innocent look."

"What look?"

"The one that says you're not going to take my advice."

"One isn't required to take advice."

He inhaled deeply. "You don't want me to insist."

Her brow came up. "You mean order me?"

He gestured, palms facing her. "Your words...not mine."

She frowned.

"Take the guards."

She scoffed. "Not when you use that tone with me."

He stood up. "George is out there somewhere!"

She spun around. He strode to her and grabbed her arm, spinning her to face him.

"What the fuck?"

"Be reasonable!"

"Don't boss me around!"

"Katarina—" He cut himself off and took a breath. "Look, I'm stressed," he said, tossing a glance at his work behind him, "and you are always physically uncomfortable now. Let's take this down a notch. I'm sorry."

She sighed. "Fine. So am I."

"Can you see my point though?"

"Yes. My point was your tone."

"I apologize, but I must insist you take the guards. This is not up for debate. I won't be able to focus on work and will follow you myself if you don't."

"I'm not in the mood for your company." She sighed. "Okay, I'll take them. I am awkward on my feet now and must keep my babies safe." She patted her belly.

"Thank you! Did you seriously consider not taking them?"

She just shrugged.

A zip of the old irritation at her withholding information rushed through him, but he pushed past it. "Be careful walking down the mountain. Hold onto the guards."

~ * ~

She took two armed guards with her and looped her arms through theirs. Her Carasivian language skills were improving, so she told them a Carasivian joke Cory had told her. They laughed and told her others. They made it to the village at the bottom of the mountain.

"There." She pointed to a woman's store.

They went into the shop. A gray-haired lady approached with a smile and bowed. "My Queen, welcome!"

Katarina chatted with her then took a coat to the dressing room. A woman knocked on the dressing room door.

"Occupied," Kat said.

"My Queen?" a female voice said.

"Yes?"

"What an honor! Would you look at a shirt and give me an opinion?"

"Sure." Kat opened the door.

The woman pushed into the dressing room and shut the door.

Kat backed up. "Miss..."

She pulled out a gun. "Quiet."

Kat gasped, putting her hands over her belly.

"Make a call and get someone to bring you ten million dollars."

Kat nodded. "My phone."

The woman pointed her gun to Kat's belly. "Don't play with me."

"I won't." She reached into her pocket and pulled out her phone.

"Say a wrong thing, and I'll shoot your belly then shoot my way out of here, killing whoever gets in my way."

"I...must get the king's permission to withdraw that kind of cash from our account," she lied.

"I see. Just don't say why, and I'll let your triplets live. This can be quiet. We get the suitcase, and my partner and I leave without a fuss."

Kat fought tears. They heard a scuffle out in the store. The stall's door flew open, and one of the guards had a man at gunpoint.

The stranger looked at Kat's captor. "I'm sorry, love."

"My Queen," the guard said. "My partner is unconscious, but I got this bastard! I approached him because he was staring at the dressing room. We argued. There was a struggle. He managed to get my partner before I got him." He shook his head as if to clear it, as if he had been struck.

"Let him go, or I'll shoot!" the woman said.

"Do and your man, then you, are dead," the guard said. "I called the king. He's racing here now. Out!" The guard backed up, and Kat and her captor stepped out.

Cory tore into the shop and looked at the woman's hand with a gun pressed against Kat's belly. "Threaten my wife and babies?" he shouted, enraged and striding toward the woman. He aimed a gun at her.

"Cory, I'm okay," Kat said.

"And you'd *better* stay that way."

"We're at a standoff," the woman said.

"No, we're not. My troops are on their way down to surround this place."

"I'm afraid the queen is my hostage. My husband and I need clear passage out of here."

"Not happening," Cory said.

"I'll shoot!" the woman said.

"Wait!" Cory stepped back with lifted hands. He then holstered the gun at his side. "Why are you doing this? For money?"

"When she turned, I saw a tattoo on her wrist. I think it means something," Kat said.

"What was it?"

"A snake biting down on Carasivia's national bird."

"King Goran made that his country's new emblem," Cory said.

"Bastard," Kat said.

"You're not kidding," Cory said.

"We don't like our king," the man said. "He threatened us. We worked for your uncle, in his espionage department. Goran, the tyrant, sent us here to snag your queen. Thought we'd get a little extra money to help us get away."

"Your woman threatened mine, and I will not tolerate that," Cory said coldly. "If you somehow escaped out of here with my wife, I'd retire as king to spend my days...hunting you." His eyes and his tone were so cold that Kat shivered.

"How hard do you think," Cory said, tilting his head, "it would be for me to find my beloved wife and triplets? Do you suppose I'd ever give up? Do you imagine I'd let you get away with taking them from me?"

"But we'd let her go once we were safe!" the woman said.

"I have no reason to believe you," Cory said. "You grabbed her on your king's orders."

Kat gulped. The energy Cory was giving off was alarming, but she imagined he was terrified under that bravado.

"I am a man who was pushed before," he added. "Never. Again."

"B...but I have a gun," the woman said.

"Cor, I had the tracer implanted in my body," Katarina lied.

"You did?" Cory asked, gaping.

"Yes," Katarina said, and then thought that maybe she should at the rate she was going.

"It's plastic. It's not a real gun," Kat's captor said, quivering. "I'm sorry for scaring her." She turned to Kat. "I'm sorry."

The woman handed Kat the gun. "Here."

Kat examined it. "She's right." She gave the gun to Cory then looked at the woman, frowning.

The woman turned to Cory. "Majesty, forgive us. We were coerced. Could we defect and become citizens here? We'd be great employees in your service."

Cory gave them a wide-eyed look. "Are you kidding me?"

"It wasn't a real gun!" she said.

Cory's gaze narrowed. "Well, now I don't have to punish you *severely*, but hire you?"

"We could give you political intelligence."

"Yes," the man agreed.

"I have zero reason to trust you."

"Majesty—"

"Quiet," Cory cut her off. "You're *very* likely going to prison after a trial in which I will testify against you."

"Hon?" Kat said to him.

"Yes, my love?"

"They might be useful."

"Sweetheart, you are a trusting, forgiving person."

"Interrogate them. Have them investigated while they are detained, and then make a decision."

He gave her a long look before nodding once. He pulled her into an embrace.

Thirty-four

A month before her due date, Cory helped Katarina lower onto their bed for a nap. He kissed her. "I love you so much. I got thousands of pictures of your pregnancy this time. My collection is awesome. I'm aiming for a father's hall of fame!"

She chuckled. "I love you too."

He sat on the bed. "You've made me incredibly happy. I hope I do the same for you."

"Yes. I'm huge this time."

"Your belly is large, but three people are in there."

"My stomach skin is going to be saggy."

He kissed her belly. "No comment."

She hit him with a pillow.

"Thank you for mothering our children." He kissed her belly again. "I love you, babies."

"Oo, the kid on the left just kicked. He or she heard you." She chuckled. "If I could have pawned off the birthing aspect on you, I would have! Then your skin would be saggy."

He fluttered more kisses on her belly. "But you'd still love me."

"Mmm, suppose so," she teased. "Hon?"

"Yes?"

"You know I've cut down on my time doing music—"

"I'm glad you're still active in it though. But it's nice to have you home now. The charitable things you do for this country... It's wonderful to eat dinner with you and our children every night, to sleep with you every night, to make love to you so often."

"I do give you a *lot* of sex."

He gave her a heated look. "The kind of explosive pleasure you give me melts the stress away."

"You're a *great* lover, always were."

He gave her a big smile. "I'm so into you."

"Could I get more involved with you, as a...co-leader?"

"I would value your increasing contributions. Is there anything in particular you want to work on? Head the council meetings if you wish."

"Maybe, we could start with...grievances—God knows why there are any the way you lead."

"Because there are over seven million, free-thinking people in this country, and I cherish their individual insights."

"Ah, well, maybe my artist side will help me come up with some creative solutions to tricky issues. That spy couple—"

"I'm sorry, sweetheart, they seemed to check out, but I just can't risk it."

"You're just mad because they threatened me."

"Damn right I am."

"You really can't hire them?"

"No."

"You imprisoned them."

"After a fair trial. Uncle Lothar's treaty with us allows for that. George never changed that. I don't have to return them. I wouldn't anyway, for your sake. George would execute them."

"The judge ordered them to a bad place."

"But, Katarina, I talked the judge into transferring them to a more pleasant place, if prison can be that at all, in exchange for giving me verifiable intelligence. And for your sake, I'll propose opportunities to make their situation better."

"Thank you."

"Why does it matter, after what they did?"

"Don't know, but I think your mother would have acted the same way."

He smiled. "On another subject, would you prefer to share my office or have your own?"

"Share yours."

He kissed her and stood. "It could be distracting at times, but if we end up doing it on the throw rug, or the couch, or against the wall, all the better. We'll approach work refreshed and in a good mood." He gave her a sexy look.

"You're a sex machine. Always want it."

"Only with you." He ran a hand through his hair and let out a hard breath of air. "Could we..." He traced a hand down her neck.

She smiled. "I'm tired and need that nap. Later?"

He grinned. "Mm, something to fantasize about. You can help me design the set-up in *our* office later."

"Thank you."

"It's my absolute pleasure, goddess of my dreams."

A look of bliss overcame her. "I feel so damn loved."

He kissed her and left the room, dimming the light.

He went to his office to do some work. His phone rang. It was George. "Fuck." He answered. "Yeah?"

"Well fuck me. You're actually happy to have that cow back!"

"Asshole!"

"Rumor has it that your sex life is even stronger than before. Will wonders never cease."

"Fuck you!"

"This will never stand. I thought I was leaving you to a life of hell with an ugly wife or a divorce scandal, but you actually like her this way. You didn't divorce her, not even after her indiscretion, and you didn't make her...disappear."

"How does it feel to be at the top of your *being a dick* class? I'm sure they'll give you a PhD for your brilliancy in the discipline."

"I thought at first you kept her to spare a scandal or for the sake of your stupid so-called honor or something."

"God, you're troubled."

"Then I heard about how you kiss her in public and give her all those lover's looks still. Those warm hugs. Can't you help yourself?"

"Your jealousy is pathetic. She will never love you!"

"Jealousy?" He laughed. "She's just plain gross now."

Cory broke out laughing.

"What's so funny?"

"You're the biggest fool on the planet." *I'm glad you no longer want my goddess of a wife.*

"Now I just have to finish this once and for all. I grow weary of the game." He hung up.

~ * ~

Cory was playing with Liam in the gardens. He used a blue toy shovel and buried a plastic figurine in the dirt. He tried to hand the shovel to Liam, kissing his head.

"Dig, son, like your uncle taught you. Make a find!"

Liam giggled and slapped his dimpled hands up and down. Cory put the shovel in Liam's hand and helped him to stab the freshly piled dirt. Liam started digging. Cory used his hands and sped up the process. He pulled out the figurine and gasped. "You did it! You made a famous discovery!"

Liam squealed with laughter. Cory picked him up and gave him kisses on the face. Liam stopped laughing suddenly, speaking to Cory with his eyes.

Cory held him away. "What is it?"

"Merr-Merr."

Cory placed Liam on his hip. "Let's go get her and have some ice cream. She should be up from her nap now."

They found Katarina in the corridor holding Merry. Katarina reached for Cory's hand. He greeted her and kissed her. The guards watching at their posts smiled.

"Good day to you, gentlemen," Cory said.

"Good day, Majesties."

"Majesty," one guard began. He looked at Katarina. "A new music magazine is coming out next week. My sister is editor-in-chief. I think you'd really like it. I'll bring a copy when it's hot off the press."

"That is nice of you, Mr. Belonof, thank you," Katarina said.

"My Queen, it's my privilege, and thank you for knowing my name."

Pride dashed through Cory. Damn, his wife was great.

She tipped her head.

The guard nodded. "King Goran used to say to me, 'Be gone with you' with a derisive curl of the lip."

Cory grimaced. "No comment." But he muttered under his breath, "My older brother is an epic asshole."

~ * ~

Alone one night, on the phone in his office, Cory demanded that George meet him on neutral territory to settle their differences, man to man, after George called his wife ugly yet again.

George laughed. "I've been thinking, American trash, those babies should have been mine."

"Not in your wildest dreams could you be so lucky."

He scoffed. "What happened between us was worth it, to hurt you."

Cory drew in a deep breath. "I will avenge her, when I figure out the perfect way. Bide your time."

"What makes you think it was rape?"

Cory curled his fist. "Don't *ever* imply such a thing about her again!"

"Well, hell. You still want that unfaithful bitch."

"You sound just like that monster, my father. You do realize that Mother wasn't murdered by a visiting official trying to kill the king."

"Yes, she was. You were there. You saw her get shot while she was jumping in front of the king to save him!"

Cory cringed. Katarina had attempted the same thing with him, not realizing how deeply she injured him emotionally with that action, bringing back the tormented memories of his boyhood.

"My *father* hired the man to do it when he found out his *unfaithful* wife had been raped to produce you. Just like him, you blamed the victim."

"I don't believe that about my mother!"

"Think, asshole, you saw your DNA test results. They didn't match those of the previous king's mother, and you know our mother wasn't even vaguely capable of infidelity."

"Fuck."

"And neither is my queen!"

"You still don't think she and baby brother had an affair. Amazing."

George's complete audacity exasperated him. "Had you been a good king, one with honor, I might never have claimed my right to the throne, or at least I would have allowed you the lavish life of a high prince of the realm and had you on my council."

"Fuck you and your charity, Corentin. You know what's odd? I hate your guts, but I kind of respect you. You used to look the former king in the face when we were kids and dare him to let you live, you in your glorious impertinence. He complied. Barely. And you dared to defy even me by marrying your current cow, though I can see why you did it at the time. She used to be *amazing*. Yeah, I think I can respect the shit out of your courage."

"Keep your respect." Cory bristled.

"Think of what Katarina and I did over and over. Obsess about it."

Cory's stomach turned. "It was once, you disgusting liar." Coldness ran through his body. He wanted to hang up, but doing so on a psychopath was dangerous for innocent people. However, George enjoyed their angry banter and never harmed anyone for it.

Cory pressed his hand against his thigh. "Your vicious crime against my wife has actually drawn her and me closer. Her incredible beauty and strength keeps me mesmerized. Her scarred face is a constant reminder of the lengths she'd go to for me and this country, her devotion and love, her dedication to me. I love her even more now, you failure fuck, and am so grateful for her. She's so damn beautiful and courageous."

"I'm so stunned I think I'll go in for a hearing check. I don't hear a lie in your voice, but I don't think the laws of physics would support the possibility of what you're saying. Katarina is a mess. How could any man stand to look at her now?"

"I dare you to say that to my face. Come on. Give me the pleasure." His breathing became hard. "And don't even think of declaring war on me again," Cory warned. "Remember that I signed some new treaties and have you surrounded. If you make a move that I deem as a war tactic, your neighbors will step up...on my side of the fight. I worked hard to achieve that, and my brilliant wife helped."

"Well, fuck me. I'm just going to have to get creative."

"You should be afraid of me," Cory warned.

George laughed and hung up.

Thirty-five

Katarina smiled at Cory as they worked in their office. He watched as she picked up a paper from her desk to the left of his, and studied it.

"Thanks for having everything translated, Cor."

"You're welcome."

"Though I'm getting better with your language. Admit it."

"Yeah, you speak it like a four-year-old now."

"Thanks!" she said cheerfully.

He broke out into happy laughter. "What are you working on, sweetheart?"

She scratched her head. "Hmm, I've decided to dig into my specialty first. I'm trying to determine if this environmental proposal makes sense. I'm analyzing some reports, looking at chemical compositions."

"Sounds good. Have you met with our scientists yet?"

"No, I do that tomorrow."

He gazed at her. "Thank you for your expertise. I know those projects will go well under your leadership."

She blew him a kiss. Suddenly, she spun sharply in her chair.

Cory sprang to his feet. "You okay?"

"Yeah." She chuckled and rubbed her belly. "Sorry. I almost forgot. I'm in need of new bass strings."

He smiled and sat back down. "Need help looking up the number in Carasivian? The English language phone book is due to arrive tomorrow."

"Naw, I got a guard's help earlier and wrote it down. He speaks English pretty well! Thanks for that."

"Give credit to Jon. He paid for all those language lessons before I was king, knowing I'd do my level best to make you fall in love with me and marry me and bring you back to the kingdom I could live in when I bested the tyrant king, George."

Her brow came up. "Really?"

"Yep."

She picked up her cell phone and dialed, speaking in her simple Carasivian. Cory couldn't help himself and watched her, charmed at her effort to practice his language. She looked at him with mild panic.

He jumped up and strode to her. "Sweetheart?"

"I don't know how to ask him for…the strings I need."

"Give me the phone."

She handed it to him.

He spoke to the salesman in Carasivian. "Hello, this is her husband. She's still learning the language."

"Sir? Is that an American accent she had? Somewhere in the western part of the country?"

"Yes. Very good ear, Mr—"

"Sanivochnic."

"Mr. Sanivochnic. We would like a dozen sets of your best bass guitar strings."

Katarina smiled at him.

"Yes, sir, very good."

"Could you deliver them?"

"No. I'm sorry, we don't offer that service."

"Very well."

"I'll reserve them in the shop for you."

"I appreciate that."

"What is the name?"

"Put them under my wife's name, please, Katarina Brodnik."

There was the sound of stumbling and a long pause.

"Hello?" Cory said.

"Uh, I uh, is this—"

"Her husband."

"You mean—"

Cory chuckled. "My name?"

"Yes," the salesman squeaked out.

"Corentin Brodnik."

"Is this...a joke?" His tone hinted at awe, and a tinge of fear.

"I assure you, it is not," Cory said seriously.

"Oh my God. Majesty, will you forgive me?"

"For what?"

"Of course, I'll personally deliver the strings to you. Right away!"

Cory stared at the phone and shook his head. He looked at Katarina. "Your strings are on the way."

"Thanks! Wow, that was fast. I could have taken my daily walk down there."

Cory shrugged and sat back down.

Minutes later, Katarina was cuddling a sleeping Merry whose head was on her baby bump. Merry's drool slid down Katarina's shirt.

"My tummy is falling asleep under Merry's cheek. I think her sibling might kick her and startle her any moment now, but I don't want to disturb Merry. She likes my heat. She giggles when my shirt moves around, but if a little foot pokes her in the ear while she's asleep, she might freak out."

Cory smiled, so grateful for the goodness of life.

~ * ~

Cory picked up the phone and answered with disgust, in no mood to talk to George. "Why do you continue to harass me?"

"Because I know you'll pick up in order to prevent me from killing one of Carasivia's citizens."

Cory flinched, remembering the one time he did hang up on George and then getting the tragic news about a villager with a note pinned to his chest.

"I have friends around that palace you stole from me, American trash. After all, many of those servants used to work for me."

"I doubt they're your friends. More like your threatened, but you'd better not even think of harming—"

"I can get people to do real damage. I sent incompetent people your way to fuck with you."

Cory grew cold. "You're insane. Get treatment."

"The former king taught me to disregard consequences, said his good looks were wasted on a jackass like you," George added. "I'm going to finish his work. He nearly had you once, but you awoke from that coma. I can forgive him that failure though."

Cory wiped his face with his hand. "I can't reason with you." So many times he just wanted to hang up on George, but he didn't dare.

"Never said you could reason with me. You stole my mother. You stole her ring, the one I was meant to have, and gave it to your ugly wife."

"Mother wanted me to have that ring, and only a goddess would be worthy to wear it after her. You should know, Mother said your energy unsettled her."

"Who do you want picked off first, your fat, unattractive wife, your dysfunctional daughter, your stupid, worthless son for coming out second after a girl—or are those kids the progeny of your cowardly, boring, sissy-ass, pretty-boy brother, whom I would love to take revenge on for siding with you over me? I'm going to make you watch. Unfortunately, you've proven to be strong, so I'm going to break you."

Cory clutched the phone. "You'll not get near my family!"

"Better keep them locked up. And away from windows. Better not let them see the light of day again, because as soon as they do... Bang! Your whole line is about to be wiped out, and then it will be easy for me to take back Carasivia. I've changed my stance on executing children." He hung up.

Cory tore down the corridor toward the nursery. The kids would have to stay indoors until he took care of George. Marina and the children weren't there. Cory asked a young nanny where they were. The girl said they went to the garden to play with a farmer's puppies.

"Thank you." He dashed away, texting Marina then signaling a guard. "Find my wife. Send her to our bedchambers to wait."

Cory opened the door to step into the garden. A shot went off, and Marina screamed. Cory ran outside and saw his son lying face first on the ground with blood soaking his shirt as Marina ran with Merry toward him.

Thirty-six

Cory scooped up Liam and ordered Marina to take Merry to his bedchambers and wait there with Katarina and tell the guards not to let anyone in. He rushed Liam to the palace doctor, shaking and crying. Liam went into surgery; Cory never left the little palace hospital. When Katarina joined him, they held hands and prayed. Cory had ordered his guards to keep Merry under heavy protection.

Katarina begged on a sob, "Is he going to die? Use your gift!"

"He's going to live," he told her once more.

"Check again!"

Cory drew a deep breath and closed his eyes. He searched within. "He's going to make it. I couldn't fake relief like this." He released a breath.

Katarina let out a choked breath of her own relief. Liam pulled through, and Cory and Katarina squeezed each other, tears running down their faces.

A nurse came in with a long face. "Your Majesties?"

Cory and Katarina stood.

"Yes?" Cory croaked out.

"Your brother...the prince—"

Cory approached the nurse. "What is it?"

"He was shot. He's unconscious. Stable for now."

Cory barely caught Katarina when she stumbled. He helped her sit then sat and pressed his hands to his face. Katarina cried again, so he lowered his hands and pulled her into a hug. "He's alive..." Cory said. "Thank God."

Moments later, he called over a guard. "I'm going to give you a list of names. Certain members of my council and certain generals. Give me a pen and paper, please."

"Yes, Sire." The guard left and came back shortly with the requested items.

Cory studied him. "You're on my side."

The guard's expression melted into sadness. "I'd give my life for you."

"Please then, don't betray me—"

"My King, no!"

Cory wrote down some names. "Get these people and no one else. Hurry back."

"Majesty." He bowed and hurried away.

Katarina touched Cory's wrist. "Do an inner search on Jon. Please tell me he isn't going to die!"

"I...I'm so flustered." Cory looked at his shaking hands then drew in a deep breath and closed his eyes. Moments later, his eyes popped open, and he made a mad dash to Jon's room. A nurse was preparing to stick a needle into a tube that Jon had in his arm. Cory shoved her aside. She fell then scrambled to her feet and ran out of the room.

Cory yelled, "Stop her!"

Two other nurses apprehended the nurse in the hall. Cory collapsed onto the floor and stared at Jon. He used his gift and discovered that Jon would live. His guards looked at him, bewildered.

"Have that tested for poison," Cory said, glancing at the drug the nurse had been trying to give Jon. "And have her detained."

"How did you know?" a guard asked.

Cory shrugged and stood. "A brother's intuition." He couldn't make his gift widely known, or every person in the kingdom would approach him every time a loved one was in danger. He put his hand to his forehead and watched Jon through tear-blurred eyes. "That was close. I need you, Jon, and I love you." He kissed the top of Jon's head then returned to Katarina reassuring her that Jon would be okay.

The guard showed up with the people on Cory's list. He ushered them into this little windowless room where Marina and Merry now were. Cory looked at the sad and scared faces and told them about Jon.

Katarina hugged him.

"I know what we need to do." He shifted.

Everyone leaned in closer.

"There are traitors among us—luckily not many, I sense—who are willing to kill infants. You all are the people I trust most." The only way for him to test loyalty for sure would be for him to look at someone or imagine them and see if he sensed death after trusting them. That didn't leave him a lot of time.

"What are we going to do?" Katarina asked.

He looked at her. "I cannot assassinate another king, and he turned me down when I challenged him to a duel."

Mouths dropped open.

"That gun I held to his head in the hotel wasn't loaded. I've wanted to kill him many times, but I'm next in line to his throne. How would that look to those people? Especially since he's my brother. Besides, I've never killed anyone." *Just beat the crap out of them.*

Katarina's eyes widened. "The gun wasn't loaded?"

Cory shook his head. "My men had loaded weapons in case my life depended on it."

"What should we do?" a general asked.

Cory smirked "There's only one thing because war is out of the question."

"George is crazy!" Katarina said.

Cory gave her a knowing look. "I have much experience in dealing with psychopaths. I studied my father, preparing for the day I was going to defeat him."

"We're short on time, Cor! George is trying to kill our family as we speak. You either have to lock him up or kill him. I prefer the latter to ever feel safe again." She pressed her face to his chest, and he stroked her hair.

"Majesties, could we assist with anything?" a council member said. George had threatened to behead the man if he ever regained power. He was furious that this council member actually showed joy when Cory took George's crown after a battle of the wits between the two in front of the nation.

"Time to get creative. And fast." Cory stood.

Katarina grabbed his arm. "Where are you going?"

"To end this." Cory took a pen and paper and scribbled out some directions. He looked at his head council member. "Implement this immediately."

"Yes, My King." The man rushed out of the room.

"Cor…"

He tapped her hand reassuringly.

"You're not going to abdicate and give him back the crown?" a council member asked.

Cory faced him. "No. He'd destroy this country."

"Not even to save your family."

"Even if he spared my family, which I doubt, he'd make the citizens of this country suffer. That's not going to happen."

The man sank back in his seat.

Katarina grabbed Cory's wrist again. "You're not going to… give yourself up and leave the crown solely to me?" She curled the material of his shirt between her fingers.

He didn't answer.

She stood up. "Cory!"

He looked at her, grinning. "I like being king because I'm good at it and make people happy. You do too, but it's not necessary to give you the position of sole ruler…unless you absolutely had to have it." He chuckled. "I wouldn't turn down the woman carrying my triplets."

Her brows rose. "I don't want sole rule. What *are* you up to?"

He winked. "Trust me."

A camera crew came into the room, filmed Cory speaking, and then left to broadcast the recording widely. Two hours later, a man came in and told him that millions internationally had gotten the message. The government's lines were ringing off the hook in support of his crazy plan. Overwhelmingly and online also, people were rooting for him. Someone brought him the mask. Cory tried it on and asked to see the people who were in or near the palace trying to kill his family. Nothing happened. He tried again. Nothing.

Katarina reached for it. "Let me try. I think that thing has a crush on me," she joked. She placed the mask to her face. "Tingles zapped my cheeks and are racing up my face and into my scalp. Get me a pen and paper!"

Seconds later, Cory shoved the items into her hand. Using Cory's back for a surface, she wrote down a list of names and places, rapidly. "There's only five of them, now Cory, being paid a ridiculous amount of money." She handed him the list.

He took it and stood, giving it to one of his guards. "I want these people arrested immediately."

"Are they getting a trial?" Katarina asked.

"Yes," Cory said. "There will be an investigation to confirm the mask's accusations."

The guard nodded. Sometime later as Cory sat with his elbows on his knees and his face in his hands, the guard returned. "It's done. They're being detained. Two of them have already admitted their guilt, and they pointed out the guilt of the other three. The two feel safer in your prison than in George's hands knowing they failed."

Cory nodded. "Thank you."

"Cor," Katarina began. "The mask made it quite clear to me that those five were the last ones he would ever convince to do something so hideous as to kill your family."

Cory kissed her before striding out of the room as everyone watched.

Guards attempted to follow. He held up his hand to stop them. Right outside the room where the reception was better, he called George.

"Goran, my loving brother!" Cory snarled.

"You did it again, fuckhead."

"You failed to kill my toddler son and my brother, you bastard."

"I can't believe what you just did."

"Do you accept now? Do you know that your own citizens are mostly behind me?"

"Meet me there at five tonight."

"My. Pleasure," Cory said with acid.

Cory's biggest ally, the neighbor directly to the west and separating him from Goran's country, agreed to let them do this on his land. Huge crowds gathered along with camera crews. The field of honor teemed with anxious people. It was a bit chilly, and Cory wore a coat.

Cory and Goran stood ten feet apart, glaring at each other. Microphones picked up their words and broadcast them to the people.

"You left me no choice after publicly challenging me. After telling everyone I shot your son and brother, but you have no proof of that."

"Yes, I do. Two of your people already admitted it and told us where to find the written contracts you signed, ordering them to do that with the promise of wealth. It seemed they doubted your word. That's why they only agreed when you signed those evil documents. Even your death threats to them alone weren't quite enough to push them to do it."

"You may kill me this day, but know that if you don't, Carasivia is mine. A duel. How eighteenth century of you." George sneered.

Cory shrugged. "Assassination was out of the question for political reasons. Besides, you're one to talk. You ruled Carasivia as if it were the Dark Ages. I'm soon to rule your new country, and know this...your people will adore me and curse your name. I'm going to put women's rights at the top of my agenda!" He chuckled. "I'm going to give the citizens freedoms they've never seen before, even better than Uncle Lothar gave them. I'm going to make them as great as Carasivia, institute things that will make them celebrate in the streets. They'll also appreciate that I speak their native language far better than you do. I paid exquisite attention as Mother taught me her French. It's going to be glorious. Have fun watching from the afterworld."

"Shut up, and let me kill you already!"

"Okay, psychopath. You can try." He touched his chest where a small, woven red heart rested.

"What is that?"

Cory smiled dreamily. "This little heart is my prized possession. My wife and children made it for me as an expression of love. They asked me to wear it, so their love would protect me," he lied. It was just part of his plan, a heart he had thrown together himself.

"I'm going to shoot right through it with your guts."

Cory's expression fell. "Again, you can try. Only one bullet in our guns."

George laughed mockingly. "Thanks for the target. I won't miss."

They had agreed beforehand that the shot had to be below the neck. Men with weapons on both sides held them up, prepared to fire should either brother lift his hand high enough to shoot above the neck.

"Oh, by the way, Corentin, I took a pill so I could prolong fucking your wife."

Cory yelled out, "Rapist!" ran, and tackled him.

They threw punches and rolled around. Cory's guards stood back with arms crossed, grinning.

"Get him, My King!"

George's guards stood around, shifting nervously, giving each other anxious glances.

"Think we should stop them?" one of Cory's guards asked.

"Naw," said another. "Let His Majesty beat the crap out of him."

"Think he'll win?" a third guard asked.

"I think our king will stop short of killing him this way."

"I agree."

Katarina gripped the guard's arm, looking at Cory. "Kick his ass, sweetheart!"

Cory punched George in the jaw.

One of George's guards looked at Cory's guards. "We should stop this."

"Why?" one of Cory's guards answered. "Goran committed a great crime against our queen. Surely, you do not condone such a thing."

"No, none of us do."

At length, both Cory and George lay on the dirt, on their backs, bleeding, clothes torn, and breathing heavily.

"A moment, asshole," Cory said. "Then I'm going to knock you unconscious. Then spit on you until you wake up. Then shoot you."

George scoffed.

Katarina approached and walked around to George's side. She spit on him.

George wiped his face and grabbed her ankle.

"Let her go!" Cory demanded, and sprang to his feet.

"Don't anyone move!"

Cory and the others froze.

"If I trip her forward, she'll land on her very pregnant belly. Then squish, there goes three babies."

Katarina trembled. Cory pulled out his gun and pointed it at George. Guards rushed to Katarina's side.

"Stop!" George ordered them. They froze.

George snarled. "Point that down, so I can stand, retrieve my weapon, and we can finish our duel."

"Let my wife go first."

"But this is fun."

"Both of our countrymen and women are seeing what a monster you are to continuously threaten a woman carrying triplets. Release her, or I'll shoot you in the head to save my babies."

He sighed and let Katarina go. A guard held out his hand, took hers, and pulled her to safety.

"Let's be done with this," George said and stood.

"My pleasure."

Cory and George turned, did their paces, and then turned again to face each other. Katarina and many others around her prayed.

The brothers lifted their guns. George aimed for Cory's heart, but Cory aimed for George's leg. Cory crumpled to the ground while George stumbled. Katarina screamed and ran to Cory, holding him in her arms. Crowds rushed to surround them. Medics hurried Cory into an ambulance, and Katarina held Cory's hand as the ambulance sped away. She looked into Cory's face, and a smile split her lips.

Cory smiled. "Help me with this."

She helped him sit up and take off the bulletproof vest. "It worked. He aimed for your chest and not your head, but it was still a risk, even with our men pointing guns at him, and I was terrified since you can't sense your own impending death."

"Naw, I knew he couldn't resist destroying a symbol of the true love I have in my life."

"Now what?"

"I'm sure I proved my point to his people. They'll overturn law to get rid of a man like him. And when they humiliate him, when he gets kicked off his second throne, I'm going to have a fucking ball rubbing it in his face. I'm going to torment the fucker. I'll hunt him down and imprison him for life."

She kissed his forehead.

When they reached the hospital, his phone rang. "Hello?"

Katarina listened to his words, and he could see she was trying to figure out what the conversation was about.

Cory hung up.

She touched his shoulder. "What happened?"

Cory grinned. "They chased him away. He got into his limo and took off as the people threatened him with death. He's officially dethroned!"

"Thank God."

"And banished from the country. His countrymen are holding prayer vigils for me as we speak and are demanding that I take over as soon as I'm physically capable. I've got to let them know I'm okay."

She hugged him. "I've got some happy news."

"What is it?"

"My parents want to move here and help out with the kids."

"Great! I'll have a suite prepared in the palace."

"Really?"

"You didn't think otherwise, did you? I'll have to get things moving quicker on that lab, so you and your parents can work together in it, and Mom and Dad can start training our babies when they're old enough."

"Thank you." She kissed him.

"You're welcome. I look forward to having Mom's famous hamburgers again. She'll have a great time working with our chef—if she wants to! She and Dad can lead a life of leisure and play with the kids all day if they'd prefer."

"It's doubtful. They're too young for retirement and love their work, but playing with the kids a lot, yes."

"And barbecuing! Picture Dad grilling up a steak and wearing his shirt that says, 'Chemists do it best because of their great chemistry.'" He smiled.

Cory's parents had been good investors and had taught him well. Cory and Katarina were making money in the private sector and were almost billionaires again. He thought of his talent with math and statistics that extended to making wise decisions about the market.

"And your book royalties. I like how you don't accept a salary from the people," Katarina said.

"That's one positive thing I learned from my father."

"People say you got your father's good looks."

"Got my mother's eyes."

"Like our daughter. Is she like your mother?"

"Yes, in many ways from what I can gather so far, but she truly is the happiest little soul I've ever known."

"So, after you lead your two countries in peace for decades and spreading it to the entire region, Merry will take over someday and continue the positive legacy of her father."

"Of her *parents*. Yes. And I will be heavily involved with the raising of our grandchildren and great-grandchildren, stressing the importance of good values."

"You're the best."

He took her hand. "You are. Had you not married me, my life would have taken a different turn. You changed me. Remember how I used to get into a lot of fights but then learned to rein it in for the sake of my love for you? Remember how serious I used to be?"

"I didn't want to *change* you!"

"Well, then you brought out my best and discouraged the rest."

"I can live with that."

"Good," he said.

"Remember how whiney I used to be? Always putting myself down?"

He smirked. "I hated that about you. I'd have to count to ten silently every time you did it. Having you confident in yourself now is refreshing. I'm proud to have you as my queen."

"Your scarred and fat queen," she teased.

"Grrrrr," he admonished her. "You displease your king, Ma'am, when you do that," he joked, but meaning it. "Besides, your eyes and your hair rock my world." He took a handful of her silky locks and let strands fall between his fingers.

She bent from the waist in a mock half bow. "Forgive me for offending you."

"Don't let it happen again." His lips turned up at one corner. "The happiness you give me infuses every decision I make. You affect a nation."

"Sweetheart, will the dethroning finally rid us of George or make him worse?"

He gazed down. "I don't know."

Thirty-seven

About two years later

Katarina pushed open the doors to her and Cory's office. Three foreign ambassadors stared at her, and Cory smiled. "My Queen?"

"Oh, sorry. I'm interrupting."

"You're never interrupting."

"I forgot that this conference was today," Katarina said. "Please forgive me. I was busy with the children. Where's Asher?"

"On his way, sweetheart."

"Majesty," an ambassador began, looking at Cory, "if we may continue. Could the queen return later?"

Cory frowned. "My wife rules this country with me."

"Yes, of course."

Cory turned to her. "You seem anxious. Do you need a word with me, or did you come to join the conference?"

She took a deep breath. "I don't think I'll join it today after all. Can you spare a moment?"

"Of course," Cory said to her. "Madam and Mister Ambassadors, if you will please wait for me."

"Your Majesty—" a second ambassador said.

Cory turned to Katarina. "My Queen, is this not something that can wait?"

"I wish it could."

"Very well." He took her hand.

"Cory, let's go into your man cave, I mean attached thinking room."

"All right." He gestured for her to lead the way then turned briefly to the ambassadors. "Please excuse me." He followed Katarina.

They pushed open a door in the back of the office and entered a corridor. From there, they opened a door on the right and walked into a small, cozy, dimly-lit room and shut the door. Katarina grabbed him by the lapels and shoved him against the wall, forcing an urgent kiss on him.

He moaned and ran his hands up her back wildly then took her by the arms and pulled her away, smirking. "I know our sex is *exceptionally* good, but you interrupted an international conference for it. Damn," he clucked his tongue. "Does much for a man's pride."

She grinned. "Your sex is that damn good, but—"

"But what?" He traced a fingertip down her neck, making her shiver.

"Let's make another baby."

He chuckled. "Now?"

She frowned. "You don't want more babies with me?"

He cupped her cheek. "Sweetheart, the thought delights me, but it's so soon. Our triplets are toddlers."

"I know but—"

"Could it not wait until you've had a longer break from pregnancy?"

She shook her head. "The mask haunted me with visions from our next child. She wants to be born. I received the message: *Today, before noon.* I was busy, and time got away from me." She glanced at her watch. "It's eleven forty-five."

He smirked again. "If you're sure."

"Please, hurry. Skip the fancy stuff." She slid up her skirt.

"Being married to you is a completely unpredictable, joyous thrill ride." He kissed her and made love to her, pressing her against the wall.

She sighed, smiling. Afterward, he passed a hand over her hair.

"Thank you, Cor."

"I adore you."

"I adore you too."

"If we weren't rushed, I could have pleasured you."

"Later, but I did enjoy it. Hey, you never use your gift."

"To check for pregnancy? No. I like the surprise. I like when you give me the happy news. But in this case, the happy news won't be news—"

"Use your gift now. Make sure."

"It's important to you."

"Yes."

He nodded and drew within. A smile came to his lips. "In nine months, we will be holding our new child."

"Thank you." She studied him. "Are you...happy about this?"

"Very. But sweetheart, you're going to take it easy. No overdoing things."

She kissed him. "Yes, sir. I'm going to go take a nap now."

They exited the man cave. He went back into his office grinning, and she went the other way, toward their bedroom. He approached the ambassadors on top of the world. By the end of the conference, they were laughing together.

~ * ~

Two years later...

Cory hung up the phone in his office.

"Who was that?" Katarina asked.

"I can't say for sure but—"

"What's wrong?"

"I think it was George."

She gasped.

"He didn't say anything, but I feel it." He shuddered. "An ugly feeling."

She grabbed his hand.

"Katarina, I want you and the kids to stay inside until this is investigated."

She nodded, rubbing her eyes and yawning.

"Those children of ours are wearing you out."

She smiled. "Your six kids are worth it."

"Take a nap, sweetheart. The nannies can feed them lunch and get playful exercise with them without us for one day."

"You're not going to the nursery?"

He glanced at his watch. "Only to say goodbye. I have to meet the ambassador at the airfield."

She took his hand. "No. Send someone."

"I wish I could, but he's only on a layover, and we really need to talk. Asher's going with me."

"Call the ambassador."

"He told me he needs to talk to me in person."

"Cory—" she said ominously.

"I love you. See you at dinner." He kissed her and headed for the door.

"Wait."

He turned around and looked at her in question.

"I just need to tell you, the best thing I ever did was to ask my impoverished best friend to marry me."

He gave her a look so endearing that she pulled him into a kiss. He pulled away. "Goddess of my dreams," he muttered, turned, and strode out the door.

~ * ~

She called him on a video conference. "I hear the plane's engine behind you. Is the ambassador leaving now? Are you coming home? Merry is tugging on my leg." She moved the camera down, and Merry waved to the screen.

He waved back. "I'll be a little later than expected."

"What do you mean?"

"The ambassador insists that I go with him to a meeting."

"No. Come home, please."

"Please, come home, Daddy!" Merry said. "I read Mommy's lips!"

Katarina squatted down so Cory could see both of them on the screen.

"Hi, my angel!" Cory said to Merry. "I need you to help Mommy hold down the fort until I get back home. Will you do that for me?"

"That American expression means be Regent with Mommy?" She broke out into rapid sign language. "For a little while? That's a big responsibility…" She paused then opened her mouth, speaking the last words. "…for a six-year old!" Merry spoke as best she could.

Cory signed his next words. "Indeed, but your mommy is not Regent, sweetheart, she's a co-ruler, as you know."

"Okay, Daddy. Maybe I'll help her pass a law…" she signed. "…while you're gone," she spoke.

He chuckled. "Make it a good one."

"Majesty, we must leave now," a voice behind him said.

"Come back tonight, Cory."

"I will. I love you both. Good to hear your sweet voice, my daughter. You speak so clearly now."

"We love you!" they said together.

"Give my love to your brothers and sisters, sweetheart."

"We will!"

~ * ~

At midnight, Katarina stretched out on a couch by the main palace door with Merry asleep in her arms. Katarina stared at the door and tried calling Cory again. No answer. She nodded off. When a guard laid a gentle hand on her shoulder, she jumped.

Merry sat up and rubbed her eyes. "Where's Daddy?"

The guard was frowning.

Kat sat up straighter. "What's wrong?"

"Majesty, Highness, please come with me," he said, and signed.

"What the hell is wrong?" Katarina screeched.

He didn't say anything but strode to the palace medical facilities. Kat's heart pounded as they made their way down the corridor. Once at the door to the small hospital, Kat's feet froze. Merry charged past her and stopped suddenly. Offering a silent prayer, Kat stepped forward and joined Merry. They peeked into a room. Asher was lying in a hospital bed.

They approached him. Merry put a hand on his arm and glanced up at Kat. "Uncle Asher is sleeping."

Kat turned to the doctor on the other side of the bed. "What happened? Is he okay? Where's my husband?" she asked frantically.

"Our ambassador will pull through."

"What happened?" she pleaded.

"There was an incident."

"Where's Cory!"

He looked down.

She dashed to his side of the bed and grasped his arms. "Where's the king!"

The doctor opened his mouth but hesitated.

"Tell me!"

Merry was staring at the doctor, watching his lips, and gripping the sheets between white knuckles.

The doctor looked at Asher. "Before he lost consciousness, he told us that he, the king, and the other ambassador were ambushed. Our ambassador was shot, and he saw Goran and some men leading King Corentin away by gunpoint. He saw Goran's men get in a shootout with our king's men. He saw Goran force King Corentin into a car saying he was going to kill him inside it. They drove away. I'm so sorry. The loss to our nation is incalculable."

Kat screamed and swayed but saw and heard Merry screaming in hysterics. Kat ran to her side of the bed, pulled her into an embrace, and dropped to the floor. They sobbed together and were inconsolable.

~ * ~

Kat was dressed in all black and surrounded by her six children in black in Cory's office. Jon approached with a case. Solemnly, he set it down on Cory's desk. The triplets and their baby sister were playing on the carpet with toys.

Liam was sitting in his father's chair, coloring at his desk. "I'm making Daddy a welcome home card," he said. "For when he comes home."

Jon looked at Katarina. "You are our queen, Ma'am, the sole ruling sovereign, having become a citizen here. Do you wish to officially make Merry your co-leader, to practice authority when she's older, or is she not to rule until you pass someday?"

Tears rolled down Kat's cheeks, and she didn't answer. Jon opened up the case. Cory's crown shone there.

Kat gasped.

Jon took Merry by the hands and looked into her face, speaking so she could read his lips. "Sweetheart, I can't replace your daddy. No one can, but I love you, and I want you to come to me whenever you need a *father* to talk to. I'll try to advise you as he would have and be there for you."

"What do you mean?" she asked.

He picked up the crown. "Touch this. It's yours, since your mommy has her own."

She backed away, screaming. "No, no, no! Daddy is not dead!"

His tears glistened.

Kat looked at Jon and said through gritted teeth, "He's not dead. They just haven't found him yet. We are not wearing black because he's dead. We are wearing black because we miss him so much it's like being dead."

"I don't see how he could have gotten out of it, My Queen," Jon said, with a broken-hearted expression.

"Put that crown away!" Kat said.

"Put it away!" Merry ordered.

He sighed deeply and complied.

~ * ~

Kat sat at Cory's desk and swiped away tears. Merry cuddled against her side. Kat tapped Merry's arm, so she'd turn her head and read her lips.

"Well, sweetheart, since Daddy isn't home yet, we've got to keep his work under control. We don't want to leave him with a big, unmanageable pile when he gets back."

"Okay, Mommy," she said sadly.

"I have my investigators searching for him. If you kids weren't so young, I'd go and search myself."

"They'll find Daddy."

"Yes, they will." Kat glanced at a paper and used sign language. "Should we okay the canal project, sweetheart? The parties involved are pretty heated about it and have strong arguments." She knew Merry was too young but wanted to give her a feel for ruling.

Merry shrugged and signed, "Let's pass a law putting cupcake machines in all the schools."

Kat smiled. "I'll handle this logically." She sat back and rubbed her eyes. Merry nodded off. Kat asked the mask for information but got nothing. Her heart screamed that Cory was alive, though.

Her secretary handed her a paper and left. She grew cold. A deadline was up. After much thought, Cory had told her he wanted to approve an important project. She argued heatedly against doing so. About to reject it, she reconsidered and signed the paper.

Later, Brendan approached wearing black. Merry was with her siblings in the playroom.

"Hi, Brend."

"I can't stand how sad you are."

Her lip trembled.

He touched under her chin with two fingers. "I wish he fucked up. I wish you were pissed off at him. Then I'd—"

"Not now."

He nodded and stepped back. "He's my brother, Kat. I don't show it, but I'm devastated. Asher and Gunther still don't talk to anyone. Neither one of them has been back to work yet. We're grieving and don't leave the palace. The country is covered in black. Everywhere you look. Cory meant a lot to a lot of people."

She got up and hugged him, crying against his shoulder. Then she pulled away and pummeled his chest with her fists. "He's not dead, damn it!"

He took her fists gently. "I know, I know. I'm just as angry as you are. Asher, Gunther, and I will stay here in this country with you, no matter what happens. We'll be more involved with the kids."

Suddenly, they heard commotion outside of the office and turned their heads.

Cory walked into the room with long hair, a beard, ragged clothes, and blood-dried wrists. Katarina fainted.

When she came to, she looked up into Cory's face as he held her on the floor. He stared at her reverently. Brendan was no longer in the room.

"He's dead," Cory said.

She struggled to sit up, and he helped her. She cried against his chest. After a while she asked, "What happened?"

"In the car, I expected him to shoot me. He didn't. He knocked me out, and I woke up in some dark, damp cell, chained to a wall."

She gasped. "H...how did you escape?"

He swept the hair from her brow. "He didn't have many people loyal to him, but one was a woman. Her brother was a warden. I was taken to his hideous medieval prison. The woman came to my cell daily to give me food."

"Did you...have to seduce her?"

Cory kissed her head. "Hm. Not physically, sweetheart."

"No sex."

"No. It was George's biggest mistake having her interact with me. He thought a woman would want him still after I came along." He chuckled.

She did too. "You may both be handsome, but you're more so, and you have far more charm." Her soft laughter turned into a sob. He rocked her.

"Luckily, she spoke five languages, and one was my second language, so we were able to communicate. I told her I was a king. She wouldn't help me escape, though, either not believing me or just being loyal to George. I had to seduce her emotionally to win her over, thinking of how I would do anything to get back to you. After finally being won over, she did research to verify my information.

She had refused to before, doing a favor for her new friend, *Goran*, who actually used a fake name. The warden and his sister were foreigners to this part of the world and had never heard of George and me before George befriended her and brought me to her. When the brother and sister found out I was a famous king who brought women's rights to a small European country, they were shocked and horrified at what George had done to me."

"And?"

"The warden had initially believed he himself was avenging his sister, imprisoning some villain that betrayed her—that's the lie she told him in order to please George. Later, the warden and his sister were escorting me out of there, finally knowing the truth. The three of us ran into George at night outside the prison. He and I came to blows. George reached under his jacket for a gun. The warden drew faster and shot him in the head. He then apologized to me, saying he didn't know who I really was when he imprisoned me. George had deceived him, and the warden was angry about being used that way. In the warden's research to verify my identity, he saw how Carasivia was in deep mourning. His sister apologized as well."

"You never got your personal revenge on George."

"Good. If anyone ever makes my life story into a movie, I'll thank God it won't be a revenge story."

Kat smiled, so proud of him. "He's gone, and that's what counts. Time for us to work on forgiveness yet again, for our own good and the good of the nation, not to mention our children and especially the future queen. Our babies need to be involved in the forgiveness process."

He traced her jaw. "My wise queen."

"I can see how it's possible that you could convince your female jailer."

"George had dwindling funds—from that secret account, and the money he stole from us—after his lavish spending and after his country closed his national accounts. He went directly to his *new* friend, the warden's sister. It seems he stumbled across the old prison and cultivated a friendship with the woman—probably seduced her.

He had planned this for a while, and it took him years to make it work. He told her I was a bad guy who hurt a lot of women."

Kat's brow rose. "What an asshole."

"Yep. I offered the warden a job in a better facility with double the pay. He accepted."

"And her? Is she in love with you? Where is she?"

Cory kissed Kat's head. "I apologized for deceiving her. Pragmatic woman that she was, she told me she would have done the same thing and wished me well."

"That's it?"

"Well, my love, that and I gave her a big enough financial reward to erase any ill-used feelings she might have had. She's currently on a yacht seeing the world. She said to say hello to the love of my life, so hello, love of my life. She's going to find her own love and told me he wouldn't be a king or a former king. I came racing here without stopping."

Kat captured his face in her hands and gave him dozens of kisses.

Epilogue

About one year after that

A banner in the ballroom read: Happy birthday, King Corentin!

People danced to cheerful music. The next day, the royal family would be flying to Cory's second kingdom to celebrate with his happy citizens there. It was also the anniversary of Cory giving *that* country their own bill of rights.

The twins ran around the periphery of the dance floor and pulled Katarina out of Cory's arms, jumping up and down. Merry rushed out a message with her hands and Liam, without even looking at her, transcribed using his telepathic connection to her.

"She says now is the time, Daddy."

"Thank you, son. But go ahead and continue your Merry mindreading. I know how much you love it. And she gets a kick out of it."

He lifted his chin. "We need to go to the little blue room for presents from your children."

"You children are my presents!" Cory ruffled his black hair and signed 'Thank you' to Merry while also facing her, so she could read his lips. They left the room and went down the corridor where nannies had their four remaining children, and Katarina's parents and Jon stood chatting. Liam ran up to his uncle and asked him an archeological question. Cory smiled. He sometimes called Jon 'doctor' now that he had his PhD. Cory's prediction about his son's interest in archeology had been right. Cory approached Jon and hugged him.

"Corentin?" Jon asked.

"You're a fine brother to me and uncle to my children. Just let me know. Whatever you need. Anything, Jon, name it, any time."

"I'm...touched."

"I'm indebted to you."

"Thank you." Jon hugged him again.

Cory clapped his shoulder and gave him a look filled with love and respect. "I would be honored and grateful if you'd mentor my oldest son to be just as good an archaeologist as you are."

"I'm completely pleased to accept. Thank you, Corentin, from the bottom of my heart."

Cory smiled. His heart glowed as he surveyed the scene. His triplets were about to enter kindergarten that year. Aleksei Jaromír waved to his father and smiled, touching the red ribbon on his chest. He had won a contest by explaining, among other things, that his name meant defender and that's what he was going to grow up and do, just like Daddy. He would be in charge of Merry's security. He waved to Merry and signed 'hello.'

Adorée "Loved Child" Katarina tilted her head, smiled, and clasped her hands together in a gesture of innocence. She was proud to have a French name like her father and her grandmother (and oldest sister) and showed an interest in languages. She loved having her mommy's name for a middle name. She also asked Asher a lot of questions about rock climbing and ambassadorship. Sometimes, Cory would be working, and he'd hear giggling in the hall. The door would come open and in would fly little Addy with one of the others in tow. "Daaaaaaaaaaaaady!" she would say. He'd sometimes call her *Katarina's daughter*, knowing how much it pleased her because she knew he adored her mother.

Dominic Jensey played quietly at a little round table with his toys. He was their serious child and didn't like to talk. He studied his world around him, which pleased his parents, but they were concerned he might be a little antisocial, being so awkward around most people. However, he showed great signs of being a brilliant scientist someday, and that pleased Grandpa to no end. Dominic would sign with Merry often, so he didn't have to talk. He also, of all the children, clung to Katarina and not Cory. Dominic would sit for hours on Katarina's lap, his back to her chest. The other five kids fought for Cory's attention. He had to work out a system of fairness with them.

Marina came over with Katarina and Cory's youngest, Grace Reynolds Brodnik—Reynolds for Katarina's maiden name. Grace clapped her chubby toddler hands together. Cory had looked into her face once and imagined a future where she worked with animals. He would help her when this day arrived and told her stories of how he rescued animals as a boy. He also envisioned walking into Katarina's studio and seeing a still very young Grace attempting to play her mother's bass guitar. She would slap a kitten sticker on the bass.

Now at the party, she first signed then said clearly and loudly, "I wuv you, Daddy."

Cory chuckled and took her, nudging her nose and giving her kisses. "I love you!"

"Mamma wants love too!" Katarina gave her little kisses and blew raspberries on her cheeks.

Grace giggled. "Ma ma ma! Eeeeeee! Wuv you."

"Mommy loves you so much."

"Ommph!" Cory looked down.

His twins had slammed into him and Katarina and put their little arms around them in a bear hug. Next, the triplets followed suit, giggling and squealing. The room was filled with laughter and love. Cory looked at his wife in wonderment, his world complete.

Merry tapped his arm, and he smiled at her.

She signed, "Daddy, open my present first."

He nodded and handed Grace to Katarina. He bent and kissed Merry's head, and then signed, "I can't wait!"

Merry ran to the table of presents, grabbed one wrapped in gold paper, and rushed back to Cory. He sat in a nearby chair. Merry jumped onto his lap with an expectant face, handing him the gift. Everyone watched.

"Open it!" Merry shouted.

Cory tore open the paper with excitement while Merry clapped her hands together. Cory stared into the box, and his smile turned into a frown. He looked up sharply at Merry and mouthed her name in question.

"What is it?" Katarina asked, drawing close. She looked into the box and gasped, looking at Merry.

Cory signed, "Sweetheart, why would you give me a slip of paper that says you abdicate your future throne?"

Merry's lower lip trembled. "Because, Daddy, I want you to live a long, long time. I'll give up my future queenship to keep you around!"

He hugged her, held her a while, and then pulled back, kissing her head and cupping her cheek briefly. "Precious girl," he signed, shaking his head. "My beautiful child, I love you."

"You like your gift, Daddy? I filled it up with love."

He nodded and swallowed past the lump in his throat, not knowing how to phrase a correction of her misunderstanding without ruining the moment. She leaned up and kissed his cheek. Katarina wiped her own tears away.

Cory took Merry's hand and led her to a private office. He signed, "You are so special to me. I'm glad you were first and are the one next in line for the throne after Mommy and me because you'll be the best at it. I'm glad you love me so much and am grateful for your gift, but please, sweetheart, honor me and be queen someday because I love you so much. It's what I want."

She squeezed him close. Leaning apart, she signed, "Okay, but make sure it's a long, long, *long* time from now."

He smiled, nodding. "I will."

"I mean it, Daddy, I'm *serious*."

"Okay. And when you're old enough, I'll send you to Uncle Lothar's country to be my regent. Though I'll miss you so much that I'll make a lot of trips there to see you."

"Maybe, Daddy. If I can bring Liam and if you come to see me every night."

"We'll see." He kissed her and led her back into the room.

Liam approached with a blue package. Merry cuddled closer to Cory's side as Cory accepted his son's gift with a big smile. He opened it and pulled out a three-inch-tall clay figurine of a woman that appeared to be centuries old.

Liam grinned. "I found it in the dirt doing an archaeology dig with Uncle Jon. He said it was priceless and let me catalogue it and do all that stuff he normally does. He says one of our ancestors carried this around for a good and happy and long life, so I wanted you to have it instead of a museum having it. I went before Uncle Jon's association and explained in detail why the artifact needed to go to you. Uncle Jon said my argument was brilliant and I won over hearts and minds. On Christmas, I'll tell you what my argument was."

Cory held out his arms and gave Liam a hug. "Son, that is wonderful. Thank you. I will find a prominent spot to put this to remind me how lucky I am to be your dad. I'm honored." He leaned away. "I love you so much."

Liam's face lit up. "I love you. Daddy, Merry's wondering right now how you're going to carry her gift around."

He chuckled and faced her. "I'll fold the slip of paper and put it in a locket that I'll wear close to my heart."

Cory leaned to whisper to his son. "Liam, you're more adventurous than any of your siblings. Of all my kids, you surprise me the most often in wonderful ways. You're the most exciting one of the bunch. Don't tell anyone I told you. It's our secret."

"Thanks, Daddy!"

The triplets bounced over, each holding a package. Cory shook his head, smiling. "Wow, I had no idea what great gifts my children had for me today. My triplets are my gift?"

They giggled.

Adorée handed him a package. He thanked her and tore it open with happy excitement, gaining more giggles. He pulled out a large folded piece of felt then opened it up. The surface of it was covered with little felt pockets, and each had hand-crafted designs like butterflies, mountains and flowers on its surface.

"It's beautiful, sweetheart! Thank you!"

"Each pocket has a message for you, Daddy. Read them! I had help with the writing, but the words are all mine."

He reached into the first pocket and read, "Reason number one. I love Daddy because he plays tea party with me."

"Pull out another, Daddy."

He reached into the second-to-last pocket and read, "Reason number ninety-nine. I love Daddy because he's nice to people and makes everyone around me smile."

"And another!" she squealed.

He pulled one out from the middle. "I love Daddy because he explains so many things to me including how good mud cookies are and I should try them, and I did, and now they're my favorite! They are made out of chocolate." Cory chuckled.

"One more right now!" she demanded cheerfully.

"All right, sweetheart." He grabbed another slip of paper from a pocket. "I love Daddy because he told me—" Cory stopped and read the end silently. "... he told me that out of all my brothers and sisters, I'm the best at languages, even though Aleksei is good with sign language, I can do French, English, and Carisivian the best, and Daddy said he was so proud of me, and it was our little secret that like people called him, I was his little word genius, and the others had some catching up to do." He looked at Addy and smiled and winked, holding his finger to his lips.

"I worked on this since right after your last birthday, Daddy," she said.

Cory gritted his jaw, so moved he thought a tear would fall in front of the room.

"Addy, this is...perfect." He kissed her.

"I'm glad."

"Whenever I'm sad, I'll draw out a message and smile, so happy to have you as my daughter. I love you, sweetheart."

Her face lit with happiness. "I love you!"

"My turn!" Aleksei bounced and handed Cory a package.

Cory's heart was racing with an almost painful love at this point as gratitude filled him up. He took his son's gift, stunned by emotion from the love his children showed him.

"Open it!" Aleksei said.

Cory took off the paper and opened the box. He stared down at a picture Aleksei had drawn for him. A small boy—Aleksei—stood in front of a mirror, looking at a man—Cory, Cory knew in his heart.

"Son, you show your talent. I love it!"

"Do you know what it means, Daddy?"

"Please, tell me in your own words."

"I want to grow up and be just as brave as you. I want to be the hero you are. Mommy told me how you saved the lives of animals and people before I was born."

He pulled his son close and kissed his head. "This is going up in my office. I can't thank you enough. The honor you give me, my son, and the happiness. I love you, my boy." He wiped a tear away, no longer able to stop it.

"You're welcome, Daddy, and I love you."

Cory leaned to whisper in his ear. "You're still the best artist in this family. Our secret."

Aleksei leaned away. "Thank you, Daddy!"

Dominic gazed down then back up at Cory and handed him a gift with more reserve than the others had shown. "Here, Daddy."

Cory smiled and thanked him. He opened his gift, pulling out a blank sheet of paper and a small jar with liquid in it.

"Son? Is this something scientific? Did Mommy help you with this?"

He nodded. "Mommy taught me how, and Marina helped me write something invisible."

"I can't wait to hear! Please, tell me." He rubbed his hands together in excitement.

"It's invisible ink made from lemon juice, Daddy. I wrote a message on the paper for you. Hold it under a light bulb."

Katarina came over with a small portable lamp and turned it on. "I came prepared." She held it near the paper.

A message appeared on the paper. "Daddy, thank you for giving me the best Mommy. I love you so much."

Cory pulled Dominic into a hug. "I love you too." He leaned back.

Dominic looked at him. "The jar has more invisible ink in it so that you can write important secret messages to your ministers. I knew you'd want something practical."

Cory kissed his head then leaned away smiling. "Thank you. I'm so glad you're a scientist like your mother and three of your grandparents. It makes me love you all the more, my son, for being special this way. You make a great scientist and make me incredibly proud."

Dominic smiled shyly and gazed down.

Marina brought Grace to Cory, holding a small box. "Sire, this is from your youngest. I helped her, but not much. Gracie put a lot of heart into this."

Cory took the gift with a big smile and opened it. Inside was a cupcake shaped vaguely like a cat.

"Meowser!" Grace said, pointing to it. "For Daddy!" she squealed. "Fwum Gwacie Weynolds Bwodnik!"

"And it's green, my favorite color!" Cory chuckled. "Thank you, sweetheart." He pulled out his phone and took a picture of it. "I'll eat it later. Thank you, my precious girl! I love you." He gave her a big kiss on the cheek. "And you, what are you best at?" He looked up briefly then tapped his lips with a finger before gazing at her again.

"Wuv you, Daddy!"

"I love you too! Ah, I know. You're the cutest!"

That earned Cory a round of "Heys" from his other kids. He laughed. "Merry is *very* pretty. I'd say beautiful, but she looks like me, and I don't want to sound stuck up."

Everyone broke out into laughter. When it stilled, Cory continued. "Liam, Dominic, and Aleksei are handsome, and Addy is adorable. Therefore, that leaves Gracie Girl to be cute! Exceptionally so!"

More children's laughter filled the room.

Cory leaned toward Grace. "You are my little animal caretaker, the best. You take great care of Meowser by feeding him treats and playing with him."

"I wuv aminals," she said.

He kissed her. "So do I."

"I'm like Daddy." She clasped her hands together.

"Indeed you are, my girl."

All the children were gathered around him. He looked at them through tear-blurred eyes.

"Thank you, my children, for the best birthday ever. I love you very much."

They gave him a group hug. Cory gave them all kisses again. He stood and looked at Katarina and handed Grace to Marina.

"Whaaaat?" Katarina dragged out, tilting her head and giving him a sweet smile.

"Thank you."

"For what? I haven't given you your gift from me yet. You're gonna *love* it. It will rock your world."

"I cannot wait," he said, then looked at their kids. "But I was thanking you for them." He gazed back at her.

His American buddies, Asher, Brendan, and Gunther walked over to them with cheerful greetings.

Brendan put a small American flag into Cory's shirt pocket. "Happy birthday!"

"Thanks! What does this mean?" Cory asked.

Brendan pointed to Asher. "Your ambassador here was successful. The deal went through."

Cory smiled and shook Asher's hand. "Thanks!"

"Anytime. Oh, later, the kids must each put on the mask. It has interesting and strange, but positive, gifts for each of them it conveyed to me."

"I can't wait," Cory said.

Merry approached Asher and stared up at him.

"Hello, sweetheart," he signed to her. "Or should I say, 'Cory junior?'"

She bowled over laughing at the familiar and much-loved joke.

"Mini Cory? The resemblance is stunning," Gunther added. "Who knew a female Cory would be so pretty."

Cory scoffed. "Katarina once said the same thing."

"Uncle Asher," Merry signed. "You have such nice-looking hair. How can I make my hair look like that?"

Brendan and Gunther laughed.

"A friend once told me a secret to use beer on my hair," Asher said.

Cory's brow lifted. "My girl is not going to pour beer on her hair."

"Daddy won't let me," Merry signed.

"Well," Asher looked at Merry. "Maybe, your mommy can formulate some wonderful conditioner for you."

"I can live with that," Cory said. He looked at her. "And Dominic can help."

"Thank you!" Merry signed. She looked at Brendan. "Uncle Brendan?" she signed.

"Yes, Cory junior?"

She giggled and took a deep breath. "I have a question. I read your lips earlier."

"Ask away, sweetheart," Brendan said.

"Why did you tell Uncle Gunther when you saw Grace that everyone was shocked when she was born a single baby, that people placed bets my mommy was going to have quadruplets after having twins then triplets?"

Brendan tried to rein in his smile but failed. He looked at Cory and shrugged. "Sorry. It was true."

Cory gave him a good-natured smile. "And kind of funny. Even though her belly was noticeably smaller." He looked at his daughter. "Good question, sweetheart. Uncle Brendan will answer it."

She looked at Brendan, and Cory could see that he was mentally translating his response to make it G-rated.

Brendan signed, "Because four comes after three."

She shook her head. "Apparently not anymore. My parents are monarchs. They can rearrange the order of numbers in this country."

Everyone who witnessed the exchange chuckled.

"That girl you were dating also said something I don't understand," Merry signed to Brendan.

"Oh?" he asked. "What is it?"

"She said the king made twins and triplets, and a single...six babies in three shots, so he must be some kind of a super stud. What is that?"

"Good lord." Cory wiped his hands over his face. He took a breath then crouched down to look at Merry at eye-level. "Sweetheart."

Brendan chuckled. "I can't wait to hear this."

Cory shot him an annoyed glance. "Uncle Brendan is an idiot." He smirked.

"Reaaaaallly?" she drew out, taking him seriously. "Maybe he shouldn't be the palace doctor then!"

"He's not really an idiot. I was teasing." He ruffled her hair. "He and his date were just being silly. They didn't mean anything by it."

"But I don't understand. What does that word mean?"

"It means..." He cleared his throat and looked up at Brendan speaking under his breath without moving his lips. "Thanks a lot, asshole."

"I didn't say it!" Brendan said, on a laugh.

Cory looked back at Merry. "It just means that Mommy and I made more babies with fewer pregnancies than most people do. But don't use the word. It's an adult word."

"Oh. Okay." Merry bounced away to join Dominic playing with marbles at a table. They signed rapidly to each other. Merry laughed at a joke he told her.

"Thank God," Cory said.

Gunther, the palace mechanic, looked at Cory with sudden concern.

Cory touched his arm. "What is it?"

"It can wait until after all the birthday celebrations."

"It's okay. Nothing could dampen my spirits now."

"It's not bad news, just intriguing."

"Oh?"

"You know I'm your ears out there. I listen very carefully."

"Yes, and I'm grateful. You stopped that assassination attempt last year. A freak follower of George's who hadn't even known him personally."

"Well, you also know Ash and I recently returned from a trip to America."

"Yeah."

"I heard something interesting while there and believe you and Kat should get on a plane and get there asap."

"Why? What did you hear?"

"Hanging around the embassy with Asher, I heard secret talk in dark corners."

"Go on."

"There was a woman there with a Carasivian accent who told another woman with an American accent that she was the sister your parents gave up for adoption on your father's insistence."

"What?" Cory's eyes went wide.

"Don't know if it's true, but she resembled you. Had blue eyes."

Cory's hands were shaking. He stilled them. "It can't be. They never said anything about a daughter. But if this is true, I want to meet her!"

"The woman was planning to get a meeting with high officials in your name and tell them her version of events that they didn't talk about. She told this woman that what she had to say would affect international relations, and the American told her she'd get her meeting. She asked why she didn't tell you of her existence. She said timing. She's still in America."

Cory drew in a deep breath. "After tomorrow night's festivities, I want you, Asher, and Brendan to join Katarina and me. We're going to America."

Katarina came over with a smile, having heard that. "Awesome! And after we do the things you need to do, I have ideas for pure fun. We're gonna have our amusement like in the old days."

Cory gave her hand a squeeze. "Our queen has spoken." He put his hands above her hips, holding her lovingly by the waist. She rested her hand on his neck and smiled widely. He kissed her.

"Love you, babe," she said.

"I love you too, sweetheart." Cory shook his head in pure happiness, taking her hand and intertwining his fingers with hers.

"Can you guys stay for my band's concert tonight?" she asked.

All three friends told her yes.

Asher looked at her. "I knew your marriage would be blessed."

"Thanks, Ash!" she said, then gazed at Cory. "How do you never tire of me?" She smiled.

Cory gave her a sarcastic look. A grin spread across his lips. "You're at it again, my love, keeping humor in our relationship."

She touched his nose.

Brendan looked at her. "You look so beautiful tonight," he said dreamily.

"You do look good," Asher added.

"Yep," Gunther said sincerely, nodding.

"Hey now," Cory said, with a chuckle. "Don't get any funny ideas!"

Brendan grinned. "Just keeping you on your toes. Kat likes it."

"Outside help is unneeded." He nuzzled Katarina's cheek. "Whether in the palace halls, the roads of the village, or the city streets, I take notice of all the men who look at my Katarina with... *admiration* then avert their eyes. I know the beauty I have as a wife."

Katarina sighed with loving happiness and dragged the back of her fingers down Cory's temple.

"You two look like you're planning on giving your six children another sibling," Brendan remarked.

Cory gave him a raised-brow look. "Hasn't anyone ever told you that you can enjoy a woman's..." he glanced over at his children playing then back, "...company without making siblings for your children?"

Gunther grunted.

"No more then?" Asher asked.

Katarina gave him a cutesy grin and shrugged. "He told me he wanted dozens of kids with me, so I guess we're only a quarter of the way done."

Cory grinned and looked back at their friends. "You guys are idiots. Good thing you're not related by blood. The questionable gene pool would have had me worried."

"Hey, I didn't say anything!" Gunther said.

The guys, Cory, and Katarina chuckled good-naturedly.

"Your kids are great," Gunther added. "All very interesting little people. Everywhere from the seven-year-old cataloguing archaeological finds to the five-year-old who knows more of the elements on the periodic table than me. And all those adorable kids speak four languages. Very, very impressive."

"I think Grace is going to work with animals someday and play her mother's bass," Cory said.

"Funny she's the only blond one. Like me," Brendan said, with a teasing tone, wiggling his eyebrows.

"Not funny. Asshole," Cory said under his breath, but he added a smile.

"Yeah, you're a *strawberry* blond, Brendan. Asher's the blond one." Katarina lifted her chin.

Cory turned to her with a smile and touched her chin. "So was my mother," he said, and gave her a soft kiss.

"I'm truly amazed at how much Liam looks like Katarina," Asher said.

"That's my boy," Cory said.

"Your good-luck twins," Asher added. "To resemble their—"

"Opposite-sex parents," Katarina interrupted. "That's what I told Cory when they were born."

Asher gave Cory his normal, happy smile, but something was missing suddenly in his eyes. "Cor, can I have a private word with you?"

Gunther tossed Asher a suspicious look.

"Sure," Cory said. He kissed Katarina then pulled Asher out of the room. They stood facing each other in the hall.

"I'm surprised Gun didn't mention it," Asher said.

"Mention what?"

"He's been obsessed with that blue-eyed woman since he first laid eyes on her. Says he wants a formal introduction and then he plans to ask her out."

Cory's brow rose. "Gunther? Obsessed? I've never seen that in all the years we've known each other. He was twice in love but not obsessed."

"I think he's thunderstruck, but he doesn't know if she is on our side, your side, or not. He pointed her out."

"Hmm," Cory said.

"Gun is your best friend, your brother, but I think he's fallen for this lady. What if she's the enemy?"

More to come...

Meet Lara MacGregor

Lara MacGregor lives in Colorado. She has written flash fiction to full-length novels, mostly historical, but other genres as well such as paranormal, especially time travel stories. She has a B.A. degree in Modern Languages with a minor in music and an M.A. degree in history. She plays guitar and piano and loves reading as many books as time will allow.

Other Works From The Pen Of

Lara MacGregor

The 12th Kiss - In 19th century London, she can fight and becomes a hero. He falls in love with her. His biggest mistake is to demand she stop her activities.

The Mask of Truth, Book One - A prince accused of murder must prove his innocence, save his country from a tyrant, and win over his true love's heart or lose all.

Letter to Our Readers

Enjoy this book?

You can make a difference

As an independent publisher, Wings ePress, Inc. does not have the financial clout of the large New York Publishers. We can't afford large magazine spreads or subway posters to tell people about our quality books.

But, we do have something much more effective and powerful than ads. We have a large base of loyal readers.

Honest Reviews help bring the attention of new readers to our books.

If you enjoyed this book, we would appreciate it if you would spend a few minutes posting a review on the site where you purchased this book or on the Wings ePress, Inc. webpages at: https://wingsepress. com/

Visit Our Website

For The Full Inventory
Of Quality Books:

Wings ePress.Inc
https://wingsepress.com/

Quality trade paperbacks and downloads
in multiple formats,
in genres ranging from light romantic comedy
to general fiction and horror.
Wings has something for every reader's taste.
Visit the website, then bookmark it.
We add new titles each month!

Wings ePress Inc.
3000 N. Rock Road
Newton, KS 67114